Praise for #1 *New York Times* bestselling author Sandra Brown

"Brown is an excellent and almost effortless writer....
The chemistry is undeniable."
—*Kirkus Reviews* on *Sting*

"Brown crafts facets and depths of characters in a
taut novel full of surprises."
—*Booklist* on *Sting*

"[An] exceptional romantic thriller... Brown
handles the romance with her usual panache and
adds some nifty plot twists that will keep readers
guessing."
—*Publishers Weekly*, starred review, on *Sting*

"Deft characterizations and eye for detail make this
a winner.... Satisfying, vintage Brown storytelling."
—*Kirkus Reviews* on *Deadline*

"Pulse-pounding...a relentless pace and clever
plot."
—*Publishers Weekly*, starred review, on *Lethal*

SANDRA BROWN

TOMORROW'S PROMISE

&

ABOVE AND BEYOND

HQN™

ISBN-13: 978-0-373-80409-2

Tomorrow's Promise & Above and Beyond

Copyright © 2017 by Harlequin Books S.A.

The publisher acknowledges the copyright holders of the additional works as follows:

Tomorrow's Promise
Copyright © 1983 by Sandra Brown

Above and Beyond
Copyright © 1986 by Sandra Brown

Printed in U.S.A.

CONTENTS

TOMORROW'S PROMISE

CHAPTER ONE

AMERICAN AIRLINES FLIGHT number 124 from New Orleans to Washington, D.C., was in trouble. At least it seemed so to Keely Preston, whose cold, damp hands were clasped tightly in her lap as she stared anxiously out the window at the frequent blinding flashes of blue-white lightning.

The first-class cabin provided a more comfortable flight than the passengers in the coach cabin must be experiencing, but then Keely always flew first class for that reason alone.

"Miss Preston." Keely jumped and whipped her head around to face the airline hostess who was bending solicitously over the vacant seat on the aisle to address her confidentially. "Would you like something to drink?"

Keely pushed back a few strands of caramel-colored hair and tried to smile with tight, stiff lips. She wasn't sure she was successful. "No, thank you."

"It might help calm you. I've noticed that you're nervous about the storm. I assure you that everything is fine."

Keely looked down at her clenched hands and smiled in self-derision. "I'm sorry that it shows." She glanced back up at the attendant and smiled with more conviction. "I'm fine. Really."

The young woman smiled her professional smile and offered, "Ring me if you need anything. We should be out of the storm in the next several minutes and will land in Washington in about an hour."

"Thank you," Keely said and made the effort to relax, to sit back against the thick luxury of the first-class seat and block out the ferocity of the storm by closing her eyes.

The man across the aisle admired her display of courage, though he sensed she was terrified. As a matter of fact, he had admired everything about this woman since she had boarded the aircraft a few minutes after he had. She was in possession of many admirable qualities.

Her hair for instance. It was soft and casually styled. He despised trendy hairstyles copied from punk rock stars or women athletes. The lady across the aisle had hair that swept her shoulders each time she moved her head. It looked well-brushed and clean and he suspected it must smell like flowers.

He wouldn't be a man if he hadn't noticed her tidy, compact figure when she had passed him on his aisle seat to find hers one row in front of and across the aisle from his. She was wearing a green two-piece knit suit. The sweater tapered to a trim waist. The skirt clung to taut hips and widened gradually to flare just below her knees.

She had damn good legs too. He noticed that when she reached overhead to toss her trench coat in the compartment over her seat. That was when he had seen her in profile and noted that the front of her sweater conformed to a ripe, but not overfull, bosom.

To anyone's observant eye he had been engrossed in

the stack of papers he had withdrawn from his brief-case soon after takeoff. Actually he had been covertly watching the woman. She had ordered filet mignon for dinner, but had taken exactly three dainty bites of it. One bite of broccoli. No bread. No dessert. She had drunk one-half glass of rosé wine and one cup of coffee slightly creamed.

He had read through several more of the official-looking documents after dinner, then stowed them again in his briefcase. He had been flipping through *Time*, but still continued to glimpse at the woman at regular intervals over the top of the magazine. Thus, he had seen and heard her exchange with the flight attendant. Now he gave up all pretense of reading and only watched her closely.

At that moment the airplane hit an air pocket and dropped suddenly. To a seasoned flier it was nothing to panic over. The woman across the aisle bolted upright and whirled her head around. Her eyes were wide with fright.

Before the man had thought about it, obeying a subconscious command he didn't stop to analyze, he was across the aisle and in the seat next to hers, holding her hands between the two of his.

"It's all right. Nothing to worry about. Just a little turbulence. No need to panic." Indeed, they seemed to be the only two in the first-class section who had even noted the sudden, and immediately corrected, loss of altitude. The attendants were still in the galley, where the unmistakable clatter of china could be heard. The other passengers, few though they were on this late-night flight, were either asleep or too preoccupied to have noticed that the handsome young man had virtually leaped across the aisle to join the distressed woman.

The warm, strong, masculine hands that gripped hers tightly were so well-groomed that Keely stared at them for a moment before she lifted her surprised eyes to the man's face. It was extremely close to hers but, oddly, not uncomfortably so.

"I'm sorry," she heard herself say. What was she apologizing for? "I'm fine. Truly. It's just…" The hoarseness in her throat shocked her. Where were the melodious tones that usually characterized her speaking voice? And why was she stammering like an idiot, which surely this man must believe her to be. Who else acted like such a complete ninny on an airplane but a hysterical, neurotic female? And why didn't she feel inclined to draw her hands away from his?

Instead she stared up into the blackest eyes framed by the blackest brows and feathered by the thickest, blackest lashes she had ever seen. There was a half-inch-long scar on his cheekbone just under his left eye. His nose was slender and finely chiseled. His mouth was full and wide, the lips dangerously close to being sensual. The jaw and chin were definitely stubborn and male, but saved from austerity by a deep dimple in his right cheek near the corner of that intriguing mouth.

"Well, what are friends for?" he asked, smiling that heart-melting, confidence-inspiring smile that had become his trademark and anathema to his enemies.

Hell, who are you kidding? he asked himself. He didn't feel like a friend. The lightning that electrified the atmosphere outside the airplane was nothing compared to the bolt that had struck him right between the

eyes and straight in the heart when he had first looked
her fully in the face.

Green. Her eyes were green, wide, full of integrity,
and sexy as hell. Her complexion wasn't peaches and
cream. It wasn't that fair. More like peaches and...
honey, sort of an apricot that would tan golden in the
summer. It was tastefully enhanced with just the right
touch of makeup.

The nose was perfect. The mouth...God, the *mouth*!
Her lips were soft and glossed with a shiny coral.

She wore small gold loops in her ears. A slender
gold chain gilded the base of her throat. She had no
rings on the hands he still held. He celebrated that fact.

Her body was trembling slightly and for one insane
moment he wished he knew what it was like to have
her quivering beneath him in unleashed passion. The
thought both thrilled and shamed him. It was obvious
she wasn't soliciting for that kind of reaction from a
man. The lust originated only in his mind, but it was
undeniably there. Yet not base desire alone. He felt
a compulsion to cover her. Not with dominance, but
with protection. To shield her. To imbue her with his
strength. It was a uniquely masculine emotion. And he
had never felt it before with any female.

Some of the voracity of his thoughts must have
shone in his eyes, for she was tugging gently on her
hands. He released them reluctantly. "I'm Dax Devereaux," he said by way of introduction and to cover
that self-consciousness that had suddenly sprung between them.

"Yes, you are," she said, then laughed softly, nervously, at her own words. "I mean, I recognize you

now. I'm pleased to meet you, Congressman Devereaux. I'm Keely Preston."

His eyes narrowed as he stared at her, his head tilted in concentration. "Keely Preston. Keely Preston. Where have I heard that name? Should I know you?"

She smiled. "Only if you drive in New Orleans. I'm the traffic reporter on KDIX radio. I broadcast from the helicopter during rush hours."

He smacked his forehead with an open palm. "Of course. Keely Preston! Well, I'm humbled to meet such a celebrity."

She laughed again and he delighted in it. Her laughter had a low, musical sound. The lovely face wasn't tense any longer. "Hardly a celebrity," she demurred.

"But you are!" He leaned forward and whispered conspiratorially. "I know people who wouldn't dare drive to work each day without your guidance from above." He cocked his head and lowered black brows over his dark eyes. They stared at her in perplexity. "Forgive me for making such a crass observation, Keely, but if you fly every day why...?" He let the question trail off and she finished it for him.

"Why was I afraid a few minutes ago?" She turned her head to glance out the window again. They had flown through the worst of the storm, though streaks of lightning still lighted up the far horizon. "It's silly, I know. It's not the flying. As you say, I do that every day. I think it was the storm that upset me." It was a lame excuse and sounded so even to her own ears. She didn't want to guess how ridiculous it sounded to Dax Devereaux.

Why didn't she just explain to him? Why not tell him that Preston was her professional name, that she had another? Why not tell him why flying sometimes terrified her, that her job in the helicopter every day was part of her self-prescribed therapy to get over her own hang-ups?

Those things were difficult to reconcile to herself, much less verbalize. She knew from experience that it made men—single, attractive men—uncomfortable when she told them of her circumstances. They didn't quite know how to catalog her. To save herself and Dax Devereaux from such an embarrassing situation, she would stick to the vague answer she had given. He seemed momentarily satisfied with it.

To change the subject away from herself she asked him, "Are you going to be our next senator from Louisiana?"

He chuckled and ducked his head in an almost boyish mannerism. She saw a few strands of silver in his thick dark hair. Beautiful hair.

"Not if my opponents have anything to do about it. What do you think?" he asked her directly.

"I think you stand a very good chance," she answered unreservedly and honestly. "Your track record as a congressman is good."

Dax Devereaux had made a name for himself in her native state. He was known as the workman's politician. Often he could be found in jeans and a work shirt talking to fishermen, farmers, or blue-collar factory workers. His critics scoffed at his tactics and accused him of insincerity and flamboyancy. His supporters worshiped him. In any event, he kept the populace aware of his activities. No one in his congressional district was ignorant of their representative's identity.

"You don't think I'm an 'opportunist, constantly

stirring up controversy for his own gain'?" he asked, quoting from a recent critical editorial.

She had read the editorial and smiled. "Well, you must admit that it doesn't hurt you to have a name like Devereaux when running for public office in the state of Louisiana."

He grinned back. "Can I help it if one of my great-great-grandfathers was an illustrious French Creole? I don't know if that's a help or a hindrance. Do you know how barbaric they behaved sometimes? Duels. They were a hot-blooded, short-tempered, snobbish bunch. One of my forefathers scandalized the family by marrying an 'American' girl after Jackson's defeat of the British. And a black sheep of the family even collaborated with the Yankees when the Union Army seized New Orleans during the Civil War."

She was laughing now. "Okay, okay. You're descended from a family of cutthroats and traitors." She looked at him speculatively. "I would think that you'd be a publicist's dream," she remarked candidly.

"Oh, yeah?" he asked and his eyes twinkled at her sudden embarrassment.

She floundered. "What I mean is your names both start with *d* and end with *x*. Surely a clever adman would do wonders with that during a campaign. And your youth and—and good looks. Sort of a John Kennedy type."

"Ah, but Mr. Kennedy had Mrs. Kennedy. I don't have an attractive wife as an asset." Keely knew that. Everyone did. His bachelorhood was a point his opponents played havoc with. Looking the way he did didn't help. Some considered a good-looking bachelor a threat and downright deadly when it came to effective politics.

She was staring into her lap. His knee was so close to hers she could feel the fabric of his pant leg against her shin. She didn't move away. Instead she raised her eyes to his and found him studying her closely. "I don't even have a good prospect for a wife," he said.

She swallowed. "Don't you?" The question was barely above a shaky explosion of breath.

"No."

That glorious sexual suppression. It was so exploited in movies, songs, and books. But it could be quite painful when one actually exercised it. The tumult that built in Keely's breast as she stared at Dax would not be squelched. For so many years it had been refused recognition, refused life. Now that it had a chance, it bloomed into enormous proportions, expanding her chest, filling her whole body, until her breathing was stifled. But before she died from that sweet suffocation, she was granted a reprieve.

The flight attendant stopped beside Dax's seat and said, "I see that the two of you have got acquainted. Can I bring you anything, Miss Preston? Congressman Devereaux?"

Dax hadn't taken his eyes off Keely and now he asked quietly, "Will you join me in a brandy?"

She tried to speak, couldn't, so only nodded mutely. He turned to the stewardess and said, "Two brandies." Keely took that time to restore herself. She ran her tongue over her lips, blinked several times, drew three deep breaths, and smoothed moist palms over her skirt. His leg was where it had been. If anything, closer. How tall was he? She hadn't had time to notice when he had suddenly appeared beside her, grasping her hands.

"Keely?"

She looked up at him. His face was serious. "If I run for the Senate, will you vote for me?" They laughed then and the tension was dispelled. They were served their brandies and she took a tentative sip. She didn't like it, but she didn't let him know that.

"Tell me about your work. It must be fun and exciting," he said companionably.

"It's much more glamorous from the outside than from within, I assure you. But I enjoy it."

"Do you ever get tired of being stormed for autographs by an adoring public?"

"Remember I'm on radio. People don't often recognize my face. But if I make a public appearance for the radio station, I enjoy a certain amount of VIP treatment."

"Maybe you should go into the more visible medium."

"Television? No, thank you!" she said with emphasis. "I'll leave the cameras to my friend Nicole."

"Nicole...? What's her name?"

"Nicole Castleman. She anchors the six-o'clock news on the television station that shares the building with my radio station."

"Yeah, I've seen her when I'm in New Orleans. Blond?"

"Yes. Men never forget Nicole," Keely said without rancor. "She and I have been best friends for years. She revels in her ardent popularity. When we're out together, she's the one who gets all the attention."

"I doubt that," Dax said succinctly. When Keely

looked up at him, she saw that he meant it. She looked away quickly.

"I wouldn't trade jobs," she said.

"It must be demanding. Doesn't it interfere with your personal life? Your family?"

It was a veiled question and one that Keely chose to circumvent. She smiled up at him. "I manage to work around it." The subject was dropped.

The seat belt light came on and the hostess came by to pick up their glasses. The pilot announced their descent into National Airport. They listened, each without hearing, to the weather conditions in the capital. They didn't look at each other, but they didn't need to. The acute awareness was there.

His hand was settled on the armrest separating their chairs. It was strong, long, with tapering fingers, and sprinkled with dark hair. A beautiful hand. He wore a gold signet ring on the ring finger. An alligator band strapped a watch to his wrist. It had a round face with bold Roman numerals. All it did was give the time of day. There was no calendar, no alarm, no chime, no stopwatch, no flashing digits, no other gimmicks. Just two slender hands that indicated the time. She liked that.

Considering his profession, one would expect him to be dressed in conservative gray. But Dax Devereaux wore camel pants, a navy blue double-breasted blazer, a beige shirt, and a tastefully striped tie.

Was there anything wrong with him? One tiny flaw? So far Keely had seen none.

Dax too was staring ostensibly at his hand. In reality, he was calculating the distance between his dangling fingers and the smooth expanse of leg beneath them. She sat with her legs chastely crossed, but the position allowed him a tantalizing glimpse of silk-encased thigh. An edge of baby-blue lace peeked from under the hemline of her skirt. His heart thudded. A baby blue slip. Was it a half-slip or a whole one with satin straps?

He cursed the lecherous track his musings were taking. They were unfair to her. And they were making him light-headed. And uncomfortable. He shifted in his seat and turned to her abruptly. "How long will you be in Washington?"

"I—I'm not sure. It depends on...several things," she answered cryptically.

"Where will you be staying?"

Keely cringed on the inside. This was dangerous. He was getting too close. He was too attractive, too appealing. Now was the time to stop it before it got started. "I don't know. I thought I'd call a hotel from the airport."

He knew instantly by the averted green eyes and the wavering tone of voice that she was lying, but he forgave her gladly. She was only being cautious. It reconfirmed his earlier assessment. She wasn't hustling. He would find her.

"It's been a pleasure, Keely." He smiled and stuck out his hand in a friendly gesture. She accepted his hand in like manner and shook it, but she was marveling over how deep that dimple was.

"Thank you for coming to my rescue." Glistening lips parted to reveal bright, straight teeth and it was all Dax could do to tear his eyes away from her mouth.

"Goodbye," he said as he stood and backed into the aisle.

"Goodbye."

He returned to his seat to gather up his belongings and prepare for the landing, which was executed without a hitch several minutes later. Keely kept her head directed toward the front of the airplane or out the window, though she was conscious of him behind her.

When the 727 came to a standstill, she sat for a moment before getting up and reaching into the overhead rack for her coat. She studiously kept her eyes from Congressman Devereaux's vicinity, though she could tell out of the corner of her eye that he was shrugging into a topcoat. She decided not to put hers on yet. He might offer to help her. Then he'd have to touch her again and that was better avoided.

She picked up her purse and a small attaché and draped her coat over her arm before she stepped into the aisle.

He was waiting for her to pass ahead of him.

"Do you have luggage?" he asked.

"Yes. You?"

He shook his head. "I'm traveling light this trip," he said.

"Oh." There was nothing else to say. She stepped into the brightly lighted portable corridor that connected the aircraft with the terminal and walked along it at a brisk pace. This was ridiculous! Why didn't she just turn around and engage him in friendly inconsequential conversation? She knew he was right behind her. Why didn't he talk to her? They were both behaving like silly adolescents. But this was best. Discretion dictated putting as much space between them as possible. It was safer.

She walked into the airport. Just as she cleared the door, a rush of reporters holding cameras and microphones undulated toward it. Curiosity urged her to turn around.

Dax was immediately surrounded by the reporters and flashing cameras. He was smiling, fielding their rapid questions, bantering with them about the lousy Washington weather. While a more aggressive reporter was rattling off a question she couldn't hear, Dax looked up and caught her eye across the throng. His smile was almost apologetic. She mouthed a good-bye, then turned away and headed for the escalator.

When her one piece of luggage had been picked off the revolving carousel and checked against the stub stapled to her ticket, she hefted it off the ground and threaded her way through the airport and out onto the sidewalk. She easily hailed a passing cab and was standing aside as the driver placed her suitcase in the trunk, when another cab screeched to a halt in the next lane.

Dax shoved open the back door and cannoned out of the cab, skirted the rear end of the taxi, and jumped up on the curb in front of her. His breathing was labored. The night was cold. His breath fogged the air between them.

"Keely…" He looked disconcerted, impatient with himself, anxious. "Keely, I don't want to say good-bye to you yet. Will you have a cup of coffee with me somewhere?"

"Dax—"

"I know. I'm a stranger. You're not the type to pick up a man on an airplane or anywhere else for that matter. I don't want the invitation to insult you. I just—"

He raked his hand through windblown hair. The collar of his coat was flipped up and framed the rigid planes of his jaw. The bottom of it flapped against his legs in the cold wind. The belt hung loose and untied from the loops. "Oh, hell," he cursed softly and shoved his hands into his coat pockets as he scanned the congested traffic. Then he looked at her again. "I just want to spend more time with you, get to know you better. It's not that late. Go for coffee with me? Please?"

How could anyone resist that dimple, that beguiling smile? Yet Keely Preston must. "I'm sorry, Dax. I can't."

Someone behind his illegally parked taxicab honked belligerently. Her taxi driver scowled at them impatiently. They were oblivious of it all.

"Are you meeting someone else?"

"No."

"Are you too tired?"

"No, it's…"

"What?"

"I just can't." She gnawed her bottom lip in vexation.

"That's no answer, Keely." He smiled gently and asked, "Do I repel you?"

"No!" The vehemence of her reply elated him and mortified her.

She looked away, darting her eyes unseeingly over the traffic, the lights of the airport that shimmered through the soft mist that was falling. "That's why I can't go with you, Dax." She spoke so softly that he had to duck his head to hear her. "I'm married."

CHAPTER TWO

HIS HEAD JERKED back as if he had been kicked in the teeth, which is exactly how he felt. He stared at the top of her head, which was bowed as she looked at the damp concrete under her feet. "Married?" he croaked. It was unthinkable, abhorrent.

She looked at him then, straight in the eye and without expression. Her voice held no inflection as she answered, "Yes."

"But—"

"Goodbye, Dax." Keely stepped around him, yanked open the door of the taxi, and fell inside, saying "Capital Hilton" to the driver, who was glaring at her with open hostility for keeping him waiting so long.

The taxi lurched away from the curb and daringly forged its way into the flow of traffic. Keely didn't even notice. Her hands were covering her face and she was pressing the middle finger of each hand on the sharp throbbing pain in the center of her forehead.

The day had finally come. The day she had dreaded for years. At 37,000 feet in the sky she had met a man. A man who made her situation that much more untenable.

Keely Preston Williams had been married for twelve years, but had been a wife for three weeks. She and Mark Williams were classic high school sweethearts.

He was the star athlete in their small hometown in coastal Mississippi. She was a cheerleader. It was 1969. Drugs, hard liquor, and loose sexual mores hadn't yet made it to the high schools in the rural South. The community in which she and Mark grew up was still poignantly naive. Regional football, community-wide picnics, and church socials were still the mode.

After graduation Keely and Mark both enrolled in Mississippi State. Mark was an athlete, and as a result of a heavy class load and grueling football practices, his grades slipped until he failed out the first semester.

The Vietnam War was still a threat to any young man, and Mark fell victim to it. As soon as the draft board was notified of his grade average, his draft classification changed and he received his induction notice. Two weeks later he was on his way to boot camp.

It had been Keely's idea for them to marry as soon as they got word of his induction. She pressured him, cried, pleaded, threatened, until she wore him down. He finally consented against his better judgment and their parents were notified to meet them on a given day in their pastor's study. They were married.

They drove to New Orleans to spend the weekend, then returned home to live that fleeting two weeks with Mark's parents before the army bus carried him off. After three months at Fort Polk, Louisiana, he was sent to Fort Wolters, Texas. He had been selected to enter helicopter pilot training.

Forty weeks of pilot's training was crammed into twenty-five. After a six-month separation Mark was granted a one-week furlough with his bride before being shipped out.

The marriage had been consummated with the tender, restrained passion of the very young, but there was still something sweetly pure about their fervent embraces just before he left for the other side of the world and a hell he couldn't have imagined even in his most horrific dreams.

Keely continued going to school, busying herself with a job after classes in order to defeat expenses. At night she would write long, involved, newsy letters to Mark. She received his letters sporadically. Sometimes they came two or three at a time, sometimes weeks would go by without her once hearing from him. She pored over his letters, cherishing each word of love.

Then nothing. For weeks, a month, she heard nothing, nor did his anxious parents. Then she was visited by an officer dispatched from Fort Polk. Mark's helicopter had been seen going down, but his whereabouts and condition were unknown. He wasn't reported dead. His body hadn't been found among the wreckage. He wasn't reported taken prisoner of war. He had simply vanished.

And to this day that was all Keely Williams knew about her husband. He was one on a list of 2,600 men still classified as Missing In Action in Southeast Asia.

For the past several years Keely hadn't been idle, but actively strove to keep the MIAs on the public's mind. She and other wives in similar circumstances had organized an action group called PROOF, taking its name from the initials of Positive Resolution Of Our Families. On most occasions Keely acted as their spokeswoman.

She leaned back on the smoky-smelling, dusty upholstery of the taxi and stared vacantly at the Washington scenery as it sped by. Twelve years. Was she any

better off now than she had been when she had first
learned of Mark's disappearance?

Drowning in a miasma of disillusionment and depression, she had finished school with a degree in
journalism. She took her degree and moved to New
Orleans. She landed a job on the *Times-Picayune* as
a "gofer" with the grandiose title of copy editor. She
stuck it out for several years, gradually working her
way into the unenviable position of cub reporter. The
events she was assigned to cover were so unimport-
ant that her stories were buried in the middle of the
newspaper.

Through the journalistic grapevine, she heard that
a newswriter at a local radio station had abruptly left,
due to an indiscretion with the switchboard operator on
company time. On her lunch break Keely had gone to
see the harried news director, charmed him into hiring
her, and started her new job the next day. She liked the
work. It was at least more kinetic than the dull stories
she had been writing.

She met Nicole Castleman in the commissary when
they reached for the same bottle of catsup at the same
time. They became friends, and when someone con-
ceived the innovative idea of putting a sexy-sound-
ing woman in the traffic helicopter, Nicole suggested
Keely.

Keely had listened to their proposal with a combination of terror and incredulity. She had never spoken
into a microphone in her life. And to get in a helicopter
every day! Mark! His helicopter had been seen going
down under heavy fire. It had exploded, but no body
was ever found. She couldn't.

But she had, seeing the job as her way of keeping

Mark's memory fresh. Over the years it had begun to dim. Also the job forced her to meet her justified fear of aircraft head-on. Keely Preston Williams hated to admit fear of anything.

Her friendship with Nicole Castleman had cemented over the years. They were able to talk to each other with sometimes painful honesty. Last night Nicole had sat cross legged in the middle of Keely's bed while she packed. She had tried to talk Keely out of coming on this mission.

"Haven't you martyred yourself enough, Saint Keely? My God! Your dedication to lost causes is your only stupid trait," she had shouted even as she helped Keely select which clothes to bring.

"Nicole, we've been through this so many times in the years since I've known you that I can almost quote it verbatim. We should just record this conversation and then every time we feel the argument coming on play the tape and save ourselves the breath."

"Sarcasm doesn't become you, Keely, so cut the garbage about a tape recorder. You know I'm right. Every time you meet with those other wives, you come back depressed and stay that way for weeks." She leaned back, displaying her lush figure, which was enviable. It was only one of her assets. She had a veritable mane of blond hair and sea-blue eyes. Her smile was deceptively angelic. That cherub mouth was capable of unleashing a string of obscenities that could make the brawniest seaman quail.

"It's something I have to do, Nicole. They have asked me to be their spokeswoman because I'm the most qualified. I've told them I would. And I will. Besides, I believe in what I'm doing. Not for myself, but for the other families. If Congress votes to have our men declared dead, then their army pay, which is automatically channeled to us, will be severed. I can't stand by and see that happen without doing something."

"Keely, I know that in the beginning, when PROOF was organized, your motives were strong. But when does this purgatory end? When the POWs were released and Mark wasn't among them, you got physically ill. I know. I was there. I saw you go through hell. Are you going to put yourself through that again and again?"

"If I have to, yes. Until I know something about my husband."

"And if you never know?"

"Then you'll have the supreme satisfaction of saying, 'I told you so.' Should I take this ecru blouse or the gray one for that navy suit?"

"Gray and navy. Wonderful," Nicole had muttered in total exasperation. "The ecru. It looks less widowish."

So now Keely was in Washington to face a congressional subcommittee on behalf of the wives and families of the MIAs to plead that the proposal to have those unaccounted-for men declared legally dead be dropped.

When she faced that assembly of congressmen, would her mind be on her plight? The plight of the others? Mark? Or would it be on the man she had met tonight? The one who had said almost shyly, "I just want to spend more time with you, get to know you better." And to whom she had had to say, "I'm married."

"Hilton," the cabby said tersely.

She realized then that they had been stopped for several seconds. "Thank you," she mumbled.

She paid the taxi fare, carried her one bag into the

lobby, and checked into the room that had been reserved for her for weeks. Subconsciously she signed the register Keely Preston, then almost as an afterthought added Williams.

Her room was cold and sterile and impersonal, as hotel rooms in large cities are wont to be. What had their room been like where she and Mark had spent their short honeymoon? She couldn't remember. She could remember very little of their time together after they were married. When she did remember him, it was as a football hero, or as the president of their graduating class, or as her date at the Valentine Prom.

When they had lived that frantic two weeks with his parents, he had been nervous and embarrassed about having Keely sleeping in his room. That first night she had scooted across the narrow mattress to embrace and kiss him. He had shied away and reminded her in hushed tones that his parents were directly beyond the thin wall. The next night he had made some feeble excuse to his curious parents and hustled Keely out of the house. They had driven to the lake, parked, and climbed into the cramped back seat of his Chevy. For Keely, that night, and the others that followed it, had been less than earth-moving. But she had loved Mark and that was all that mattered.

Keely shivered in the cold room as she slipped out of her coat. She switched on the stereo system built into the bedside table, reset the thermostat, and began unpacking her suitcase, smoothing out the wrinkles of each garment before carefully hanging it up. She was almost done when the telephone next to the bed rang.

"Hello," she answered.

"Keely, this is Betty Allway. I was just checking to see that you had got here all right."

Betty was a decade older than Keely and had three children. Her husband had been missing for fourteen years, yet the woman refused to give up hope. She, like Keely, wouldn't take the legal action herself and have her husband declared dead. They had met several years ago and had served on PROOF committees together and corresponded often. As always Keely was inspired by Betty Allway's undaunted courage.

"Hello, Betty. How are you? The children?"

"We're all fine. You? Was your trip from New Orleans pleasant?"

A startlingly accurate vision of Dax Devereaux flashed through Keely's mind. Her heart did a somersault. "Yes. Uneventful." Liar, she accused herself.

"Are you nervous about tomorrow?'

"Oh, no more than I usually am when I have to face a group of grim congressmen carefully guarding the purse strings of the nation."

Betty laughed good-naturedly. "They couldn't be as intimidating as General Vanderslice. We've been through worse. And you know we all have confidence in you."

"I'll try not to let you down."

"If things don't work out like we want them to, it won't be because of you, Keely. What time should we meet in the morning?"

They made plans to meet in the coffee shop of the hotel and go from there to the conference room in the House of Representatives.

Keely hung up, trying to shrug off the despondency that had suddenly cloaked her, and began peeling off her travel-rumpled clothes. She was down to her underwear when the telephone rang again.

Betty must have forgotten a detail. "Hello," she said for the second time.

"You don't wear a wedding ring."

She gasped softly and clutched the half-slip she was holding in her hand against her body like a shield, as though Dax could see her through the telephone wires. She collapsed on the bed, her knees refusing to hold her.

"H-how did you know where to find me?"

"I put the CIA on your trail."

"The—"

"Easy, easy," he laughed. "Can't you take a joke? Actually my taxi followed you to the hotel."

She didn't say anything. He completely disarmed her. She was trembling, twirling the cord of her telephone in her fingers, staring at the striped bedspread, dreading the moment she would have to hang up, when she wouldn't be able to hear his soft breath in her ear.

"You haven't commented on my observation," he finally said to break the silence that neither considered uncomfortable.

"What? Oh, you mean about wearing a wedding ring? Yes, I do wear one, only not when I know my hands are going to perspire as they do when I fly. That's why I didn't have it on tonight."

"Oh." He drew in a deep, remorseful breath. "Well, you can't blame a guy for jumping to the wrong, albeit hopeful, conclusion then." When she didn't respond, he asked, "Can you?"

She laughed then, though there was really nothing funny about the situation. "No, I can't blame a guy for jumping to the wrong conclusion. I should have told you right away that I was married."

Another silence hung between them, this one slightly more tense than the last.

"You didn't eat your dinner on the plane. You must be hungry. Why not go out for a bite with me?"

"Dax!"

"Okay. I'm sorry. Perseverance runs in my blood."

Another silence.

"I can't go out with you, Dax. Please understand. You do, don't you?" It was suddenly vital to her that he did.

A soft expletive sizzled through the cables followed by a deep sigh. "Yes, unfortunately I do."

"Well…" she paused. What did one say at this point? It's been nice knowing you? See you around sometime? Good luck in your Senate race? What she said was "Good night." It wasn't quite as definite as goodbye.

"Good night."

She sighed regretfully as she replaced the receiver. She could almost hear Nicole screaming in her ear, "Have you lost your ever-lovin' mind?"

If they argued constantly about Keely's involvement in PROOF, it was nothing compared to their go-around about Keely's love life, or more to the point, the lack of one.

Nicole loved men. And they loved her. She went through them with the neglect that most women go through a box of Kleenex; she used and discarded them almost daily. But while she was with one, she loved him without limitation. Her men came in all shapes, sizes, and pedigrees. She adored them all.

How Keely could have stayed faithful to her husband for twelve years was beyond Nicole's comprehension. "My God, Keely. Twelve years of living with one man would be ghastly enough, but twelve years of living with a fond memory is absolutely asinine."

"He's not 'one man.' He's my husband," Keely said patiently.

"If this husband of yours comes home one day, which I hate to say I doubt, do you think you'll pick up where you left off? Come on, Keely. You're more intelligent than that. For godsakes. No telling what he'll have gone through. He won't be the same person you remember. You're not the rosy-cheeked cheerleader any longer either, my friend."

"Thanks," Keely cut in dryly.

"That's not a dig, it's a compliment. You're a woman, Keely. You need men—or if that's asking too much of your outdated morals—a man. I'll loan you one of mine."

Keely had laughed in spite of her pique. "No, thank you. I don't know any of yours that I'd have. Except for Charles, maybe." She slanted a shrewd glance at her friend.

"Him? He's not one of 'my men.'"

"No?"

"No!"

"He's in love with you, Nicole."

"Love! He's never even tried to take me to bed. All he wants to do is bug the hell out of me, which he does so well."

"He doesn't cater to your every whim, if that's what you mean."

"We're not discussing Charles and me," she said crisply. "We're discussing you and a man."

"Okay," Keely said dramatically. She planted her hands on her hips and faced Nicole. "Suppose I met *a man*. Do you think *a man* would be content for long to squire me around to movies and dinner without exacting some form of payment?"

"No. You're attractive, intelligent, and sexy as all get-out. He'd want to get you in the sack ASAP."

"Exactly my point. I couldn't do that, Nicole. I'm married to someone else. So, end of affair. End of friendship. I'm back to square one."

"Not necessarily. You *could* go to bed with him. You might even fall in this 'love' you put such stock in. You might even see your way to having Mark declared—"

"Don't say it, Nicole." The warning in Keely's voice silenced any argument.

Nicole hung her head in contrition and studied her well-manicured nails. Finally she looked up at Keely and smiled a repentant smile. "I'm sorry. I went too far." She came forward and embraced her friend warmly, kissed her on the cheek. "I only nag you because I love you."

"I know you do. And I love you. But we'll never agree on this subject, so let's talk about something else. Okay?"

"Okay," Nicole conceded. Then she mumbled. "I still think a terrific roll in the hay with some mean stud would do you a world of good."

If Nicole knew that Keely had passed up an invitation to go for coffee with Dax Devereaux, one of the country's most eligible bachelors, she would no doubt strangle her.

It's not to be, Nicole. Sorry, she thought as she switched on the fluorescent light in the bathroom. A good hot shower was what she needed to ease the tension that contracted every muscle in her body. Then she would curl up in bed and study her notes for her speech tomorrow.

The shower, as it turned out, was lukewarm, but it sufficed, and she felt better when she stepped out and wrapped her washed hair in a towel and pulled on her thick terry-cloth robe. The blue hotel towel and her yellow terry-cloth robe clashed, but what difference did it make?

She was flipping on the lamp beside her already turned-down bed when there was a soft knock on her door. With the characteristic caution of a woman who lives alone, she walked carefully toward the door and checked to make sure the chain lock was in place. "Yes?" she queried softly.

"Room service."

She slumped against the door and pressed her forehead to the cold surface. Vainly she tried to calm the immediate acceleration of her heartbeat. She opened her mouth to speak, found that it had gone dry, and swallowed hard. "Are you insane?" she managed to rasp.

"I must be," Dax said. "This is one of the dumbest things I've done recently, but..." She could imagine his shrug. "May I come in?"

"No."

"Keely, your reputation, not to mention mine and my campaign, will be shot to hell if anyone comes down this hallway and sees me at your door. It would be just like Carl Bernstein and Bob Woodward to find me here. So please open the door before something disastrous like that happens. I have something for you."

Some intuitive niggling in the back of her brain told her that he wouldn't go away until he saw her. She unlatched the chain and drew open the door. Dax was standing on the threshold with a tray in his hands. He was dressed in a casual shirt and jeans. He wore a bellman's cap on his head.

She laughed as she sagged weakly against the jamb. "What are you doing here?"

"I live here," he said and brushed past her, setting the tray on a small round table.

"You *live* here?"

"Yeah. Upstairs on the top floor. It's not practical for a bachelor to own a house in D.C. Expensive as hell. So I keep a suite of rooms here."

"That's why it was so convenient to follow me. You were coming here anyway," she teased.

"It made it easier. I would have followed you anyway." He wasn't teasing.

She shifted uncomfortably and glanced at the tray, which was draped with a white linen cloth. "What is that?"

"Room service," he said by way of a flippant explanation and took off the cap with a flourish. "I never lie."

Until then she had forgotten about the towel wrapped around her head, the homey terry-cloth robe, and her bare feet. Embarrassment climbed up her neck to blossom in her cheeks. She made to scurry past him. "I'll only be a minute."

"You look fine," he said, laughing and reaching out to grab her arm. If he hadn't touched her, it might never have happened. As it was, he did touch her.

It was the warmth of his fingers along the inside of

her wrist that did more to halt her rush from the room than did the strength of his grasp. She skidded to a stop but didn't turn around to face him. His laughter subsided then died altogether.

It was with the merest tugging on her wrist that he turned her around to face him. Her eyes were wide with guilt and apprehension, his full of supplication. Gradually they inclined toward each other until his hand came up and cradled her cheek. Ebony eyes sought out and adored each feature of her face. His thumb stroked across her quivering mouth. Of their own volition her lids shuttered her tear-flooded eyes.

Dax hesitantly bent his head and brushed his lips across hers. White heat seared through him. Her breath escaped from slightly parted lips in a thin, anguished whisper. He stared down at her mouth, at the incredibly fragile eyelids fringed by long lashes, and succumbed to the temptation again. He touched her lips with his.

Instinctively she moved closer. Bodies brushed, eased away, touched, fused. Then primeval hunger seized them. Caution was thrown to the wind, the barriers were broken down, and a flood of sexual tension that had been building since they first saw each other burst free of the dams of conscience and prohibition.

He clutched her to him as his mouth melded into hers. Strong arms, yet gentle, wrapped around her back and molded her against his body with such an exquisite fit that Keely was made dizzy by the sensations. Her hands found their way to his waist and settled lightly on his belt. Then around to his lower back. Then up to explore the smooth muscles under his soft shirt.

The towel became dislodged from her hair and fell to the floor. Her wet strands were ravaged by his fingers before they cupped her head and held it immobile while the exploration of her mouth deepened.

His mouth moved over hers, testing each angle, delighting in each nuance, savoring the taste. His tongue slid persuasively along her bottom lip before it dipped repeatedly into her mouth, taking and giving equally. The plunder increased in tempo and ferocity until it became too evocative, too fiercely passionate, too erotically symbolic, for them to ignore. They broke apart under the impact.

A tear trickled down Keely's cheek and she covered her mouth with a shaking hand. Dax held on to her shoulders lightly, searching her face, his dark eyes pleading for her understanding. She pulled herself free and flew across the room to the wide window. She leaned against the cold pane of glass, squeezing her eyes shut against her shame, sobbing in dry, heaving gulps.

Dax didn't follow her. Instead he dropped into a chair. His knees were spread wide, his elbows propped on them, his face buried in his hands.

After a while he rubbed his face hard. He looked at the woman still cowering at the window. "Keely, please don't cry. I'm sorry. I shouldn't have come here. I swore to myself that I wouldn't touch you, but…" he dwindled off lamely.

"It's not your fault," she said barely above a whisper. "I shouldn't have let you in." After a soul-searching moment she added, "I wanted to."

He was sitting in the chair, forlornly staring at the carpet between his shoes, when she turned around. "Dax, I haven't been fair to you. I want to tell you about me, my life. There are things you should know. Then you'll understand."

He looked up at her then bleakly. "You don't need to tell me anything, Keely. I know all about you. I'm one of the congressmen you'll be appealing to tomorrow."

CHAPTER THREE

HAD HE WHIPPED a switchblade out of his pocket and threatened her life, she couldn't have been more stunned. Speechless, she stood there and stared at him. "That's impossible," she husked.

He shook his head. He made no other movement.

"But your name isn't on the list. I've had a list of the members of that subcommittee for weeks. Your name isn't on it." She was trying desperately to remain sensible, to set the world right again, to get things back on the proper footing.

"Congressman Haley from Colorado was voted last week to serve on the Ways and Means Committee. My constituents thought it would be a good idea for me to replace him on this one when the chair became vacant."

Keely still maintained her post in front of the window. Was it a bulwark she had erected in her mind? She had to leave its tenuous security sometime. Unconsciously she tightened the tie belt on her robe and pushed herself away from the window. She walked toward the bed, only to stop several feet from it. Her hands had nothing to do, so she crossed her arms defensively over her chest before facing him.

Anger championed her shame. "Well, Congressman Devereaux, you've certainly armed yourself with an arsenal of rebuttal, haven't you?" she asked scathingly. "My carefully planned speech about how we still hope that our men are alive will be worth only so much smoke, won't it?"

"Keely—"

"You should be proud of yourself. Tell me, do you go to this much trouble on every political issue you want voted your way?"

"Stop that!" he snapped. "I didn't know who you were until I got upstairs to my room. I had reams of paperwork to read over, to familiarize myself with, before tomorrow. Quite by accident I read that the spokeswoman for PROOF was one Mrs. Keely Williams. How many Keelys do you know? When I checked the desk downstairs and found out that a Keely *Preston* Williams was in Room 714, I put two and two together. I swear I didn't know about you until then."

"But when you found out, you didn't waste any time getting down here to see just how sincere we grass widows are, did you?" She covered her face with her hands, furious with the tears that wouldn't be stemmed.

"Dammit, my coming here, my kissing you, had nothing to do with tomorrow, or the outcome of the hearing, or anything else."

"Didn't it?" she flared.

"No!" he roared. He was standing now, facing her, hands on hips, as angry and distraught as she. When he saw the visible pain on her strained features, he emphasized more softly, earnestly, "No."

She turned away from him, hugging herself tightly, fearing if she didn't hold herself together physically, her spirit would shatter and fly apart. If she had felt torn between decisions before, divided by loyalties, the interference of Dax Devereaux in her life had compounded her quandary a hundredfold.

"You can't understand," she whispered.

He longed to go to her, take her in his arms, reassure her that everything would work out well, but he dared not. The dejection he read in her posture indicated the terrible confusion that gripped her. It was better to let her solve it in her own mind. "Maybe I *can* understand. Why don't you tell me?"

She faced him again with glaring accusation in the green eyes. Hastily he added, "Not as Congressman Devereaux. Explain it to me as Dax."

She sat on the edge of the bed, tense, her shoulders hunched in self-protection. He returned to the chair. Quietly, methodically, and with no dramatic gesture or inflection, she told him a capsulized rendition of her courtship and marriage to Mark Williams, his disappearance, and the resultant havoc it had wreaked on her life.

"I have neither the status of a widow nor of a divorcée. I'm married, yet without a husband or home or children. I live as a single woman, but am most definitely not."

She stopped talking, but she didn't look at him, only stared at her lap. After a length of time he asked quietly, "You never considered freeing yourself?"

Her head shot up. "You mean have Mark declared dead, don't you?" she asked incisively. Involuntarily he flinched under the harsh quality of her question. "No. In spite of stringent advice against it, I've remained faithful to my husband and the belief that he's still alive. On the outside chance that he does come home someday, I want to be here for him. There would be no one else. Since he was reported missing, his father has died. His mother is in a nursing home. She is no longer able to take care of herself. The grief…" She sighed and rubbed her forehead with her fingertips. "Mark's paycheck goes to support her. I don't keep any of it for myself." Now she looked at him. "Dax, it's her and the wives with children who desperately need that money. If that bill is passed to have our men—"

She broke off abruptly and raised her chin defiantly. "But then, you'll hear my formal speech tomorrow, won't you?"

He stood up then, looking as tired and despondent as she. "Yes. I'll hear it tomorrow."

Without another word he walked to the door and opened it. On the threshold he turned to face her. "Don't forget to eat something." He indicated the long-forgotten tray with a quick jerk of his chin. "Good night, Keely," he said softly. Then he was gone.

Keely stood in the middle of the suddenly empty room and stared at the closed door. A hopelessness that she hadn't acknowledged in a long while smothered her like a shroud. She felt desolate and lonely. So lonely.

And in spite of it all, she longed to feel again the strength of Dax's arms and the urgent pressure of his mouth.

HER CRITICAL APPRAISAL of the image in the mirror determined that she looked as good as she could. Maybe she shouldn't have listened to Nicole and brought the gray blouse instead. It had a simple rolled collar that tied in a chaste bow. The one she had brought had tulle-lined lace inserts on the collar and across her collarbone. Well, she sighed, it was too late now. Maybe that touch of femininity relieved the severity of the navy suit with its straight skirt and blazer.

Navy suede pumps, a matching purse, and her cashmere coat the same color as her caramel-colored hair completed her ensemble. She tucked her trim leather attaché under her arm and took the elevator down to the lobby to meet Betty Allway for breakfast.

"You look gorgeous as always," Betty remarked with a spark of envy tempered by honest admiration. "How do you stay so slender living in New Orleans, the eating capital of the world? I'd weigh four hundred pounds in a month."

Betty's good humor was infectious and Keely found herself chatting about her work and asking Betty about her children. The older woman supplied her with an animated tale about each one of them.

"The baby was only four months old when Bill was reported missing. He's never seen him. Now that 'baby' is a strapping basketball player on the high school team." A touch of sadness came into her usually optimistic eyes and Keely reached over to cover the workworn hand with her own.

"It never gets easier to accept, does it?" Keely mused aloud. "We learn to live with it. But I don't think we ever truly accept it."

"I know I can't and won't. Until I've got a positive confirmation of Bill's death, I'll go on believing that he is alive." She took a sip of coffee. "By the way, we may have a fly in the ointment. Congressman Parker, the chairman of the subcommittee, called me this morning."

Keely thought she knew what might be coming, but

she said a cool "Oh?" before taking a small bite of her English muffin.

"One of the congressmen I thought we could count on for support has been chosen to serve on a standing committee. He's been replaced by a Daxton Devereaux from Louisiana. Do you know him?"

Keely edged away from a direct answer and said, "Everyone in Louisiana has heard of Dax Devereaux." Cautiously she asked, "Do you think he'll be an opponent?"

Betty stared concernedly into her coffee cup while an unobtrusive waiter filled it for her. "I don't know. From what I understand, he's politically ambitious. He's a likely candidate for the Senate in the next election."

"That doesn't really mean anything. He may see taking our side as a point in his favor."

"What about his economic policy?"

"I'm not in his congressional district, so I don't really know," Keely answered truthfully.

"I've heard that he advocates tax cuts. He's a fanatic for trimming down government spending. That definitely worries me."

Keely tried to interject a bright nonchalance into her voice when she said, "Well, the jury is still out. There are ten other men on that subcommittee. Let's not concede defeat yet."

"Never!" said Betty heartily and then laughed without humor. Her steady gray eyes met Keely's over the cluttered table. "I know it's not fair, Keely, but we do depend on you so much to do our talking for us."

That was the last thing Keely wanted to hear this morning. She felt like Judas. "I know you do," she said. "I'll do my best." What would Betty think of her if she knew she had been kissing Dax Devereaux last night with an abandon that even now made her blush in remembrance?

"We'd better go," Betty said briskly. "Let's not give them the satisfaction of our being late. The others will meet us there."

They settled the bill and went outside. The rain was gone, but a cold, biting wind was sweeping through the capital. They hailed a cab, and the driver fought morning rush-hour traffic to deposit them in front of the House of Representatives.

Keely had never dreaded anything more than she did facing Dax. Her night had been a restless one. She had dreamed of Mark and that always upset her. It had been a regular occurrence when he had first left for Vietnam. Even after he was reported missing, he had played key roles in her dreams.

Over the years, however, the dreams had become less frequent and dimmer, more nebulous. When he invaded her subconscious mind, he was still a youth, a nineteen-year-old boy. Now, if he were alive, he was a mature man. What did he look like? She had no idea, and that haunted her. The man to whom she was linked by name and holy vow she might not even recognize if they accidentally met on the street.

"Keely?" Betty's tentative nudging roused her from her reverie, and she asked, "Are we here already? I was rehearsing my speech in my head." When had she started lying so blatantly and with such constancy? Since she had met Dax. Since she had talked to him, laughed with him, touched him, kissed him. Since she had admitted only to herself that, for the first time in years, she wanted to experience the physical loving of a man.

There were three other women who met them in the corridors of the Congress. They, too, were actively campaigning to prevent the MIAs from being classified as dead. Keely knew them all and greeted them warmly.

A page ushered them into the chamber where the subcommittee hearing was to be held. Keely was seated at a table with a microphone mounted on it. Betty was beside her. The others took seats behind them.

Keely took her notes out of the attaché, stacked them neatly, arranged her purse on the table, anything to keep her eyes from scanning the room, though she didn't think Dax was there yet. Pages, aides, reporters, and the other committee members moved around the room, greeting each other, shaking hands, talking, reading newspapers or briefs. Keely took off her coat and a page rushed to help her. She was thanking him graciously over her shoulder when she saw Dax walk into the paneled room.

Their eyes met and locked. Each was powerless to control the intense attraction, so they graciously surrendered to it and allowed themselves the luxury of looking at each other. For a moment they were held captive by the other's presence in the room, oblivious of everyone else. Keely saw mirrored in his face the same yearning she felt. It held on tenaciously. All through the restless night when she had awakened from her dreams, it hadn't been the security of Mark's arms she longed for, but Dax's. The whispered words of comfort she imagined hadn't come from her husband's lips, but from a mouth juxtaposed most alluringly to a deep dimple. It had been Dax's eyes, dark and fathomless, that had warmed her chilled soul.

Their binding gaze wasn't broken until another congressman moved in front of Dax and took his hand in a hearty, backslapping handshake. Keely faced the front of the room again, tugged the hem of her skirt down over her crossed knees, and read—or pretended to read—the papers she held in her damp hands. How could she possibly live through this?

A few minutes later the hearing was called to order. Congressman Parker of Michigan, the chairman, made his opening remarks and introduced each member of the subcommittee to the representatives of PROOF. When he introduced Dax Devereaux, Betty's elbow touched Keely's right ribs gently. She wasn't sure what that covert gesture was supposed to convey and she didn't turn her head to look at Betty and find out. Dax was obviously the youngest member of the subcommittee. He was unequivocally the most handsome. But was he friend or foe? There were eleven congressmen serving on the committee, the majority party having the advantage of one. Dax was of the majority.

Congressman Parker adjusted the half-glasses on his nose and peered over the silver rims at Keely. "Now, Mrs. Williams, I think you have prepared a statement on behalf of PROOF. We should like to hear it at this time."

"Thank you, Congressman Parker." She addressed the members of the committee, the press, and then in her well-modulated, softly Southern voice, presented the case for PROOF. She neither read her copious notes nor quoted anything by rote. Instead she spoke conversationally, with conviction, but on a personal level, as though she were addressing each committee member on a one-to-one basis.

In conclusion she said, "It is our most sincere hope that you, as esteemed and knowledgeable representatives of the American people, will table this proposed bill. That you will keep those classified as Missing In Action alive until we are all satisfied to the contrary."

No one moved for a moment, impressed by her informative collection of facts and her unemotional, but puissant, presentation of them. Then under the cover of the restless shifting of people who had sat still and quiet for a long time, she heard Betty's "Bravo." Her acclaim was echoed by the women sitting behind them.

"Thank you, Mrs. Williams." Congressman Parker looked down either side of the table, which was set up panel-fashion to face the women, and queried, "Gentlemen? Does anyone have points for discussion?"

For the next hour and a half Keely and her group fielded questions and asked many of their own. Points were scored and lost on each side, but most of the committee members seemed in sympathy with the lobbyists if not in agreement with them.

Keely tried to keep her eyes off Dax, but it was almost impossible. He didn't contribute anything to the heated discussion, but sat back, his fingers tented over the bridge of his nose, and listened closely. She wished she knew what he was thinking.

Only one of the congressmen was openly hostile, Congressman Walsh from Iowa. His questions bordered on belligerence, and he made what he considered to be valid observations with an attitude of condescension.

"Mrs. Williams," he addressed Keely directly in a

bored, half-amused voice. "Forgive me for pointing out that your appearance doesn't exactly denote poverty. Most of you who are married to or mothers of the MIAs have made new lives for yourselves. Don't you feel the least bit guilty about bleeding the federal government of moneys that may best be appropriated elsewhere?"

Keely bit back a nasty retort that would tell the congressman in no uncertain terms what she thought of him and his heritage. Instead she said levelly, "I don't think any of us should feel guilty about accepting pay for a job done, do you, Congressman? Our husbands or sons are considered to be still in the service of their country. They should be paid just like any other soldier."

"Mrs.—"

"Please, may I finish?" she asked coolly, and he grudgingly assented. "There is more involved here than money. If our MIAs are declared dead, then whatever measures the government and the army are taking to provide us with information will desist immediately. We must not let that happen as long as there is the slimmest chance that these hundreds of men are still alive, possibly being held prisoner or surviving by whatever means they can."

The sanctimonious, pompous man leaned back in his chair and crossed his stout arms over his protruding belly. "Do you actually, in all honesty, believe that your husband, or any of these men, is still alive?" Before she could answer, he turned his shiny balding head toward Dax. "Congressman Devereaux, we haven't heard from you. You served in Vietnam, did you not?"

Keely's surprised eyes riveted on Dax and she was disconcerted to find him staring straight at her. "Yes," she heard him answer. She had no idea he was a veteran of the war.

"In what capacity?" the older man persisted.

Each eye in the room was now trained on Dax. "I was a Marine captain."

"For how long were you in Vietnam?"

"Three years."

"A Marine captain sees quite a lot of action, I would imagine," the man drawled unctuously. "Basing your answer on what you experienced there, would you say it's even conceivably possible that these missing men are still alive?"

Dax sat forward and rested his folded hands on the table in front of him. He studied them for a long moment before he answered the loaded question. "The war in Vietnam broke all the rules of warfare. I wouldn't say that it was conceivably possible that small children could be bribed to walk into a group of GIs and pull the pin on a hand grenade, but I saw it happen. Nor is it conceivably possible that commanding officers could be shot by their own men who were strung out on drugs, but I saw that happen too. During one skirmish I sustained a minor flesh wound. An old Vietnamese civilian gave me a drink of water and bandaged my wound before the medic could get to me. The next morning his head was mounted on a pike not ten feet from where I was sleeping." He fixed hard, cold eyes on the flustered congressman and said with a brittle voice, "In a war of such atrocious impossibilities, anything is conceivably possible. That's the only way I know to answer your question."

There was not a breath in the room. Tears blurred

Keely's vision as she watched Congressman Parker call the meeting adjourned for lunch.

THERE WAS A flurry of people gathering up their coats and briefcases, laughing and chattering in a vain attempt to alleviate the dark mood Dax Devereaux's words had cast over the room.

The women of PROOF congratulated Keely as a group and then singly for her eloquent expression of their petition and hugged her in turn. She pulled on her coat and neatly replaced the papers in her attaché case. It was an extreme effort not to look at Dax, who was being besieged by constituents and reporters.

"Keely, thank you," Betty said and hugged the younger woman to her. "You were wonderful. I don't know if we'll succeed or not, but at least we gave it our best shot."

"We're not done yet. I don't think Congressman Walsh is finished. If anything, I think D—Congressman Devereaux's elocution angered him and made him even more resentful to us."

Betty looked at the retreating bulk of the man as he imperiously shoved his way past eager reporters. "That big blowhard," Betty scoffed. "He's only trying to get his name on the six-o'clock news. I'm afraid that if they compare him to Dax Devereaux, he'll come out looking like a fool—which I personally think he is." Her eyes surveyed the room and latched on to Dax as he was being interviewed by a network television reporter. "Have you ever seen a man as gorgeous as that one?" she whispered to Keely.

"Who?" Keely asked with feigned ignorance even as her heart started thumping in her breast. "Oh, you mean Congressman Devereaux? I guess he is rather charismatic. But you're not the first woman in the country to notice, you know."

"My guess is that he'll go far, at least with the women voters." Betty giggled girlishly. "Who could resist that dimple? And what he had to say—"

"Excuse me, Mrs. Allway, Mrs. Williams."

They turned to face a serious, middle-aged man in a brown tweed suit that could have stood a good pressing. His sparse salt-and-pepper hair was sticking out around his head as though he had just come in from a gale wind. He looked at them through wire-framed glasses that were popular a decade ago. "Yes?" Keely replied.

"I'm Al Van Dorf of the Associated Press."

"Hello, Mr. Van Dorf," Betty answered for both of them.

"It seems that the two of you more or less represent PROOF, at least you've always been more vocal than some of the others. I was wondering if you'd join me for lunch. I'd appreciate an interview with you."

"Keely?" Betty deferred to her. Keely took an instant liking to the reporter. He didn't seem the aggressive, boisterous type. She liked the fact that he seemed nervous about asking them to lunch.

"I think that would be all right."

"Thank you," Van Dorf said. "Both of you." He included Betty in his self-effacing smile. He handed Keely a piece of paper. "Here's the name of the restaurant. The reservations have been made. I'll meet you there in say—" he consulted a wristwatch "—half an hour. That should allow us time to get there."

"Fine. We'll be there," Betty said.

"Ladies." He shifted his tape recorder from one hand to the other and gave them an old-fashioned half-bow before scampering off, just as a television reporter approached the women for a statement. Betty backed away, leaving Keely to face the lights and cameras alone.

By the time they edged their way out into the corridor, said goodbye to the other women of PROOF, answered the questions of the competitive reporters, and wended their way through the miles of hallway to the outside of the Congress, they barely had time to flag a cab and get to their luncheon appointment.

In the taxi Keely brushed her hair and applied fresh lipstick while Betty powdered her nose. They were only a few minutes late when the taxi pulled up in front of a quiet-looking restaurant on an avenue not far from Embassy Row. They hurried inside and were greeted by a maître d' who was escorting them to a table before they could even identify themselves.

Keely almost stumbled on the well-worn carpet under her pumps when she saw Dax sitting along the wall on the banquette. Van Dorf, Congressman Parker, and Congressman Walsh stood as the two women approached the table. Betty seemed as alarmed as Keely as they were greeted by the small assembly.

"Mrs. Allway, Mrs. Williams, I'm glad you could make it," Van Dorf was saying in a much more assured voice than he had used on them in the congressional chamber. What had happened to his shuffling timidity? "You know these men, of course, but let me reintroduce you. Congressman Walsh from Iowa, Congressman Parker from Michigan, and Congressman Devereaux from Louisiana."

The ladies extended their hands to be shaken by each of the men. Dax shook Betty's hand and said, "A pleasure, Mrs. Allway." As his firm fingers closed around hers, Keely dared to raise her eyes to his. They were warm and gave off a hungry look that she hoped fervently no one else could discern. That's why she was so shocked when he said, "Mrs. Williams, how nice to see you again."

CHAPTER FOUR

KEELY COVERED HER gasp of surprise by saying, "Hello, Congressman." His fingers pressed hers quickly before releasing them.

"You know each other?" Congressman Parker voiced the question all the others were silently asking.

Keely knew that Betty Allway's eyes had gone wide with disbelief and that her mouth had formed a moue of perplexity, but she dared not look at her friend.

"Yes," Dax answered easily. "We were on the same flight last night and introduced ourselves then. Mrs. Williams." He moved aside, allowing Keely to slide onto the banquette between him and Parker. Taking his cue from Dax, Congressman Walsh, oozing charm, held Betty's chair for her and she sat between him and Al Van Dorf.

Keely admired the aplomb with which Dax had handled the awkward situation, though she thought him dangerously honest. What would the other congressmen think? Would it disturb them to know she and Dax had met beforehand? Apparently not. Parker was already studying the menu through his half-glasses. Walsh was boisterously hailing a constituent sitting at another table. Only Betty seemed somewhat shaken. Keely noticed that her hand was trembling as she took a sip out of her water glass.

Dax, seemingly unaffected, helped Keely off with her coat while chattily asking Van Dorf about a recent banking scandal the reporter had uncovered. The hand that smoothed down her back as he adjusted the coat along the banquette belied his indifference to her.

The waiter took their drink orders and Van Dorf asked, "Does anyone mind if I smoke?" Without waiting for a response, he lighted up a short unfiltered cigarette. He talked around it as he set his tape recorder in the middle of the table. "I thought it would be beneficial if we had a casual, off-the-cuff meeting away from the hearing chambers. The issue at hand involves money, politics, foreign policy, the military, and human emotions. I think you can all see why I consider it to be an important news story. Will you indulge me and speak candidly?"

"Everyone knows how I feel about this," Walsh huffed.

"We can always count on you, Congressman, to be vocal about your position on any topic," Van Dorf said. The stodgy representative from Iowa missed the subtle insult. Van Dorf's eyes, which had looked at Keely and Betty with such humility only an hour ago, now shone with rapacious incisiveness behind his glasses. Had the man undergone a personality change? Keely was coming to realize that she had been hoodwinked, as had many of Van Dorf's former victims.

She picked up the stiff linen napkin folded over her place setting and laid it in her lap. Dax was doing the same. Keely's eyes glazed in shock when Dax clasped her hand under the table and gave it a hard, quick squeeze. When he brought his hands back to the tabletop, his innocent expression gave away nothing. Keely hoped her rapid, shallow breathing could be accounted for by the off-color joke Congressman Walsh had just told.

When the waiter came back to take their lunch orders, Keely said, "Caesar salad, please."

When Dax had asked for a steak sandwich, he turned to her with a mock scowl. "That's not much lunch for a growing girl."

She laughed softly. "That's why I don't eat much lunch. I don't want to grow."

"You don't eat enough anytime."

"I ate—" She was about to tell him that she had eaten a half of one of the four sandwiches he had left in her room last night when, out of the corner of her eye, she caught sight of Van Dorf across the table. He had the look of a fox. It was a silly notion, but she could almost imagine that his ears had grown sharp and pointed as he strained to hear their conversation without appearing to do so. "I guess my appetite isn't very active," she finished.

Since Betty was conversing with Walsh and Parker, it looked quite normal for them to be talking together, but Dax sensed, as she did, Van Dorf's interest. He turned toward the reporter and asked, "Al, are you still playing racquetball when you're not chasing down a hot lead?"

Dax had an uncanny knack for tapping into someone's vulnerability. Van Dorf automatically launched into a detailed account of his latest bout, of which he was the victor. Keely wondered what the reporter would think if he knew that the shin of her crossed leg was being safely protected by Dax's calf beneath the table.

During the meal the chatter was limited to generalities. No one broached the subject that weighed so heavily on all their minds. But when their after-lunch coffee had been served, Van Dorf changed the tape in his recorder and lighted another pungent cigarette. "Do you think your husband is still alive, Mrs. Allway?" he asked brusquely.

Betty, taken completely off guard, sputtered around the sip of hot coffee she had just taken. "I—I couldn't…. Why…"

Keely quickly came to her rescue. "That isn't the point of the hearing, Mr. Van Dorf. Whether Bill Allway or my husband or any of the MIAs is alive isn't the issue here. Our immediate goal is to see that channels to confirm or deny their deaths are kept open. And at the same time to allow their families to collect money rightfully due them."

"Do you agree with that, Mrs. Allway?" Van Dorf asked.

"Yes," Betty replied, her equanimity restored.

"I'm curious to hear what the army has to say this afternoon," Parker said. "Do you have any idea what their stand will be, Mrs. Williams?"

"The last time we had a meeting with military personnel, they were supportive. I hope their attitude hasn't changed."

Walsh leaned back in his chair and said expansively, "Now, little lady, you—"

"Please don't address me as a 'little lady,' Congressman Walsh. I find it offensive," Keely said firmly.

Walsh looked momentarily nonplussed, then he grinned patronizingly. "I assure you I didn't mean—"

"Of course you did," Keely said. "Your opinion of

us is all too apparent. You consider us to be a group of hysterical women wasting your valuable time. I wonder what your attitude would be if we were a group of men making an appeal. Would that give us more credibility? I assure you that there are numerous men in our organization, Congressman. Fathers, sons, brothers. They are just as concerned and resolved as we, but they find it harder to address such an emotional issue publicly. For that reason you'll find more women actively engaged in our efforts."

There was a silence around the table. Finally Congressman Parker said quietly, "I'd hate to think that anyone serving on this or any other committee would be blinded by prejudice of any kind." He glanced balefully at Walsh.

"Well, I certainly meant no offense and I wouldn't want to be accused of being chauvinistic. I apologize, Mrs. Williams," he blustered.

Keely's tone didn't soften, but she said, "Apology accepted. I'm sorry I broke your train of thought. What point were you about to make?"

And so it went. For the next half hour ideas were exchanged and discussed. All the while Van Dorf looked on with almost lascivious curiosity, his eyes darting around the table like a ricocheting bullet. His recorder didn't stop. When he was presented with the check, he scrawled his name across it and stood abruptly. "I guess it's time we all made our way back. Thank you for consenting to this luncheon. The maître d' will hail cabs for us," he said as they all stood.

"I think I'll walk a few blocks," Parker said. "Mrs. Allway, may I help you with your coat?" He matched action to words as he escorted Betty toward the door.

"Devereaux, do you want to share a cab with me?" Walsh asked.

"Thank you, but I need to stop by my office. I'll take my own."

"Then if you don't mind, I'll grab the first one."

"Not at all," Dax answered as the other congressman lumbered off.

Van Dorf, after pocketing his cartridge tapes, rushed toward a cigarette vending machine. Keely and Dax were granted a few moments of relative privacy.

"Remind me never to get your dander up," he whispered near her ear while holding her coat as she slid her arms in. "You've got sharp claws."

"That ignorant, bigoted buffoon," she said. "He's laughable. Imagine him holding a congressional seat. It's frightening."

"You were superb." His hand rested against her waist. Only to the casual observer would it appear that he was escorting her in a detached gentlemanly manner. To one more observant his touch would look like a caress.

"Why did you tell them we had met before?" she asked over her shoulder.

"For your information, Van Dorf is ruthless. He's after the next Watergate story. Be careful of him, Keely. He's a wolf in sheep's clothing."

"I likened him to a cunning fox rather than a wolf. He led Betty and me to believe that we were his only guests for lunch. He failed to mention that you congressmen would be here. He made a self-effacing, pleading invitation, while all along he was baiting a trap."

"That creep. I'd like to cram that tape recorder of

his down his throat. Or somewhere even more appropriate."

Keely couldn't stop the laugh that threatened. She turned to face him. "Remind me never to get your dander up," she taunted. He smiled, deepening the dimple. "Your fiery Creole heritage is showing."

"Is it? I'm sorry."

"Don't be. It's rather attractive."

"Do you think so?"

She looked around nervously. Betty and Congressman Parker were standing by the door watching for the promised taxis. Van Dorf was cursing the vending machine that had taken his change but hadn't come forth with the cigarettes. Walsh had left.

"Why did you tell them that we had met last night?"

"That was your original question, wasn't it? You see, when I'm around you, I have a hell of a time keeping my mind off— Never mind. To answer your question, if Van Dorf or anyone like him had seen us talking together last night and then we pretended never to have met today, that would pique someone's curiosity. Telling the truth is always the best policy."

"And if someone had seen you either coming into or going out of my room last night, what then?"

His eyes twinkled with devilish humor. "Then telling a lie is always the best policy."

She laughed. "You're a politician, all right."

He wasn't offended. Indeed, he laughed. His smile softened measurably when he asked, "How are you? Did you get any rest last night?"

She wished he wouldn't look at her with such concern. His eyes touched on each feature of her face and they grew warm under his interest. Why wouldn't her heart slow down? It beat so strenuously that it stirred the lace across her chest, a fact that Dax's wandering eyes took note of. "I didn't sleep too well, no."

"I take full responsibility for that."

"You shouldn't."

"But I do," he stressed. "I shouldn't have upset you. And don't deny that I did. When you first told me at the airport that you were married, I should have left you alone. That would have been best."

"Would it?"

"Wouldn't it?"

Pulled together by some invisible, inexplicable force, they felt themselves moving closer. Dax could feel the blood rushing to his extremities. His fingertips throbbed with it, with the need to touch her. The scar under his eye twitched. Too vividly his lips recalled the feel of her mouth beneath them. His eyes bored into hers.

Reflexively she licked her lips and he followed the sensuous course of her tongue with his eyes. "Yes," she said breathlessly. "It probably would have been best."

"I've forgotten the question again."

"Keely?"

"What?" She spun around guiltily when Betty called to her from the door. "Is the cab here?" she asked on a gulping breath.

Betty eyed her flushed cheeks and agitated breast suspiciously. "Yes."

They said their goodbyes to Dax and their thank-yous to Van Dorf who was demanding his lost money from the management. Congressman Parker went out with them.

When they were situated in the back seat of the

drafty taxi, Keely ineffectually fumbled with the clasp of her purse. "You don't have to tell me, but I confess I'm curious," Betty said.

"About what?" Keely strove for nonchalance, but knew she wasn't fooling anyone. Especially herself.

"Come on, Keely. This morning when I asked you about Dax Devereaux, I presented you with a golden opportunity to tell me about your meeting him last night. You didn't."

"I didn't think it was important."

Betty reached out and took Keely's damp hand in her own. She held it until Keely raised her eyes and looked at the older woman. "Women are characteristically more perceptive than men. Hopefully no one else at that table noticed the undercurrents running between you and the handsome congressman every time you looked at each other, but I did. I'm not being nosy. Your personal life is none of my business, Keely. I don't presume to censure you. I'm only cautioning you to be careful. Don't do something that will open you up for criticism, something that could jeopardize your reputation and integrity, not to mention PROOF."

Keely shook her head emphatically. "I would never do anything that stupid, Betty. You must know that."

"I know you *think* you wouldn't. I may seem old and dried up to you, Keely, but I'm a woman who hasn't had her man for over fourteen years. A man with Dax Devereaux's charm could tempt a saint to fall from grace."

Keely turned her head away, her eyes staring sightlessly at the Washington Monument that pointed toward heaven like an accusing finger. "I know what you mean."

The afternoon session of the hearing was taken up

by the dull, routine, monotoned recitations of an army general. He read one affidavit after another from various branches of the military. The names and ranks were impressive, but the documents shed no new light on the issue. The general straddled the proverbial fence whenever an exasperated Congressman Parker tried to pin him down to a definitive statement. He had been coached to keep his comments generic and his opinions qualified. When the gavel banged on the block, dismissing the session for the day, everyone greeted it with a collective, bored sigh of relief.

Keely lost sight of Dax as he left the chambers. She and the other members of PROOF arranged to meet at Le Lion d'Or and treat themselves to a lavish dinner.

"We deserve it after two hours of General Adams," Betty said.

They went to their separate rooms when they arrived at the Capital Hilton. Keely wasn't looking forward to the evening as she should. Even a hot shower, careful grooming, and dressing in her coral print crepe de chine dress didn't generate any enthusiasm for the hours ahead. By an act of will, when she met Betty in the lobby, she pushed her despondency aside.

The meal was sumptuous, the atmosphere serene, the service without flaw. By tacit agreement the women who joined Betty and Keely didn't talk about the hearing or speculate on its outcome. They discussed fashions, the latest Hollywood scandal, their children, hairstyles, movies, books, and diets. They laughed, knowing what Congressman Walsh's comment would be if he saw them at the expensive restaurant.

Keely contributed to the conversations, ate and drank her fair share but by the time she waved good-night at her floor of the hotel and got off the elevator, she was exhausted and ready to fall into bed.

All evening her mind had strayed to thoughts of Dax. She saw him as he had been on the airplane, solicitously clasping her hands, reassuring her. He came to her mind looking as he had last night wearing the bellman's cap and holding the tray on his shoulder, laughing and teasing. Then her mind homed in on what she most wanted to forget—his eyes, his mouth, passionate and hot and hungry, his hands.

She slammed the door behind her when she reached her room, slung her coat over a chair, and tossed her purse and room key onto the dresser. "What in the hell am I doing?" she angrily asked her image in the mirror. "You're only torturing yourself, Keely."

Her limbs felt like lead appendages as she undressed. She flopped down onto the bed when she was at last washed, creamed, and brushed. Reaching for the alarm, she cursed under her breath when the telephone rang.

"Hello." Would it be Dax?

"Hi! Whatcha doin'?"

"Nicole! Hi." She ignored a pang of disappointment and put it down as indigestion.

"You sound tired," Nicole said.

"Do I? It's no wonder. I…uh…I didn't sleep well last night and today was hell. That congressional chamber seems to have walls that close in the longer you're there. What's happening at home? Everything all right?"

"Fine. Charles roped me into having dinner with two sponsors tonight. You should have seen their wives. Charter members of the Blue Hair and Mink Club of

Suburban America. D-o-w-d-y! And Charles was his typical pain-in-the-posterior self."

Charles Hepburn was one of the television station's most successful salesmen. He sold more commercial time to more local clients than all the other salesmen together. His quiet, efficient manner attracted potential sponsors even before they enjoyed his thorough personal handling of their accounts.

"Nicole, you're not fooling me. You adore him."

She sighed theatrically. "I guess he's okay. If there's absolutely no one else around and absolutely nothing else to do."

Keely laughed in spite of her dour mood. Nicole had the gift of cheering up even the most dismal of days, for she never let herself get depressed.

"Hey, the newspapers here are full of Dax Devereaux being on that subcommittee. I didn't know that, did you?"

"Not until I got here, no."

"Well?"

"Well what?"

"Oh, hell, Keely. Are you going to make me drag it out of you? Have you met him?'

"Yes."

"And?"

"And what?"

Nicole's expletive made Keely cringe. "You're going to melt the cables if you don't stop talking like that over the telephone."

"Don't be coy with me," Nicole said crossly. "What do you think of Devereaux?"

"I don't know much about him. I've barely met him, Nicole."

"Oh, for sweet Pete's sake! You know he's the most gorgeous hunk of male flesh that's been available in a long time. If you've laid eyes on him at all you know that. And it's more than eyes I'd like to lay on him."

"Nicole!" Keely cried. "When did you meet him?"

"I haven't—not really. He was at a party last summer, and while I didn't actually *meet* him, I certainly knew he was there. He squires that Robins broad around. You know, the one who married that nice old man who conveniently croaked about six months after the nuptials and left her all that glorious money, the house in the Garden District, the cotton plantation in Mississippi, and the fleet of ships."

Keely's throat constricted. Dax and Madeline Robins? Had she known that? She was surprised to realize how much it hurt to visualize Dax with the flamboyant and merry widow who was touted for her beauty.

"Are you still there?" Nicole demanded when Keely failed to respond.

"Y-yes. I'm just tired, Nicole. Thank you for calling, but I really need to get to sleep."

"Kid, are you all right? You sound funny. Is everything there okay?" Nicole had dropped her cheerful bantering and Keely knew the concern in her friend's voice was genuine.

"Yes," she sighed. "It's just, well, you know, Nicole. I don't want to upset you by talking about PROOF."

"Oh, that. Well, that's why you're there, isn't it? And you know how I feel about it, so I won't belabor my point."

"Thanks."

"It wouldn't hurt if you had a wild fling while you were there though. Go to a triple-X-rated movie and sit next to a real pervert. Or have a hot and heavy affair with a visiting despot from some wonderfully decadent country."

"Goodbye," Keely called in a high singsong voice.

Nicole laughed. "Party pooper. Bye."

Without another word Nicole hung up. Keely was smiling when she replaced the receiver. She never remembered laying her head on the pillow and closing her eyes.

WHEN THE TELEPHONE rang again, she didn't realize at first that several hours had passed. Groping in the dark for the instrument, she finally found it, but missed her ear twice before fitting the receiver to it. "Hello."

"Good morning."

Her eyes sprang open. What a delightful way to be awakened—with a man's voice. This man's voice.

"Is it morning?" she asked. Her words were muffled by the pillow.

"Did I wake you up?"

"No." She yawned. "I had to get up to answer the phone."

"Very funny."

"No, it wasn't. It's too early for humor. What time is it?"

"Seven."

She rolled over and confirmed the time by the digital clock on the bedside table. "Oh, my God," she groaned. "I've overslept."

"What's the harm? The hearing's not till ten. You've got plenty of time."

"I know. It's just that I'm used to getting up early for my job. I feel self-indulgent when I sleep late."

"What time do you usually get up?"

"Five."

"Ugh! Why?"

"Because we're in the helicopter by six-thirty. Rush-hour traffic, remember?"

"I only called because I didn't get to say goodbye yesterday afternoon. I had mounds of paperwork to do in my office, and I knew I couldn't see you alone anyway."

"I went to dinner with the other ladies last night." Whom had he had dinner with? "I was exhausted when I came in. I was history once I got into bed."

"You needed the rest. You'll have another long day today."

"Yes."

There ensued a silence rife with so many things left unsaid. Unspoken words hung between them, dancing along the line that connected them, begging to be uttered. "Well, I guess I'll see you later, then." Dax said at last. It wasn't at all what he wanted to say.

"Yes." Was that the best her brain could do? She was repeating herself like a parrot.

"Goodbye." A low sigh.

"Goodbye." A low sigh echoed.

"Keely?"

"Yes."

"While you're sitting behind that table all prim and proper today, know that at least one man in the room is wishing he could be holding you."

The line went dead in her hand.

CHAPTER FIVE

FOR ANOTHER DAY and a half the hearing droned on. PROOF found an ally in a POW who had returned home when the prisoners were released. In a poignant speech he related how he and the other prisoners of war never gave up hope and faith in their country. Even when they were subjected to the vilest indignities, he told his rapt audience, he and the men imprisoned with him never even considered that they would be abandoned and forgotten.

Keely and the other PROOF delegates celebrated this small victory, but their jubilation was short-lived. A representative of the Treasury Department testified to the amount of money it cost the taxpayers to pay the salaries of these men yet unaccounted for and possibly long since dead. Congressman Walsh and a few of the others nodded sagely as they listened to the financial report. Keely wished Walsh's fat stomach would suddenly start paining him in proportion to its size.

Through the hours of close confinement in the committee room she adroitly avoided any encounter with Dax, intentional or otherwise. He too had apparently decided that contact with her would be disadvantageous, for he didn't make any overtures toward her.

They appeared to be strangers, unaware of each other, but beneath the surface the awareness was a choking reality. Keely often felt Dax's eyes on her. Remembering their early-morning telephone conversation, she blushed to the roots of her hair, whether she met his eyes or not. Glancing at him was an urge she didn't resist often enough.

His mannerisms were becoming endearingly familiar. His tasteful neckties rarely remained knotted for longer than an hour. Impatient, restless fingers would tug on the knot until it loosened. The collar button of his shirt would be freed from its hole. The strong, tanned column of his throat would expand with his now unrestricted breathing.

He sat leaning back with his elbow propped on the padded maroon leather arm of his chair. His chin rested on his thumb, three fingers covered his upper lip and mouth, and his index finger lay along his cheek pointing unerringly to the faint scar just below his eye.

He listened carefully; he watched intently; he jotted down notes with a rapid scrawl.

He looked at Keely.

Once, his steady gaze was so compelling that she courageously, albeit unwisely, met it. Her heart skidded to a jarring halt. Her breath was trapped in squeezing lungs. Perspiration lubricated her palms. Her stomach knew the fluttering of a million wings. His eyes let her know that his thoughts were no more on what the speaker was saying than were hers.

The finger lying along his cheek lifted in a silent hello. The motion was so subtle that no one would even see it unless the salutation was meant for him. Keely saw it and acknowledged it with a brief lowering of her eyelids. The message said more than merely hello. It said: *I wish I could talk to you. I wish we weren't in this particular place at this particular point in time, doing what we're doing. I wish...* So many things that were impossible.

At noon of the third day, when Congressman Parker adjourned them for lunch, he recommended that they take the rest of the afternoon and the next day off.

"We've had three full days of discussion, I think we all need time to digest what we've heard, assess our opinions, do our own research, and clear out the cobwebs, so to speak, before a final discussion." When the motion was unanimously agreed to, he banged the gavel and the committee hearing was adjourned.

"What a break," Betty said gratefully. "I need a day to do my hair and nails. I'm running out of money too and need to find a bank. What about you, Keely? Want to get in some shopping this afternoon?"

Keely smiled, but shook her head. "I don't think so, Betty, but I'm sure some of the others will go with you. If you don't mind, I'm going to beg off. I think I'll go to my room and collapse with a good book or a good nap."

Betty laughed and patted the younger woman's arm. "Then I'll say goodbye. See you later for dinner?"

Keely considered for a moment then said, "Sure. Call me when you get back to the hotel."

Betty turned and walked away, but not before glancing worriedly behind Keely. Before Keely could wonder why, she felt the light tap on her shoulder. Dax was there, smiling too widely, too brightly, too openly, to denote intimacy. "Mrs. Williams," he spoke quickly. "I haven't had a chance to talk to you since we met at lunch the other day. I hope you aren't finding the hearing too tedious."

"Not at all, Congressman. I more or less expected things to move slowly. It will be to our advantage, I think, for all of you to weigh the issue carefully."

He nodded in deep concentration as though she were expounding on something of great importance. He moved closer, folded his arms over his chest, and studied the toes of his polished loafers. His voice was so low she could barely hear him when he said, "How are you really?"

"Fine."

"I have to go to a damn cocktail party tonight at the French Embassy. I was told to bring a date if I wished. You wouldn't consider..."

The invitation was left dangling, but she supplied the rest of it. "No, Dax," she murmured. "You know that wouldn't be wise."

His grim expression perfectly suited the topic they should have been discussing—the MIAs. "Yeah, I know," he muttered. "Well, let's hope things work out for the best for everyone, Mrs. Williams," he said more loudly and stuck out his hand for her to shake. Their eyes locked when their hands clasped and, for a heartbeat, the rest of the world fell away. All too soon it came back.

"Hey, Congressman," Al Van Dorf said from behind them. "I wondered if I might get a statement from you about that armaments proliferation bill being talked up in committee."

"Sure, Al. Enjoy the time off, Mrs. Williams," Dax said politely.

"Thank you. I will. Mr. Van Dorf." She nodded her goodbyes and left the two men. Leaden legs carried her out of the chambers. It took several minutes for her to hail a cab on Pennsylvania Avenue. She didn't mind. She almost wished she had agreed to go shopping with Betty. The afternoon hours yawned before her. Anything was better than sitting morosely in a lonely hotel room, yearning for things that couldn't be.

AS IT TURNED OUT, she remembered very little of that dismal afternoon. She returned to her room and immediately fell asleep, not waking until Betty knocked on her door several hours later. They decided to stay at the hotel and eat at Trader Vic's because of the inclement weather.

When they were done with their meal and crossing the lobby toward the elevator, Betty said, "I bought a new suit today. Why don't you come up and I'll model it for you. There's an old Robert Taylor-Barbara Stanwyck movie on television tonight. Of course, you probably don't remember them."

Keely laughed. "I certainly do! You won't mind the company?" She hated the thought of returning to her room. After her nap she knew she wouldn't be ready to go to sleep for hours.

"No, I'd love it. Let's really misbehave and order up a bottle of wine," Betty said with adolescent enthusiasm.

Several hours later Keely was feeling mellow after drinking a few too many glasses of wine and watching the sentimental, romantic black-and-white movie. She and Betty had giggled like schoolgirls over the wine and cried over the tender love story. She left Betty yawning sleepily and weaved her way down the deserted hallway.

The elevator doors swished open. Keely was instantly sobered when she saw Dax leaning against the back wall. His previous gloomy slouching posture was replaced by one of rigid attention, as though an order had been snapped by a drill sergeant intolerant of laziness. He uncrossed his ankles and dropped the overcoat that had been draped over his shoulder and held by one finger. His face broke into a wide grin. "Going up?"

"No, down."

"Come along for the ride," he invited. When he saw her hesitate and glance around apprehensively, he said, "No one can blame us for meeting accidentally in a public elevator when we're staying in the same hotel. Besides that, what could possibly happen in an elevator?" He was teasing, but Keely's eyes dropped involuntarily, but significantly, to the lushly carpeted floor of the cubicle. "Forget I said that," he growled. "Get in."

She stepped through the sliding doors and they closed behind her, sealing them in, separating them from the rest of the world, creating their own universe.

She cleared her throat self-consciously. "How was the party?"

"Loud. Smoky. Crowded."

"Sounds fun."

He hadn't given a damn about the party, could barely remember it though he had left it only minutes ago. He had had a terrible time. He had eaten the rich canapés, all the while wondering what Keely's favorite foods were, wishing they could be sharing a peanut butter sandwich and popcorn in front of a fireplace, on a couch, in a bed...

He had drunk perhaps a tad too much of the limitless liquor, wondering if she liked chilled white wine. While listening to the shrill voice of the buxom, over-jeweled wife of a foreign diplomat, he was seeing Keely's mouth, shimmering with spilled wine. He imagined his tongue lifting golden droplets from the petal-soft lips.

The other men at the fete had ogled a senator's secretary whose well-known figure had been touted and tasted by every male on Capitol Hill. Tonight the generous body had been encased in a tight red dress. Pendulous breasts and broad hips had swayed invitingly. Only a week ago Dax's comments on the woman's anatomy would have been as clever and imaginative as anyone's. Tonight she had seemed obscene and stupid. His thoughts had centered around a much daintier figure. Softly feminine, yet neat. Curvaceous, yet compact. Touchable, yet…untouchable.

"You're home," she said softly. The elevator had ascended to the top floor and the doors had slid open. Across the hallway was his suite of rooms, void of warmth. The only source of heat in which he found comfort this night was standing with him in the elevator, looking at him with bemusement.

"Where were you just now?" he asked.

"In Betty's room. We watched an old movie and demolished a bottle of wine."

"Red or white?"

She closed her eyes as if savoring the vintage. "Golden," she whispered. Her eyes flew wide when his anguished groan filled the small cubicle like the roar of an angry, thwarted tiger. His finger pressed the button for the seventh floor and it lighted up as the doors closed. "What—"

"I'll ride with you to your floor," Dax said by way of explanation.

"You shouldn't."

"You don't have to remind me."

She looked away, hurt by his sharp tone. "I'm sorry," he said contritely. "I'm not angry at you. I'm mad at—"

"I know," she interjected quickly. The less said, the better.

The elevator stopped on her floor and the door opened, but before she could step out, he pressed another button. She didn't notice which one and it didn't matter. The doors closed again. "Dax—"

"I'm picking you up tomorrow morning in front of the hotel. Ten o'clock. Dress casual."

"I can't," she objected, shaking her head.

"Can't dress casual?" he teased. For the first time she saw the familiar smile, the one that deepened the dimple and lightened his dark eyes from ebony to chocolate.

She gave him a withering look. "I can't meet you."

"Sure you can."

The elevator stopped, the doors opened, and Keely and Dax were both surprised to see a middle-aged couple standing on the other side. They had almost forgotten that they weren't the only two people in the world. "Good evening," Dax said genially. "Where to?"

"Three," the man said.

Dax pushed the specified button for the man and leaned negligently back against the wall as though he were only a casual passenger in the elevator. "Are you from out of town?" he asked.

"New Mexico. Las Cruses," the man answered. The woman was staring at Dax's discarded coat still lying on the floor. She raised myopic, suspicious eyes to Keely, who smiled sickly. The woman grasped her husband's arm as though seeking protection from these immoral, large-city types.

"Ah, there's a fine university in Las Cruses," Dax said.

"New Mexico State," the man said proudly.

"Right!" Dax snapped his fingers. Keely could have throttled him. He was enjoying himself.

The elevator stopped at the third floor and the man ushered out his disapproving wife. "Have an enjoyable stay," Dax said with a smile that should have graced a Chamber of Commerce brochure. The doors closed again. "Now, as I was saying…"

"No, *I* was saying that I can't go anywhere with you, Dax."

"We're taking the day off. Having an outing. We've both been cooped up in that stuffy room for too many days and it's beginning to play on my nerves. And if I may say so, you're looking a little peaked yourself."

In fact, the opposite was true. Her cheeks were flushed from recent embarrassment and wine consumption. Her eyes were large and shiny remnants of her uninterrupted sleep that afternoon and tearful enjoyment of the movie. Her hair was beguilingly mussed. She had never looked more beautiful, more alluring, sexier.

His eyes riveted on her lips, which had parted with the intention to argue, but any arguments died unspoken. Even without the benefit of artificial gloss, her mouth shone with its own dewy softness and he longed to drink of it.

"Why can't two friends spend a few hours in each other's company?" They weren't friends and never would be and they both knew it. But his gravelly words took up time and space necessary to keep him from crushing her against him as he ravaged that kissable mouth.

They didn't speak again, only looked at each other, saying more silently than verbal communication would allow them. This time when the doors opened on her floor, he pressed the Door Open button.

"Ten o'clock tomorrow."

"Someone—anyone—might see us. Van Dorf..." Her objections meant nothing. There was no doubt in either's mind that she was going to meet him.

"No one will notice. I borrowed a friend's car. It's a silver Datsun. I'll circle the block until you come out on the K Street side. Don't look furtive or guilty. Just open the car door and get in."

"Dax—"

"Good night." He placed his index finger on her breastbone and pushed her gently across the threshold of the elevator. He wasn't trying to get rid of her; he was removing the temptation to commit a criminal offense. He released the button on the panel and the doors closed between them.

For long moments Keely stared at the doors, not seeing them, not seeing anything. Dazedly turning toward her room, she was already in a quandary about what to wear the next day.

HER FINAL CHOICE was a pair of gray flannel slacks, a black turtleneck sweater, and a herringbone blazer that matched both. Black suede boots would keep her feet warm, as the weather was cold and rainy, not yet conceding that spring was imminent. She had no idea where Dax was taking them, so she wanted to be prepared for any eventuality. At five minutes to ten she picked up her overcoat and left her room.

Her heart was thudding with guilty anticipation as she crossed the crowded lobby with what she hoped looked like nonchalance. No sooner had she reached the broad doors than she saw a low, sleek silver Datsun slow to a crawl beside the curb. Pushing the door against the strong wind, she whisked through it, ducked her head to be sure it was Dax behind the wheel of the car, and opened the door. They both laughed when she plopped into the deep leather seat and sped away.

"Good morning," he said, taking advantage of a red traffic light to turn his head and look at her.

"Good morning."

"You're right on time."

"Punctuality is one of my virtues. How many times did you go around the block?"

"Three. Impatience is one of my virtues." They laughed again with the sheer pleasure of being alone together. He resented the light for turning green and forcing him to pay attention to his driving.

"Where are we going?" Keely asked, not caring.

"Mount Vernon."

"Mount Vernon!" She looked through the tinted car windows at the drizzle and low-hanging, ominously threatening clouds. "Today? Who would go to Mount Vernon on a day like today?"

He stopped at another traffic light before answering her. Swiveling to face her, he tweaked her nose. "No one. That's why we're going there."

She acknowledged his astuteness with a slight bow. "You're not a senatorial candidate for nothing, Mr. Devereaux. You're positively brilliant."

"Sometimes I'm so smart it's frightening," he boasted and got an elbow in his ribs for punishment.

She didn't bother him while he threaded his way through the traffic on Constitution Avenue toward the Lincoln Memorial. She folded her coat behind the bucket seats, placed her shoulder bag beneath her legs, and tuned in a stereo radio station agreeable to them both.

They crossed the Potomac River on the Arlington Memorial Bridge and took the Memorial Highway along the river toward George Washington's homestead. The woods that lined the road were still-naked reminders of winter.

"This will look lovely in a few weeks when the dogwoods and redbuds start blooming," Keely mused.

"Yeah. I love it at home when all the flowers bloom. We have azaleas on all four sides of the house, and it's a magnificent sight when they're in full bloom. We hire a man whose sole responsibility is to take care of the flowering shrubs."

"We?"

"Well, that's not quite accurate. I still consider the main house my parents' home. Several years ago they moved to a smaller house on the other side of our property. Ostensibly the move was to keep my father from having to climb stairs, but I think it was to make me feel lonely rattling around in that large house all by myself and to provide an incentive for me to find a wife and start having grandbabies."

"Why haven't you?"

"I haven't found anyone important enough to me to share my life with." His eyes wavered from the scenic highway to look across the narrow space of the car at her. "When I do find her, I'll fight like hell to get her into that house with me."

Her throat closed as tightly as the fists she clenched in her lap. She looked away from the compelling force of his eyes. "What's it like? Your house. Is it antebellum?"

He faced the road again. "No. The Devereauxs did have an ancestral home, but it was razed by the Union Army during the war. It took us until 1912 to recover our losses from the war and Reconstruction and build another. I love it, but I'm not going to tell you much about it. I want you to see it for yourself sometime."

"Is it in Baton Rouge?"

"Twenty miles from there."

"How much land do you have?"

He shrugged self-consciously. "Enough to farm profitably and raise a few horses."

"Are you dodging my questions? You're not giving me straight answers, Mr. Devereaux, a talent you've no doubt perfected from dealing with reporters."

He laughed. "You've found me out."

She didn't press the issue and he didn't volunteer any more information. Obviously he was embarrassed by his family's wealth. It had been the topic of many unflattering editorials.

The remainder of the fifteen-mile trip was passed in companionable silence. When the car pulled into the parking facility, it joined few others. Where usually there were dozens of tour buses, today only one was parked in the lot provided them.

"See? What'd I tell you?" Dax asked. "We'll have the place virtually to ourselves. I doubt if George and Martha ever had it so good." He chucked her under the chin before lifting his overcoat from behind his seat and getting out.

He opened her door and held her coat while she slipped into the arms. His hands settled only slightly and briefly on her shoulders before he clasped her elbow and steered her toward the gate.

The lady in colonial costume behind the grilled window said, "You certainly didn't pick a very nice day to visit us, but I hope you'll brave the rain and see all the outbuildings too. Tours start every twenty minutes or so. We don't keep to a rigid schedule except during the summer when we're crowded. There's a group waiting to go up to the house now. You can join it. A guide will be along shortly."

"Thank you." Dax flashed his famous smile. "I wanted to come on a summer day, but this is the only day my sister could come."

Keely gazed up at him in stupefaction. She felt her lower jaw drop to hang open stupidly. When they walked away, Dax's gait was jaunty. "You're crazy!" Keely admonished under her breath.

Dax didn't look at her. He was busy fishing his collapsible umbrella out of his deep coat pocket. He pushed the button and it mushroomed open with a loud pop. "Do you really think people are going to believe I'm your sister?" she demanded, stopping on the gravel path leading up to the house.

He looked down at her as he held the umbrella over them as protection against the light rain. He studied her objectively. "No, I guess they won't. We'd better practice the act. Here, hold this." He thrust the handle of the umbrella into her surprised hand.

"Sis!" he exclaimed, grasping her by the shoulders.

"Look at what a beautiful woman you've grown into." He lowered his head and kissed her soundly on the mouth. "Let me see you."

Stunned by his playacting, Keely stood docilely while he unabashedly opened her coat, then moved aside the lapels of her jacket to rake his eyes appreciatively over her sweatered chest. "Never would I have guessed when you were all arms and legs and flat chested that you'd round out so nicely."

Vexed, Keely opened her mouth, but she didn't have a chance to rebuke him before he rushed on. "You look gorgeous in any color. Do you know that?" His banter took on a different tone. Her cheek was grazed with gentle fingertips. "You're wonderful in black. I like you in that green you were wearing on the airplane." His voice lowered and became husky. "And you're delicious in yellow terry cloth. Is there any color in the rainbow that dulls your eyes, or makes your complexion sallow, or fails to make your hair come to life?"

His thumb mesmerizingly traced the curve of her jaw. She saw herself mirrored in the dark depths of his eyes and was shocked at the wistful expression she saw on her face. He shouldn't stand so close, but she didn't want to destroy this moment by pointing that out.

His fingers really shouldn't touch her lips. It was far too intimate a gesture and destroyed the brother/sister act. But even as her mind objected, her lips obeyed his urging and parted slightly.

His head was lowering dangerously close when a party of four came hurrying along the path behind them. Dax backed away from her. "Come along, sis," he muttered, taking the umbrella and ushering her toward the small group of tourists waiting at the base of the rise on which the stately house sat.

After only a short wait a guide came down the path and led the soggy, but undaunted, group up the hill to the house. The guide's spiel was rehearsed, but thankfully, she made the recitation colorful and conversational. Like the others in the group, Keely and Dax listened. They climbed the stairs, they peered into roped off rooms, they noted what should be made note of, and they wouldn't remember any of it later.

When the official tour was over, they were again invited to view the outbuildings and grounds. Most of the others trailed off toward the tack room and kitchen. Keely and Dax headed toward a small building that housed personal effects of the Washingtons.

"Did you ever think," Keely said, "that if you ever become president, two hundred years later people will be traipsing around your house looking at your razor?"

"I use a disposable razor, but remind me to always keep my false teeth polished." They laughed and quite spontaneously he hugged her.

They walked to the tomb where the Washingtons were interred. Dax said quietly, "Did you know it was rumored that Washington was in love with another man's wife?"

"He was?" Keely asked on an uneven breath.

"Yes. So they say."

"How tragic."

"Maybe not," Dax countered. "The love he had for that woman may have been something very special."

"Yes, maybe." Why did she feel like crying?

"It certainly doesn't take anything away from what he did for his country. I can't see that it matters much."

"Not now," Keely said thickly. "But then, when it was happening, it might have mattered a great deal to those who were involved."

His sigh stirred her hair that had somehow come to rest against his lean cheek. "I guess you're right."

They left the grave site and made their way back to the main compound. Trying to shrug off the pensive mood, Dax suggested they eat a snack before starting back. "I understand the restaurant here isn't too bad. And we certainly don't need a reservation," he said as he opened the door leading into the virtually deserted dining room.

Maple tables and chairs were arranged in neat rows across the hardwood floors. Each window was flanked by starched white ruffled curtains. Brass candlesticks with tall narrow chimneys adorned each table and cast a soft glow on the provincially papered walls.

Only three of the colonial tables were already occupied. Fires were glowing in the fireplaces and Dax led Keely to a table near one of them and close to a window that overlooked the manicured grounds. A waitress rushed to take their orders for clam chowder. When they had done justice to the soup, Dax signaled her and she scurried over again.

"We'd like dessert too. What have you got?"

"Homemade pies are our speciality. Cherry, apple, and pecan."

"Terrific. We'll have two pieces of cherry."

"No, I want pecan," Keely interposed.

Dax looked comically thunderstruck. "You can't come to George Washington's house and not have cherry pie. It's anti-American."

She laughed, but said to the waitress, "Pecan, please."

"Okay," Dax said grudgingly. "And we want two scoops of vanilla ice cream on each."

"No, I want whipped cream on mine."

He turned and glared at her. "Who's doing this, you or me?"

She and the waitress laughed at his villainous scowl. "You didn't ask me what I wanted and I want whipped cream."

Dax shook his head in frustration then asked with exaggerated courtesy, "Coffee?"

"Tea," she replied primly.

The waitress, pen poised over her tablet, was shaking with laughter. "Cream?" she asked.

"No."

"Yes," Keely answered at the same time.

Dax looked up at the waitress and said in a loud stage whisper, "She thinks she's a liberated woman."

The waitress leaned down and said to him, "I like to see marriages where each partner is considered an individual." Then she walked away with her skirts swaying saucily behind her.

Keely stared down at her left hand, which lay on the tabletop. It was a natural enough mistake. There was the simple gold band encircling her third finger. Out of her peripheral vision she saw Dax's hand move closer until it covered hers.

"She thinks you're married to me," he said softly. "As long as she thinks that and she doesn't recognize either of us, I suppose it's all right if we hold hands." His long fingers laced with hers and squeezed tightly.

"I suppose so," Keely said, returning the pressure.

They stared at the fire that popped and hissed cheerily. They stared at the rain that fell monotonously and heavily and ran in wide rivulets down the panes of glass. It blurred the scenery, softened the sharp angles of the world, dimmed the harsh light of reality, and made it easy for them to pretend for a while that things weren't as they were. And because they couldn't help themselves, they stared at each other.

The warm ambience of the restaurant surrounded them like a cocoon. The clatter of china and silverware in the kitchen couldn't override the silent messages each transmitted. The movements of the other patrons or waitresses didn't distract their eyes from the other's face.

"I just noticed for the first time that your ears are pierced," Dax commented. "Did it hurt?"

"Like hell."

His grin was wide, but he didn't laugh aloud. "You'd never make a politician, Miss Preston. You're far too straightforward."

Miss Preston. Not Mrs. Williams. Here with him now, she was Miss Preston. "How did you get that scar under your eye?"

"Is it unsightly? I'll have plastic surgery."

"Don't you dare! It's—" She was about to say beautiful, but amended it for fear he would take umbrage at such a feminine adjective. His dark brows arched in silent query at her pause. "It makes you appear very rakish," she said.

"I'm a regular swashbuckler. As a matter of fact, there was a seedier Devereaux involved with the Laffites."

She squinted her eyes and tilted her head. "Yes, I can see you as a pirate."

"Maybe I should have *my* ears pierced. No, just one of them, I think. That's much more…rakish."

They were laughing when the waitress set down the tray between them.

"Do you want something else?" Dax asked when they were finished.

"Are you serious? I can barely breathe," Keely said.

"Do you want to race to the car and burn off a few of those calories?"

"I'll be lucky to waddle," she confessed as he held her coat for her. They settled the bill and regretfully left the warmth of the restaurant for the cold outside. They splattered through puddles as they dashed for the car. The rain was coming down more earnestly than it had all day.

The cold motor took some coaxing to get started, but then it roared to life, and Dax carefully steered it out onto the highway.

"It's really coming down," Keely remarked worriedly when they had driven a few miles through sheets of rain. Even with the rapid, insistent cadence of the windshield wipers, the road was obliterated by a virtual wall of water.

"It's crazy trying to drive in this. I think there's…" His voice trailed off as he searched the side of the road through the foggy windows. "There it is," he exclaimed and pumped the brakes until the car slowed enough for him to turn into the innocuous side road.

"I'm going to stop here until this lets up."

CHAPTER SIX

THE LANE WAS rutted and the sports car bumped along it for several yards before Dax braked it to a stop. He parked under the semiprotective branches of an oak and cut the motor. The ensuing silence was deafening. The radio's music ceased abruptly. The windshield wipers stopped their drumming. The motor's throb no longer vibrated. Only the rain persisted.

Dax reached across the seat and touched her shoulder. "Are you warm enough? Do you need your coat?" They had taken off their outer coats and folded them behind the seats again before leaving Mount Vernon.

"No, I think the heater had time to warm up the car enough for now."

"If you get cold, tell me. I can either get your coat or let the motor idle for a few minutes." His hand slid down her arm and took her hand. He massaged it. "Your hand is freezing."

"I know. I can't ever get them warm."

"Put them in your pockets."

"It doesn't help."

"Then put them in my pockets." He was only half teasing.

"Then what would you do to keep yours warm?" It was a challenge she couldn't resist issuing.

His eyes twinkled through the gloomy atmosphere.

"I'd think of something," he answered in a low rumble. His fingers aligned with hers and he pressed each one in turn. He studied the contrast of his hair-sprinkled hand with the smooth frailty of hers. Then he raised her hand to his mouth and lightly brushed his lips across the fingertips.

"If I had to accidentally meet the wife of an MIA on an airplane, why did she have to look like you? Be you?" His mouth was moving against her palm now, talking into it, kissing it.

"You shouldn't say—"

"Shh. If I can't do anything else, at least let me talk, Keely." His hot tongue darted quickly into the center of her hand and her breath caught in her throat. "But then if you hadn't looked like you, I doubt if I would have gone barreling across the aisle of that airplane like some misplaced Sir Galahad to rescue you, would I?"

She couldn't answer. His tongue was sliding between her fingers at their base, slowly, leisurely. It was too sexy a gesture to allow, but too blissful to stop. He covered his mouth with her hand and lifted his eyes to hers.

The air in the small enclosure was redolent with ungratified passion. Their breath created a moist veil on the inside of the cold car windows. Each sound was amplified in the silence. When Dax leaned closer to her, the rustle of his clothing sounded like leaves in an autumn breeze. Each sight was magnified. He could almost count the dark lashes on her lower eyelid. The corner of her mouth quivered slightly with each breath. It was a beautiful mouth, and he had claimed it as his the first time he saw it.

Keely never remembered feeling quite this helpless—knew indeed that she had never felt this way in her life. She was floating weightlessly, yet a heavy pressure made her lower body ache with longing. She felt imbued with a strength she had never before experienced, but her muscles seemed to have liquefied. Her whole body tingled with life, yet she knew this panting desire closely resembled dying.

She didn't know she had reached for him until she saw her hand smoothing back a damp, errant strand of dark hair from his forehead. She watched as her thumb stroked across the faint scar beneath his eye.

Only her name, spoken with the reverence of a prayer, hovered between them before his lips caressed hers. Had she closed her eyes she might never have known that he touched her, so light was the touch of his mouth on hers. But she had been watching and now saw him draw back. Disappointment swamped her. She wanted to know the heat and urgency of his mouth. He had told her impatience was one of his virtues. She was desperate for a display of that impatience now.

But Dax wasn't about to rush this moment or take advantage of her mood. He took her hands and slipped them under his sweater, pressing them against the hair-roughened skin. "Warm them on me." He dropped the sweater back into place and held her face cupped between his palms. Cautiously she moved her fingers against the skin that was as hot as a furnace. He watched her expression. Her eyes closed as she became braver and moved her hands in ever widening circles. Lips, soft and pliant, parted as she emitted a sigh. His mouth was suddenly there, resting on hers, drawing in the breath she expulsed so sweetly.

His tongue slipped past her lips and traced the row

of teeth. A gentle nudge was all it took for her to lift that barrier. The tip of his tongue found hers and explored it with erotic leisure. Then he searched each crevice of her mouth, wantonly investigating, sensuously seeking out the places that, when found, caused her to strain against him.

His tongue withdrew, but hers followed. Tentatively, maidenly, she parted his lips and they opened for her. He was surprised at her inexperience, the youthful awkwardness, the timidity with which she kissed him. He accepted the timorous flutterings of her tongue until they became well-planned strokes. When it slid along the roof of his mouth, he groaned and crushed her against him.

Breaking apart to draw breath, he rasped against her ear. "Don't ever be afraid of me, Keely. There is no need to be." He had taken her shyness as fearful caution.

"I know, I know. It's not that. It's…I'm afraid I'm not good at—I was so young and it's been so long—"

"You're sweeter because of that. If only you knew how much sweeter. And you'll learn. We'll learn together."

He hooked a finger in the high collar of her sweater and lowered it to avail himself of the skin underneath. Nibbling lips wandered along her neck to her ear. He teased her earlobe with his tongue and caught at the gold sphere adorning it with his teeth. They laughed softly. Her laughter turned into gasps of ecstasy when he probed the inside of her ear with his tongue. She shuddered.

"Are you cold?" he asked.

She shook her head, just barely, not enough to dislodge his mouth. "No."

"Tell me."

"I will." Cold? She would never be cold around him. His mouth was relentless. She never thought a man could be so sensitive to what a woman wanted... needed. Dax seemed to glean and anticipate her every carnal wish. He wasn't greedy and fumbling. Every move was slow, practised, and choreographed to bring her pleasure.

The increasing palpitations in her throat frightened her. She feared she might not be able to breathe much longer. Her hands moved restlessly under his sweater around to his back, seeking a handhold before she slid off the edge of the world.

He kissed her again, deeper, with a hunger tempered by caring. His hands eased from her cheeks down to her neck and encircled it. His thumb charted her collarbone. When he lowered his hands to embrace her, they ghosted over her breasts.

God help me, Dax requested silently. *Don't let me touch her. If I do, I'll never be able to let her go.*

He felt her imperceptible reaction. Her soft, rapid breaths struck his mouth like puffs of cotton. He felt the muscles of her thighs contract as they lay against his. His hands lingered indecisively, waiting. Catching her bottom lip between his teeth, he worried it gently. Meeting his fervor equally, she murmured something incoherently and raised herself to just beneath his hands.

Emboldened by her response, his good, honorable intentions dissolved and his hands closed over her. Their sighs of pleasure echoed each other. By slow degrees Keely relaxed and offered herself up for his further exploration. She leaned back into the car seat and locked her hands behind his back, pulling him closer.

He kneaded her gently, caressed her. He learned her by the sensitive employment of his hands. He closed his eyes and visualized what he was touching—the texture, the color. It was agony not to see, but heaven to imagine. He had felt the bra immediately, but knew it couldn't be much. For as he cupped her and lifted her with his palms, his thumbs fanned her nipples, which were aroused and impertinently demanding his attention.

"So lovely," he murmured as he pressed his face into her round softness and breathed deeply of her fragrance, which had permeated the knit of her sweater. With nose and mouth he nuzzled her while his fingers continued their tender torment. "You feel so good," he whispered just before his lips closed around one distended nipple. His tongue dampened her sweater.

"Oh, Dax!" She shoved against his shoulders with the heels of her hands. He bumped his head on the ceiling of the car as he jerked upright.

"Did I hurt you?" he asked, alarmed.

No, no. It wasn't pain she was feeling. Mark had touched her there, but had never done anything as intimate as Dax just had. Never had she felt a spear of pleasure piercing her so deeply that it went straight to her womb and opened up a floodgate of desire that overflowed until she wasn't able to contain it. It had thrilled her, frightened her, terrified her.

He could read the fear on her face and blamed himself for putting it there. Guiltily, wearily, he shook his head. "I'm sorry, Keely. I only wanted to touch you, to kiss you."

Sadly she stared out the windshield as he slipped the car into gear. The rear wheels spun, trying to gain traction on the mushy turf. Finally the car lurched forward and Dax maneuvered it back onto the highway.

The rain had lessened significantly to a dreary mist. The windshield wipers clicked back and forth, making the only sound in the car. When the radio had come back on with the motor, Dax had switched off the silver knob. He cursed the slow bumper-to-bumper rush-hour traffic as they approached the city.

The brakes screeched when he pulled the car to a halt outside the hotel. He was a long time looking at her and when he did, he was struck to see tears glistening in her eyes. Her mouth was working with emotion.

"Keely—"

"It was a beautiful day. Forgive me, Dax, for— It wasn't your touching me that I was frightened of, but of my not wanting you to ever stop."

Before he could reply, she was gone and running toward the doors of the hotel.

SHE LAY HUDDLED under the covers, clad only in her underwear. She wasn't sure how much time had elapsed since she had let herself into the cold, lonely room, stripped off her clothes, which still lay where she had dropped them, and crawled into the false sanctuary of the bed. Convinced that she needed rest, she tried to sleep, but it eluded her.

Her mind wouldn't let her escape from this maelstrom of indecision and guilt—guilt over betraying Mark, if not in deed, then certainly in thought, guilt over leading Dax on so shamelessly. He would despise her after today. She couldn't blame him.

Her heart jumped in her chest when she heard the light tapping on her door. She had put out the Do Not Disturb sign when she came in and had taken the telephone off the hook. But whoever was on the other side of the door wasn't taking her at her word.

She threw back the covers and padded to the door, putting her eye to the fish-eye peephole and seeing a man dressed in a hotel uniform. "Yes?"

"Mrs. Williams?"

"Yes," she repeated, this time in affirmation.

"Are you all right? I'm Mr. Bartelli, an assistant manager here at the hotel. A Mrs. Allway has been trying to reach you and hasn't been able to get through. She was worried and requested that I come check on you. Are you well?"

"Yes, Mr. Bar—Bartelli. I only wanted to rest undisturbed. I took the telephone off the hook. Please tell Mrs. Allway that I'm fine and that I'll see her in the morning." She could have offered to call her friend herself, but she didn't want to speak to anyone.

"Very well. You're sure we can't do anything?"

"No, I'm fine, thank you."

"Good night. I apologize for disturbing you."

"Good night." She watched in the distorted glass his minuscule figure disappear down the hall.

Since she was already up, she decided to take a shower before going back to bed. It worked well to soothe and relax her. Almost too well. Feeling languid and warm as she stepped out of the shower, she caught her reflection in the mirror. Her skin was rosy from the hot water. Her breasts tingled from the shower's invigorating spray. Watching herself in the mirror, she raised her hand and lightly touched the pink crown. It pouted in instant recollection of Dax's touch, his lips. Unbearable heat spread like an ink stain over her skin.

Ashamed and embarrassed by her own physical need, she got back into bed and pulled the covers tightly around her. Never had the bed seemed so empty and unwelcoming. Yielding to an immature temptation, she laid the extra pillow against her, snuggling to it, rubbing her hands along it, wishing that it were warm vibrant skin covered with springy hair, wishing that it would speak to her the words of a lover. But there was no surcease to be found either physically or spiritually.

The pain in her heart conquered her control and she gave way to tears.

IN THE MORNING she felt somewhat better, or at least determined. She had been playing with fire and she had no one to blame but herself for getting burned. Time and again she had told Nicole it wasn't worth the time and effort to become involved with a man, because it could only end in disaster. She hadn't heeded her own words where Dax Devereaux was concerned. It was only a shame she couldn't gloat to her friend in New Orleans that she had been right. Nicole, nor anyone, would ever know about Dax. What was there to tell? It was over before it was begun.

Her cinnamon-colored crepe dress didn't quite match her military posture, but she convinced herself it did. She peeled her hair back into a sleek bun on the nape of her neck and disdained any jewelry. She didn't want to look or feel feminine and vulnerable.

Earlier she had called Betty Allway and they agreed

to meet and ride to Capitol Hill together as they had done that first day. When they arrived, Keely entered the subcommittee chamber with a straight back and raised chin, looking neither left nor right. She took her chair and then buried her nose in notes that blurred before her eyes.

Only when Congressman Parker called the hearing to order did she raise her eyes. Purposefully she didn't look in Dax's direction, yet she knew he was there. She could see him out of the far corner of her eye. He was wearing a gray jacket, a light blue shirt, a maroon tie. She refused to allow her eyes to waver from Congressman Parker's face.

"We are going to hear this morning one more time from the army. Colonel Hamilton is going to read an affidavit documenting strides the various military branches have taken toward finding the MIAs. Colonel Hamilton, you have the floor."

For two hours the colonel took advantage of his platform and read every word of the affidavit in a nasal monotone. Had Keely not been strung so tightly by nerves, she would probably have gone to sleep. Several times Congressman Walsh's snore rose above Colonel Hamilton's steady drone.

Keely studied her cuticles, the wood grain in the table, the spiderweb in the chandelier. She didn't look at Dax. Betty shifted uncomfortably beside her and once leaned forward to say, "I'm glad he's such a bore. This might really damage our case if he were the least bit interesting and anyone were listening." Keely only smiled. What would her friend think if she knew what a traitor she was?

A few minutes before noon Colonel Hamilton finally wrapped up his remarks. Congressman Parker banged the gavel to get everyone's attention again and looked down at Keely. "Mrs. Williams, before we adjourn, would you like to say anything more?"

Keely hadn't expected this unscheduled courtesy and nervously moistened her lips with the tip of her tongue. She sat up straighter in her chair and surprised herself by speaking in a level voice. "Only that we have said all that should be necessary. Speaking for all of us, I can't believe that you, as representatives of the American people, would even consider introducing a bill that would declare any citizen of our country dead, when proof of that death is nonexistent.

"True, it may save tax dollars, but what is a man's life worth? Can something that intrinsic be appraised? Personally, I feel that at least some of these men may yet be accounted for, found to be alive, but if they aren't, don't their families deserve to be honored, repaid for the suffering they have endured? If Congress declares these men dead, and severs their pay, then America has just cast off one of her children in the cruelest of manners."

Congressman Parker smiled at her with secret approval while her constituents applauded. He glared down either side of the panel tables as if daring anyone to dispute her. When no one did, he picked up the gavel and banged it loudly on the block. "We are adjourned until two thirty when we will reconvene to announce our decision. Members of the subcommittee will please take a brief lunch and meet back here at one forty-five for discussion." The gavel crashed again and they were dismissed.

Keely was surrounded by photographers and reporters. She answered what questions she could, avoided others, and methodically threaded her way toward the door. When she was free of the room, she broke through the throng with an apology and dashed for the ladies' restroom. Betty was close behind her.

"You were wonderful, Keely. Thank you." The older woman hugged her tight, but when she pulled back, she was struck by Keely's shattered features. "Are you okay? You're as pale as a ghost."

"No, I'm fine. Really." One wouldn't have believed it by the deep breaths she was pulling in. "It was so crowded in there and all the people and flashing lights on those cameras. I don't want to be the focus of attention."

"Then you shouldn't look so tragically, beautifully, heroic." When Keely's lips didn't show even the faintest smile, Betty said quickly, "Why don't I go out ahead of you and fend them off. I'll wait for you at the top of the stairs. Take your time." At the door of the lounge she paused and turned around. "Keely, I think we've won."

For the first time Keely smiled back. "I do too."

"See you in a minute."

Keely collapsed onto a stained, threadbare chair and covered her pale face with her shaking hands. It was over, or almost so. Everyone was lauding her, and she didn't deserve it. *I don't, I don't,* she averred as she breathed deeply. Forcing herself to move, she went to the sink, washed her hands, smoothed her hair, and applied fresh lipstick, which made her paleness even more noticeable.

Picking up her coat and purse, she opened the door and stepped into the empty hallway. She was looking the other way, and when she turned around, she pulled up short and gasped when Dax loomed largely in front of her.

"Easy, easy, this is only another of our chance meetings," he said under his breath and behind a camouflaging smile.

She glanced over his shoulder and saw Betty's silhouette at the end of the long corridor. "What are you doing here?"

"I work here," he quipped. She tried to brush past him, but he caught her arm and said, "I'm sorry. I don't mean to be cute, but dammit, I want to talk to you." He released her arm and when she didn't move away, he rushed on in a quiet undertone. "I tried all night to call you, but your phone was off the hook. I called down to the main desk—anonymously, I might add—and asked the hotel management to check on you. I was informed by Mr. Bartelli that he already had. You were fine, but only wished to be left alone."

"That's right, I did…do."

"Then you're out of luck."

"Dax—"

"Shh. Here comes Radar Ears Van Dorf. Are you on the eight-fifty flight to New Orleans?"

"Yes."

"We'll talk then." He raised his voice. "So, speaking off the cuff, I'd say that the committee will table the bill, Mrs. Williams. Well, hello, Al. Why aren't you eating lunch like all the other nice press boys?"

"Because I'm not nice," he said, smiling that obscenely cunning smile. "Mrs. Williams, you were as eloquent as always. Do you mean everything you say?"

Taken off guard by his blunt question, she replied heatedly, "Of course I do!"

"Okay, okay. I was just asking. By the way, I tried to reach you for comment all day yesterday. You were out. The doorman at the Hilton said you'd left that morning in a silver sports car."

She resisted the urge to glance worriedly at Dax. Instead she answered calmly. "That's right. I went sightseeing with a friend."

"It wasn't exactly an ideal day for sightseeing, was it?"

"No, it wasn't."

"But you went anyway. Hmm. Wouldn't want to tell me who that 'friend' was, would you?"

"No, Mr. Van Dorf, I wouldn't. It's none of your business."

Van Dorf stroked his chin as he looked at her. She met his incisive stare unflinchingly and only hoped he couldn't see her heart as it hammered against her ribs. He turned his foxlike face toward Dax. "You weren't available either, Congressman. Funny, isn't it, that you two are either together, like now, or nowhere to be found?"

"I'd say it was a downright shame that I wasn't available for an interview with you yesterday, Al. You know I never pass up an opportunity for free publicity." Dax's smile was so genuine, that Keely almost believed it herself. How far could anything Dax said be trusted?

"If you gentlemen will excuse me, Mrs. Allway is waiting for me." Without another word she moved past them and by a sheer force of will kept herself from running down the hall in cowardly retreat.

IT WAS NO surprise later that afternoon when Congressman Parker announced to the anxious members of PROOF that, for the time being, the bill that would have declared the MIAs dead was to be tabled. He thanked everyone involved for their time and adjourned the hearing one last time.

An undignified period of celebration ensued. PROOF members weepily hugged Keely and Betty. Sympathetic members of the press came over to offer their congratulations. The committee members who had obviously argued in their favor came by personally to congratulate Keely on their victory.

Across the room she felt the magnetic pull of Dax's eyes and met them. Al Van Dorf's speculation had been a warning and Dax wasn't about to jeopardize either of their reputations by publicly talking to her again. His eyes were warm with gladness over her triumph. But they bespoke more than that. They held a pride for her, the woman she was, and her knees went weak under his silent praise.

He ducked his head slightly before turning away, as though to say, "I'll see you later." But he wouldn't. After a hasty lunch she hadn't tasted, didn't even remember, she had gone back to the hotel, packed her bags, and sent them on to the airport via the hotel's limousine service to be checked in with the airline.

Then she had called and changed her reservation to an earlier flight. She and Dax had done nothing that either should be ashamed of—yet. They shouldn't press their luck. This time she had escaped unscathed, and it had made her more resolute than ever not to become involved with a man until she knew what had happened to Mark. "I'm still married," she had repeated to herself like a catechism. And now she said the words again as she watched Dax's retreating back, fighting the urge to run to him and beg to be held and supported by his strength.

Betty was disappointed to learn that she was leaving. "I thought maybe all of us could go out and celebrate tonight. I know none of the others are leaving until tomorrow."

"I'm sorry, Betty, but I need to get back. The radio station wasn't too thrilled with me for taking time off." That wasn't true. Her employers were proud of her stand on the topic of MIAs and never chastised her for taking time off to further PROOF's cause. Another lie. Ever since she met Dax… "I've already called them and told them I'd be there tomorrow. Have a glass of champagne for me."

"We will." Betty laughed. "Several, I'm sure. Take care of yourself, Keely. You can't know how much you mean to us. No one could be a better spokesperson than you. Thank you again."

Keely hailed a cab outside the Congress and it took her straight to National Airport. She went through all the mechanics of boarding a domestic flight without conscious thought. Her mind was on what Dax would do and how he'd feel when she wasn't on his flight. Would he be worried? Angry? Both? Would he demand to know which flight a Mrs. Keely Williams had taken? Or would he ask for Keely Preston? He would ask for neither. He couldn't afford to.

What had he wanted to talk about? He hadn't seemed angry like he had been the evening before when he had let her out at the hotel. What would he have said to her tonight? It didn't matter. Nothing could change their circumstances.

She tightened her seat belt before the airplane taxied

and took off. She declined dinner and pushed her seat back into a reclining position, feigning sleep to prevent constant attention from the stewardesses.

The flight was routine. There were no thunderstorms. Nor was there anyone to hold her hand.

CHAPTER SEVEN

"WHY WON'T YOU come with us?"

"I've told you, Nicole. I don't want to."

"That's no reason."

"It's the best reason."

"I'm sick of the Sulky Sue role."

"Then leave me alone," Keely shouted and, planting both hands on the edge of her desk, shoved her chair back. Pushing out of it, she went to the grimy second-story window and looked down on Chartres Street. It was a drizzly day in the French Quarter, perfectly matching her mood. She had been avoiding Nicole for the past few days, but her friend had finally trapped her in her office at the radio station.

Actually her "office" was little more than a closet at the end of a long, murky hallway at the back of the building. Into the room had been crammed two ugly olive-green steel desks. Keely shared the office with the midnight-to-six disc jockey, whom she had never even met. She knew him only by the picture of him and a leggy blonde that was signed: *It was fun, Cindy*. The photograph was stationed on his littered desk in what could be presumed was a place of honor.

Keely sighed and closed her eyes. She wished when she opened them that the rain would have washed away some of the dirt on the window. But it wouldn't. Nor would the dull ache around her heart have disappeared. None of that was Nicole's fault, however, and she regretted having snapped at her friend. Nicole's nagging was a product of concern. Keely turned to face her now, though she remained standing at the window.

"I'm sorry," she said. "I'm in a foul mood and I shouldn't take it out on you."

Nicole hitched her shapely hip over the corner of the disc jockey's desk, upsetting the picture of Cindy. "You certainly shouldn't. To look at you one would think I was your last friend, so you'd better treat me nice." She crossed her arms over her generous breasts and eyed her friend speculatively. "I'm dying of curiosity, you know. When are you going to break down and tell me?"

"Tell you what?" Keely asked innocently and found a thread on her cuff that required her undivided attention.

"Tell me why you've been dragging around here like a damn zombie since you got back from Washington last week. Tell me why you look like hell, and why you won't confide in your best friend about something that's obviously upset you."

"Is that a new pair of earrings?"

"Don't you dare try to get me off the subject, Keely Preston," Nicole warned. "I want to know what happened to you up there that made you even worse off than you were before. And God knows that was bad enough. So lay it on me. I'm not leaving this room and neither are you until you tell me."

"Who set you up as judge of how bad off I am?" Keely asked crossly.

"I did, since you apparently need a keeper to prevent

you from closing a shell around yourself like a damn clam or something. What gives, Keely?"

Keely took the few steps back to her desk and flopped down in the creaking chair. She leaned her head on the cracked imitation leather and closed her eyes against the perpetual headache she couldn't seem to shake. "You know what gives, Nicole. You yourself said I'm this way every time I do something for PROOF."

"Yes, but you scored a great victory this time. You should be happy instead of miserable. And don't deny that you're miserable, because I know better. You make Hamlet look like a comedian."

Keely smiled, but the attempt didn't quite make it to a full-fledged laugh. "I *am* happy about what we accomplished. I'm just tired."

"Try again."

"I don't want to be around people just now, that's all." *I met a man, a wonderful man. He kissed me, touched me, like no other man ever has. I think I've fallen in love. What am I going to do about it?* What would Nicole's reaction be if Keely said aloud what she was thinking?

"That won't do, Keely. You need to be with people. Come on and go to this reception with us tonight. We won't stay long, I promise. When you say it's time to leave, it'll be time to leave."

"I don't want to."

"But you *need* to, dammit!" Nicole said in exasperation. "Dress up. Have a drink or two. Dance. Live, Keely." She jumped off the desk and dug her fists into her hips. "If you don't come with us, I'll have to endure Charles all by myself. You wouldn't wish that on me, would you?"

Keely did laugh then. "Why don't you give that guy a break? I know you're crazy about him and just won't admit it. All right, all right." She put up her hands to ward off Nicole's objections. "You wouldn't be with Charles by yourself. You said you had a spare man."

"We do. And frankly, he's as dull as Charles. If I can stand it, you can. The point is you'll be in a public place instead of holed up at home and you'll be in the company of other human beings instead of by yourself. Come on."

"Where is it and what is it?" Keely asked in resignation.

"It's at the Marriott. Formal. Something for the Arts League. Charles is going to represent the television station since it's airing public-service announcements for the League. We'll pick you up at eight."

"I don't know, Nicole," Keely demurred.

"Eight o'clock," Nicole said firmly. "And for God's sake, do something with your hair. I hate it all slicked back like that. You look like Jane Eyre."

"You're certainly literary this morning. First Hamlet, now Jane Eyre. Have you read either one?"

Nicole laughed good-naturedly as she sashayed toward the door. "Heavens, no. I only read porn. Keeps me in practice." She winked wickedly before the door closed behind her. Then Keely heard her call from halfway down the hall, "Eight o'clock."

Eight o'clock. Would she feel up to facing the world by then? She doubted it. She hadn't felt like facing it so far. Erroneously she had thought that once she got away from Washington and back to work, memories of Dax would soon fade and she would forget all that had happened. It wasn't to be. The longer she was away from him, the larger he loomed in her mind. Every minute of the day she wondered what he was doing, whom he was with, what he was wearing, what he was feeling, if he thought of her.

It was wrong. It was insane to perpetuate an impossible dream, but she couldn't help herself. She stared often at the telephone, willing it to ring. In some secret corner of her mind she had thought—wished—that he would call. After all, she wasn't on his flight as she should have been. Hadn't he been the least bit concerned about what had happened to her? Of course, if he had been in New Orleans the past few days, he would have heard her on the radio and known she was at least alive.

Apparently his disinterest indicated what he felt about their interlude in Washington. It had been just that, an interlude. A disappointing one for him, she was sure, since she hadn't "come across." Dax Devereaux didn't have to fool with a woman like her, since many were far too willing to accommodate him.

Nicole was right. She was at a dead-end street and she must turn around and go in a different direction or keep running into the wall. Tonight she would make an effort to return to the world of the living. Checking her watch, she noted that she was due at a sponsor's meeting and she hadn't even read through the agenda.

Taking a compact out of her purse, she grimly admitted that Nicole was right. She did look like hell. Her complexion was sallow, her eyes lackluster, her hair a disgrace. She hadn't done her nails since her return from Washington.

"Okay, Keely, you've mourned long enough," she said to her reflection before snapping the compact shut. Before reading the copy for her commercial about the virtues of a steel-belted radial tire, she telephoned a beauty salon and made an appointment for the works.

NOT BAD, SHE thought critically as she looked at the results of her two hours in the salon and another hour spent at home on personal grooming. She had had a half inch taken off the bottom of her hair, getting rid of the cursed split ends. It had been arranged in a casual top knot, soft but sophisticated, with tendrils grazing her cheeks and nape.

She had put an oatmeal mask on her face, and now her complexion was glowing radiantly. She had applied her makeup tastefully and well, and if that sad look in her eyes wasn't completely gone, it was somewhat screened.

When the doorbell rang, she picked up her evening purse, swung her black satin cape over her shoulders, and went to meet her "date."

As Nicole had said, he wasn't very exciting, but he politely introduced himself as Roger Patterson as he escorted her down her brick sidewalk to the car waiting at the curb. He was the liaison between the Arts League and the media. Keely thought he had chosen his profession unwisely, for he was a self-effacing type that one would forget five minutes after meeting him.

He held the door of Charles's Mercedes open, and she settled in the back seat. "You look sensational," Nicole enthused.

"How do you know?" Keely asked cryptically. "You haven't even seen me yet."

"You had only one way to go. Unless you had died."

"You *do* look lovely, Keely," Charles Hepburn spoke to her via the rearview mirror.

"Hello, Charles. How are you?"

"I'm well, thank you."

"Did you meet Randy?" Nicole asked, turning around to them from her position beside Charles in the front seat.

"Roger," he corrected quietly.

"Oh, I'm sorry."

"Yes, we met," Keely said quickly and gave her date an easy smile.

Keely's house was actually a duplex carved out of an old house in the Garden District. The area was known for its lovely homes, some of them previously neglected, now being restored and converted from enormous one-family dwellings to apartments and condos.

Charles drove them up St. Charles Avenue to Canal and then toward the Mississippi River to the Marriott. He left his car with the valet service. They entered the hotel by the side door and traversed the sprawling lobby crowded with tuxedoed men and formally attired women. "I think the receptionist is up on the third floor in one of the ballrooms," Roger said unnecessarily since there were signs to that effect posted throughout the lobby on brass easels.

"Oh, I love affairs like this. But then I love affairs of any kind," Nicole said naughtily. She was actively taking note of who was there and what they were wearing and whom they were with.

They were walking toward the escalator past the open bar when Nicole exclaimed, "Madeline Robins is wearing her famous diamonds, I see. They really look tacky with that dress. Who is she— Oh, it's Dax Devereaux. Look, Keely. You met him, didn't you?"

Keely's heart had dropped to the floor and she had stumbled over it. Roger put a tentative hand under her elbow when her footsteps faltered. She looked in the direction of Nicole's gaze and her breath lodged in her throat when she saw the shining black hair, delicately sprinkled with silver at the temples, and knew that it could only belong to one man.

Even as she spotted him, Dax leaned back to laugh at some amusing remark the stunning woman next to him had said, and his black eyes lighted on Keely. His reaction at seeing her was as volatile as hers at seeing him. His grin fell, and the flash of white teeth disappeared. He looked as if he had been struck a physical blow and couldn't quite believe it.

"Are you going to speak to him, Keely?" Nicole asked expectantly.

"N-no." Keely stuttered, looking away from him hastily. "He's with a group. Perhaps I'll see him later. I barely know him, after all. He probably doesn't even remember meeting me."

Nicole's look frankly said, *Liar*. But she didn't pursue the matter as they rode up the escalator. Under the pretense of straightening her cape, Keely glanced over her shoulder down onto the lobby below and her eyes locked with Dax's as he watched her progress up the conveyor.

She forced herself to turn away and join the others' chatter as they rode up to the third floor. At the coat check she allowed Roger to slide the cape from her shoulders and disappear with it into the throng of men who were doing likewise.

Charles gasped when he took Nicole's fox coat from around her. "Your eyes are buggin' out, Charles," she teased. Indeed, she wore an eye-popping dress. It was black georgette. The long sleeves were slit from cuff to shoulder, and the neckline was slit from neck to waist. It intimated more than it revealed, but the effect was startling. As always she looked gorgeous.

Though she didn't realize it, Keely looked just as stunning. Her black taffeta tulip skirt, called that for its rounded hem that became a slit to just above her knees, provided an enticing view of her legs. The cerise blouse was moderately plunging and fitted her bosom and waist like a second skin, but the ruffled collar that stood against the back of her neck and the soft peplum at the top of her hips kept it from feeling sexy. Her black satin sandals were by Jourdan and had a thin line of rhinestones around her ankles in lieu of a strap.

"Listen to that heavenly music," Nicole said, undulating in rhythm to the orchestra's dance music. "Come on, Charles, and dance with me."

He glanced worriedly at her breasts swaying unrestrained under the sheer fabric and said, "All right, but if you get carried away and come out of that dress, I'm taking you home."

"And then what?" she asked invitingly as she dragged him onto the dance floor.

Keely laughed. She liked Charles Hepburn and knew that he was in love with Nicole. He was older, at least forty-five, but his receding hairline inspired confidence. His body was perfectly maintained by daily workouts in a downtown gym. His small frame was wiry and bespoke a strength that would have done a much younger man proud. He was mild mannered and courteous to a fault. Keely sometimes thought Nicole would treat him better if he'd lash back at her just once, but his patience imitated Job's.

No matter how many times Nicole vehemently denied it, Keely thought she cared more for Charles than she was willing to admit. Perhaps his serious, mature nature frightened her seemingly carefree friend. As Keely watched them dancing, she was convinced more than ever that whatever their feelings for each other were, they ran deep. Nicole was brushing herself against Charles and smiling in a way he couldn't resist. His hand stroked her back. Keely wished they would stop fooling themselves and each other and admit their mutual affection.

"Would you like to dance?" Roger interrupted her reverie hesitantly. She had almost forgotten him.

"I don't think so right now. Maybe later. I would like something to drink." She wasn't much of a drinker, but seeing Dax, especially with Madeline Robins, had upset her more than she wanted to give credence to.

"Yes, of course." Roger seemed relieved to be of some use to someone. "What would you like?"

"Something cool. A vodka Collins?"

"Vodka Collins. I'll be right back." He wove his way through the crowd and was soon swallowed up by it. Feeling self-conscious at being left alone, Keely located a table with four vacant chairs and claimed it for them. She signaled to Nicole and Charles as the dance finished and they left the floor.

Settled with drinks, they passed the first hour of the reception in easy companionship. People they knew stopped by frequently to chat. Ones they didn't know came by to meet and be met. She knew Nicole was a celebrity, but it never ceased to amaze her that people thought of her in that light too. Often when she was introduced and the person put her face with the familiar voice on the radio, they became tongue-tied and effusive.

Society's stars were out. A few of the New Orleans Saints were there; several celebrities who were performing in town had been invited to attend the fundraising function. It was a glamorous crowd, exciting. The food on the buffet tables was sumptuous. The dance music couldn't have been surpassed.

And Keely was ready to leave within a few minutes of her arrival.

Miserably she had noticed that the table Dax and Madeline shared with three other couples wasn't far from where she was sitting. She was forced to watch his attention on the other woman. He got her drinks. She ate off his plate and he playfully slapped her hands away. She kissed his cheek. He helped her find a lost earring. They danced. They whispered. He kissed her lightly on the mouth.

Keely excused herself and found the ladies' lounge, staying in there an inordinate amount of time. When she came back, Nicole and Charles had disappeared and she saw Roger on the other side of the huge room chatting with the symphony conductor. She took a sip of her watery drink to give her hands something to do.

"Do you get your jollies by standing up men in airports?"

The slippery glass, beaded with condensation, nearly fell through her fingers. She set it down on the tablecloth and turned her head to see Dax leaning over her with both hands braced on the back of her chair.

"No. I wasn't in a very jolly mood that day."

"I was. Until I got to the airport, on the airplane, waiting for you, and not knowing what in the hell had happened to you."

She lowered her eyes from his accusing ones. "I'm sorry."

"Then dance with me."

"Where's Madeline?" she asked cattily.

"Do you care?"

"Don't you?"

He only shrugged and took her hand to pull her to her feet. Since she had been seen dancing with Roger and Charles and several others, it wouldn't look all that strange for her to dance with the congressman, would it?

His touch burned her skin and she couldn't have stopped herself from being drawn into his arms under the penalty of death. The song was a slow, love ballad. The strains of the music surrounded them. The lights were appropriately dimmed. His hand was on her back, pressing, caressing without even moving. His mouth was against her hair.

"Do you know what I'd like to be doing?"

She shook her head.

"Nibbling your rhinestones."

It took her a moment to realize what rhinestones he was referring to. The only ones she had were the ones around her ankles. She laughed breathlessly. "Shame on you."

"Those are without a doubt the sexiest shoes I've ever seen. I might develop a real shoe and foot fetish and become a dyed-in-the-wool pervert."

She looked up at him in mock dismay. "What! And ruin your political career?"

"Or enhance it." He laughed and pressed her head back against his shoulder. "Sexual fantasies are 'in' now, you know. Lately I've become an expert at them. Want to hear some?"

"No. I'd be too embarrassed."

He tilted his head to look down at her. "You probably would be," he whispered. "You play a very active role in them."

"Dax, you shouldn't talk to me this way."

"All right, I'm sorry," he said, then belied his contrition by expanding his chest and flattening her breasts against him. He executed a flawless turn, giving him an excuse to splay his hand on her back and bring her closer. "Is it okay to tell you how beautiful you look tonight?"

She lowered her eyes, only to raise them again. She couldn't keep from looking at him. It was a constant internal war. For every time she looked at him, it necessitated raising her head from his shoulder. "Yes, and thank you. You look very distinguished in your tuxedo too. It suits you."

"Who's the man?" he asked abruptly, adroitly dancing them to the darkest corner of the floor.

"What?"

"The man you're with. Is he someone I ought to start hating?"

She colored with pleasure at his jealousy. "No. I only met him tonight. I really came with Nicole and Charles."

"Good." He smiled and she returned it. His arm tightened around her, but no one would have noticed unless they saw the melting expression in each of their eyes.

She pitied every other woman in the room for not knowing what it was like to be held in Dax's arms. The hard pressure of his thighs sent an exquisite thrill up her own as they rubbed together. In the hand held by his she felt the hypnotizing massage of his thumb in her palm. His breath was hot and fragrant on her face and she barely restrained herself from gulping in great amounts of it to fill her own lungs.

He too was thrilling at the opportunity of holding her. Her breasts gentled against him. The tops of them swelled between the ruffles of her blouse and he was made dizzy by the sight and the sweet smell that rose from that velvet cleft. He longed to press his mouth there, to feel the texture of her skin against his lips, against his tongue. He ached. And the ache was made more profound by the way she naturally curved up against his middle, fitting him so well it made their dancing evocative of another act.

All too soon the song ended. His wistful smile matched hers as he escorted her back to her table. She pulled up short when she saw the Robins woman standing beside it talking animatedly to Nicole.

Dax propelled Keely forward until they reached the group. "There you are, darling. I wondered when you were going to remember who you came with." Madeline was smiling, but her eyes slithered menacingly over Keely.

"Madeline, this is Keely Williams. Or Preston, if you prefer her professional name. She is actively involved with the MIA issue. We met recently in Washington." Dax said all of this unemotionally, as though he didn't feel the mounting tension around the table. "Keely, this is Madeline Robins."

"Mrs. Robins," Keely said coolly.

"How nice to meet you," Madeline said with a voice well-trained to conceal unspoken epithets. "It's such a pity about your husband. Nicole was just now telling me how bravely you face life without knowing whether you're a wife or a widow."

There was no way to respond to that, so Keely didn't even try. Nicole broke in. "Keely, we haven't met the congressman."

"Oh," she said, tearing her eyes away from Madeline who had possessively linked her arm through Dax's. In the shiny metallic green dress Madeline wore, Keely thought her long limbs resembled drooping seaweed as she tenaciously clung to Dax. "I'm sorry. Congressman Devereaux, this is my friend Nicole Castleman, Charles Hepburn, and Roger…uh…"

"Patterson," the man supplied and stuck out his hand. "Congressman, I've been wanting to meet you for a long time. I'm an admirer of yours."

"Thank you, Roger. Call me Dax."

God bless Nicole, Keely silently offered up as her friend took over. She flirted harmlessly with Dax, saying how long she had wanted to meet him, but always missed him. He said he felt like he knew her from having seen her so often on television. He chatted with Charles, asking about rates politicians had to pay for television-commercial airtime.

"Call me later in the week," Charles said. "We'll set up an appointment and I'll discuss it with you. Generally speaking, the more commercials you buy, the cheaper the rate per commercial. If your commercials run during the news shows, they are more expensive, but you reach the greatest number of people."

"I'm lost." Dax laughed helplessly. "I'll need your expert opinion, so I'll take you up on your offer to discuss it."

"I'll look forward to it. It will soon be time for you to start planning a media campaign," Charles added. "It can be expensive. I hope you're prepared for it."

"I'm helping him be prepared for it," Madeline said, snuggling closer to Dax. "I've already got a campaign fund started. I'm going to see to it personally that Dax is elected to the Senate."

A look of annoyance momentarily tightened Dax's mouth, but then he smiled genially. "I need all the help I can get."

They chatted inanely about the reception and estimated how much cash it was raising for the various arts. The weather was discussed at length. Then an awkward silence ensued. They had said all that could be said in a group of strangers.

"It was nice to meet you, Mrs. Williams," Madeline said by way of dismissal.

"Thank you," Keely replied, and only courtesy forced her to say, "It was nice meeting you too."

Dax shook hands with Charles and Roger, kissed Nicole on the cheek with an old-world flourish, and did the same for Keely. His mouth touched the skin of her face only fleetingly, yet her body sang with sensations when he raised his head and for a moment his eyes met hers. "I enjoyed our dance, Mrs. Williams. It was a pleasure to see you in a less austere atmosphere. Congratulations again on your victory in Washington."

"Did you support us, Congressman Devereaux?"

she asked goadingly. The others might just as well have not been there. Dax filled her field of vision. His voice was the only sound she heard. The depth of his dark eyes was her firmament.

"Do you even have to ask?" The dimple beside his mouth deepened with his smile. Regretfully he straightened and took Madeline's arm. "Good night, everyone."

Roger held Keely's chair for her. As she sat down, making a production of smoothing her skirt, she heard Madeline purr, "I think everyone who should see us here has seen us. I'm more than ready to leave whenever you are, darling."

Keely's throat squeezed shut and even the hasty swallow of the fresh drink Roger had had waiting for her didn't help relieve the tightness. Charles made some mildly humorous remark, but when she looked up with a stiff smile plastered on her face, she saw that Nicole wasn't laughing either. Instead she was staring at Keely. Her blue eyes lifted to the retreating couple, then dropped back to Keely. Her eyelashes fluttered guilelessly and her mouth curved angelically. Keely didn't trust that innocent expression for a moment and was immediately suspicious of the gleam in her friend's eyes.

They availed themselves of the dessert buffet then decided they had had enough of the gala.

While the men were getting the wraps, Nicole sidled up to Keely and said, "Devereaux's some hunk, isn't he?"

Keely answered levelly. "Yes, I suppose he could be called a 'hunk.'"

"You told me when I called you in Washington that you'd barely met him."

"I had."

"You could have fooled me by the way he danced with you. You two seemed real chummy out there."

"He was only being polite."

"Uh-huh. And I'm a three-toed aardvark, but let's skip that for now. What do you think of Madeline Robins?"

"She's all right, I guess."

Nicole leaned forward and whispered, "And you're a liar, Keely Preston. She's on the make and you know it and you don't like her any better than any other woman does." She pursed her pretty mouth and said, "I wonder how involved the congressman is with her."

"Is there any doubt?" Keely asked bitterly. Where was Dax taking her now that, as Madeline had pointed out, everyone who needed to see them had seen them? To her mansion? His house in Baton Rouge? A room in this very hotel?

"Oh, I'll grant she has the hots for him," Nicole said. "But somehow I get the notion he's not quite as ardent as she is."

"I wouldn't know about either's love life and I care less."

Nicole only smiled blandly as Charles draped her coat around her shoulders. As they left the hotel Keely was grateful they didn't see the other couple. She tried to act unaffected, but wished more than ever that she hadn't come tonight. She should have gone with her first instinct and stayed at home, letting her desire for Dax Devereaux die a slow, graceful death. Now the wounds had been reopened just when they were about to heal. Now she had that recovery process to go through again. Only this time there was an additional irritant in the wound. Madeline Robins. And how many others?

She shook Roger's hand graciously at her door and thanked him for the evening. "I hope you enjoyed yourself," he said, and Keely doubted that he had had any better a time than she had. Charles honked a goodbye when they pulled away from the curb.

Inside her own house she let go her rigid control and slumped against the door. Tiredly, dispiritedly, she crossed to the sofa table and switched on the small brass lamp. Dropping her cape and purse on the loveseat-sized sofa, she leaned down and unfastened the tiny buckles that held the rhinestone bands around her ankles. Dax's words came back to her and she blushed. She told herself it was only the blood running to her head from her bending position, but his suggestion induced all kinds of sexual visions. She kicked the sandals from her feet, reducing her height by several inches without the high heels.

She undid the covered buttons down the front of her blouse as she was crossing to the staircase. The doorbell pealed loudly.

Did I leave something in the car? was her first thought.

Hastily rebuttoning her blouse, she opened the door a crack, peering out.

"Hi," he said.

"Hi," she answered.

CHAPTER EIGHT

INSTINCTIVELY HER HAND went to the wall switch to turn off the porch lights.

His voice, tinged with humor, came to her out of the sudden darkness. "Do you think we're under surveillance?"

"I don't know. Could we be?"

She felt, rather than saw, his careless shrug. "I'm willing to take my chances."

She moved aside and let him through the door. He took three steps into the room and looked around it with appreciative eyes. Keely was proud of her house. The building had been in sad disrepair ten years ago when someone had bought it and divided the rambling structure into two separate condominiums. It had been completely restored and modernized then, but when she bought her half three years ago, she had decorated it to suit her.

The exterior of the house typified early New Orleans with its used red brick, white shutters, and black iron grillwork on the windows and around the narrow balcony on the upper floor. Keely had furnished it with a tasteful combination of old and new. Fruitwood antiques she had picked up in attics and out-of-the-way shops were mingled with pieces upholstered in contemporary fabrics. Stark white woodwork accented the sand-colored walls. Muted shades of rose, blue and green were used as accent colors in throw pillows, framed graphics, and the padded fabric that covered one wall in the dining room. The effect was beautiful.

"I like your house," Dax said without turning around. "It looks like you."

"A hundred and seven years old?"

He turned to face her then and the twinkle in his eyes was mischievous. "It's amazing how you relics are holding up." He shook off his overcoat and came back to the door to hang it on a brass hall tree. He pivoted slowly until they were standing face-to-face.

It might have been hours, years, small eternities, or it might have been only seconds that they looked at each other. For however long, it was enough to convey all the longing, need, and frustration that each had suffered since last they were together.

The facades of decorum were torn down and all that was left standing was the naked desire that each had for the other. There were no observers, there were no rules, there were no conventions that had to be satisfied. For the moment it was only them, and they put away conscience, yielded to the attraction that continued to haunt them, and lived only for the present.

He extended his arms slowly and closed them around her. Her arms lifted to his shoulders. Their bodies gravitated toward each other, until they touched from breast to knee in one unbroken line.

He lowered his head and nuzzled her hair, her ear, her neck. His lips made a pass across her jaw, up to her cheekbone, over her brow, and down her nose until they came to rest at the corner of her mouth.

"I couldn't stay away from you. I tried. I couldn't."

His mouth closed over hers and it blossomed open. He drew on her as though she were the energy supply necessary for his life force. She gloried in her ability to sustain him and hoped his appetite for her would never be satisfied.

His tongue played havoc with her senses, first plunging deep, then teasing with rapid, elusive dartings. The sensual lingual stroking went on and on, robbing her of breath, yet bringing her to life. Every cell in her body was awakened to his touch, his smell, his taste, and the low sounds that emanated from his throat. Her breasts were imbued with desire, much as a mother's would be with milk. They ached to be relieved of this tingling fullness. Conversely, her womb contracted against a vague emptiness that longed to be filled.

His arms relaxed, but only enough to cradle her face between his hands and look down into her swimming eyes. "Why did you do that to me, Keely? Why did you leave without a word of goodbye? Do you know how frantic I was at that airport? How was I to know you hadn't been abducted or something? Horror scenes out of the worst nightmares came to my mind. Why did you do it?"

"Dax," she groaned. "I thought it was best if we didn't see each other alone again. Things were...are... getting out of hand."

"I'm sorry about what happened after we left Mount Vernon. Keely, I'd never do anything to hurt or insult you. My God! I wanted to apologize to you. I tried, but you took your phone off the hook and then the next day there wasn't an opportunity."

For torturous moments his fingers lightly explored

the features of her face, gliding over them, comparing textures. "Despite what my adversaries say, I *do* have some moral fiber. I know you're another man's wife. If you were my wife, I'd kill any man who touched you." Now he pulled her close in a smothering embrace. "But God forgive me, I want you."

"Ask for my forgiveness too, Dax."

He didn't need a second invitation. His tongue delved past her lips and swept her mouth like a searing torch. His body melted along her in a heart-stopping juxtaposition.

She knew she was slipping from a world held together by gravity into one of random bliss. His mouth drew her beyond the boundaries of conscience and regret and she never wanted to return. Without anchor, aimlessly, she floated in a sea of passion. In her thirty years she had never known the seductive power of a man's touch. Desire rioted through her veins, seeking an outlet, electrifying her nerve endings until they hummed.

"You're beautiful," he said against her mouth. "While we were dancing, I wanted to do this." His head came down to kiss the valley between her breasts just above the edge of her bra. His head oscillated with agonizing slowness, stroking her not only with his mouth, but with nose and chin as well. His hand closed over one breast and treated it to a lazy massage. The top curve of the other was kissed by parted lips and a languid tongue. He kissed again. And again. Lower. And lower still until…

"Keely, Keely." Her name was an agonized cry ripped from a hoarse throat. He rested his forehead on hers. "We can't do this any longer, Keely."

"I know."

"I can't bear it."

"Neither can I."

"I have to go."

"I understand."

"Are you getting up at five tomorrow?" he asked, taking his overcoat from the hall tree and pulling it on.

"Yes." She tried to smile, but her lips quivered uncontrollably.

He checked the tailored wristwatch. "You won't get much sleep. It's late."

She couldn't have cared less. "Are you driving back tonight? To Baton Rouge?"

He shook his head. "No. I have business here tomorrow. When I'm in New Orleans, I stay at the Bienville House. Do you know it?"

"In the Quarter on Decatur?" He nodded. "I know it, but I've never been inside."

"It's clean and quiet."

"I suppose it is." They were saying nothing they wanted to say, only biding time until they would have to part.

"Who lives in the other side of the house?"

"An older couple. He's a philosophy professor at Tulane. They share the house with a Great Dane that's taller than I am." Another attempted smile. Another failure.

"You were lucky to get the side that—" His amiable mood finally played out and the temper erupted with volcanic impetus. He cursed viciously as he slammed his fist into his opposite palm. "*Dammit!* What in the hell am I standing here babbling for? I don't give a damn who lives in the other side of your house. I'm only talking to keep my hands off you. I don't even know what I'm saying. I'm only thinking of how I want to be making love to you, naked and freely, and not like two grappling adolescents.

"I want to see you naked, Keely. And I want to lie down beside you naked. I want us to maybe hurt each other a little, and soothe each other a lot. I want to kiss your breasts and stomach and watch your face while I'm doing it. I want to know what your thighs feel like.

"If any of this disgusts you, I'm sorry, but it's what I feel, what I've felt since I first saw you on that damn airplane." His voice had risen to a level she had never heard before. At his sides his fists clenched and un-clenched as though he were trying to grip the reins of his temper and haul it in, but couldn't.

"It's not just something I feel in my loins. I could satisfy that anywhere. But it's something I feel in my brain and in my heart too. I deluded myself into think-ing I could be your buddy, your pal. But I can't, Keely. I can't be with you and not touch you. Do you under-stand? These clandestine meetings compromise us both and, speaking for myself, will soon lead to insanity. It will be best for both of us if we don't see each other again. Goodbye."

Without another word he flung open the door and closed it behind him with finality. Keely stood motion-less, though tremors of anguish were tearing through her body.

He's right. He's right. We've known all along that nothing could come of this. It's better this way. It is. It is.

Then why was her face bathed with tears?

"HERE WE ARE at eight fifty-six and I'm going to let Olivia Newton-John take you into the second shift this morning. One more word from you, Keely. How do things look from up there?"

Keely spoke into the small microphone that curved around her cheek from the headpiece she wore. "It's looking good, Ron," she said to the rush-hour DJ. "The police are still working that six-car pileup on the Pontchartrain Expressway at the Broad Street exit. All but one lane are still closed. Anyone going that direction may want to consider an alternate route. All in all it's been a rather calm morning."

"Thank you, darlin'. How about coffee later?"

"No, thank you, Ron. I'm all tied up today."

He groaned heartbrokenly. "Folks, our angel in the sky has a heart of stone."

Keely switched off her mike as the DJ said his farewells to their audience and switched on the promised recording. Every day they carried on that ridiculous repartee over the airwaves and their listeners seemed to eat it up. She often received fan mail that asked her not to be so hard on poor old Ron who was obviously in love with her. Little did the writers of such mail know that he was married, had three children, and lived in relative peace under his real name in Metairie.

She sighed as Joe Collins, the veteran helicopter pilot, banked the aircraft and changed their direction. As usual, her knuckles whitened a bit as the ground tilted. Her husband had disappeared after a helicopter crash. She never forgot that.

"You all right this morning, angel?" Joe teased, though his eyes were concerned as he looked at his passenger.

"Yes." Keely smiled wryly. "I didn't get much sleep last night." That was true. After Dax left her, she had passed the hours in dreary contemplation until it was time for her to shower and dress for work.

"You're sure that's all?" Joe asked her as he set the chopper down on the Superdome parking lot where he picked her up every morning and afternoon.

"Yes. I've just got a bad case of the doldrums. Nothing to worry about."

"I'm not convinced, but I won't pressure you into talking. See you this afternoon."

"Sure." She stepped out of the chopper, grabbed her things, and slammed the door shut. She ran under the rotating blades until she had cleared them and then turned to wave as Joe lifted off.

Keely trudged to her car and unlocked the door. She had thought seriously about calling in sick this morning, but decided she would be better off going to work as though nothing had happened last night. It was better to stay busy than to mope around her empty house, thinking about her empty life.

She drove through what lingered of rush-hour traffic into the French Quarter, which always had traffic jams. At that time of day the narrow streets, not suited for modern traffic, were crammed with delivery trucks making stops to the many restaurants and shops in the Vieux Carré. She finally pulled into the parking lot on the roof of one of the old buildings and walked the block to the studios of KDIX.

Yesterday's rain had stopped and a watery sun was trying to shine, an attempt that Keely found offensive. She wanted nothing to brighten this day. She was in a black despair and she wanted the world to know it.

For a long time she stared out the window of her office, reliving those moments when Dax had held her, kissed her. She had vivid recall of everything he had ever said to her. She believed everything he had ever said. That's why she didn't doubt that he wouldn't see her again. They couldn't be "friends" and nothing else. The chemistry between them was too electric. Every time they were together they betrayed not only Mark, but their own principles. She didn't need him in her life, complicating what was already an untenable situation. And he certainly didn't need her in his. His adversaries would have a field day should he have any relationship with the wife of an MIA, especially one as visible and vocal as she.

Determined not to dwell on Dax, she went to her desk and mechanically reduced the pile of unanswered mail, returned telephone calls, and spoke at length with the producer of the morning show. Since she had to work a split shift and report on the afternoon traffic as well, she usually took off at noon and didn't have any obligations until three-thirty when she met Joe again at the Superdome.

It was almost time for her to leave when the door to her office burst open and Nicole rushed in. "Thank God you're here," she said, out of breath. "You just saved my life."

Keely couldn't help but laugh at her friend's obvious relief. Her beringed hand was splayed across her heaving chest in a gesture of thankfulness.

"Tell me quick what I did," Keely said.

"You're going to be the live interview on the noon news."

"Guess again."

"Keely, don't go cute on me. I'm not kidding. Our scheduled guest just called and he's sick and can't come. Unless you want our viewers to see fifteen minutes of my vacation slides, you're going to take his place. I'll interview you about the MIAs and what happened in Washington last week. It's current and newsworthy. So what's the problem?"

She didn't feel like living much less like going on television—that was the problem. "Nicole, any other day I would, but I don't feel well today. I look worse."

"Bullfeathers. You look gorgeous as always."

"I have circles under my eyes!" Keely exclaimed.

"So do I," Nicole shouted back. "Makeup works wonders. Besides, you wouldn't let a few dark circles under your eyes stand between me and ruin, would you?"

"Nicole, I know if you thought real hard, you could call in a favor on someone. How about the mayor? He's always good for last-ditch efforts."

"He's boring as hell too. You've got a good story here, Keely. Get yourself together. We go on in ten minutes," she said, checking her watch. "God, I haven't even looked over the script. Come on." She went to Keely's desk and, grabbing her by the arm, hauled her to her feet.

"I've got the cramps," Keely whined.

"Take an aspirin."

"This dress is—"

"Beautiful."

They had reached the door. "Oh, hell, why not?" Keely asked herself under her breath.

"That's the spirit," Nicole said as she pulled Keely down the hall. At the door of the ladies' room she stopped. "Do whatever you need to do and then come on down. The interview will be after the weather segment, about twelve-twelve, but get there quick so you can be wired for sound. And if I start asking stupid questions, interrupt with a lengthy explanation. I haven't boned up on this." She shoved Keely through the restroom door.

Peering into the wavy mirror over the water-stained sink, she tried her best to bring some semblance of cheerfulness to her face. She added blusher to her cheeks, darkened her lipstick, and brushed her hair. The jade silk shirtwaist dress would show up well on camera. At least she wasn't wearing a stripe or check that would "crawl."

Checking her wristwatch, she noted that it was straight up noon. She left the restroom and walked down the concrete staircase to the wide thick doors of the studio. The red On Air sign was lighted, but she opened the door wide enough for her to squeeze through. The studio was darkened except for the circle of light around the news desk where Nicole and her co-anchor, a young man, were reading the news.

She let her eyes grow accustomed to the darkness before gingerly stepping over the cables that stretched across the studio floor. When a commercial came up on the monitor, the floor director detached his headpiece from one of the cameras and came up to her, taking her arm.

"Hello, gorgeous," he said freshly. "Allow me to escort you to the interview set if you please. Will you have an affair with me?"

"Only when your wife gives you permission, Randy," she laughed. "How are things?"

"Chaotic as usual. Thanks for helping out today. Some wouldn't want to share the set with Devereaux."

"Dev—" The name died on her lips as she stepped up onto the set under Randy's guiding hand and saw that Dax was already seated on the small sofa and wired for sound.

"I think you two know each other," Randy said as he gently pushed Keely down beside Dax and handed her a microphone. "Don't let that snag your silk," he warned.

"Randy, we're thirty seconds out of the break," one of the cameramen called.

"We'll be coming to you out of the next break," he said before skirting back to his camera and replacing his headphone.

"Why didn't you tell me?" Keely asked out of the corner of her mouth.

"I didn't know," he replied under his breath, making an overt show of straightening his necktie.

Her head whipped around. "Didn't know?"

"Not until this morning. Nicole called me early, full of apologies. Said to be here at noon. Here I am."

Keely adjusted her weight away from his warm presence so close beside her on the small sofa. Tugging on the hem of her skirt, she mumbled, "She duped us both. The same act was played on me. I didn't know you were going to be here. She said I was saving the show because their interview guest wasn't able to come. I'm sorry."

"I'm not."

She looked at him again, but before she could speak, the studio lights glared on, illuminating the set. "Hello, sexy!" The director's voice boomed at them from the glass booth suspended above the studio floor. Keely realized that they had gone into another commercial break. The cameramen were deftly wheeling the three cumbersome cameras toward them and focusing on her and Dax. "Oops, sorry, Congressman. I was talking to our own Keely there."

"Hello, Dave," Keely said, shading her eyes against the bright lights and waving to the man behind the control board in the booth. Unexpectedly her voice reverberated through the studio.

"Give me a level please," they heard Dave say. Then to Keely he said over the speaker, "Try again, this time for a mike check."

"Hello, Dave. This is Keely Preston with a mike check. One, two, three."

"Sounds grrrrreat, honey throat. Congressman Devereaux, will you be so kind?"

"Hello, Dave. How is the new baby?"

"Well, I'll be damned! That's right. Last time you were here my wife was in the hospital. Thanks for remembering. Both are doing well."

"Good," Dax said.

The disembodied voice then said in exasperation, "Nicole, will you please get your sweet tush on the set? We're into the last sixty seconds."

Keely had noticed that Nicole had jumped from the news set and raced over to the studio mirror to check her perfect hair. Quickly now she crossed the cavernous room and plopped down on the chair opposite the sofa, clipping a microphone to her collar. "Goodness," she said breathlessly. "This has been some day. Hello, again, Congressman Devereaux." She studiously ignored Keely, and Keely knew just how flustered her friend was. Since when did Nicole say "goodness"?

"Call me Dax, please," he said.

Nicole smiled. "I will, but not during the interview."

"Coming to you on camera two, Nicole," Randy instructed quietly, replacing Dave's booming directions. "Fifteen seconds."

"Ready, you two?" Nicole asked. Without waiting for an answer, she faced her camera, licked her lips, and smiled. When the red lights on the front of the camera flashed on, she said, "Today on the interview portion of our show we have with us our own Keely Preston and Congressman Dax Devereaux."

For the next seven minutes Keely and Dax fielded Nicole's questions and brought up points she failed to mention. The interview went smoothly. Keely and Dax seemed interested in each other only through the issue they were discussing.

Once when he was speaking with his controlled, convincing voice, Keely turned her head to look at him. He used his hands to make a point and it occurred to her how familiar the gesture was. Each point he made was concise, clear, explicit. He never minced words when someone's welfare was concerned. Some might label him a zealot. Keely admired him as a man of strong convictions.

"Thank you both," Nicole said when she closed out the interview and the news show concluded. She stood up, taking off her microphone. "I can't tell you how I appreciate your dropping everything and doing this for me."

"I'm glad I could do it," Keely said, barely containing her fury, while fumbling to free herself of the microphone. She knew exactly what Nicole had had in mind by inviting both of them on the show. Keely had denied having any undue interest in Dax when Nicole had grilled her about him last night. She should have known Nicole wasn't a fool, and if she was attuned to anything, it was to the relationship between men and women. "Excuse me now. I have work to do." Without another word to either of them, Keely brushed past Dax and left the studio.

She was trembling as she climbed the stairs to the second floor and navigated the labyrinth of corridors to her own secluded office. She sank into her chair and covered her face with both hands, breathing deeply. This time fate had had help, but it had brought Dax and her together again. She had reconciled the fact that Dax would hold no place in her life.

Last night, in frustration and anger, he had come to that conclusion and, showing more discipline than she ever could have, had said that he wasn't going to see her again. Now, only a few hours later, they had been together, sitting in close proximity on the same sofa, breathing the same air, and it had been painful to be that close and pretend indifference.

One thing was certain, she wasn't going to sit in this gloomy office nursing her wounds. The faster she was away from this building, the better.

She was taking her coat from the hook on the wall when the door quietly opened and Dax slipped inside, shutting the door behind him.

They looked at each other for long, silent moments, Keely's hands frozen in the process of lifting her coat down. He kept his back to the door, as if keeping opposing forces at bay.

"Where are you going?" he asked at last.

She put her coat on. A defense mechanism? Yes.

She felt exposed, vulnerable. Irrationally and irritatingly her heart was pumping in her chest. "Out. I take several hours off in the middle of the day."

"Oh," he answered, but made no move to get out of her way. *God, she's beautiful,* he thought. Last night he had meant every word he had said. It was lunacy for them to continue these secret meetings. He despised lying and sneaking. In this context it added an element of seediness to the feeling he had for Keely, and for that reason alone he wanted no part of secret rendezvous.

There was no way he could turn off his desire for her, so he would eliminate the temptation. A clean break. Surgical severance. Cold turkey. Unconvinced but determined, he had walked into that television studio. Seeing her had obliterated even the smallest shred of resolve.

Dignified, he had sat and answered Nicole's questions logically and concisely, and all the time he had been making love to this woman in his mind. He hadn't been immune to her nearness. Her body radiated a heat that beckoned to his. He was aware of each move she made, no matter how slight. Watching the gentle rise and fall of her chest, he logged each breath she took.

"I came to tell you that I didn't know you were going to be on that program today. I was as surprised to see you as you were me."

"I didn't think you had anything to do with it. The whole thing smells of Nicole. She arranged it."

"Why? I mean, beside the fact that she thought we'd make an interesting interview."

"I don't think she'd have thought we'd be nearly so interesting if she hadn't seen us dancing together last night." Keely looked away from him. "She…uh…she started asking me leading questions afterward." Knowing now her leaving would be a futile attempt to put this all behind her, she slipped out of her coat and rehung it on the hook in the wall. She dropped her purse on top of her desk and sat down in the squeaky chair.

"What kind of questions?" he asked, coming to the side of her desk and hitching a hip over the corner.

"Questions about you. How well I got to know you in Washington."

"What did you say?"

"That I'd barely met you."

"And what did she say?"

Keely looked up at him and replied solemnly, "She said that she couldn't believe that by the way we were dancing together."

He leaned forward and captured one of her hands. His thumb smoothed over each long, oval, manicured nail. "What else did she ask?" When he lifted his eyes, it was only as far as her mouth. As if sensing his appraisal, her tongue darted out. It was such a dainty pink thing to wield such power. Seeing it made him tremble inside.

"She wanted to know if I considered you a hunk." A smile tugged at the corner of her mouth.

A smooth black eyebrow arched over an amused eye. "A *hunk*? Now, that is interesting. And I can't wait to hear what you said." He leaned closer to her, over her.

She had to tilt her head back to look him in the face. "I said I suppose you could be called a hunk."

He cocked his head sideways and asked teasingly, "You said that about me?"

His smile was infectious and she responded, saying coyly, "In a moment of weakness."

They laughed together softly. His index finger came up to investigate the tilting corner of her mouth. It stroked leisurely along her bottom lip until it found the opposite corner just as intriguing. His hand left her mouth only to curl his fingers around her neck beneath her collar and draw her up toward his descending lips. His other hand lightly brushed past her breast when it slipped under her arm to press against her spine and arch her up to him.

The clicking of the doorknob was like a gunshot in the room and they sprang apart. Keely bolted out of her chair, but Dax stood in front of her, facing the door, as though to protect her. They sagged in relief when they saw Nicole standing just within the door. She closed it behind her quickly.

"For godsakes. You two are a case. Don't you know that if you're taking *that* kind of lunch hour you should lock the office door?" Hands on hips, she admonished them like an aggravated parent.

Keely pushed Dax aside and rounded the desk. "Nicole, I could easily strangle you for the stunt you pulled today. Why did you do it?"

Completely unaffected by her friend's anger, she hopped onto the DJ's desk, upsetting poor Cindy again. "Don't pretend to be angry about seeing each other again. It was obvious to me last night that you two are dying to jump on each other's bones, so I appointed myself matchmaker, that's all," she admitted happily. "It worked, judging from what I saw when I came in. I'm only disappointed that I didn't find you in a more compromising position."

"Nicole!" Keely exclaimed, her cheeks flaming with hot color. "Dax...I mean...we..."

Dax came up behind her and placed a reassuring arm around her shoulders. "Nicole," he said calmly, "apparently you noticed that Keely and I became attracted to each other while we were both in Washington. It was accidental. Neither of us planned it, but it happened. Each of us sees the futility in our developing a relationship. She's married." He looked down at Keely sadly. "And I'm running for the Senate. Having an...affair with a married woman wouldn't make for good politics, even if Keely would consent, which she would never do. Last night after the gala we decided that we shouldn't see each other anymore, privately or publicly if it could be avoided. That's why we were both rather disconcerted to see each other today."

"Last night?" Nicole asked sharply, coming off the desk. "After the party? Where?"

Dax glanced at Keely and when she nodded, he added, "At her house."

Nicole slumped back against the desk. "Jimineeeee. Did anyone see you there?'

"Why?" Keely asked, not liking the way Nicole was gnawing her lower lip.

"Well, I'm not the only one who noticed the... warmth...with which you two danced. That's why I came up here. This is the first edition of the evening paper. I thought you ought to see it."

For the first time they noticed the folded newspaper she held in her hand. She extended it toward Keely. With a sinking feeling in the pit of her stomach, Keely unfolded the front page of the society section. There, in a picture no one could miss, were Dax and she dancing, holding each other tightly. His face was bent low over hers, which was raised to his like a flower to sunlight. Their smiles were intimate, more telling than the way he held her. Under the picture the caption read: "Congressman Devereaux and Keely Preston, wife of an MIA. Their turn around the dance floor turned heads."

"Damn," Dax cursed under his breath and flung the newspaper to the floor. "Damn."

Keely folded her arms across her middle and turned away, going to the window and staring out.

Nicole cleared her throat. "You'd better get your stories straight," she warned. "Someone's bound to pick up on this. Dax, did anyone see you at Keely's house?"

"I don't think so. I parked at a restaurant on St. Charles and walked over."

Keely turned around and stared at him. "You did? I didn't know that."

"You didn't? How did you think I got there?"

They took the steps necessary to bring them together. She shrugged. "I didn't think about it. You were just there." She picked at a piece of lint on his jacket lapel. "You shouldn't have done that. It's a dangerous neighborhood after dark. You could have been mugged."

"I'm a hunk, remember?"

"No, I mean it," she said earnestly. "Weren't you cold?"

He smoothed back a strand of her hair. "When I left? Are you kidding?" The private joke was chuckled over.

"Yoo-hoo. Remember me?" Nicole said and they turned toward her with glazed eyes as though they truly had forgotten her presence in the room. "Personally I hope you tell the world to mind its own bloody business. I would love nothing better than for you to start—or continue—a hot and heavy affair. But if valor comes before lust, which I sadly suspect it does in this case, you'd better be prepared for the repercussions this picture is bound to generate. Incidentally, there's an accompanying story you failed to read that hints strongly there may have been more going on in Washington than that subcommittee hearing. By the guilty looks on your faces, I think their suppositions aren't too far off base."

She went to the door. "Please remember that I'm not the enemy. I'm a friend. And I'm sorry about doing what I did today. Had I seen the paper first, I probably would have come up with something less public to bring you two together." She squinted her eyes. "On the other hand, that could be your excuse for last night. You had been invited to come on today's show to talk about the MIA issue and you were only rehashing what had happened in Washington. It isn't much, but it may be all you have."

With that she was gone. Dax and Keely stared at the door even long after it had closed. Finally they turned to each other. He sighed and rubbed the back of his neck. "I guess the decision has been made for us."

"I guess so. I'm sorry, Dax. I wouldn't have jeopardized your Senate race for anything in the world."

"I know. I knew exactly what I was doing when I asked you for that dance. I deceived myself into thinking that I could hold you platonically." He gestured at the paper lying at his feet. "A picture's worth a thousand words."

"We'll just have to make sure that we don't give them any more fuel. You said last night that we shouldn't—couldn't—see each other again, no matter how innocently. What happened today should reinforce that decision." She looked up at him. "I'm still married, Dax. Whatever else is a contributing factor, that one remains the same, and it's the one that makes all the others so vitally important. I'm married."

He went to the door, but turned to her before opening it. "You'll be okay, won't you? What if you're cornered and asked to comment on the picture?"

"I'll plead stupidity. I met you in Washington. We went to lunch with a group of congressmen, a noted journalist, and another member of PROOF. I respect the stand you took for our cause. I fully endorse you for the Senate. Beyond that, nothing."

He nodded his head bleakly. He looked like a man going to the gallows, delaying his departure for as long as he could. "If you ever need me for anything...."

Her eyes answered for her.

Then he was gone and the pain was unbearable. Blindly she groped her way back to her desk and lay her head down on her arms. The shrill ring of the telephone was a rude interruption to her gentle weeping.

"Yes," she grated into the receiver.

"Ms. Preston, this is Grady Sears at the *Times-Picayune*."

She gripped the receiver harder and mustered all her poise. "Yes?"

CHAPTER NINE

THAT WAS ONLY the first in a series of similar calls. The persistent reporters were vastly disappointed by Keely Preston Williams's calm responses to their barrage of insinuating questions. When asked if she and Congressman Devereaux were romantically involved, she laughed lightly.

"I'm sure the congressman wouldn't be at all flattered to have his name romantically linked with an old married lady's."

"Your husband has been missing for over twelve years, Mrs. Williams. And you're not exactly old. The congressman's romantic encounters are legion."

Are they? How many have there been? Am I just one among many? "I don't know anything about Congressman Devereaux's love life past or present."

"How do you account for the intimacy with which you two were dancing?" This asked with a leer. "Pictures don't lie, Mrs. Williams."

"No, but they can be misinterpreted. The congressman and I were celebrating a mutual victory in Washington. He supported PROOF's cause. If he uses as much finesse during his campaign as he did on the dance floor, he'll be certain to win the election."

This last was said through a tight throat and stiff smile. She sounded like an idiotic, simpering female, but that was better than sounding like a guilty corre-spondent in a tangled love affair.

All the interviews followed the same pattern. Since she and Dax didn't provide another opportunity to fan the flames of scandal, it was dying a rapid death. Just when she thought she had dodged even the most in-cisive reporters, she learned she had yet to dread the worst of them.

It was four days after she and Dax appeared on the news program. Joe was returning her to her car at the Superdome after a hard day. Three never-say-die re-porters had called her for further comment.

"Looks like you have company," Joe shouted over the loud clapping of the rotary blades as he set the chopper down.

Keely had already seen the car parked beside hers and now she saw the man opening the door and sliding from behind the wheel. It was Al Van Dorf.

"Looks like I do," she said grimly. Thanking Joe for returning her safely, she waved him off, and rather than run from under the blades as she usually did, she walked with a measured tread toward her car. Van Dorf had positioned himself between her and it.

He watched the helicopter lift off and bank sharply in the direction of the hangar, where Joe kept it when it wasn't being chartered.

"Never ceases to amaze me how things fly," he said, still looking at the diminishing helicopter.

"Hello, Mr. Van Dorf. What brings you to New Orleans? Did you run out of things to write about in Washington?" *Easy, Keely,* she cautioned herself. It wouldn't be in her best interest to antagonize him. She softened her sarcastic words with a gracious smile and could tell by the probing look he turned on her that he didn't know if her question had been intentionally snide or not.

"Let's just say that there are more interesting things to write about down here right now." The feral eyes gleamed at her from behind the outdated eyeglasses. His smile was slow in coming and insolent when it finally materialized. "Like you and Congressman Deveraux for instance."

Her look of total bewilderment was worthy of an Oscar. "I—I don't understand. Congressman Devereaux and *I*?"

"Why don't we go somewhere and have a drink and talk about it." He moved to take her arm. She eluded him gracefully but left him with the distinct message that she didn't want to be touched.

"No, thank you, Mr. Van Dorf. I'm on my way home."

"Well, then, I guess we'll just have to talk here." He reached into his breast pocket and pulled out a folded page of newspaper. Keely knew immediately what it was. He studied the picture of them dancing with an objective tilt of his frazzled head. "You take a nice picture, Mrs. Williams."

"Thank you." She could fence with him as long as he could with her.

"Would you say the congressman takes a good photograph? He's a handsome devil."

"Yes, he is. Very handsome." Her ready reply surprised him. He seemed almost angry that she wasn't showing any nervousness. Taking advantage of his guard being down, she asked, "What did you wish to speak to me about, Mr. Van Dorf?"

He eyed her shrewdly. This lady was no easy case. If she was going to play rough, then so was he. "Is Devereaux as good at lovemaking as he is at debate?"

If the question was geared to shock her, it was successful. For a moment she was too stunned to speak. When she did, she found it difficult to form words with her rubbery lips. "Your inference is unforgivable, Mr. Van Dorf, and I don't choose to honor it with a denial."

"Aren't you and Devereaux lovers?"

"No."

"Then how do you explain this picture?"

"How do you explain it?" she fired back. Shock had been replaced by anger and she barely contained her impulse to strike against that knowing smirk that twisted his mouth into an ugly grimace. "People dance together all the time. Do you imply that the President is having an affair with every woman he dances with at a White House reception?"

"Yes, people dance together all the time, but rarely with such sublime grins on their faces."

"Congressman Devereaux is a charming man. I find him intelligent, charismatic, enthusiastic. I admire him for the stand he took on the MIA issue. I respect the courage with which he faces his critics. Admiration and respect. That's all I feel for him." *Liar,* her mind accused, making her even more determined to put Van Dorf off the track. "How you detect something illicit from one dance is beyond me. Do you consider that good journalism?"

"It's not just one dance, Mrs. Williams," he replied coolly. "It's all those covert looks and smiles in Washington. It's a rainy day that neither of you can or will account for. It's a gut feeling I have."

She laughed mirthlessly. "If your 'gut feeling' is your only source of information, you'd better find others more reliable. I have never been Congressman Devereaux's lover." That was the truth. "I will never be." That remained to be seen. "Nor do I want to be." That was a lie. "Now, I've granted you all the time I intend to. I would think you'd have better things to write about than 'covert looks and smiles,' all of which are only figments of your exploitative imagination."

With that, she pushed past him and went to her car, unlocked the door with shaking hands and got in. She was pulling her coattail free of the door when he asked her, "What does the congressman think of you?"

"Ask him."

He smiled that lazy, smug grin. "Oh, I intend to. You can bet on it."

She slammed the door, started the engine, and, controlling an urge to race out of the parking lot, drove away at a reasonable and, what she hoped was, an unperturbed speed.

Later that night, as she got into bed, she was still quaking with anxiety. What could she have said that she hadn't? What had she said that she shouldn't have? Did Van Dorf believe her? Probably not, but he would have nothing else on which to build a story. If he did print a story hinting at a relationship between them, he'd look like a fool. He had no proof, no definitive facts. His material would be purely conjecture. And when it came to the bottom line, they were innocent.

Of course he might stumble upon the fact that Dax had been at her home after the Arts League benefit. It would take some strong convincing on their part to persuade him that nothing had happened, especially since he was prepared to believe the worst. But in fact, nothing *had* happened. They had absolutely nothing to feel guilty about.

Everyone believed her to be Dax's lover. Could no one imagine that Dax could have a platonic relationship with a woman?

For the past two days Dax's sexual exploits and his long list of "companions" had been counted and recounted. Vehemently she had denied being the next name on that list, but that's what she was automatically suspected of being. Had she submitted to Dax's lovemaking, would that be all she was to him? Another notch in his belt? No, no. Yet…

She had read an interview with Dax in last evening's paper. When asked about the now infamous photograph with Keely Preston, he had answered glibly, "I wish they had printed the picture of me with the representative of the Longshoremen's Union. It was a much better picture of me, though that burly longshoreman wasn't near as pretty as Mrs. Williams."

He had laughed it off, made light of it. Of course under the circumstances that's all he could have done. But maybe that's how he really felt. Maybe he wasn't suffering as much as he had told her he was.

Tears blurred her vision as she stared across her bedroom at the bookcase. The photograph taken of her and Mark on their wedding day was in its place on the third shelf. The bride had bangs and two long skeins of hair hanging over either shoulder to her breasts. Her pure wool dress was hemmed at least six inches above her knee and looked ridiculous with the white patent leather boots that hugged her calves. A traditional wedding dress had been out of the question. There hadn't

been time to select one. But had she really got married
looking like *that*?

Her burning eyes slid to the young man in the picture. Mark. *Where are you? What happened to you?
Do you live? My sweetheart Mark. For you were a
sweetheart. Kind, generous, tender, fun, all of those
things. The perfect first love.*

In the picture his hair was cut in early Beatles fashion with long bangs sweeping his eyebrows. That was
only days before the army had sheared off his hair at
boot camp. His pants and the sleeves of his jacket were
too short and tight for his athletic frame. His shoes
looked tiny in contrast to the then fashionable bell-
bottom cut of his trousers.

Both of them were wearing silly smiles, quite
pleased with themselves for having done such a grown-
up thing as getting married.

She sat up to look at the photograph more closely.
The girl in the picture seemed someone else. She had
no relevance to the woman Keely Preston Williams was
now. She was as foreign to Keely as a stranger. This
Keely couldn't relate to that girl child.

Nor, if Mark were still alive, was he that same young
man. She couldn't attach a face, a voice, a smile, a personality, to the man Mark would be if he should come
back. The boy in the picture was gone, vanished. And,
just as surely, the girl no longer existed either.

Keely lay back down and stared at her ceiling. She
tried to remember what it felt like to be kissed and caressed by Mark, but all she could focus on were Dax's
kisses and caresses. She didn't recall ever losing all
sense of time and space when Mark kissed her. Perhaps
her heart had accelerated and her palms had grown

moist with anticipation, but she didn't remember that weighty warmth invading her limbs or that liquid, melting sensation that was debilitating and life-giving at the same time.

Closing her eyes, she beckoned to an imaginary lover. When he came, he didn't have the young, blond good looks of her husband, but dark hair and eyes, inherited from French Creole ancestors. His movements weren't fumbling and apologetic, but practiced and patient.

No clumsy hands roamed her body, but ones sure of their talent to arouse. They didn't grope for erogenous places, but went to them unerringly, touched them reverently. Greediness and haste were anathema.

His kiss was deep, engaging every part of his mouth and hers in a sensuous ballet. Teeth, lips, and tongue were erotic instruments that tantalized, stroked, sipped, and probed.

A dimpled mouth murmured something against her breast before raining light kisses on the soft flesh. A tongue swept the nipple silkily as though coaxing it to relax, but the pouting tip became harder.

The persuasive hands stroked downward, touched, found. She welcomed her ghost-lover. He accepted the invitation, whispered accolades in her ear, praising her femininity even as he claimed it.

Together they moved, giving and receiving equally. That aching void that was so much a part of her was filled. She became one with this lover who breathed love words in her ear as his body spoke a poetic language all its own.

Writhing in unfulfilled longing, Keely arched her hips upward, begging her imaginary lover for release. It came over her like a warm blanket, smothering her momentarily until she was clutching at air to fill starved lungs.

Ever so slowly she coasted down. Her eyes fluttered open and she dazedly wondered what had happened to her. Realization brought with it an inundation of shame. For when she had beseeched her lover for surcease, it hadn't been her husband's name she called out, but that of Dax Devereaux.

Her pillow absorbed the scalding tears of bitter remorse.

"WANNA TAKE SOME sandwiches to Jackson Square for lunch?"

As with most of Nicole's telephone conversations, this one was without preamble. "I don't—"

"Have you got anything better to do?" Nicole demanded with a touch of asperity.

"No," Keely admitted.

"I'll see you at the front door in half an hour. I'll bring the sandwiches."

Since that day she had played the trick on Keely of getting her and Dax on the news show, Nicole had given her wide berth. They had spoken occasionally on the telephone and met in the hallways at the studio, but there hadn't been the usual camaraderie between them, and Keely missed it.

At the appointed time she went downstairs and met Nicole at the front door. They exited the building on Chartres and walked the few blocks east toward the historic square. This was one of Keely's favorite places. With Saint Louis Cathedral, the Presbytere, and the Cabildo on one side and the Pontalba Building on the adjacent side, she sometimes envied missing all the memorable events that had occurred here or near this landmark. She satisfied herself with strolling among the sidewalk artists who lined the walkways around the square with their wares.

Today the sun was shining and a pigeon was happily sitting atop Andrew Jackson's head as they entered the square from the north gate in front of the cathedral. Early spring flowers were just now hinting at the promise of blooms. Selecting a deserted bench, Nicole dug into the paper sack and extended a wrapped sandwich to Keely.

"The suspense is killing me," she said, biting into an egg salad on wheat bread. "Am I or am I not?"

"Am you or am you not what?"

"Forgiven." Nicole said the word softly and looked at Keely with such contrition that Keely couldn't help but laugh. Laying her sandwich in her lap, she put her arms around her friend and hugged her tight. "You are and I'm sorry too. I've missed you."

Nicole pulled away and blinked back rebellious tears. "Well, thank God that's over. I thought I'd have to wear sackcloth and ashes the rest of my life. And I look ghastly in gray."

Her retort didn't fool Keely. She had been emotionally moved and had obviously missed their shared confidences as much as Keely had. "What you did was hitting below the belt, but at the time that was the least of my worries," Keely said, shaking her head. It had been two weeks since she had seen Dax. Wasn't time supposed to heal all wounds? She had disproved that fallacy. The longer she went without seeing him, the more she craved the sight of him.

"Do you want to tell me about it? That is, what I can't piece together."

Keely slid a look in Nicole's direction. "And what have you pieced together?"

Nicole wrapped the remainder of her sandwich back in the cellophane and opened a canned soft drink. Offering another one to Keely, she said, "I think you must have met somewhere in Washington, been instantaneously attracted to each other, known from the beginning that things could get sticky considering your stations in life, and your consciences and libidos have been battling it out ever since."

Keely looked absently at the statue of Andrew Jackson, where more pigeons had now lighted. "That about sums it up."

"Keely, why are you martyring yourself? If you want to have an affair with him, have one. So he's a congressman, he's still a man. And who really gives a flying fig in this day and age who sleeps with whom? Be selfish. Think about yourself for a change."

"I have to think of him too."

"Why? He's a big boy. He went into this with his eyes open. Knowing you, I hardly think you enticed him beyond the point of no return, did you? Wasn't he the aggressor?"

"Well, yes, but...I told him right off that I was married, but I didn't refuse to see him either. It was so... he was..."

Nicole mumbled an expletive under her breath. "Have you slept with him?" At Keely's shocked look she hurriedly justified herself. "Well, hell, I don't see any reason to beat around the bush about it. Have you?"

"No," Keely said, barely above a whisper.

"Then no wonder you're miserable. Why for god-sakes are you feeling so ashamed? It's not a permanent condition. Sleep with him and get him out of your system. It's not as if you're in love—" She broke off with a sharp intake of breath. Putting her hand under Keely's chin, she yanked her friend's face toward her and saw the tears beading in anguished green eyes.

"My God," she whispered. "You *are* in love with him. With Dax Devereaux. Jimineee, Keely. When you do something, you do it up big, don't you? I encouraged you to have a nice, uncomplicated affair and you choose a congressman hoping to be a senator and then you go and fall in love with him to boot."

Keely was stung by Nicole's chastising tone. "I wouldn't want to have an affair with him if I didn't love him. I'm not like you. I can't separate sex from love. With me they're one and the same. I can't treat going to bed with a man as casually as you do."

The moment the words left her mouth, she wished to recall them. She covered Nicole's suddenly limp and lifeless hand with her own and pressed hard. "I'm sorry," she rasped. "I wouldn't have said that had I not been so upset. You know I don't censure you. What you do, how you feel about things, is your business."

Nicole snorted a short laugh. "Hell, if anyone knows my reputation, it's me." She stared into space for a moment and then turned her head with its glorious riot of hair toward Keely. "Didn't it ever occur to you that I might rather be like you?"

"Me?" Keely asked, genuinely incredulous.

"Does that surprise you? I don't know why it should. Maybe you don't realize how unique you are. You stand for something. You were given values, standards to live by. They weren't preached at you. You learned them by example.

"I'd love to be ladylike the way you are. My language is deplorable and I know it. My behavior is outrageous and I know it. I would like to have refinement, speak softly and with gentility. I'd like to have the respect people have for you." She uttered that hard laugh again. "Fat chance of that."

Keely hesitated before asking quietly, "Why—why do you…go…with so many men?"

"You mean sleep with so many, don't you?" Her question was tinged with bitterness, but it was aimed at herself, not at Keely. "I guess I'm only living up to what was always expected of me. My mother deserted my father and me when I was too young to remember it. But he never let me forget it. Every day of my life he reminded me how like her I was—a born slut, no good, doomed to a life of sin and immorality. He took out all his anger at my mother on me."

She traced the nap of her twill skirt with her finger, remembering the painful past. "I've analyzed myself, you see. I'm looking for someone to love me, hoping to find in each man I'm with the father-affection I never had. From the day I needed a training bra my father called me a tramp. He was right. I am a tramp. A high-classed one, but a tramp just the same."

"Don't say that about yourself, Nicole. You're not! You have a great capacity to love, you've just never channeled it in the right direction. I think you're afraid to love someone, afraid that they'll reject you the way your father did."

"We were talking about you, remember?"

"Now we're talking about you. Behind this tough I-don't-give-a-damn facade you show the world, there's an insecure, lonely woman begging to be loved for herself and not for the flamboyant image she projects. And a sensitive man is bound to see that woman." She looked at Nicole's averted face and said, "Charles Hepburn perhaps."

Nicole laughed in earnest now. "Talk about rejection! I've tried every trick in the book to get that man in my bed, and he's turned me down flat. It's not that *I* want *him,* it's that he *doesn't* want me. It's become a matter of pride with me. A challenge." She covered her heart with her hand and said theatrically, "He holds great stock in commitment."

"Good for him."

"Well, he can forget it if he thinks I'd give up every other man for *him*." They were quiet. Nicole moved a pebble along the concrete with the toe of her shoe. "No matter what I've said to you in the past, I do respect you and your ideals."

Keely smiled. "And I covet your courage. Sometimes I think morality is little more than fear of reprisal."

Nicole moistened her angelic mouth and asked hesitantly, "What does Dax feel for you, Keely?"

"I don't know. He's said things that made me think that…but then…" She trailed off without finishing.

"Will you give me credit for knowing a little more about men than you do?" Nicole asked. When Keely looked at her and nodded, she said, "I think he's got it as bad as you do. Wait a minute and let me finish," she said, stepping on Keely's attempt to interrupt. "Don't get mad or anything, okay? I made a play for him myself."

Keely felt her jaw drop in disbelief and Nicole rushed on. "Now, I said not to get mad at me. Hell, it was worth a try, wasn't it? At the time I only guessed that you two may have something simmering on the back burner. It was after the interview when you went stalking out of the studio like an offended saint. I put all my 'come on' powers into play, but the man was totally unresponsive. Zilch. No go. He didn't even play along, pretending to be interested, but rudely kept turning his head looking at the door you'd gone through."

"That hardly proves anything."

"No, but when I saw you together, he was...I don't know...attentive, protective. Knowing his reputation with females, most of which is exaggerated conjecture, I'm sure, I didn't expect him to be so..." She searched for a word and came up with "Absorbed."

"Whatever else he is, he is not on the make. I'll admit I've turned down few offers, and in all modesty, few of mine have been turned down. It's not something I'm particularly proud of. What I am proud to tell you is that your man didn't even see these." She cupped her breasts, lifting them and then letting them fall. "He didn't see this hair or these eyes, all of which have been known to drive men crazy. He saw only you, Keely." She stopped speaking to judge the effect her words were having on Keely.

"Take that for whatever it's worth. If I were to gamble on it, I'd bet that you and the congressman haven't had the last chapter written yet."

Keely shook her head in denial. "No. I appreciate everything you've told me, but it was over before it ever got started."

"Strictly off the cuff," Nicole said haltingly. "If you

had your choice tonight, who would you rather be with? Dax or Mark?"

Keely jerked upright as though she'd been slapped. "That's not fair! There's no way I can answer that."

Nicole looked at her sadly and said in a sympathetic undertone, "You just have."

CHAPTER TEN

KEELY AND NICOLE were weak with laughter as they pushed open the heavy studio doors on their way out. They were clutching each other, leaning into each other, giggling like sorority girls. It had been two weeks since their picnic lunch in Jackson Square. The confidences shared that day had added a new dimension to their friendship. Today Nicole had talked Keely into having dinner with her between the evening newscasts.

"Can you believe it? I mean *really,* can you believe it?" Nicole gasped, dabbing at the tears in her eyes. "When I said…when I said…when…" They collapsed into another fit of giggles as they made unsteady progress down the hallway.

"You must share the joke." They turned together to see Charles Hepburn walking toward them. Dax Devereaux was with him.

The laughter seemed to be sucked from Keely's body by a giant vacuum. Her mouth was still open in a wide smile, but no sound came out. She couldn't draw a breath. Seeing Dax had robbed her of even involuntary functions.

"Oh, Charles," Nicole said, going to him and wrapping her arms around his neck. She was still laughing helplessly. "Did you see the newscast?"

"No, Dax and I were just concluding our meeting. What happened?"

"It was a disaster. You'll probably lose all the sponsors you've so carefully stroked. But it was so funny!"

Her laughter was infectious. Dax was smiling. Charles looked at Nicole as if she were a delightful and precocious child and said, "Well, tell us."

"Okay," she said, straightening and clearing her throat. "I was introducing this news story about CPR. They're holding free teaching sessions in the public schools this week." She inhaled deeply to suppress the giggles that were already making her voice ripple. "Anyway, the last thing I said was, 'Pay close attention. The next thing you see might very well save your life or the life of someone you love.' They rolled the tape, but instead of the news story about CPR it was a laxative commercial!"

The men joined the laughter. Nicole fell against Charles like a rag doll. He caught her to him, hugging her while they laughed. "I had just said it was going to save their lives and here was a box of laxative on the scr-screen. You fin-finish, Keely. I can't."

Keely cast a fleeting look at Dax then spoke to everyone in general. "Well, they dumped out of the commercial and came back to Nicole. She was laughing so hard she could barely speak. When she finally did, instead of going back to her script, she handed the whole thing off to the weatherman."

They all laughed again and for a moment she was distracted by Dax's deep dimple and flashing teeth. "The poor man wasn't expecting it. He didn't even have his coat on. Luckily his mike was clipped on. Anyway, like a real trooper, he started jabbering about highs and lows and pressure systems and only then realized that a cigarette was dangling from his mouth."

"That's when it really got funny," Nicole chimed in. "I guess he thought no one would notice if he just let the cigarette casually fall out of his mouth to the floor. But he'd forgotten all those papers and things he uses. The cigarette fell right into a big pile of them around his feet and started smoldering. So here he was stamping on the floor, trying to put out the cigarette and waving that pointer of his. It looked like a magic wand that had a will of its own." She was doing a comical imitation of the stomping foot and waving stick and they all laughed again until they were gasping for air.

When he was somewhat restored, Charles said, "You'll probably all be fired in the morning. I may recommend it myself."

"Are you kidding? Management wouldn't dare fire us. It was the most spontaneous, entertaining newscast they've ever had. We probably won points with the viewers."

While she and Charles bantered the issue, Dax and Keely were thirstily drinking up the sight of each other. She was thinking that the lines around his eyes looked more finely etched, as though he hadn't been getting enough rest. He was thinking that her eyes looked enormous and green in her pale face.

She was thinking that the sprinkling of silver hair at his temples was more obvious. He was thinking that her hair looked lovely as it framed her face. He knew it smelled like flowers.

She was thinking that the dimple beside his mouth was more beguiling than ever. He was thinking that her mouth had never looked more kissable, parted as it was with her quick, light breathing.

She was thinking that his necktie was always perfectly knotted. He was thinking how enticingly the slender gold chain lay against her throat.

She was thinking that he'd never looked taller or stronger. He was thinking that she'd never looked more delicate or feminine.

She was recalling her vivid fantasy and blushing prettily. He was conjuring up fantasies even as he stood there, his blood flowing with unerred direction to the center of his body.

"What do you say, Dax."

Dax and Keely jumped slightly, caught unaware by Charles's question. "What? I'm sorry," Dax said. "I missed the question."

"I asked if you minded if I invite Nicole and Keely to dinner with us."

Dax looked back at Keely, his eyes shining. "No, of course I don't mind. I rather like the idea. Not that I don't find your company interesting, Charles." He looked back at the man and smiled.

Charles laughed good-naturedly. "I take no offense. Frankly, I'd rather have the ladies along to decorate our table too. We'd planned on going to Arnaud's. Does that suit you?" he asked them politely.

"Yes," Nicole enthused, glaring at Keely with a look threatening that she'd better not protest. For good measure she said, "You and Dax could probably talk about radio advertising. I'm sure you know more about that than Charles does."

"I'd be glad to help any way I can," Keely said meekly. The discussion was rhetorical and they all knew it. Nicole had only provided them with an excuse should they be seen together.

The die was cast. Keely had had nothing to do with this accidental meeting. Dax seemed amenable to the suggestion that she and Nicole accompany them to dinner. Of course, what else could he do? Worriedly she glanced up at him, an apology in her eyes. But his eyes were shining down on her with a warmth that told her he didn't mind the situation in the least.

Without speaking, he took her lightweight raincoat out of her hands and held it for her. She turned her back and slid her arms into the sleeves, keeping her distance. She thought if he touched her, she would crumble. But miraculously she didn't. He leaned forward until she felt his chest against her back. His head came down level with hers and he turned to speak into her ear. "Is this all right with you?"

His voice was a caress, low and vibrating, like the music of a cello. She tilted her head to one side and turned slightly to look at him. So close. His clean, brisk, citrusy cologne was intoxicating. The tip of her nose almost touched his chin, shadowed this late in the day by a hint of beard. Short sideburns tapered beautifully into the hair that grazed the top of his ear. It looked so soft. Her fingers ached to touch it.

"Yes, it's fine with me." Her whisper was husky and intimate and said more than the words she had uttered.

"We'll have to walk a block to where my car is parked. I hope you don't mind, Dax," Charles said as he draped an arm around Nicole's shoulders and led her toward an exit.

"Not at all," Dax said.

Once on the narrow, uneven sidewalk, Dax placed

his hand under Keely's elbow. Any gentleman would have done the same. It was only a courtesy. But would anyone else make such a mundane gesture feel like erotic foreplay?

He wrapped his fingers around the bend of her arm. His thumb wedged itself into the crevice of the elbow joint. Sliding back and forth, it stroked sensuously. Then he rolled his thumb over the two round bones, moving her skin, reminding her of other caresses in other places.

In the back seat of Charles's Mercedes they sat calf to calf, knee to knee. Touching nowhere else, they stared at the contact spot, feeling the heat that rose from it. With each movement of the car, the hosiery covering her knee slid along the flannel covering of his.

Nicole and Charles kept up a lively conversation. Keely and Dax responded in desultory tones, as though to say, "Don't bother us, we're busy thinking of each other."

Charles found a parking space on Dauphine so they only had to walk a block down Bienville to the restaurant. The maître d' knew his stuff, for he called each of them by name and deferentially escorted them to Charles's reserved table in one of the more intimate corners of the restaurant.

Usually Keely reveled in the European ambience of Arnaud's. She liked the crisp, understated, elegant decor, the hushed, accented voices of the waiters. Even the dishes and cutlery wouldn't dare clatter loudly in this restaurant and destroy the atmosphere.

Tonight she was aware of nothing but the man sitting adjacent to her. Under the pretense of sharing a menu, they looked at each other. It was an opportunity

for his shoulder to press hers, for his thumb to caress
her index finger. When Charles asked for their choices,
they were flustered and embarrassingly unprepared
to tell him. Quickly they ordered the trout meunière,
and, being relieved of that duty, happily went back to
staring at each other. Charles took it upon himself to
complete their order for them, guessing correctly that
they wouldn't care what they ate.

"Dax and I spent most of the afternoon together,"
he said after the waiter left their predinner drinks on
the table.

"Did you?" Nicole asked. "Did you buy some television time?"

Dax placed his forearms on the table and leaned
forward slightly. "Charles has got a stupid client, I'm
afraid. The more he tried to explain my options, the
more confused I became. And it's so expensive, not
even counting the—the production costs." His inflection rose on the last words, making them a question.

"Yes," Charles said. "Before we can run a commercial for you, you have to have a commercial." He
smiled genially. "I'll happily recommend some production houses for you."

"I've been thinking. I should hire professionals to
take care of all this for me. They could better coordi-
nate all the media ads. What do you think?" Obviously
Dax respected Charles's business acumen.

"I think you'd be greatly relieved of a lot of tedious
responsibility so you could better concentrate on other
things."

The waiter had brought a linen napkin-lined basket of French rolls. The hard golden crusts kept their
white centers soft and doughy. Dax broke off a piece

of one, buttered it liberally and handed it to Keely. The pillows of his fingertips touched hers at the moment their eyes held and locked. Only the barest movement of flesh on flesh electrified them. The magnetic field that surrounded them was only broken when an obsequious waiter served them crocks of onion soup.

The restaurant wasn't crowded on this weeknight, but nevertheless they were wary of curious eyes and made the supreme effort of appearing no more than dinner companions. Throughout the meal the conversation was light and amusing, peppered as it was with Nicole's naughty statements, which she said only to aggravate Charles and try to shake his stoicism.

"Would anyone care for dessert?" Charles, acting as host, offered.

"I'm too full right now," Nicole said.

"I'd like some coffee," Keely said and Dax concurred. When it came, he automatically added cream to hers and stirred it for her. The natural intimacy of the gesture wasn't wasted on Charles and Nicole, but the knowing look they slanted at each other went unnoticed by the other two diners.

In the foyer of the restaurant as they were shrugging into their coats, Nicole said, "I like to walk a while and then go for dessert. And you know what I like best? Beignets at Café du Monde."

"You want to walk all the way to Café du Monde?" Charles asked.

"Sure, Grandpa. Aren't you up to it?"

"I'd probably make it there, but I doubt if I could make it back. Besides, you don't have time. You have to go back to work, remember?"

"We can take a cab from there back to here. And

there is a network movie on tonight that runs late, so
the news will be late too."

Charles looked at Keely and Dax who were standing close together, not caring what the plans were, so
long as they didn't have to leave each other right away.

"Dax? Keely? Are you game?"

"I don't have any plans," Dax said.

"Neither do I," Keely said.

It was settled. They were thrilled. They could have
an evening together and as long as they were protected
under the auspices of business, they could always justify being seen together.

"Let's go down Bourbon Street," Nicole said and
Charles groaned. "Come on, you old fuddy-duddy,"
Nicole taunted.

"Nicole," he said patiently, "Bourbon Street is noisy,
dirty, crowded, immoral, and decadent."

"I know. I adore decadence," she said, her blue eyes
dancing. She grabbed Charles by the arm and virtually dragged him the half-block to the intersection of
Bourbon and Bienville.

They mingled with the throng, which was nothing
to what it would be in a few weeks during Mardi Gras.
The sounds and smells of Bourbon Street, New Orleans, were uniquely its own. The spicy aroma of sea-
food gumbo mingled with those of beer and the musty
dankness that was inherent to the French Quarter. Live
jazz blared out into the streets from the many night-
clubs and blended discordantly with Cotton Eyed Joe
being played by a country-western band. Barkers in
front of the topless bars swung open the doors teasingly while touting the physical attributes of the danc-

ers within. One could usually catch a glimpse of bare skin illuminated by flashing colored lights.

On the front of one such entertainment hall was a sign that read: "World-Famous Sex Acts Performed." "I wonder what makes them world famous?" Charles asked pedantically.

"Well if you have to ask, it's for sure you've never seen them performed," Nicole quipped. He sighed tiredly and, placing an arm around her shoulders, steered her away as though she were a recalcitrant child.

They meandered farther down the legendary street until the neighborhood became less commercial and more serene. They turned onto St. Peter Street, which would eventually lead them to Jackson Square, and the café.

The street was deserted and dark. Walking by twos, Charles and Nicole led the way, going past closed shop fronts, art galleries, and grillwork gates that protected alleys leading into private inner courtyards.

Dax raised his arm from the middle of Keely's back and settled it along her shoulders, pulling her closer. "How have you been?"

"Fine. You?"

"Fine."

"You look tired. Have you been working?"

"Yeah. I've been in Washington for the past three weeks. The congressional calendar is full. We're trying to get in all our business before the closing of the session."

"Oh."

"I had dinner at the White House with the President and the First Lady."

"Truly?"

"Yes." He grinned boyishly. "Business, of course, but it was nice to be invited."

They walked in silence then Dax said, "I read what you said in the newspapers."

"I read what you said too."

"Don't believe everything you read."

She turned to look at him. "No?"

"No," he said, shaking his head.

"Like what for instance?"

"Like for instance that I think of you as an admirably courageous woman who is fighting for a great cause and that I have no romantic inclinations toward you."

Her heart was pounding in her temples. "I shouldn't believe that?"

"The first part, yes, the second part, no. If you only knew how romantically inclined toward you I was, you'd be afraid to walk down this dark street with me. You'd know why I haven't eaten or slept properly in the last month. You'd know why I count at least ten new gray hairs every morning. I hope it's true that they say that gray hair inspires confidence."

They had reached Jackson Square now. The gates around the park itself were locked for the night, but they walked in front of the Pontalba Building, ostensibly looking in the shop windows on the street level, but seeing nothing.

"Did you have a tough time with the reporters?"

"Not really," she answered. "For a few days, that's all."

"I'm sorry, Keely. I'm accustomed to it, but I know you're not. I wish you could have been spared that."

"I survived. Van Dorf was—"

"Van Dorf! He came to see you?"

"Yes. He was at my car one day when Joe deposited me at the Superdome."

"That jerk," Dax growled. "One of these days…. He didn't hurt you, did he?"

She laughed softly and smoothed the lapel of his raincoat in a comforting gesture. "No. He only implied some rather nasty things."

"What kind of things?"

She averted her eyes away from the probing strength of his. "He only said…you know…asked me things about you."

"What did he ask?" he persisted.

Flushing, she tried to look away, but he wouldn't allow it. He captured her chin in his hand and forced her head back until she had to look at him. "What did he ask?"

She licked her lips. "He asked me if you were good in bed."

"He what!" His hands went to her shoulders and gripped hard. "He asked you that? So help me, Keely, if he prints one libelous word about you—"

"But he didn't and he won't. He may be ruthless, but he's not stupid. He knows he has nothing to write."

"What did you tell him?"

"The truth. I don't know."

He tried to contain the smile that suddenly threatened, but failed, and finally gave in to it. "Take a guess."

She leaned away from him and looked sharply into his mischievous eyes. "What?"

"Take a guess as to how I am in bed."

"No!"

"Come on. Be a sport. Take a guess. I'll give you a hint."

"I don't want a hint."

Ignoring her, he leaned down, settled his lips against her ear, and whispered, "I'm not world famous yet, but I'm working on it."

He lifted his head slowly, studying her reaction, while she puzzled through what he had said. Then remembering the earlier conversation between Charles and Nicole in front of the nightclub, she burst out laughing. He caught her behind the head and pressed her face into his shirtfront as she laughed. His fingers interlaced behind her head and his thumb slipped under her hair to massage behind her ears. Eventually her laughter subsided and she raised her head. She watched his mouth as he spoke.

"I want to kiss you so bad I hurt. But this is a bit too well lighted and public, don't you think?"

Dumbly she nodded. Reluctantly he released her and they went to join the other couple at the street corner who were waiting for the light to change. They crossed Decatur and went past the Washington Artillery Park to the Café du Monde. Over a hundred years old, the café was still one of the most popular spots in the city. Serving only beignets, the fried doughnuts covered with powdered sugar, and coffee, it never lacked for customers during its twenty-four serving hours each day.

They chose a table on the covered porch even though the evening was cool and misty this close to the river. The chairs were chrome and green vinyl, the tables gray Formica, but it was for the hot coffee and doughnuts that one came to Café du Monde. That and to watch the constant flow of traffic—pedestrian, horse drawn, and motor—that circumnavigated Jackson Square.

They ordered two helpings of doughnuts, three black coffees, and one café au lait for Keely. In a matter of minutes the hot fragrant sugar-coated doughnuts were served with steaming mugs of strong chicory coffee.

They fell onto the doughnuts ravenously. Each bite unsettled the fine sugar on the doughnuts until a soft white cloud seemed to drift over the table and cost them all valuable eating time while they laughed. Faces, hands, and clothes were also dusted with the confectioners' sugar, but it was a messy hazard they gladly suffered.

Keely and Nicole each got a plate of leftover sugar to blot up with moistened fingers. Nicole was licking hers clean, her motions deliberately provocative, when she said, "Let's go up on the levee." Her eyes half closed as she eyed Charles seductively.

"You have to go to work."

"I have time." Without waiting for permission or assent, she left her chair and went toward the tunnel that connected through to the boardwalk built along the levee, affectionately named the Moonwalk. Lampposts with appropriately dim lights had been strategically placed along the walk, shedding enough light to keep one from stepping off into the Mississippi River, but not too much to destroy the romantic atmosphere.

The others followed Nicole's lead, and by the time they came out of the tunnel, she had already selected a bench for her and Charles. By tacit agreement when he sat down beside her, Keely and Dax walked farther on. They became absorbed by the shadows and swallowed by the mist that was lightly falling as they claimed their own bench. Lights on either bank of the river made wavy reflections on the surface of the water. What wasn't so pretty in the daytime looked magical by night.

Dax curved an arm around her shoulders and pulled her under its protection. She lay her head against the hard bicep. Her eyes were closed. She could feel his breath on her face, drawing nearer. Gently he blew against her eyelids, her mouth. It opened slightly to take in the air he expelled. Then his lips touched hers.

Now, after having been denied so long, they extended the torture, heightened the anticipation, perpetuated the excitement. He kissed her with closed lips once, twice, a third time. The light brushings couldn't really qualify as kisses, but more as caresses of mouth against mouth.

Cupping her palms over the hair above his ears that she had longed to touch before, she closed her hands around his head. His tongue played temptingly along the line where her lips came together, flicking and stroking until her own came out to meet it. Her tongue became a wild thing, forever imprisoned but now freed to do what it would. It outlined his lips, delved into the dimple, tormented the corners of his mouth until it opened under her probing. She swept the honeyed cave, taking up his nectar and leaving hers. Her tongue slipped behind his teeth and glided over the roof of his mouth. With deep anguished moans they fell apart.

They stared at each other without speaking. Their eyes wandered freely, giddy with the privacy they'd been granted and taking liberties otherwise prohibited. Hair, eyes, ears, noses, mouths, were perused at leisure until they could bear it no longer and came together again with hungry passion.

Their mouths fused, dispelling the doubts that had clouded their minds. Did she mean all those frivolous things she had said about admiration and respect? Has he truly left a trail of brokenhearted mistresses? How much does she pine for her husband? Does he love Madeline? Does she miss me? Does he miss me?

At long last he released her lips only to bury his mouth in her mist-dampened hair. "God, Keely, these past weeks have been hell. I've thought of nothing but you."

"I've been miserable, confused. I thought maybe you meant everything you told those reporters."

"No. You know better. Open your coat, please. I want to... There... All of that was just words, something to say. I never meant any of it."

"I thought so, but you weren't here..." They kissed.

"I wanted to call, but I thought up all sorts of nightmares about wiretaps and...don't bother with the buttons. I just want to feel your hands on me...yes...oh, sweet..." They kissed again. "...wiretaps and all, you know...you taste so good, Keely."

"Are you worried about things like that?" she asked on a soft groan as he captured her earlobe with his teeth.

"More for your sake than mine.... This is so soft..."

"Dax..." She sighed. "What did we do to make such a stir? Yes, touch me...."

"You feel so right.... So many people saw us dancing. I wasn't aware of the audience we were drawing. I wasn't aware of anything except holding you and wanting you…. Oh, yes, sweetheart…there." He pressed his hand over hers, trapping it against his shirtfront.

"I want you, Keely. I want to make love to you, to be inside you. I want you so bad I taste you with every pore."

CHAPTER ELEVEN

HER FINGERS FURROWED through his hair, holding his head tightly against her breasts. She groped for something to say. There were no words of comfort she could share with him, because she was as bereft as he. Did he know she ached for him as badly as he did for her?

Charles spared her having to offer any trite platitudes. She saw him strolling toward them, stopping at a discreet distance to stare out at the river. Keely nudged Dax, softly saying his name, and he sat erect, following the direction of her gaze. Charles cleared his throat loudly. "Excuse me, but Nicole must get back to the studio. Of course, if you wish to stay—"

"No," Dax said gruffly, finding it necessary to clear his own throat. "We'll go too." He stood and offered his hand to Keely. She hastily buttoned her coat, picked up her belongings, and joined him to follow Charles's hollow footsteps down the boardwalk.

Nicole was languishing on the bench, looking smug and satisfied. Keely shot an inquiring look in Charles's direction, but his bland expression gave away nothing. Still waters ran deep, Keely thought with a smile.

They retraced their way back to the front of Jackson Square. "Since your cars are parked in the KDIX parking lot, I thought we'd all walk Nicole back to work and then I'll get a cab to my car from there," Charles explained with the thoroughness of a scoutmaster.

"That's fine," Dax said. He placed a firm arm around Keely's waist as they walked along the fog-shrouded sidewalks. "To hell with my image. It seems to get worse the harder I try to improve it." He set their pace, slowing in order that Nicole and Charles would be well enough ahead of them to give them privacy.

"What did Madeline think of the publicity linking your name to mine?" Keely asked.

"I don't know. I didn't ask."

"You don't care then about her opinion?" she asked shyly.

"Not where you're concerned. She's got a lot of money, she's nice to look at, and on occasion, she can be fun. But she's also got a vicious streak. She's possessive and grasping and ambitious and jealous."

"Have you and she...?" Keely couldn't bring herself to ask the question and sucked her chin against her chest, staring at the wet concrete under her shoes.

They had almost gone a block before he answered. "I don't think it would be fair to Madeline or any other woman for me to answer a question like that."

"I'm sorry, Dax. I had no right to ask that." She gnashed her teeth, wishing she hadn't even hinted at the question.

"You have every right, so don't apologize. I'm glad you asked. It means a lot to me that you care about such things. Most people don't these days." They had reached their destination and paused at the corner of the building. He closed his arms around her and spoke gently. "I promise you, Keely, that since I met you, I haven't been with anyone else."

Joy bubbled inside her, and as she clung to him, she squeezed her eyes shut in ecstatic relief. The idea of him being with someone else had plagued her. Now her heart sang, albeit unfairly, to know he hadn't slaked the passions she'd induced on someone else's body. Feeling guilty over her selfishness, she pulled away to look up at him as she said, "You didn't have to tell me that."

"But you're damned glad I did, aren't you?"

Was she so transparent? Did he already know her that well? "Yes," she said honestly.

His finger traced her hairline as he murmured, "It wouldn't be fair to take another woman to bed, Keely, when I'd be wishing it was you lying with me."

"Dax—"

"I came back here to see if the two of you were making out all right—no pun intended—but you seem to be doing fine," Nicole teased. "Charles has magnanimously consented to see me home properly, so he'll be staying through the newscast. You're welcome to stay too."

"I need to get home," Keely said. "I have to be up at five, remember?"

"And I'll see Keely to her car," Dax said. He went to Charles and shook his hand. "Thank you for an enlightening day and a wonderful dinner. I enjoyed it all. As soon as I've firmed up someone to handle the media campaign for me, they'll be in touch with you."

"KDIX will appreciate your business. Good luck, Dax."

"Thank you. Good night, Nicole."

"Good night, everyone," she called back airily as she sailed through the employee entrance that led to the studio. She was dragging Charles behind her like a queen with a conquered foe.

Dax looked after them pensively. "They're in love with each other, aren't they?"

"Yes. Charles knows about it. I'm not sure Nicole does yet."

"What a pair! Who would ever guess they'd choose each other?"

Keely smiled, but it was a sad expression. "I'm not sure such choices are ours to make."

Dax caught her meaning all too well. "No, I guess they're not," he said huskily. "Some things just happen, don't they?"

The parking lot was eerily dark and deserted as they walked up the ramp to where their cars were parked. Besides her compact, the only other car on the lot was a chocolate-brown Lincoln.

"Is that yours?" she asked.

"Yes."

Done with conversation, he slipped his hands inside her coat, settled them on her waist, and pulled her to him as he backed her against the car. Her feet were trapped between his. Touching from ankle to chest, he leaned forward and took her lips under his.

She lost all perspective of the environment under the demands of his mouth. The muffled sound of traffic below, the mist that cloaked them like an ethereal veil, the hard surface pressing into her spine, all vanished with his touch. His mouth and the sensuous way it possessed hers were her only sources of reference.

When at last he lifted his mouth from hers, it was only far enough for him to speak. "Keely, would you even consider coming to my house for the weekend?"

He paused for her to respond, but shock had rendered her mute. He pressed his advantage and rushed on. "I don't want you to misconstrue my invitation. There are no strings attached. I'd just like for you to come to my house and meet my parents."

It was such a dear, desperate, appealing invitation that Keely's heart was breaking that she must refuse it. Even though his intentions were honorable, Dax knew as well as she did that staying in the same house together overnight would be torturous and dangerous.

But not wanting to turn him down outright, she waltzed around a refusal. "Do you think that's wise?"

"It's positively crazy." His finger traced the delicate bones of her jaw. "I thought coming to your room at the Hilton was the dumbest thing I'd ever done. Inviting you to spend the weekend at my house outdoes that. Nevertheless, I'm asking."

"I'd like to meet your parents, but what would you tell them about me?" Suddenly she wondered how many women Dax had taken to his house for a weekend and it pained her to estimate.

"I'd tell them that you are a lady I hold in high regard. My father will exercise all his Southern gentlemanly charm on you and my mother will deluge you with recipes and antidotes for every catastrophe."

She laughed and toyed with the brass button on his jacket as she asked casually, "Does anyone live with you? A housekeeper or anyone?" Her voice was high-pitched and wobbly.

He lifted her chin with his finger and looked long and deep into her eyes. "She goes home after dinner."

"Oh."

He didn't release his hold. Rather he kept her head

tilted back as he said, "Keely, I wouldn't expect you to change your mind about anything on the short drive from here to there. Nor do I want you to compromise any standard you've set for yourself or for me. If it'll make you feel any better, I'll supply you with nails and a hammer and you can seal yourself into your appointed bedroom as soon as the sun goes down." He smiled, but she felt that he meant it. "I just want us to have some time alone. To talk and walk. We can work in the garden, or ride horses, or go fishing, or neck, or take a boat out, or rearrange the furniture, or—"

"Wait! Back up."

"Well, the furniture in the library needs rearranging. I've been think—"

"No, before that."

"I have a small lake on the property and we could—"

"Before that."

"Let's see." He squinted his eyes, feigning concentration. "Oh, you mean the part about necking?" His lips curled into the devilish grin she adored and he said, "I just threw that in to see if you were paying attention." She laughed and he added, "But it's a hell of a good idea."

He laid his forehead on hers while he swayed them back and forth as they hugged. "Will you come?" he asked softly.

Maintaining their position, she answered soberly, "I can't, Dax. You know that. I'd love to, but I can't."

He was silent for a while, absorbing what she had said, swallowing his disappointment. "I promise to be on my best behavior."

"But I may not be on mine. Rather than relaxing, I

think we'd both be tense and uptight, and that wouldn't be any fun."

"I won't let that happen. I promise to be relaxed."

"The risk we'd run of having someone find out I was there would be too high. We'd both be ruined should that happen."

"It's always a possibility, but I'd take every precaution to see it was kept a secret." He pushed his fingers through her hair until they rested on her scalp. "Please come, Keely." When he felt the negative shake of her head, he urged hastily, "At least say you'll think about it. I'll wait until the end of the week for your answer. Just say you'll consider it."

Her answer would probably be the same at the end of the week, but this was a small concession she could make. "All right," she said, lifting her eyes to his. "I promise to think about it."

SHE THOUGHT ABOUT IT. All day. All night. All week.

By Wednesday she was in an abominable mood. It seemed that asinine drivers chose that day to have an orgy of fender-benders that tied up traffic on major arteries and kept her and Joe frantically trying to keep up with them and inform commuters of the hazards they posed.

"Keely, what the hell is going on today?" the afternoon DJ asked her after he had started a Willie Nelson record.

"I'm doing the best I can, Clark," she snapped back into her microphone. "We've had five accidents reported in the last twenty minutes."

"Well, it sounds like you're rambling all over town," he grumbled.

"We are! I'm getting airsick flying around up here in circles. I don't orchestrate these accidents you know."

"Okay, okay. Sorry. Just be more concise, please. You've taken up far too much of my airtime."

Keely switched off her communicating device and Joe laughed when he heard her mumble, "Conceited ass."

At one minute to five on Thursday morning her telephone rang.

"Hello."

"Well?"

"I don't know yet."

He hung up.

At seven-thirty that evening her telephone rang again. She was contemplating her answer over an omelet. "Hello."

"Well?"

"Give me until midnight."

During the long evening hours she pondered the dilemma. Dax had promised that he wouldn't consider her going home with him a reversal of her convictions. She trusted him. He would never force or coerce her into his bed. It was herself that she didn't trust.

During the past week she had guiltily dragged out pictures of Mark, written letters to his mother, looked through her high school yearbook and scrapbooks, trying to convince herself that she still loved him. Yet she couldn't conceive of him as anything except a two-dimensional image on a piece of paper. He wasn't flesh and blood, and light and heat, and sound and smell.

How long was she going to cling to this fond memory? It was more than remotely possible that Mark had been dead for years. Was she going to waste her life, her youth, her love, on stubbornness that she had convinced herself was honor?

She freely admitted to herself that she loved Dax. This was no adolescent infatuation, but the love of a woman for a man. It carried with it no idealistic illusions, but all the pain and heartache that went hand in glove with true loving. She and Dax weren't children, innocent of the injustices that could be handed down. Hopefully, they would have the fortitude to face them.

Her decision was made then. She would spend the weekend with Dax. She wouldn't be aggressive, nor resistant, but would respond with love to whatever circumstances presented themselves. They would both know when and if the time was right.

With that glowing thought she attacked her closet with a vengeance, looking for just the right clothing to take with her. Horseback riding, fishing, walking, all the things he'd said they'd do ran through her mind as she made her selections and set them beside her opened suitcase. Two days? In half an hour she had already picked enough clothes to last at least two weeks.

The telephone rang at ten minutes to twelve. He's early! her heart sang. He couldn't wait to hear her answer any more than she could wait to give it.

Picking up the receiver, she shouted, "Yes, yes, yes. I'll come."

There was a silence on the phone, then a woman's voice said, "I'm sorry. Is this Keely Williams?"

The voice rang familiar. "Yes," she answered cautiously.

"Keely, this is Betty Allway."

"Betty!" she exclaimed, intensely embarrassed at the way she had answered the phone and wondering guiltily how she was going to explain herself. But why should she? All that guilt was behind her now.

Before she could say anything, Betty was speaking again, and this time Keely heard the tension in her usually friendly voice. "Keely, I've got some news."

Slowly, like the balloons that were leaking their helium, Keely gradually sank down on the edge of her bed. Her eyes went straight to the picture of Mark on the bookcase. "Yes?"

"Twenty-six men have come out of a jungle in Cambodia. They made their way to a Red Cross refugee camp. The Red Cross notified our military, which received permission to go in and pick them up. They're being taken to Germany first for immediate first aid and observation. As a matter of fact, they're already there. The day after tomorrow they're being flown to Paris. We've been invited to go and meet them."

The silence was long and palpable. Betty didn't interfere with Keely's roiling thoughts. She let the younger woman digest the news and all that it portended.

When Keely spoke, it was with a hoarse croak. "Is—is Mark—"

"The army hasn't released any names yet. I'm not even sure that they've identified all of them. As you can imagine, some of the men are delirious with malnutrition or disease. All I know is that they number twenty-six."

"When were you called?"

"About an hour ago. General Vanderslice called me from the Pentagon. They're pulling together an official delegation from the United States to go over there. The State Department, the Congress, the military, you and

I and PROOF, and a selected group of media representatives will be invited to go on a government-chartered plane. For the time being, until we ascertain the condition both mentally and physically of these men, they'll be kept more or less isolated."

"I see." Keely looked down at her hand and was surprised to see that it was shaking violently, as though she had a palsy. Perspiration was inching down her sides and the backs of her knees. A loud roaring in her ears handicapped her hearing.

"Will there be any problem with your going, Keely? I don't know how long we'll be gone. I would say at least three or four days."

"N-no. Of course I'm going." She knew she was about to weep and she crammed a fist against her tight thin lips. "Betty, do you think—"

"I don't know," Betty answered intuitively. "I've asked myself if Bill is one of them a thousand times already, but there's no way to know. I hated to even tell my children for fear they'd get their hopes up too high. Fourteen years is a long time to wait for this day. Now that it's here, I dread knowing. I only have to convince myself that I'll be happy for whoever is on that list of men."

"Yes. I will too, of course," Keely said disjointedly. She ran her hand over her eyes abstractedly. Every muscle in her body had contracted when Betty had told her the news and now that she was forcing herself to relax, she found it painful. "When do we leave? Where?"

"The plane leaves from Andrews Air Force Base at six o'clock tomorrow evening."

"Tomorrow?" Keely asked weakly. So soon. Not enough time to prepare oneself mentally.

"Yes. We'll be met at National and escorted to Andrews. Pandemonium will reign, I'm sure, so be ready for it."

"I'll see you there then. I don't know when I'll be arriving. I'll call the airlines right now."

"There are only twenty-six of them, Keely."

Twenty-six out of over two thousand. They were both thinking how slim were the chances that either of their husbands would be in that group. "I know, Betty. I'll try to remember that."

The older woman sighed. "I'll see you tomorrow." She hung up.

Why were they not rejoicing? Because they were afraid to. Yet. Keely's eyes stared vacantly at the clothes strewed across her bed and when it came back to her why they were there, she folded her arms over her stomach, gripping it as though in agony, and rocked back and forth. Her keening wail could have issued out of the jaws of hell.

When the telephone rang a few minutes later, at straight up midnight, she didn't answer it.

CHAPTER TWELVE

THE SPACE BETWEEN her shoulder blades burned with fatigue. Keely hunched her shoulders, drawing them up under her ears as far as they would go, held them there for several seconds, then let them drop again. She closed her eyes and rolled her head around on her neck, stretching it.

The room was crowded, stuffy, and overheated. A pall of cigarette smoke hovered overhead, clouding the chandeliers that dripped crystal. The long reception room in the American Embassy in Paris today looked like anything but a formal parlor. Coatless men, unshaven and grim, leaned against the walls, arranging themselves in small groups to converse in hushed tones. At intervals the groups shifted as though programmed on a timer.

Reporters checked and rechecked their recorders. Photographers fiddled with cylinders of film and flashing devices. Television news teams monitored their batteries carefully, making sure they would have power when they needed it.

Only the military men in their crisp uniforms didn't seem wilted and disgruntled. Instead they briskly entered and left the room periodically on official duties nonapparent to anyone else. Keely had guessed that their business wasn't really necessary but contrived to give the impression that everything wasn't as stagnant as it seemed.

She and Betty sat side by side on a small sofa. For hours they had been in this room awaiting word, any kind of word, on the men who were now, as rumor had it, in another part of the embassy. But rumors had come and gone. Some had proved to be correct, most had not. Keely doubted the veracity of anything she heard.

For fifteen hours, since the motorcade had rolled through the streets of Paris from Charles de Gaulle Airport to the embassy and disgorged the official delegation, they had been sitting in this room.

Everything that could be said both privately and publicly had been said. All they could do now was wait. Reading was out of the question, as words held no meaning to them now. The view from the windows facing Avenue Gabriel had lost its fascination. Talking was an exhausting exercise. Thinking was impossible. So they sat silently, staring vacantly, praying unconsciously. Waiting.

The flight over the Atlantic had been grueling. Keely was interviewed by numerous reporters, all jealous and greedy of her time. Congressman Parker, who had been asked to be part of the delegation because of his chairmanship of the recent subcommittee hearings, had finally come to her rescue, asking the reporters to let her rest for a while. In a fatherly gesture he had patted her on the shoulder and urged her to try to sleep.

But sleep was made impossible by the presence of two other passengers on the airplane. One was Congressman Devereaux. The other was Al Van Dorf.

A television reporter had been asking her an involved question when Keely saw Dax come through the door of the aircraft. Her tongue stumbled over an answer to the question, but she didn't hear the next one over the pounding in her ears. She had had to ask the reporter to repeat it.

Dax's eyes met hers only briefly, but they communicated an encyclopedic amount of information. They told her that he was as bewildered by this situation as she. They told her that he was torn between hope that Mark was one of the few men who had made it out of Cambodia alive and distress to know what his sudden reappearance would mean to them now. His eyes wished her happiness, but selfishly admitted wanting to share that happiness. They told her he didn't want to be here but had to be here. He couldn't stand by somewhere else awaiting word and not know immediately if the name Mark Williams appeared on that all-important list. The strongest message his eyes bespoke was that he wanted to hold her.

All of that was conveyed in one puissant glance. She hadn't dared to look at him during the remainder of the flight nor since they had been ushered into this reception room and erroneously told that a spokesman for the army would be with them shortly.

Even had she been inclined to look at or talk to Dax against all common sense to the contrary, the eagle-sharp eyes of Al Van Dorf prevented her. He watched her like a scientist watches a cell under a microscope. Keely knew that each move she made, each word she spoke, were being carefully chronicled in his notebook. She had come to loathe the sight of that green looseleaf tablet and the busy pencil. For all his covert surveillance, he had approached her but once.

His strolling gait had brought him to the small sofa

on which she and Betty sat. He stood in front of her, forcing her to look up at him like a petitioner. "Mrs. Williams, are you optimistic that your husband is among these twenty-six men?" He fired the question at her without preliminary small talk.

"I'm trying not to be too optimistic," she replied.

"Do you hope he is?"

She jerked her head up and glared at the reporter with stormy green eyes. "Either you are incredibly stupid, Mr. Van Dorf, or the question is unworthy of you. Either way, I refuse to answer it." She could feel Betty's surprised eyes on her, but she continued to stare down Van Dorf. At last she won, and he dropped his eyes to his hateful notebook and made a notation that she knew was intended to frighten her.

Betty cleared her throat diplomatically. "Mr. Van Dorf, I'm afraid that both Mrs. Williams and I are rather too wrapped up in our own thoughts to be very cordial about answering questions just now. If you'll excuse us, please," she said.

Van Dorf bowed to her slightly but said, "I have one last question for Mrs. Williams." Turning back to her, he asked, "Did you know that Congressman Devereaux was coming along on this trip?"

"No. Not until I saw him board the airplane." That was an honest answer.

Van Dorf grinned that foxlike grin and asked suggestively, "Why do you suppose he did?"

Keely knew the question was asked in hopes of dismantling her composure. She looked up at him placidly and answered, "You should ask Congressman Parker that. He himself told me he had invited Congressman Devereaux to come."

"Seems strange," Van Dorf mused aloud, "that out of all the congressmen in Washington, he would choose Devereaux."

"Not at all," Betty said. She was on Keely's team even though she wasn't sure what game they were playing. "Congressman Devereaux served on that subcommittee, as you well know, Mr. Van Dorf. He supported our cause and was against that bill. He's a veteran of the Vietnam War. Why you're surprised that he should be here, I can't fathom. Now, please, neither I nor Keely feel like talking."

Van Dorf didn't take hints too well, but he ambled off after staring down Keely once more with deadly eyes behind the deceptively meek eyeglasses.

"Thank you," she said to Betty when he was out of earshot.

"What is it with him and you? Why does he keep asking you about Devereaux?"

"I don't know."

"Are you sure?"

She looked quickly at Betty, but then away guiltily. She was spared having to answer when one of the Marines stationed at the embassy marched up to Betty.

"Mrs. Allway?"

"Yes?"

"Will you come with me please at the request of General Vanderslice?"

Betty looked quizzically at Keely, who shrugged her shoulders, then stood up to be escorted by the uniformed man through the ornately carved doors.

Another hour went by, in which Keely sat alone. At any given time she knew what Dax was doing, though her eyes never singled him out. He ran a weary hand around his neck. He shook off his suit coat and draped it over the back of a chair. He unbuttoned his vest. He looked at her. He coughed three times, crossed to the table where ice and canned soft drinks were available. He poured a Coke into a plastic cup, took one swallow, and then abandoned it on the table. He looked at her. He locked his fingers high over his head, stretching expansively. He conversed in undertones with Congressman Parker. Together they looked toward the door through which Betty had passed with the Marine, then started talking again. He looked at her.

The door behind the podium was flung open by two Marines who barely had time to clear it and snap to attention before General Vanderslice bustled through. Not one of his silver hairs was out of place. His uniform jacket buttoned over his solid torso with a meticulous fit. His eyes darted over the room, assessing the situation even as he strode toward the mounted microphone. His carriage was a textbook of perfect military bearing.

Everyone in the large room ceased speaking as though a switch had been turned off. All eyes riveted onto the commanding presence of the general, who placed a sheaf of papers on the lectern.

"Ladies and gentlemen, your patience is commendable. I know how anxious you have been. I realize the limitations of comfort this room affords. I know you've had no rest since the long flight. I apologize for the delay, which seems inherent to an occasion of this importance." His speech was as precise and clipped as his body language.

He cleared his throat and glanced at the papers under the microphone. Keely looked down at her clenched hands, her heart slamming against her ribs. Her glands refused to secrete any saliva, and her tongue, when she tried to swallow, only stuck to the roof of her mouth.

"I want to introduce a man to you. Often in my military career, I have paid homage to men others considered to be heroes. Through whatever motivation, these men exhibited inconceivable courage and valor."

He paused and drew a deep breath. "William Daniel Allway was a major when he was sent to Vietnam sixteen years ago. This morning he has been promoted to the rank of lieutenant colonel."

Keely clamped her fingers over her mouth to cover her cry of joy. Bill Allway! Betty's husband. Tears ran unchecked down her cheeks, but she wasn't even aware of them as she looked toward the doors behind the podium to see a tall, bony man in an ill-fitting army uniform leaning against Betty's supportive arms.

General Vanderslice turned toward the couple and said kindly, "Colonel Allway, will you and Mrs. Allway come forward, please."

The cacophonous racket that roared through the room was only a small element of the pandemonium that broke loose. Cameras popped like fireworks. The applause and cheering was deafening. Many, caught up in the enthusiasm of the moment and forgetting decorum, jumped onto chairs, whooping and hollering, giving Bill Allway a true hero's welcome.

Keely jumped to her feet, applauding tearfully for the safe return of her friend's husband. One thing was undeniably certain: Mark Williams was not among these few men. Had he been, she would have been called away for a private reunion with him as Betty had been.

When the celebration finally began to recede to

a dull roar, Bill Allway approached the microphone. He was thin to the point of emaciation. What hair he had left was white. His cheeks were sunken, his nose pinched, his eyes ringed with dark circles. But he was radiant as he clutched his wife to him tightly.

General Vanderslice tried to be heard over the ruckus. "As most of you know, Mrs. Allway has faced her husband's long absence with the same indomitable spirit that he has shown. I know, because I've had more than one run-in with her." Laughter rumbled through the room. "I can't tell you what pleasure I felt to know that Bill Allway was one of these returning men and that Mrs. Allway, because of her involvement in PROOF, was also here. Colonel Allway, as top-ranking officer and leader of the returning MIAs, has requested the privilege of introducing them to you. Colonel Allway."

Bill and Betty unabashedly clung to each other as he assumed General Vanderslice's position behind the lectern. He looked down at her and kissed her lightly on the mouth. Again the crowd went wild.

Betty looked beautiful. Love exuded from her as her eyes stayed glued on her husband. He finally brought his shadowed eyes back to the crowd and addressed the suddenly hushed room.

"It's…it's…so good to see American faces again." His voice cracked and he ducked his head self-consciously. He shouldn't have worried about the tears that flooded his eyes. Many eyes in the crowd were moist with emotion.

"You are all curious, I know, to learn how we made it out, where we've been, and how we got there. You'll be briefed thoroughly, I promise." He smiled, and the stretching skeletal expression was heart-wrenching. "It will take days and even weeks to fill you in on the details that, in my instance, encompass fourteen years. As you must understand, the armed services will have to analyze the information we've brought out with us before it becomes public knowledge."

General Vanderslice interceded momentarily. "There will be a press conference immediately after we identify the men with Colonel Allway." He stepped back and Bill Allway had the floor again.

"The names will be read alphabetically along with the soldier's hometown and the date he was reported missing."

Television cameras from all over the world were aimed at both Bill Allway and the doorway through which each soldier would pass.

"Lieutenant Christopher David Cass, Phoenix, Arizona, June 17, 1969. Lieutenant George Robert Dickins, Gainesville, Florida, April 23, 1970."

Each man was applauded and cheered. Keely, like everyone else in the room, was bursting with happiness for each of the depleted soldiers who passed shyly through the door. They had survived years of deprivation, disease, starvation, torture, and battle, and yet they seemed afraid of the lights, the people, the cameras, the attention. They all sported new haircuts. Their uniforms were new, if loosely fitting. And their faces bore the ravages of their experiences like identifying badges.

When he had read through the list and twenty men stood solemnly at the front of the room, Bill Allway said, "There are five men unable to be introduced here. Two of them are critically ill, so we are withholding their names for a few hours until they can be examined and their conditions more accurately appraised."

He drew Betty closer to him and continued. "I'm not a chaplain, but if Chaplain Weems will indulge me, I'd like to offer a prayer."

Even the most steadfast atheist couldn't argue with an appeal like that. Every head in the room was bowed, save for the photographers holding the video cameras in focus. A hush fell over the room. Bill's voice was as scratchy as sandpaper, but had he been a renowned orator, he couldn't have commanded such keen attention.

"Father, it is with exultant hearts that we come to You in thankfulness for life, for deliverance, for freedom. We pray for the countless men still struggling for survival. They remain nameless and faceless, yet You know them. Make them aware of You. Those of us who have been in hell know that Your presence can be felt even there. We, who against all odds, are alive today, pray that our lives will be lived honorably and to Your glory. Amen."

If previously there were any dry eyes left in the room, there were no longer. A subdued General Vanderslice approached the microphone while Bill Allway assisted his wife off the platform. "We ask your indulgence. It has been suggested that the press conference take place two hours from now in this room. That will allow you to take a much needed break and give these men time to collect their thoughts. I'm sure you can all understand a certain confusion and bewilderment on their part." He consulted a silver wristwatch and said, "The press conference will begin at three o'clock. Thank you all."

The door closed behind the returned soldiers as they

filed through it. Bright lights were switched off. Cameras were replaced in their metal boxes. Cigarettes were lighted. Coats were retrieved. The lighthearted, jubilant, and triumphant mood prevailed as members of the press corps, dignitaries, and advisers gravitated toward the wide double doors.

Keely, no longer a focus of attention, dropped back onto the couch and stared absently at the carpet. Only when another pair of shoes, black loafers, came into her field of vision, was she cognizant of her surroundings. She raised her eyes slowly up the long legs, past the belt buckle with the congressional seal stamped into the gold, past the necktie long since loosened for comfort, to the face she loved.

The rich dark eyes begged her forgiveness, forgiveness for feeling a twinge of relief that Mark Williams hadn't walked through the door. Her eyes told him that she understood his relief. Her lips couldn't quite produce a smile.

"I'm sorry. Do you believe me?" he asked for her ears alone.

"Yes."

He shoved his hands in his pockets and stared over her head at the picture on the wall of Washington crossing the Delaware. "What will you do now?"

She dropped her head and noticed a coffee stain on her skirt. She must truly look a mess. When had she last showered, slept, changed her makeup, eaten? She couldn't remember.

"I don't know," she said, shaking her head. "Right now I can't think past a bath and a few hours' sleep."

"It was an unfair question."

She looked up at him again. "No, it wasn't."

Most everyone else had left, but they weren't aware of it. He knew by the look on her face that she was suffering and he cursed his inability to comfort her. *I want to hold you, Keely.* "Are you going to the hotel before the news conference?"

Dax, I need you. "Yes. I guess so."

He moved aside as she stood up and gathered her belongings. *You look so helpless.* "Have you got everything?"

I feel so helpless. I need your strength. "Yes. I was told our luggage would already be at the hotel."

"Good." *Do you want me to hold you?*

Yes. "Yes."

"Do you know which hotel they've designated you? They had to divide us up from what I understand. Tourist season." *I wish you were in my room.*

"They told me I'd be at the Crillon." *I wish I were staying with you. I'm afraid when you aren't with me.*

Thank God. I can keep an eye on you. "Me too."

Thank God. You won't be far away. "Good."

They had reached the front of the building now where members of the delegation were being loaded into waiting limousines. Actually it would have almost been easier to walk, since the hotels were so close, but since the courtesy was being offered, no one was refusing it.

"We have room for one more for the Crillon," said one of the embassy attachés. "Mrs. Williams?"

She turned and looked beseechingly toward Dax. She didn't want to leave him. "You'd better go on and take full advantage of the time allotted," he said kindly, thinking he'd die if he couldn't touch her soon.

"I'll wait. I don't— Thank you again, Congressman Devereaux, for your concern. I'll never give up hope."

He knew by her sudden switch in tone and dialogue that Van Dorf was more than likely lurking near them. A quick glance over his shoulder confirmed it. "I'm holding up the others. Goodbye." She shook hands with Dax perfunctorily and then went down the steps to be whisked away in the limousine.

Dax stood there, bereft, looking after the black limousine. "She seems upset," Van Dorf commented at his side.

Dax shot him a deprecating look. "Wouldn't you be, Van Dorf? She had a glimmer of hope that her husband might yet be alive, and not only was he not among the men who have come back, but she still doesn't know his status or hers."

"Surprising," Van Dorf said offhandedly.

Against his better judgment, Dax took the bait. "What is?'

"Her seeming concern over her husband."

Dax could feel his blood rising. "Why is it surprising?"

Van Dorf laughed scoffingly and it was a nasty sound. "Oh, come off it, Congressman. You're a man of the world. She's a hot little broad. How long do you think a sexy looker like her can live without a man? One month? Two?" He laughed again. "Surely not twelve years."

The French temper that flowed with every beat of Dax Devereaux's heart had never been so provoked. His hands formed iron fists at his sides and it was all he could do to keep them there and away from Van Dorf's throat.

"In your case, Van Dorf, ignorance isn't bliss, but a pity. You obviously don't recognize honor and decency in anyone else because you've never found them in yourself."

Dax stalked away, still marveling over the fact that he had kept himself from murdering the man. Van Dorf watched his angry departure, smiling with evil relish.

KEELY BATHED, WASHED her hair, and cleaned her face before collapsing across the bed. She awoke an hour later when her tiny travel alarm went off. She sat up, groggy and befuddled. The short nap might possibly have done more harm than good.

Dragging herself off the bed, she considered skipping the press conference, but immediately decided against that. She had to go. Her absence would appear graceless and would no doubt be noted in news accounts. Especially those written by Van Dorf. She hadn't even spoken to Betty yet and she wanted to meet Bill.

Her dress was a straight sack that she belted with a gold link belt. The green color was springlike, but the long cuffed sleeves would keep her warm. She brushed her hair and didn't even bother with electric curlers. Its natural wave was enough for now, encouraged as it was by the early Parisian spring humidity.

Arriving back at the embassy, she noted that the reception room had been swept, cleared of debris, and aired. A long table with a row of microphones had been set up instead of the single lectern that had been used that morning.

She took a seat in the last row of chairs and graciously accepted numerous condolences, assuring the sympathizers that she was grateful for the safe return of the men who had made it. Officially she said, "I think this only reinforces that our government's efforts to secure information about the MIAs not be abandoned. There is still a very real possibility that many more men are in Vietnam and Cambodia struggling to get out alive. I hope that what we hear from the survivors today will shed some new light on the problem."

She saw Dax come in and take a position next to Congressman Parker along the wall in front of the windows. He nodded imperceptibly and she drew strength from even that small gesture.

As promised, General Vanderslice began the proceedings on time. The returnees took seats behind the table, Bill Allway in the middle, Betty seated in an extra chair directly behind him.

The barrage of questions began and for the next two hours the men were quizzed in a dozen languages. It was learned that ten of the men had escaped a prisoner of war camp together and over a period of a year and a half picked up the other sixteen men. During the months they had been together, three of their original number had died. Their names were read and duly recorded. The stories they related were incredible. What they had lived through was incomprehensible and the more their audience heard the more appalled it became.

Before dismissing the conference, General Vanderslice announced that the men had consented to an interview session the following morning. Everyone stood and applauded the soldiers as they left the room.

Keely waited for the throng to thin out before she stood to leave. Just as she was pulling on her light raincoat, Congressman Parker came up to her. Dax was with him. "Mrs. Williams, would you care to join Congressman Devereaux and me for dinner?" he asked politely.

Should she? The senior congressman didn't know he would be acting as a chaperon, but his presence would serve as her and Dax's protection from speculation and suspicion.

She was about to give him her affirmative answer when a Marine came up to them and saluted smartly. "Excuse me, Mrs. Williams, but Mrs. Allway sent for you. She needs to talk to you about the men still in the hospital."

Keely's heart lurched. Could this be happening now? Was this another shot in the dark? Or did Betty know…?

"I—I'll come right now," she stammered to the Marine. Turning back to Dax and Congressman Parker, she said, "I'm sorry, but—"

"No need to apologize, Mrs. Williams. This may yet be news of your husband," Parker said.

She avoided Dax's eyes as she followed the Marine's lead out the room and down a gloomy hallway into a deserted office. She was impressed first by the quiet. All day her ears had been adjusting to a din, now the silence caressed her ears gently and she welcomed it. Her escort left her alone.

A door opened on the other side of the empty office and Betty and her husband stepped through it. For a moment they looked at each other over the expanse of desks and carpet, then Keely rushed to the couple and threw her arms around Betty.

"I'm so thrilled for you, Betty. My joy couldn't be any greater."

"Keely, Keely," Betty said in her ear. "I'm sorry. I shouldn't be so happy."

"Of course you should!" Keely pulled away to look at the older woman's concerned face. "You should be ecstatic. And I know from watching you today that you are." She turned to the gaunt man standing beside Betty. "Hello, Bill," she said. "I've heard so much about you. Welcome back." She extended her hand for him to shake but, at the last moment, impulsively hurled herself at him and hugged him tight. Her embrace didn't offend him. She felt his thin arms enfold her.

"Betty has told me about you and how you've campaigned for the MIAs. I only wish your husband were with us."

Keely then remembered why she had been summoned. She searched their faces but saw no suppressed good news behind their compassionate expressions.

"The men in the hospital...?" She left the question open-ended.

Betty shook her head sadly and took Keely's hands between hers. "I'm sorry, Keely, but no, Mark isn't one of them. That's why I called you in here so Bill and I could talk to you alone. I didn't know how much hope you were holding out, and I wanted to spare you any false optimism."

"Keely." She turned blind eyes toward Bill Allway when he spoke her name in that gravelly voice. "After Betty told me about Mark, we immediately questioned the others if they knew anything about a helicopter pilot by that name. We gave them the date his chopper went down, any detail we knew that might be helpful. No one could provide us with any information. Of course the soldiers still hospitalized haven't been interrogated."

Keely turned her back on them and walked to the window, staring out over the Paris skyline that was being lighted now in the dusk. "Thank you both for your consideration. In view of the fact that you haven't seen each other in fifteen years, I'm humbled that the few hours you've been together you've spent much of it thinking about me and Mark. Thank you," she repeated.

"Keely—"

Not able to bear any more sympathy, she whirled around and interrupted Betty before she could say any more. "I'm fine, really. You two need time alone. Go on. I'll be fine. Indeed—" she tried valiantly for indifference "—Congressman Parker has invited me to dinner." She peeled her lips back into what she hoped was a smile. In the waning light of the office the Allways must have been fooled.

"If you're sure..." Betty hedged.

"I'm sure. Now go."

"We'll see you tomorrow," Bill said.

"Of course. Good night."

They left through the door from which they had entered and she was alone. More alone than she had ever been in her life.

She felt like she was on some kind of emotional pogo stick, being catapulted up into an emotional upheaval only to be hurled again to the bottom. She hated this conflict of emotions she felt. She wanted to be delirious with happiness for the Allways, and she was. But she couldn't help but be jealous that Betty's sentence was over.

Or was it? What would the Allways' marriage be like now? Could they pick up where they left off after fourteen years of separation? Having seen them together, Keely thought their chances were extremely good.

But what of her and Mark? How would she have felt today if she had been called out to meet a man, a man she didn't know, a man she was bonded to by marriage vows and legality, but no longer felt an affinity for? At the first sight of him would all the feelings of love she could no longer conjure come rushing back? Would she have flung herself into his arms? Or would she have been frightened to think that this stranger was her husband—this stranger she didn't recognize because all traces of youth and exuberance had been cut away by war as cleanly as by a surgeon's scalpel? Betty had had the advantage of years, of knowing her husband as a man before he went to war, of learning the ins and outs of his personality. She and Mark had had no such luxury.

The walls of the office were suddenly claustrophobic, and she left, avoiding the crowd at the end of the hallway and exiting through another door. Getting her bearings, she walked toward the Champs-Elysées. The avenue was jammed with honking, belligerent traffic that characterized the city's perpetual rush hour. Pedestrians crowded the sidewalks. As Keely walked, skirting the moving mass, she found it offensive that to so many people this had been just another workday. Some had no more to worry about than what they were going to eat for dinner or if they should stop at the dry cleaners tonight or wait until tomorrow.

The Place de la Concorde was thronged with laugh-

ing tourists and Parisians impatient with laughing
tourists. As she was jostled through the crowd, she
wondered idly how many times the horses of Coysevox
at the entrance of the Tuileries Gardens had been photographed. Little of the world-famous square with its
obelisk in the center attracted her attention for more
than a moment at a time. Her thoughts were elsewhere.

Pont de la Concorde took her across the Seine onto
the Left Bank. One of the bateau-mouche dinner ex-
cursions glided beneath the bridge as she crossed it.
She didn't even see the beautifully lighted boat. She
just walked.

On the Boulevard Saint-Germain, she stopped at an
intersection to wait for a break in the traffic. Much to
her distress the man standing next to her was finding
her fascinating and wasn't taking her ignorance of the
French he was pouring in her ear as discouragement.
He moved closer, almost knocking her off the low curb.
She regained her footing and shot him an annoyed look,
which he took as a challenge and smiled.

With foolhardy bravery she ran in front of a tour bus
to cross the street. Upon reaching the other side, she
was grateful that she had escaped both a sudden death
and the amorous attention of the Frenchman. A few
blocks farther on she felt the pent-up weariness finally
manifesting itself. She sat down on a sidewalk bench
and stared sightlessly, dejectedly, in front of her. She
only wanted to be left alone, to be invisible, to evapo-
rate. She was tired of coping.

The ingratiating voice intruded again, this time as
her ardent pursuer sat down close beside her on the
bench. She was glad her knowledge of the language
was limited. His tone was lewdly suggestive. She shook

her head forcefully and tried to scoot away, but to no avail.

Then another French voice, this one growling and threatening, came from behind her and her aggressor jumped to his feet, made a placating gesture with his hands, and fled down the sidewalk as though the hounds of hell were after him.

She looked up to see Dax standing behind her. He didn't speak, but came around the end of the bench and sat down beside her. The understanding smile, the black liquid eyes that related so much, the security that he represented, were her undoing.

When she fell toward him, his arms were opened to receive her and to cradle her head against his chest.

CHAPTER THIRTEEN

HOLDING HER STILL and tight, he didn't disturb her bout of weeping. The slim shoulders under his arms shuddered with the sobs that seized her. He bent his head over the soft brown hair and inhaled the fragrance as he would have inhaled her sorrow if he could.

He wasted no energy worrying about the curious picture they must make. All his thoughts, his being, were absorbed by this woman. She was so very precious to him. He had admired her strength of character, her beauty, her achievements, the career she had made for herself. Now this new fragility awakened in him yet another emotion. His passions surged to the surface and he became fiercely possessive and protective. He might very well have killed anyone who attempted to hurt her.

Long after the tears were spent and only dry sobs shook her, he held her. Whatever would be said and done would be initiated by her. The violet sky deepened to a darker indigo and then gradually faded to black, and still they sat, wrapped around each other.

When she raised her head, she looked away, wiping her mascara-streaked cheeks and smoothing back her hair. He didn't admonish her grooming efforts and tell her she looked beautiful. He thought she was beautiful, despite her dishevelment, but he knew she wouldn't want to hear it. She would be self-conscious now, shy of him, and ashamed of her loss of control. He would give her free rein. She would chart the course, set the pace.

"Will you walk with me?" she asked.

He stood and gave her his hand. She accepted it, but dropped it when she had taken but a few steps. He didn't try to regain it, though he wanted to surround it with his hand in a symbolic gesture of the protectiveness he felt. They walked slowly, not talking, looking through a shop window when something struck her fancy. Only slight smiles, soft sighs, poignant glances, were used to communicate.

He had no idea how long or how far they walked. It didn't matter. He was faintly surprised when she paused and faced him. "Are you hungry?"

He smiled. "A little. Are you?"

"Yes."

"Then I'll be glad to buy you dinner."

"Where?"

"You choose."

"All right."

The first restaurant they came to was passed over because it was crowded and noisy. The next one's bill of fare featured only cold sandwiches and she admitted to being hungrier than that.

The third one they came to was perfect. It was typically French with checked tablecloths, dim candles, and one lone daisy in a bud vase on each table. The sidewalk dining area had been closed for the night, but the low-ceilinged interior suggested an aura of welcome intimacy.

As soon as the garçon had showed them to a table, Keely said, "May I be excused for a moment?"

"Of course." Dax didn't sit down until she had disappeared through a narrow shadowed opening leading to the back of the restaurant. When she came back to the table he saw that her face had been cleaned, her hair had been brushed, and she had applied fresh lipstick. He didn't touch her when he held her chair.

She munched on a piece of hard crusty bread. "I didn't know you spoke French."

He smiled humbly. "Only one of my many accomplishments."

"What did you say to him?"

"The waiter?"

"No, the man who followed me."

He was momentarily distracted by the tongue that glided across her lips to pick up vagrant bread crumbs. He found it hard to remember what she had asked him. "Uh…oh, that. Well, it isn't found in any dictionary," he grinned. "Do you know what you want to eat?" he asked, opening the well-worn menu.

"I'll let you order. I'm fond of coq au vin."

"Then you're in luck because it's right here," he said, pointing to the menu. "Coq au vin. Salad?" She nodded. "Soup?"

"I don't think so."

The waiter stepped forward. If the tuxedo he wore was shiny and his cuffs a bit frayed, they didn't notice as Dax gave him the order. As a matter of fact, neither of them could ever recall what he looked like. They were only looking at each other.

"Did you want a drink?" Dax asked.

"No. Coffee after dinner."

"Okay." He leaned his elbows on the table and cupped his chin in his fists.

She looked through the curtained windows at the steady stream of traffic on the boulevard. "How did you know where to find me?"

He wished she would look at him. Her voice sounded remote and her despondency was killing him. "I met Betty and Bill Allway in the hall. They told me what they had discussed with you. I thought you might need…someone. When I went into the office where they said you'd be, you were already gone. I ran like mad to catch sight of you. Your long legs sure can cover ground."

The attempt at humor worked and she laughed as she finally turned her head to look back at him. "Anyway," he continued, encouraged. "I only followed you to see that you were all right. When I saw that guy getting fresh, I closed in."

"You were just in time."

"Sure you weren't just being coy with him? I may have ruined a good thing." The first interjection of humor had worked, so he pressed for two times in a row.

This one was successful too. She laughed again and he could see a discernible difference in her posture as she began to relax.

By the time their salads arrived, they were chatting easily, though about nothing pertaining to what had brought them to Paris, to this small café, in the first place.

"He'll be offended if we don't drink any wine with dinner. This is Paris, you know," Dax leaned forward across the table and whispered conspiratorially.

"Watch it, you're getting salad dressing on your tie."

He looked down quickly. "Oops. Sorry." He picked

up the drop of vinegar and oil from his tie and licked it off the end of his finger. "What about the wine?"

Keely glanced at the waiter who was hovering nearby in an expectant attitude and she suspected that he could understand their English perfectly. "Well," she demurred, "if you think he'll be offended if we don't…"

Dax took his cue and signaled the waiter over. He was at the side of their table before Dax had completely lifted his hand. The order was given and accepted in French. Keely sat and watched, bemused.

The waiter went briskly toward the rear of the restaurant and was back in an uncannily brief space of time. He carried a chilled carafe of white wine on a tray.

"This is the house wine, guaranteed to be excellent. Or so he says," Dax said to her. He went through the wine-tasting ritual, comically swishing it around in his mouth like mouthwash and rolling his eyes. The waiter tried to look aghast, but found the performance so entertaining that he looked down at Keely and smiled as though the two of them were patronizing a willful eccentric.

Dax swallowed loudly. "Wonderful, beautiful!" he exclaimed and gestured that the waiter was to fill their glasses. He did and left the carafe on the table.

"Oh, Dax! I just remembered Congressman Parker. What did you tell him?"

"That I had jet lag. I made your excuses too."

"Thank you."

The food was delicious. The chicken was cooked to perfection, as were the small white potatoes, green beans, and baby carrots. No sooner had he taken away their empty plates than the waiter brought out parfait glasses of chocolate mousse with a mound of whipped cream and chocolate shavings on top. They delved into those and when she could only eat half of the rich dessert, Dax finished it for her, complaining that she had eaten off all the whipped cream.

The carafe of wine was empty and they sat, mellow and satisfied, over cups of coffee. The dishes were taken away by a deferential subordinate of their waiter. When only the sputtering candle and the drooping daisy in the center of the table were left between them, Keely knew the time had come for them to talk.

"Dax," she opened slowly, "I know that you'd never ask, but you must want to know what I'm feeling."

"You're right on both counts. I'd never ask. And it's up to you whether you tell me or not. My only job is to be here if you need me."

She raised swimming eyes to his and her mouth trembled deliciously and dangerously. "I *do* need you."

"You've got me." He wanted to reach across the table and take her hands between his, but his motion to do so was arrested when he saw her fold her hands together at the table's edge.

"I don't know if any of this will make sense. I haven't categorized my thoughts, so I may ramble."

"I won't mind."

She drew a heavy, shuddering breath. "I think that I must not be a very nice person. Today I was sickened with disappointment. But the heartache I felt because Mark wasn't among those soldiers wasn't for him. It was for *me*."

She slumped against the back of her ladder-back chair and toyed with the tablecloth at the edge of the table, pleating it between her fingers to fit the rim. "All

I could think of when I realized that he wasn't one of the twenty-six men, was that my travail wasn't over. Not only was he not among the living, but I still don't know if he's among the dead either. I've progressed nowhere, but only remained stationary."

She lifted her eyes briefly as though to check to see if he were listening. She needn't have worried. He was hanging on to her every word.

"And then when those pitiful specimens of men faced that room of us so bravely, so…warily, I saw myself for just how selfish I am. Or am I?

"All afternoon we listened to those men recounting their experiences. Time and again they stressed that they had lived as they had to, doing whatever was necessary for survival. I suppose that would encompass every aspect of living, wouldn't it?"

She didn't expect an answer, so he gave none. She darted him a fleeting look and licked her lips before she continued. "What I mean is that those MIAs said they knew of American servicemen who didn't necessarily want to come home. What if Mark has a life there he doesn't want to leave? He may have a wo-woman and children. He may have lived with her for years. She, not I, would be his real wife.

"I had to face an undeniable truth about myself today, especially after I saw Bill and Betty together. It's not really Mark that I miss. He may very well be dead. But if not officially, he's been dead to me for many years. What I miss is the status of being married. Had it not been for Mark, whom I loved very much at the time, I might have chosen to live singly for years. Or had his death been reported, I might have chosen to marry again. But as it turned out I didn't ever have a choice.

"I've grown accustomed to the fact that I may be a widow. What I can't reconcile is that I still don't *know.* Fate has robbed me of having a choice in the direction my life will take." She looked at him then, pleading with her eyes for his understanding. "But I *do* have a life, Dax. And I don't want to waste it."

For long moments they didn't speak. The waiter, ever watchful, didn't approach the table. Something in the way the man looked at the woman, the way she stared into his eyes, the way they seemed oblivious of their surroundings, kept him at his discreet distance.

When at last the heavy silence was broken, it was Dax who broke it. "You're wrong, Keely. You make a great deal of sense. And you are positively entitled to a few selfish thoughts. You have one uncommon virtue that you don't credit yourself with."

She raised her head and met his glowing gaze across the table. "What?"

"You're totally honest, with yourself and now with me. Very few of us are willing to admit to shortcomings, or even to recognize them. Yet you've confessed to a questionable selfishness when a truly selfish person wouldn't even see themselves as such."

"Are you just saying that to make me feel better, to absolve me of guilt?"

"No."

"Are you sure?"

"Yes. I'm trying to be honest too."

She sighed and he thought he detected relief in that sigh. She tried to smile. "I *did* ramble, though."

He caught her effort to relieve the portentousness of the moment. "A bit," he said, smiling.

"I still have ambiguous feelings about...everything."

"You most probably always will, Keely."

"Yes." A melancholy tone crept into her voice and she stared out the window for a moment, lost in thought. Then she looked at him again. "Thank you for being...for being you."

"I didn't do anything."

"You listened."

"That's not much."

"It's a lot."

Covering his self-consciousness over praise he didn't feel he merited, he said, "Shall we leave or would you like something else?"

"No, thank you."

They stood and Dax left a roll of French francs in the center of the table. He saluted their waiter before he followed Keely through the door.

"What now?" he asked, taking her arm companionably. "Sightseeing, a nightclub, or home to bed?"

It took him a moment to realize that she was resisting his guiding hand and he glanced back to where she stood rooted to the sidewalk while Parisians hurried past her.

His eyes locked with hers and held. He took two steps back until he was standing inches from her, searching her eyes for what he wanted so desperately to see. "Keely?"

Her eyes didn't waver. If anything they widened, deepened, darkened, until he was drowning in their green depths. "I want you," she whispered. "I need all of you." He couldn't hear her, but he read the words on her lips.

She saw him swallow, saw the Adam's apple bob in his throat before coming to rest again. He hadn't misinterpreted her meaning. His hands came up to rest on her shoulders. He came half a step closer until she could feel the fabric of his clothing rustling against hers.

"You know——" He tried to get the words out, but they stuck in his dry throat. He had to make a second effort. "You know that I want that more than anything else in the world, and I will hate myself later if I change your mind. But, Keely, you're extremely vulnerable right now. Your emotions are running high. We've shared an intimate dinner with candlelight and wine and this is Paris, the most romantic city in the world. I'd never want you to look back on this night and think that I had taken advantage of you and your state of mind."

His grip became tighter, his voice more urgent, breathless almost. "Are you sure, Keely? Because if we go to a room together and get even the least bit comfortable, there'll be no stopping me this time. I want you to know that. *Are you sure?*"

Romance was still very much alive in Paris. There was even a smattering of applause by passersby when she came up on her tiptoes, placed her hands on his cheeks, and kissed him gently on the mouth.

THE ROOM THEY checked into was in a small family-owned hotel on one of the side streets off the Boulevard Saint-Germain. It was only four stories tall, and the second story was given over to several sitting rooms and a kitchen available for guests' use with certain stipulations that were painstakingly explained to an impatient Dax and Keely.

They were led up wooden stairs to the third floor. Each floor was only two rooms deep divided by a central hallway, and there were only eight rooms on each floor. The wainscoting was oak. The wallpaper was outmoded. The runners down each hall were tasteful Oriental imitations. All was spotlessly clean.

Dax conversed fluently with their hostess, a short, plump, rosy-cheeked woman with luxuriant white hair piled carelessly on top of her head. He translated their conversation, telling Keely they were lucky that an occupant had left earlier that day. They had been given the corner room that had two windows. She smiled at him as they followed their hostess's quick, surprisingly light footsteps down the hall.

Indeed the room did have two windows perpendicular to each other in the corner of the room. They were shown how to open the exterior shutters once the windows were raised. The bathroom was proudly opened and they were treated to a demonstration of how the faucets worked, how the commode flushed, how the shower nozzle in the narrow tub was to be handled, and how to use the bidet. Her cheeks flaming, Keely refused to meet Dax's amused eyes.

After being assured that they didn't need any more towels, an extra blanket, nor wine or coffee, their hostess departed. She graciously, but firmly, refused Dax's offer of a tip and closed the door behind her after wishing them a good-night.

Alone now, they were suddenly stricken with bashfulness and nerves. Their eyes didn't know where to look. They didn't know what to say. Their hands seemed idle and useless.

Keely finally slipped off her coat and draped it over the old-fashioned Boston rocker in one corner of the room. The cushions on it matched the patchwork-print pillows decorating the bed, which was covered with an ecru chenille spread. The fringed border grazed the polished wood floor.

Keely moved out of his way as Dax took off his lightweight overcoat and laid it across the opposite arm of the rocking chair. There was a chest of drawers with a framed oval mirror hanging over it. Keely went to it and stared unseeingly at her reflection before making a show of fluffing her hair. Dax was at the window fiddling with the latch.

At the same moment they turned to each other wordlessly. As if programmed to move with synchronized motions, they walked toward each other, meeting in the center of the room. His hand was raised to caress her cheek. They jumped apart when a timid knock was magnified in their ears to sound like a battering ram against the door.

Dax lunged toward it and pulled it open. Apologizing profusely, their hostess handed him a bouquet of fresh flowers in a china bowl. She had arranged the flowers that morning, but had failed to bring them up. Dax took the bouquet, thanked her, and closed the door again.

He stood awkwardly, holding the flowers as though at a loss as to what to do with them. He looked at Keely.

"They're pretty," she said. "Why don't you put them on the chest of drawers?"

"Yeah." He sounded grateful for the idea and rushed

to place the flowers on the chest as though their container were burning his hands. He inspected the flowers. They could have been a rare masterpiece. "They look good there."

"Yes, they do."

He turned to look at her again. "Uh…would you like to use— You can have the bathroom first."

She looked toward the door to the bathroom. "I'm not sure I need—I mean, why don't you go first."

He smiled tensely, briefly, so that it was really just a nervous jerking motion of his mouth. "Okay. I'll be right out."

The door closed behind him and immediately Keely heard the faucets running full blast and wondered what he could possibly be doing that would require so much water.

She gazed around her in perplexity. What should she do? Undress? Get in the bed? Should she take off everything or just partially undress? God, she couldn't believe her stupidity. She was thirty years old and she didn't know how one went about going to bed with a man.

She decided to split the difference and only take off a few garments. That would indicate interest, but not aggression. With that in mind, she stepped out of her shoes and unbuckled her belt. What to do with them? The closet? Yes.

She went to the narrow door and opened it. She placed her shoes neatly on the floor and hung her belt in a hook behind the door. Now what? Panty hose were the least sexy garment she could imagine. Better to dispose of them now than have to worry about them later.

The water in the bathroom was suddenly turned

off. She panicked, fearful that he would come through the door and catch her ungracefully peeling off her panty hose. She virtually ripped them from her legs and balled them up. The doorknob on the bathroom door rattled noisily. She threw the panty hose into the closet and slammed the door shut just as Dax opened the bathroom door.

He looked at her curiously. "All done," he said. "It's yours."

"Thank you." She grabbed up her purse and brushed past him toward the sanctuary of the bathroom. There was no sign of all the water he had splashed. He must have dried the basin with the damp towel that hung from the shower curtain rod that encircled the tub.

Needlessly she washed her hands. Needlessly she brushed her hair. She dabbed perfume from a tiny purse vial behind her ears and on her neck. She wished she hadn't cried earlier. Her eyes still showed evidence of her weeping, but there was no help for that. Taking a deep breath, she left the bathroom, switching off the light behind her.

Dax had turned off the overhead light and left on only a soft lamp beside the bed. The bed! It was turned down. The linens were snowy white in the softly glowing light.

Dax was shirtless and his feet were bare. Since the clothes he had taken off weren't visible, she wondered if he had seen the discarded panty hose when he put his clothes in the closet.

She dumped her purse in the rocker on top of her coat. When she turned around, he was standing close.

He took her breath away. Broad shoulders sloped down to the wide muscles in his chest. His ribs were leanly covered with taut skin and tapered down to a flat stomach and narrow waist. It was all forested with dark springy hair that grew in a fascinating pattern.

Was it her imagination, or was his hand trembling when he reached up to smooth it down from the crown of her head, past her ear, to rest on her shoulder? Still keeping space between their bodies, he leaned down to kiss her sweetly on the mouth. The kiss was excruciatingly tender as his lips pressed upon hers, held, then moved. Lips parted, tongues touched, mouths opened, passions ignited.

"Keely," he grated against her lips. His hands roamed up and down her back. "I've waited so long for this and now I can't believe it's happening."

"It's happening." He moved closer and she felt the angles and planes of his body adjusting to fit hers. "Dax," she said anxiously, "I'm nervous."

His self-derisive laugh was a soft puff of air against her ear. "I am too."

"You are?"

"Yes." His fingers tangled in her hair and forced her head back. "But I want you, Keely. I want you." His mouth claimed hers again in a consuming kiss. His breath in her ear had caused cold chills to race along her spine. Instinctively she moved toward him for warmth, and all the loneliness she had felt that day, had felt in her lifetime, was incinerated by his heat. His arms closed around her. His mouth sipped at hers and she knew what it was to be cherished. Her fear and anxiety vanished. This was Dax. She wanted this as badly as he. This wasn't a performance. This was a sharing experience. When the time came, she would know what to do.

He stepped back from her and, staring directly into her eyes, brought his hands to the back zipper of her dress. His eager fingers finally released the tiny hook from its eye, then he drew the zipper down with agonizing slowness. His eyes never left hers and the only movement apparent was the leaping flames of desire.

When the zipper tab was at last at the end of its track, he pulled aside the two back panels of her dress, slipped them over her shoulders and down her arms until they were freed. Rather than simply drop the dress to the floor, he stooped down, and she placed her hand on his bare shoulder for support as she daintily stepped out of it. He straightened and almost reverently folded the dress over a low footstool in front of the rocker.

His eyes showed supreme discipline when he faced her again and looked, not at her body, but into her eyes. His hands closed around her throat gently while his thumbs stroked along her moist lips. They parted slightly and his fingers detailed the row of perfect white teeth. He felt the soft purring vibration in her throat when his thumbs glided down her slender neck to her collarbone. Tracing it with sensitive fingers, he marveled at its delicacy.

Then all ten fingertips combed down her chest so slowly that she closed her eyes, begging him silently to hurry, but all the while reveling in the time he was taking.

His fingertips brushed across the top curves of her breasts. Skin on skin was such a delicious sensation. But it wasn't enough. They both ached for more. His hands closed over her and she leaned into his palms. Only then did he lower his eyes from her face to watch what his hands were about.

He unclasped the front fastener of her peach-colored bra and the veil fell away. His eyes riveted on the desire-swollen breasts as he removed the brassiere and tossed it away.

Keely had expected him to touch her again, so she was mildly surprised when his hands caught her wrists and brought them around his neck, overlapping them and securing them behind his head. Then his hands stroked down the undersides of her arms, over the valleys of her underarms, the sides of her breasts, and around to her back as he pulled her against him. "Keely, you feel so good," he ground out with an insufficient breath.

She buried her face in the curve of his shoulder and languidly moved her torso against his. The crinkly hair teased her skin and set all her nerve ends laughing in sheer joy at the differences in their bodies.

He kissed her then and she could tell by the hot insistence of his mouth that he was suffering from and thrilling to the same driving desire that had her whole body sensitized to a high level. His mouth explored hers thoroughly then trailed down her neck and chest to her breasts.

"Let me taste you, Keely."

"Yes, Dax, yes."

He bent over her and she fell across his arm for support. Her head went back and her back arched as his open mouth first skimmed her breasts randomly, then closed around one nipple, drawing on it gently.

She had never known such erotic possession. Out of all the men in the world, was it Dax alone who knew how to use his lips and tongue, his whole mouth, to bring pleasure beyond description? It seemed that there was a cord that wound through her from the tip of her breast to the secret part of her body. When Dax's tongue touched her nipple, she felt that touch deep inside her womb. Her femininity became full and warm with an ache that demanded to be assuaged.

Her fingers slid upward from his neck where he had placed them to weave through his thick raven hair. She felt her arms lower even as his head moved down to kiss the underside of her breasts and continue downward to count her ribs with nibbling lips.

Dropping to his knees, his hands smoothed over the satiny half-slip that was the same peach color as her bra. He placed his mouth against her stomach. His breath was hot and moist as it filtered through the fabric.

Then the elastic waistband was lowered over belly and hips until her slip dropped around her ankles in a frothy, lacy heap. His hands spanned her naked waist, his thumbs pressing into her navel. Then as his hands slid around to her back, his mouth replaced his thumbs and gave that shallow indentation ardent attention. He kissed it as he would have her mouth.

His palms were warm as they slipped beneath the scant swath of cloth that was her panties. His hands molded to the curve of her hips. Then the panties went the way of the half-slip over her hips and thighs and past her calves to the floor. What was revealed was revered with eyes and hands and mouth that looked and touched and kissed. With his tongue he branded the skin of her stomach, hips, and thighs until she couldn't bear any more and, with a desperate cry, felt her knees buckle and thump against the wall of his chest.

He was ready. Standing quickly, he pulled her

against him and caught her under the knees and back and lifted her to carry her to the bed. She was laid down with a care usually reserved for breakable objects.

He was away from her only long enough to rid himself of his clothes. The zipper of his pants rasped softly in the room. The snap clacked loudly. Then in one swift motion pants and underwear were gone and he was splendidly naked and looking down at her hungrily. Had he not been Dax, the starved, glazed look in his eyes would have frightened her. Instead she felt an answering hunger deep in the pit of her stomach.

"Keely, beautiful Keely," he said as he gradually lowered himself over her and gathered her to him. She absorbed his weight, adjusting her body beneath his and awakening them anew to the precision with which they fitted.

He pressed into her and a sharp, near virginal cry alarmed him. "Oh, God, Keely!" he cried in anguish and cupped her head, holding it protectively against his shoulder. "Darling, did I hurt you?"

"No, no," she sobbed. "Please, Dax. It's wonderful…please, Dax…" she begged.

The magic was spun. Her arms came from around his back to intertwine with his. Tightly laced fingers lay on either side of her head on the pillow. Thighs stroked thighs. Stomachs kneaded each other in a rhythmic cadence. Hair-roughened chest pressed smooth breasts. Mouths fused. Spirits sang. Essences were exchanged.

Shaken and weak, they lay perfectly still, his head beside hers on the pillow. Long moments passed while they savored the interlocking intimacy of their damp bodies. His voice seemed to come from far away, though she could feel his lips moving on her ear. "This is what my life has been for, Keely. This moment. This is why I was born. To be here with you like this. Do you understand?"

She could only nod. She did understand because she felt the same way, only she was too swept away by the miracle of it to say so.

CHAPTER FOURTEEN

"HOW LONG HAVE I been asleep?" he asked when he
opened his eyes. She was watching him. Waking up
had never been this nice.

"A half hour or so. I don't know. It doesn't matter."
Her fingers wandered over his cheekbones, down the
aristocratically shaped nose, across the lean cheek, to
the silver hairs at his temple.

He shifted his weight, rolling over to face her and
splaying his hand on her back to draw her closer. "How
could I have slept?"

"I think you were worn out," she said mischievously,
draping her arm over his shoulder.

He swatted her bottom playfully. "And you weren't?"

"Oh, yes, I was," she laughed. "But I couldn't have
slept." An inquisitive finger slid along his lips and she
wondered how they could be so firm and yet feel so
soft against her body.

He captured her hand and murmured against the
palm, "Why is that?"

"Because that's never happened to me before," she
said quietly, watching his reaction. "Never like that."

His eyes across the pillow sparkled with a happy
pride he was trying hard to keep at bay. "No?"

She shook her head. "No." Comparisons weren't
fair to Mark. She had told Dax all he needed to know.

"I'm glad. I'd be less than honest to say I wasn't."

Her emotions were too strained to say more. She groped for a more neutral subject. "Is this where you were wounded in the war?" she asked, tracing the puckered white scar beneath his shoulder blade with her finger.

"Yes. Luckily it was a piece of shrapnel that had lost most of its momentum before it got to me." She kissed the spot. "It's ugly because it took several days to get to the medics. By that time it was badly infected. They had to gouge out about a pound of flesh. It left quite a hole."

"Please don't tell me." She kissed his chin. "And the one under your eye?"

"My cousin and I got in a fight when I was about thirteen." He saw her disappointment and laughed. "Sorry, nothing more dramatic than that."

"How dare he pick on you." The seductive tone of her voice caught his attention and he watched in wonder and surprise as she knelt over him. Her hair fell softly around her face. The planes and valleys of her body were cast in sharp relief by the soft glow of the lamp. Light and shadow highlighted gentle mounds and tapering curves. Almost shyly she bent down and kissed his mouth.

His hand came up to clasp the back of her head and hold her over him. But he let her be the aggressor. Her tongue probed his mouth timidly until she breached the barrier of his teeth. Then she explored at leisure.

Her tongue made repeated dipping forays into his mouth. He was reminded of a child licking an ice-cream cone, who after each lick, returns his tongue to his mouth to savor the taste.

Pulling up only slightly, she kissed the scar under his eye then the dimple beside his mouth. Her lips settled on his neck and in one long, sensuous, fluid motion slid down to his chest. His fingers became twisted in her hair as he clenched his fist convulsively. His other hand settled in the curve under her hip and with only the slightest suggestive tug she raised one thigh over his.

"Keely, that's wonderful," he said as her lips sucked at his skin. His words were barely audible.

It gave her a heady, gratifying feeling to know she could bring him this much pleasure. She kissed her way down his stomach, delighting in his uneven breathing and murmured phrases.

Her mouth followed the tapering design of hair that became silky around his navel. When she examined that crevice with her tongue, his knee trapped her thigh against his. Her lingual exploration continued, and she found a thicker, rougher thatch. Dax's short ragged breathing stopped altogether. His fingers entangled in her hair, pulling it painfully. The muscle beneath her cheek contracted spasmodically.

She hesitated but a moment before kissing him again.

"Oh, God…sweet…" He lifted her, shifting them until she lay beneath him.

He pressed her back against the mattress with his kiss. It was a deep, drugging kiss that involved not only their mouths but their bodies as well. When his tongue pressed deeper into the hollow of her mouth, it was symbolic of another possession, another void he filled.

He raised his head and looked down at her. "The most beautiful sight I've ever seen was your face in that instant you knew what it was to be a woman fulfilled. Shine for me again, Keely."

The words he whispered heightened her love because she knew that her fulfillment contributed to his. His hands, as they stroked down her sides and over her hips and thighs, were like the touch of a velvet glove. His mouth on her breasts was alternately rapacious then soothing and brought her closer to what he wanted to see.

As her tumult built, so did his. What he wanted to witness was almost denied him. For at the last moment they did that little bit of dying together.

AT DAWN THEY LEFT. Their hostess, who apparently ran the hotel single-handedly, was distressed over their hasty departure. Repeatedly Dax assured her that the room had been more than satisfactory, but that other matters prevented them from staying any longer. She looked sad standing at the concierge's desk as they left her hotel.

Paris was barely awake. The streets looked washed clean from the nocturnal rain. Merchants and vendors were rolling down their awnings and preparing for a day of business. The aroma of fresh coffee and croissants filled the air.

They stopped at a sidewalk café not yet open and asked the proprietor for a take-out order. He grumbled, but being a true Parisian at heart and having a penchant for lovers, he relented and filled a sack with croissants and gave them plastic cups of steaming coffee. They munched as they strolled without undue haste.

They didn't speak of why they had to go back to the Crillon, they simply knew that they must. Instead they whispered and laughed in intimate exchanges that brought blooming roses to Keely's cheeks and gave Dax's grin a satyric quality.

"You love me so well," he said.

"Do I?"

"You love me well. Perfectly."

Her eyes dropped to the half-eaten croissant. "I couldn't stand it if you thought I was forward or crude—"

"God, no." He collected the refuse of their breakfast and shoved it into a trash receptacle. He came back to her, reaching out to smooth her cheek. "You are totally female, Keely, and I love all the physical parts of you that make you female. I also like your daintiness and delicacy, your ladylike demeanor and prim mannerisms.

"I also adore that you shed them like clothing before you come to bed with me. But never in a million years could you be crude. Don't even think such a thing."

"Dax," she said softly, tears shimmering in her eyes.

"I can't stand this any longer," Dax muttered impatiently and hailed a taxi.

"What?"

"I want to kiss you right now."

"No one's looking," she challenged.

"They will be if I kiss you the way I want to," he warned.

He hustled her into the back seat of the cab and gave the driver their destination. "I told him to take the long way," he said to Keely before he fell on her with the desperation of a dying man seeking sustenance.

He kissed her aggressively, hungrily, powerfully, as though he wanted to stamp his seal of ownership on her. She knew that in an endearing way he was convincing himself that even if they weren't securely locked in their small room, she still belonged to him.

When she managed to pull her mouth free, she pushed against his chest. "Dax, the driver."

"Let him get his own girl," he growled.

She laughed, struggling against him and only exciting him more. Before she knew what he was about, his hands were inside her coat. "Dax! Do you realize what you're doing?"

"Uh-huh." He smoothed his hands over her unfettered breasts beneath the soft dress. He had talked her out of wearing the bra this morning. His touch set off a chain reaction of sensations throughout her body and she strained against him.

The ardency of his kisses and the persuasiveness of his hands depleted her consciousness. They could have been driving for hours or merely minutes when she finally realized that the cab driver was calling something in French over his shoulder. "Dax," she murmured and firmly pushed him away. "He's saying something to you."

He sighed, sitting up and straightening his clothes. "The Crillon is in the next block."

Dax paid the driver and hauled her out of the back seat by pulling on her hand. She fell against him, laughing, and his arms enclosed her briefly before they turned toward the hotel.

Keely froze.

Walking toward them were the Allways. Their arms were linked around each other's waists. They were smiling happily, but their smiles turned to expressions of shocked dismay when they saw Keely and Dax in an embrace resembling their own.

The four stared at each other in stunned silence. It must have been the Allways' idea to have a quiet, private breakfast away from the throng of reporters and prying eyes. The interview session was to begin at ten o'clock. They were hoping for a couple of hours alone before an exhausting day.

Seeing them had been more than a mild shock to Keely. It had been an assault. A piercing spasm of guilt struck her in the heart, and following the millions of capillaries that radiated into every part of her body, the guilt pervaded her, seeped into her, until she was saturated with it.

She had betrayed these friends. They had remained faithful to each other, to their wedding vows, and to their conviction that their partner was surviving, if for no other reason than to see the other again.

She had betrayed her husband by sleeping with another man. Her sexual unfaithfulness was only a particle of her adultery. She had given all of herself to Dax, freely and wildly. She had retained nothing, held none of herself in reserve for Mark lest he return one day. Everything had been given to Dax and there was nothing left to give to anyone else.

She had betrayed herself by thinking she could put away every moral conviction she held dear in the name of love. Her loving Dax couldn't justify her betrayal of Mark. Love based on betrayal and deceit could never be blessed. She knew that and, until last night, had stood by that principle. But now in the light of day and in view of two who had withstood untold adversity to finally be brought together, she saw that she had been deluding herself. Love was never free. The price must always be paid.

"We were just going out for breakfast," Bill Allway said calmly, breaking an awkward silence that Keely wasn't even aware of.

"Would you like to join us...?" Betty asked graciously, but her voice trailed away to nothingness before she even completed the invitation. There was no condemnation in her eyes, but Keely felt like a scarlet letter had been branded on her chest. The evidence couldn't be more incriminating. She and Dax had got out of a taxi just minutes after dawn with their clothes rumpled and their faces flushed. What other conclusion could be drawn except the correct one? She thought that if she didn't die from guilt she would surely die of shame.

"No, thank you." Keely answered Betty's invitation for both of them.

Dax stood by silently and stared at her.

"Well, then, we'll be getting on our way," Bill said. "Betty?" He took his wife's arm and all but dragged her away. She was staring at Keely and Dax as though she still couldn't believe what her eyes had seen.

"Look at me," Dax hissed when the Allways were out of earshot.

"No," she said and turned away from him.

Her arm was practically wrenched from the socket as he whipped her around to face him. "Look at me," he commanded.

She jerked her head up and stared at him mutinously and his heart twisted when he saw the hard, closed, determined expression on her face. "I know what you're thinking, Keely." His voice was tight with suppressed tension.

"You couldn't possibly imagine what I'm thinking."

"Yes, I can. You're awash with guilt over what happened last night." His hands came up to grip her shoulders. "Seeing Betty and Bill set your conscience working overtime again. They are a lovely, happy couple, Keely. I couldn't be happier for them. But what happened to them doesn't have anything to do with you and Mark."

"It has everything to do with it," she argued stubbornly. "Betty was faithful. I wasn't."

"Faithful to whom? To a man you can barely remember? To a man you'll probably never hear of again?" He despised the cruelty of his words but he couldn't afford to be kind.

"Up until yesterday, Betty didn't know her husband was alive. Now he's back with her. Something could happen just that fast and Mark would be home expecting his wife to be waiting for him."

Dax looked around him impatiently as though he couldn't stand to hear what she was saying. Frustration screamed from every cell of his body. Finally his roaming, directionless eyes returned to her. "That is a very slim, remote possibility. What happened between us is a sure thing." He softened his voice to match the warming depth in his eyes. "I love you, Keely. I love you."

Her hand flew to her mouth and mashed her flattened lips to her teeth. She squeezed her eyes shut and shook her head. "No," she wailed softly. "Don't say it now. Not now."

"I'll say it until I know you hear me. I love you."

She fought his restraining hands with newfound

strength and gained her release. "No! It's wrong, Dax.
It always has been. Don't you see? I'm still not free to
love you. It will never be right for me to love until I
know that Mark is dead."

She stumbled backward, fearful that he might come
after her and take her in his arms and she would be
doomed again. "It isn't possible. Leave me...leave me
alone. Please."

She turned and fled, nearly knocking down a man
standing in the door of the hotel. It was only after she
had reached her room and collapsed on the bed in a torrent of tears that she sat bolt upright and took a heaving, shuddering breath of fearful realization.

That man had been Al Van Dorf.

DAX RACED DOWN the concourse, his heart pounding
with each footfall. He barely noticed his exertion. With
the least bit of encouragement he felt he could fly.

To think that only this morning he was in the depths
of despair when he watched with an empty heart as
Keely ran away from him. He had all but flattened Van
Dorf when he made some snide remark about whether
they were coming or going.

He had pushed past the man and stormed to his
room, ready to do combat with anyone brave enough
to test his temper. He never remembered feeling that
helpless and angry in his life.

For hours he had paced his room and with each hour
his frustration mounted. Looking at the situation from
an objective point of view, he could see that there was
no right side nor wrong side. No easy answer or simple
solution was going to jump out at them. Their problem
couldn't be solved by careful deductive reasoning. It

could only be resolved by making a judgment call, by weighing one strong emotion against another equally strong. It was a decision involving Keely's conscience. God! He was afraid what her decision would be.

Congressman Parker had called his room and he had all but yanked the telephone out of the wall in his haste to answer it, thinking that maybe Keely had had a change of heart. "Yes," he barked.

"I surrender," Congressman Parker laughed.

Abashment and disappointment did battle, and disappointment won. "I'm sorry. What can I do for you, Congressman?"

"I'm glad you offered your services, because I *do* have a favor to ask. I'm expected to attend those interview sessions today, sort of be on hand should any question pertaining to legalities or congressional options arise. I'm also expected to go to the hospital and visit those soldiers as a representative of the administration. I doubt if the President would object if I asked one of his pet congressmen to fill in for me there. Would you mind?"

Dax ran a hand through his hair. He might as well. He wasn't up to another day in a crowded room filled with photojournalists and reporters. If he stayed here, he'd only think about Keely and that wasn't getting him anywhere either. "Certainly. Give me time to clean up. What info do I need before I go?"

"We lost one of those boys, Dax. Last night. He just couldn't pull through."

"Damn!"

"Yeah. I'll send a folder down to your room with stats about each one of them. When you're ready to go, ask the desk to send a car. Take your time. There's no hurry. Oh, except for the plane leaving tonight."

"What plane?"

"Some had requested that they be sent right home and the President has agreed. So those who feel up to it are returning tonight as well as anyone on the original delegation who wants to go on home."

"What time does the plane leave?"

"Nine o'clock. From de Gaulle. I'll jot down all the particulars in one of the folders."

"Thank you."

"Thank you, Dax. Say hello to those soldiers for me."

So he had gone to the hospital as a substitute emissary. God, what if he hadn't gone? What if the corporal named Gene Cox had been asleep? What if he had been the unfortunate one to die during the night?

He shivered even as sweat rolled down his torso. His coat flapped against his legs and he hefted his bag into a sturdier grip. His feet thudded on the carpeted concourse. He could see the gate. It was still crowded. Good, the plane hadn't taken off yet. Thank God the government hadn't made an exception and done something on time.

He ignored the curious stares directed at him. He ignored Congressman Parker's signal for Dax to join him. His eager gaze swept the waiting room until it found the woman sitting all alone on the far side of the room looking out at the black night where only the blue runway lights relieved the stygian darkness. He could see her reflection in the glass, her desolate expression.

He dropped his bag where he stood and elbowed his way toward her. She saw his image in the glass as he loomed up behind her. His heart was rent in two at her immediate and visible distress.

"I've got to talk to you," he said urgently.

"No," she said, not turning around. "It's all been said."

He knelt down beside her chair and spoke softly. "If you want the whole world to hear this, witness this, then fine. But I believe I've got something to tell you that you'd rather hear in private. So what's it going to be?"

She turned to look at him then. He met her rebellious gaze levelly. He saw her belligerence waver, then fade. "Very well," she said and stood up, waiting for his lead.

He indicated with his head that she was to follow him. Obediently she did so. Most of the other waiting passengers were too tired or apathetic to notice their departure. When they reached the wide central aisle of the airport, Dax looked around until he saw a deserted alcove that housed pay telephones. He took her elbow and steered her toward it.

She turned to him as soon as they had reached the alcove that offered them only a modicum of privacy. "What do you want?"

He could forgive the cold haughtiness with which she faced him. He could forgive it because he knew that within a matter of moments her feelings would be quite different. Best to get the worst of it out of the way and proceed from there.

"Keely," he began gently, "Mark is dead. He's been dead since the day his chopper went down almost twelve years ago."

There were no manifestations of the emotional tumult she must surely be experiencing. There were no tears, no audible gasps, no hysterics, no gladness, no sorrow, nothing but a stoic mask and impenetrable green eyes that gave away nothing.

"Did you hear me, Keely?" he asked at last.

She nodded before she spoke. "Y-yes." She swallowed and cleared her throat. "How did you…how do you know?"

He told her then about his going to the hospital in lieu of Congressman Parker. "After my official duties were over, the four MIAs and I began talking as one vet to another. Just out of curiosity's sake, I asked each of them the circumstances behind his disappearance. One of them, an army corporal named Gene Cox, mentioned the date of a helicopter crash. Keely, it was the same day Mark's chopper went down.

"I asked Cox what had happened and he said the helicopter had been hit and was already burning when it crashed. He and the pilot were able to get out before it exploded. They crawled into the jungle, which he said was 'creeping' with Viet Cong. Both of the pilot's legs were broken and he must have had internal injuries. He died within an hour of the crash. Cox covered him with some thick foliage, hoping that the Cong wouldn't find the body and— Well, wouldn't find it.

"Then Cox was captured and taken prisoner the next day." He took her hands in his and squeezed them tightly. "Keely, the helicopter pilot's name was Mark Williams. He was a tall blond guy who spoke with a Southern accent."

He had expected her to possibly slump against the wall or perhaps to lean into him for support as she tried to assimilate what he had told her. He had planned to hold her close, not as a lover but as a friend, until she was ready to talk about what this meant to them. He had expected tears perhaps over the wasted life of a young man, maybe even a little bitterness over the war to which he had been sacrificed.

In all his imaginings he hadn't anticipated the reaction he got.

She jerked her hands free of his as though flinging off something hideous. The only sound she made was a laugh, harsh and without mirth, but rife with contempt. "How could you, Dax?" she asked, loathing dripping off every word. "Whose conscience are you trying to salve—mine or yours?"

He stared at her in mute astonishment. "Wh—"

She laughed that horrible laugh again. "I've no doubt that this soldier Cox told you his story. But I find it a shade too coincidental that the pilot's name was Williams and that he spoke with a Southern accent. Did you think I was so gullible that I'd believe that?"

His jaw, which had been hanging slack in puzzlement, was now hardening as he tried to get control of his quickly slipping temper. In deference to the situation he managed to contain it. "I'm telling you the truth, dammit." He pushed the words through his teeth. "Why would I lie about something this important?"

"Because I told you this morning that I couldn't belong to you, that we couldn't have a life together until I knew about Mark's fate. I think you conveniently worked his name into the story this soldier told you. That would make a neat, tidy little package, wouldn't it?" She shook back her hair with an angry toss of her head. "You have a reputation for getting what you want,

Congressman Devereaux, by fair means or foul. I think you've just lived up to that reputation."

His proud ancestors could tolerate just about anything except a slur on their family name. So could Dax. But any intimation that his integrity wasn't sound was the one thing he would never forgive.

He straightened to his full height and looked down at her with violence smoldering in his eyes. "All right, Keely. Believe what you will. Sacrifice your life too. Hoard your love like a damn miser. I think you actually thrive on your self-imposed martyrdom. It sets you apart, doesn't it, from the rest of us animals? But be forewarned, the human race finds saints immeasurably tedious."

She whirled away from him and crossed the concourse to the boarding area. Though his heart was being chiseled away piece by piece, his pride wouldn't allow him to call her back. How could she believe him capable of something so despicable after last night? Last night… He covered his face with his hands, trying to wipe out the memories of shared joy, ecstasy. It was impossible that she could think—

"Your woman run out on you?"

Al Van Dorf's drawling voice thrust Dax abruptly back into the present. He dropped his hands and jerked his head around to see the smirking grin he detested. Van Dorf was leaning negligently against the wall just inside the alcove. His mocking arrogance was the last straw for Dax's tenuous composure.

He lunged at the reporter and his Marine-trained instincts took over. Before the man realized what had happened to him, he had been uprooted, yanked farther into the shadows, and pinned against the wall. Both hands had been clamped behind him by an iron fist. His eyeglasses had been knocked askew. Dax's knee was rammed up into his crotch, causing him to squeal a high, pitiable screech. A hard forearm was pressed like a crowbar across his throat.

"You've opened your wise mouth once too often, Van Dorf."

"I saw—"

"You saw *nothing*. You heard *nothing*. *Nothing* you can prove, anyway. If you ever make one of your sly innuendos to me again, I'm going to sue you for so much money that even if I lose, your reputation as a credible journalist will be so shot to hell that no news service or two-bit rag will touch you with a ten-foot pole. Not only that, but I'll beat the bloody hell out of you. Do I make myself clear, Van Dorf?"

For emphasis, he pushed his knee higher and the man whimpered, confirming what Dax had always suspected—he was a coward. "I asked you a question, Van Dorf. Do I make myself clear?"

The man bobbed his head up and down as far as Dax's stranglehold would allow. The devil eyes that glared at him threatened that the congressman might yet change his mind and go ahead and kill him. It was with vast relief that he felt Dax's hands gradually relax.

"What I said goes double for Mrs. Williams. If I read one word of insinuating copy with your byline on it, I'll kill you."

Then, in a gesture of disdain, he turned his back on Van Dorf, who was still struggling for air. He strode back to the boarding gate, picked up his bag where he had left it, and went to stand in formidable solitude against the wall, waiting for the long overdue airplane back to the United States.

CHAPTER FIFTEEN

THE MOON WAS on the right side of the aircraft. Keely
was staring out a window on the left side, so only a
diffuse silver glow alleviated the black night. The stars
seemed far away. The clouds below the aircraft were a
thick, seemingly impenetrable blanket.

"Are you sleeping?" The question roused her from
her stupor and she turned her head to see Betty Allway leaning across the aisle seat. Since the reporter
who had been sitting beside Keely originally had taken
her rude silence as a hint that she didn't want to talk
and moved to another seat, she had been sitting alone.

"No," she answered the older woman's question.

"Do you mind if I sit beside you for a while?"

Keely shook her head and picked up her raincoat,
which had been lying in the seat to discourage anyone
else from sitting there. "What's Bill doing? Sleeping?"

"Yes," Betty said. "He gets frustrated because he
tires so easily. I'll have to keep an eye on him so he
doesn't do too much when he first gets home. I'm sure
his inclination, and the army's, will be to try to make
up for the past fourteen years in a few weeks. I'm going
to fight them both to see that that doesn't happen."

Keely responded with a warm smile. "You're entitled to a little possessiveness, I think."

They sat in awkward silence for a moment. Keely

couldn't forget Betty's surprised expression when she had seen her and Dax getting out of the taxi that morning at dawn. It was a wonder the woman would speak to her at all. After all the heartache they had suffered together, she hated to lose the friendship of a woman she had long admired.

"Keely," Betty said hesitantly. "I don't want to butt in where I'm not wanted or needed, but you do look like you might need someone to talk to. Is that the case?"

Keely's head fell back onto the seat cushion and she closed her eyes for a moment before responding. "I guess I'm just feeling the letdown. The past three days have seemed like a lifetime and I'm exhausted. I never did carry fatigue well." She tried to smile, but it turned out to be a travesty of that expression.

"No, Keely. It's more than that. And I think it has a lot to do with Dax Devereaux." She leaned over the vacant seat between them and took Keely's hand between her own. "Are you in love with him?"

She was tempted to lie, to answer vehemently in the negative. But what good would it do? Betty had seen them together on so many occasions she was bound to have put the pieces together to form a complete picture. She had heard Van Dorf's leading, provocative questions. The woman could think no less of her than she already did. She rolled her head toward the other woman, though she didn't raise it off the cushion. Meeting Betty's eyes openly, she said, "Yes, I'm in love with him."

"Ah," she said thoughtfully. "I thought so. May I overstep the bounds of curiosity and ask since when?"

"Since the night I arrived in Washington for the subcommittee hearing. We met that night on the airplane.

I didn't know then that he was on the committee and he didn't know that Keely Preston and Mrs. Mark Williams were one and the same."

"I see."

"I don't think you do. I—we—never intended it to happen. We both fought it. Particularly me. But—"

"You don't have to justify love, Keely." She continued to hold Keely's hand, stroking it absently as she said, "Does he know how you feel about him?"

"I don't know. I'm sure he must, but I...we had an argument of sorts. He did something—" She rubbed her forehead with her free hand. "Never mind. A relationship between us is impossible for so many reasons."

"Mainly being?" Betty asked leadingly.

Keely looked at her in surprise. "Mainly because I'm still married and I don't know if my husband is alive or dead. Your situation has changed, Betty, but mine hasn't, remember?" She instantly hated the sarcastic tone she had used. "I'm sorry," she said contritely. "Please, Betty, I'm sorry. I don't know what I'm saying."

"Don't apologize, Keely. I think I can understand the emotional conflict you're suffering. Perhaps you've suffered long enough. Maybe you should consider having Mark declared dead and marry your congressman." Had the woman said she was going to jump out of the airplane, Keely couldn't have been more stunned. After all the years they had campaigned on behalf of the MIAs, after their avowals that they would never give up hope on their men being accounted for eventually, she couldn't believe her ears had heard Betty right. "You can't mean that."

"Yes, I do," Betty said firmly.

"But—"

"Let me confess something to you, Keely. For these past years I've taken advantage of you. No, let me finish," she said when Keely was about to object. "You did our cause a world of good. You were a perfect representative for us. You are bright, beautiful, and successful. You added a credibility to us that I played to the hilt. Somehow, with you as our spokesperson, we didn't seem so much like a group of hysterical females.

"Ever since our last trip to Washington, I've felt ashamed of myself for encouraging you, albeit subtly and without malice, to waste your youth and vibrance and love on Mark's memory. I even remember cautioning you about jeopardizing your reputation with a man like Dax."

"I never did anything I didn't want to do, Betty. I felt, and do still feel, as strongly as I ever did."

"But now you've got another cause, one equally important, to rally behind. If you love this man, and I think you do or you wouldn't be wallowing in so much guilt, you should be with him, Keely. If his behavior is any indication, I think your feelings for him are reciprocated. He needs you. He is alive and he's here in the present and in the flesh. Mark is not and may never be."

Keely faced her friend angrily. "How can you say that? Less than a week ago you had no idea that Bill was ever coming home. Now he's here. You waited all those years, you were—were faithful." To her chagrin tears were rolling down her cheeks.

"Yes. And I had three children to consider. I'd also had ten beautiful years with Bill, which weren't as easy to forget as a few weeks. We had a life together. You and Mark didn't. I can't tell you what to do, Keely. I can only say that if you want to be with Dax, you should be. Don't sacrifice your happiness and his forever."

Keely was shaking her head, unaware of the tears that continued to flow. "It's too late, Betty. I don't agree with what you've said about deserting the cause I've fought for so long. I can't just drop PROOF. Others are still depending on me. Especially now that these MIAs have returned, we have new hope, perhaps channels of investigation we didn't know existed will open up. But all of that aside, Dax and I were doomed before we were begun. If ever there was a spark of love between us, it's gone now."

She looked at Betty and the older woman thought she had never seen such naked sadness and disillusionment on a face so young. "I'll get over this depression once I get home to New Orleans and back to work."

SHE DIDN'T KNOW how wrong that prediction would prove to be. She was so exhausted by all that had happened in Paris and by the ceaseless interviews she had granted during her brief layover in Washington, that when she arrived home she took her telephone off the hook and barricaded herself in her apartment, sleeping around the clock for almost twenty-four hours.

When she finally woke up, she realized that Mardi Gras week was in full swing. Finding a parking space was unheard of. Waiting for a table in a restaurant took hours. To walk down a sidewalk one had to detour around the bleachers set up along the parade routes and dodge revelers, who were generally inebriated and noisy. In her current state of mind the merrymaking was repugnant.

She called her producer, begging for several days

vacation she had accumulated. After receiving his grumbling consent, she packed her car and drove to Mississippi to visit with her parents.

They were sensitive to her dark mood and trod lightly around her. She ate well, slept as well as dreams would allow, and took long, solitary walks along the Gulf shore. A short visit to the nursing home where Mrs. Williams stayed almost negated what strength she had built up, and she came away from the institution feeling that nothing would ever be right in the world again.

When she returned to work, everyone treated her with effusive, deferential kindness. She felt like a mental patient who had just been released. She despised the patronizing tones everyone used when talking to her and the pitying looks and the false jocularity.

Nicole, who couldn't bear depression of any kind, steered clear of Keely, except for a few commiserating telephone calls. She didn't bring up the subject of Dax Devereaux. Once she mentioned that she had read of his rapidly growing popularity because of his activities concerning the returned MIAs. Keely made no comment, so Nicole took the hint and dropped the subject. Just by looking at her, anyone could tell that Keely's self-possession was eggshell thin. Nicole, like everyone else, didn't want to be the one responsible for cracking it.

After three weeks of avoidance Nicole invited herself over for dinner. "Can you believe it? I've got a Saturday night without a date. I'm coming for dinner. Make that spaghetti casserole with all the gloriously fattening cheese in it."

Keely laughed. "If there's anything I hate it's a shy guest. What else would you like?"

"That layered chocolate thing with the cream cheese and pecans."

"Anything else?" Keely inquired dryly.

"Loaves of French bread."

"Anything else?"

"No," Nicole said flippantly. "I'll bring the wine."

She did. At seven o'clock that evening Keely, jean and sweatshirt clad, answered the door to Nicole, equally sloppy, carrying a jug of red wine under each arm.

"This is going to be a blast. I'm going to eat myself into oblivion. When one doesn't have a date for Saturday night, there's only one consolation—blow your diet. Besides I heaved my guts up yesterday and couldn't hold anything down all day. I deserve a feast."

"Nothing serious or catching, I hope," Keely said, leading Nicole into the kitchen.

"I don't think so. Just one of those twenty-four-hour bugs."

"Well, just in case, don't breathe on my plate."

"Just get it ready and—" She broke off when the doorbell rang. "Damn! Who can that be? I look like hell and didn't want anyone to see me."

"I don't know who it could be," Keely said. "I didn't invite anyone else."

"Well, I'll get rid of them, whoever it is. I don't intend to share any of that delicious-smelling food."

Nicole flounced through the door and Keely was distracted by the boiling spaghetti. She didn't turn around until she heard Nicole call her name in an uncharacteristically subdued voice. "Keely, there's a man,

a soldier, to see you." Her blue eyes reflected her bewilderment.

"A soldier?" she asked on a high note and dropped
her wooden spoon onto the countertop.

Nicole nodded.

Keely went past her, drying her hands on a dish
towel as she walked into her living room. The soldier
was standing nervously, twisting his cap in his hands.
He was pale and thin and had the sallow complexion
of one who had been recently ill. His hands and feet
looked too large for his spare body. His ears seemed
abnormally large under his military haircut. He was
around thirty years old, though the lines running down
from either corner of his mouth should have belonged
to an older man.

"I'm Keely Preston Williams," she said by way of
introduction. "You wanted to see me?"

"Yes, Mrs. Williams. I'm Lieutenant Gene Cox."

The name struck her right between the eyes and she
staggered back a step or two before she clutched the
back of a chair for support. Her ears rang so loudly
that she almost didn't hear Nicole's gasp of concern.
She warded off her assistance, however, and tried to
pull herself together. "Won't you please sit down?"
she said hoarsely.

The soldier was obviously distressed that he had
brought on such a drastic reaction. Keely's face had
drained of color and her lips looked blue. He sat down,
fearing that if he didn't do as she asked, she might
fly apart altogether. Keely collapsed on the chair and
leaned forward. "Why did you come to see me?"

He glanced fleetingly toward Nicole as if seeking
her advice about talking to this deranged woman, but

at her nod he brought his honest, open eyes back to Keely's strained face. "Well, I've known about you since Paris. I was in the hospital, but we were kept informed about what was going on. I think it was the chaplain who told us about PROOF and all." He looked down at his hands, which were still twisting the cap. "Everything happened so fast, I get confused about who told me what."

"I'm sorry," Keely said gently. "I don't mean to rush you. Take your time and tell me what you came for."

"Well as I said, I knew about your work in PROOF and that you were in Paris. Excuse me, Mrs. Williams, but didn't Congressman Devereaux tell you what I told him in the hospital? I mean when he left that day after we figured out that it was probably your husband I went down with, I felt sure that he'd go straight to you and tell you."

Keely ignored Nicole's soft cry of dismay. She nodded her head. "Yes, he told me, but—"

"Well, I saw him in Washington last week. I finally got to come home five days later than everybody else. I was pretty sick," he said bashfully. "I'm sorry, I'm off the track again. I saw the congressman in Washington and asked him how you had taken the news. He said you weren't convinced that it was really your husband who was flying that chopper. 'Course I can't be certain either, but I brought something today that might clear it up for you."

He was digging in his breast pocket and Keely's heart began to thud. It couldn't be! But it was. Gene Cox was taking a medallion on a silver link chain out of his pocket. She recognized it immediately.

"The Mark Williams I went down with was wearing

this with his dog tag. Just before he—he...uh...died, he asked me to get this back to you if I ever made it out. When I got captured by the Cong, they took my dog tag and his, but they weren't interested in this, so they gave it back to me. I've kept it all this time. I didn't know if I'd ever have an opportunity to return it to you or not, but I hung on to it. I never bartered it for food or anything. I promised that GI I wouldn't." He was attacked by self-consciousness again when he extended the oxidized medallion toward Keely.

Her fingers could barely close around it, they were trembling so hard. She looked at the St. Christopher medal she had given Mark on their wedding day. Turning it over in her palm, she read the inscription she had paid extra to have engraved there: "God keep you, my husband." It was also dated. Tears flooded her eyes as she stroked her thumb over the blackened silver.

"Is it his, Keely?" Nicole asked quietly from behind her.

She only nodded. Her throat was closed to speech.

Gene Cox shifted uncomfortably on the sofa and said, "I wish I could tell you he didn't suffer, but he did. His legs were broken, and he kept vomiting bl— But he died like a hero. Even with his legs the way they were and the chopper exploding and burning debris flying, he wanted to look for the other boys. I think there were three of us besides him in that chopper. I really can't remember. I only remember that I had to fight him like hell to get him out of that clearing and under the cover of the jungle. When—when the end did come, he was peaceful-like about it, you know? He said something about better this way than to come home to you a cripple."

"He was wrong," Keely said hoarsely.

"Yes, ma'am. But I guess I know how he felt." He cleared his throat loudly again. "My—my wife's been married to another guy for three years now. She came to Washington last week to see me. I barely recognized her. And she sure as hell didn't recognize me."

Keely raised her eyes to him. "I'm sorry."

He only shrugged, made a fist, and coughed unnecessarily into it. He stood up. "Well, I hope that settles things for you anyway."

She went to him and, without reserve, hugged him tenderly. "Thank you so much," she whispered in his ear before backing away.

"I'm glad I could do it. I wish I had answers for all the others. See, sometimes we thought we were the only twenty-six guys left over there. It's spooky to think there are a hundred times that many still unaccounted for. We had no idea." He turned toward the door.

"Lieutenant Cox, I have one more question."

"Yes?"

"Did you show Congressman Devereaux the St. Christopher medal?"

"Yes."

Keely's hands clasped together at her waist. "What did he say?"

The soldier's eyes darted to Nicole again then back to Keely. "He…uh…he said it would mean more if I brought it to you myself."

Before he left, he wrote down Keely's address, promising to stay in touch with her. He volunteered his services to PROOF in any way the organization could use him.

When he closed the door behind him, she laid her forehead against the hard wood. The metal was still impressed into her palm and she squeezed it tightly.

"Come sit down," Nicole said, taking her by the shoulders and turning her away from the door. She let herself be led to the sofa and sank down on it. Nicole sat beside her, smoothing her hair and rubbing her back.

"Now you know, Keely. I'm sorry about Mark, but now you know."

"Yes."

"I know it's hard right now, but in a few days you'll feel such a sense of relief that it'll be like rebirth. You can go on with your life." She continued her soothing ministrations as she asked, "Keely, did Dax tell you about Mark in Paris?" Keely nodded. "And you didn't believe him?" Nicole's voice told of her incredulity that Keely could be so stupid.

"No!" Nicole was flung back by the impetus with which Keely leaped to her feet. "I didn't believe him," she cried, anguished.

"Why would you not believe him? For godsakes, Keely, what was wrong with you?"

"I don't know," she groaned, hiding her face in her hands. "I thought he was playing a low trick."

"Trick! Dax Devereaux doesn't have to play tricks."

"I know, I know, but I was so confused. It was too incredible, too coincidental, and I was feeling so guilty—" She floundered when she realized her slip.

"Guilty? Why?" When Keely tried to avoid her eyes, Nicole went to her and clamped her hands on either side of Keely's face. *"Why?"*

"Because we had slept together," she shouted and pushed Nicole away.

"So?" Nicole shouted back.

"So?" She rounded on her friend, aghast that she hadn't caught on yet. "So I was still married to Mark. I didn't know until *after* I had spent the night with Dax—"

"Oh, no!" Nicole threw back her head in exasperation. "Don't stand there and tell me you're going to feel guilty about betraying a man who had already been dead for twelve years!"

"But I didn't know—"

"You already said that and I'm sick of hearing it," Nicole yelled. "You can't mean that after living the life of a vestal virgin for twelve years, you're consigning yourself to another interminable purgatory. You slept with a man you love! Your husband has been dead for twelve years. Explain to me your sin."

"You don't understand," Keely said impatiently.

"You're damn right I don't. I could overlook some senseless, unbalanced person for hanging on to grief and guilt for years as some sort of security blanket. But you're an intelligent, vital, beautiful woman, and there's something pathetic and sick in your wasting your life this way. How many crowns in heaven can one person use? Huh? Well, I'm tired of you and your self-righteous self-sacrifice. Feed on your misery, culture it until it destroys you more than it already has, but count me out. I've had it."

She spun away from Keely and, after retrieving her bottles of wine from the kitchen, stormed out the front door.

Tossing on her bed, she tried to block out the visions, turn off the sounds, erase the memories, but they refused to be eradicated. Nicole's desertion had hurt. Keely had cried herself to sleep last night after feeding all the food she had prepared to the garbage disposal. She had spent Sunday morning working up a profuse sweat repotting the plants on her patio. But the work had run out and she had been cursed with hours of time in which to brood. She had never been so grateful as when the hands on her clock indicated it was late enough to go to bed.

But sleep wouldn't come. After her mind had replayed its recording of her argument with Nicole, it switched to the morning she and Dax had awakened in each other's arms.

They had decided that before they left the small hotel they would avail themselves of the bathroom that their hostess had been so proud of.

"Let me celebrate you," he had whispered as they stood facing each other in the narrow European tub.

"I never have had very good aim with one of those," she said about the hand nozzle of the shower.

"I have terrific aim."

"You sure do," she crooned and pressed herself up against his nakedness.

One black wing of an eyebrow arched over his eyes. "Do I detect a double entendre?"

"I don't know what you mean." She fluttered her eyelashes innocently.

"Like hell you don't," he growled and bit her playfully on the shoulder before he leaned down to turn on the faucets. "How do you like it? Hotter or cooler?"

"Hotter."

"One hot shower it is," he said and then they both hollered as ice-cold water sprayed on them.

"You did that on purpose," she accused when the water temperature finally adjusted and she had her stolen breath back.

"No, I didn't. I swear," he laughed as her nails raked down his chest.

When they were properly wet, they shared the soap, lathering each other until they looked like two snow-people. "You're going to wash all the skin off," she said when he had given his attention to her breasts, delicately rubbing them with soap-slickened fingers.

"Then I'll just have to move on to someplace else." His soapy fingers were only championed by his use of the nozzle spray when he meticulously rinsed every place he had washed.

"I need a shave," he mused aloud, running his hand over his jaw as he studied his reflection in the mirror over the basin. They had eventually quit the tub in favor of drying each other with fresh-smelling, fluffy towels.

"You certainly do. You look positively piratical."

"How do you think people would react to a bearded congressman?"

"Grow one sometime and see."

"I might just do that. But are you sure you want me to? It can get awfully scratchy."

"Oh, it would be understood beforehand that we wouldn't kiss or anything while you were growing it. How long does it take to grow a nice, soft beard? Several months?"

"Would you be impressed by my unusual virility

if I could do it in a couple of weeks?" His grin was smug, a modern Tom Sawyer and his Becky Thatcher.

"No," Keely said saucily and skipped out of the bathroom.

He tackled her on the other side of the door, spun her around, and backed her toward the bed until the backs of her knees caught on the edge and she collapsed. "Then I'll have to think of something else to impress you."

His mouth was like a live electric wire that had snapped in two. It danced erratically across her stomach, striking at will, shocking each place it struck, electrifying her whole body with shooting sparks.

Then it became more tame, traversing the delta of her abdomen and leaving soft, damp kisses in its path. Her thighs knew the thrilling rough scrape of his bearded cheeks. She was burning, burning, and his lips both fueled the flame and melted against it. Her fingers burrowed through his hair. She called his name over and over, though she was never sure that she spoke it aloud.

He raised himself from his knees and made a slow climb up her body. His stubbled chin abraded her skin in a way that made her shiver. He paused at her breasts. His tongue leisurely stroked the nipples while his hands admired the full round shape. When he was face-to-face with her, his body stretched over hers, powerfully declaring his need between her thighs, he asked, "Are you impressed?"

Now Keely buried her face in her pillow and screamed her torment. Would she ever forget? No, no. That night, that dawn, was the most precious day of her life. The night she had spent with Dax bore no similarity to the nights she had spent as Mark's bride. That passion had been furtive and under cover of clothing and darkness.

She and Dax had cavorted nakedly without embarrassment or shame. She knew his dark, muscled body by touch, by smell. He knew every inch of her intimately. She had never known what it was to love and be loved by a man until she had spent that night with Dax.

Acquainted now with all the pleasures he could give her and she could return, her body throbbed with desire for him. She longed for his fervent, passionate kisses as well as the tender ones. She craved to hear once more his rushing breath in her ear and the quiet love words he had chanted.

"I love you, Keely."

She could see his face as he had said that. Why hadn't she, at that moment when he spoke the words she longed to hear, thrown herself into his arms and begged never to be released?

It was too late now. She knew that the rigid, hard jaw and the blazing black eyes he had speared her with when she had accused him of lying meant that whatever love he had felt was destroyed by her doubt. Even if she called him to beg forgiveness, he would never love her again. He would always remember the time she mocked him when he tried to tell her something that would change the course of their future. Nicole was right, she was a fool.

Should she call him? Should she put down her fear and hesitation and call him, asking for his forgiveness? Yes!

She was reaching for the telephone when another thought struck her. He knew about Gene Cox bringing her the medal! What had the soldier said? *He said it would mean more if I brought it to you myself.* Dax knew, but he hadn't made an effort to contact her. He knew she was free, but he hadn't come to her seeking a reconciliation.

She was free, but he wasn't.

He was still running for the Senate. She had seen his picture with Madeline Robins in the Sunday paper. Madeline had given him a lavish welcome-home party last night after his return from Washington.

So while Keely was listening to Gene Cox's story, Dax had been partying with Madeline. While her best friend was scorning her, deserting her, he was dancing with Madeline. Laughing.

He had said he loved her. Maybe he did. But would it be the best thing for him to have her in his life right now? What would it do to his career? The name Keely Preston was too fresh on the public's mind. She would have to officially announce Mark's death soon, but people had seen her and Dax together before the MIAs returned. They would be the subjects of gossip and speculation. They weren't out from under the shadows of scandal yet.

He needed the Madeline-types in his life who could help him win his Senate seat. He didn't need Keely Preston Williams.

She felt like she might very well die without him in her life, but she knew that he certainly couldn't live with her in his.

Obligation and responsibility forced her to drag herself out of bed when her alarm went off at five. She dressed and applied her makeup mechanically. She managed to gulp down one cup of coffee before she left her house and drove to the Superdome.

The morning was warm and humid with the promise of spring. There were clouds on the horizon where the sun would soon rise, but the sky overhead was clear. She had a few minutes to ponder the deep lavender-gray sky before she heard the clatter of the helicopter blades and saw it flying over the buildings of downtown like a giant mosquito.

Joe set it down with ease. Keely locked her car and ran toward it. The terrific wind tried to tear her clothes and hair off, but she was used to that and knew that it rarely did any permanent damage.

"Good morning," she shouted over the racket as she climbed inside.

"Hi there, good-lookin'," Joe greeted her. "I brought some doughnuts this morning. Help yourself."

"Thanks," she said as she buckled her seat belt and the helicopter lifted off the ground.

The morning was routine. Her earliest report came at six fifty-five when she reported that traffic was still light and that all ramps leading onto the freeways were clear of congestion. It was proving to be a beautiful morning, so weather wasn't a consideration.

It was while she was joking with the disc jockey during her second report that she heard the loud bang that sounded like a car backfiring, then a still silence when the helicopter's motor died an instant death.

"Godamighty!" Joe cursed.

Keely spun her head around and saw that his hands were busy at the controls. She broke off midway into her sentence about an upcoming rock concert. Panic rose in her throat like scalding bile. "Joe!" she shouted, wanting him to sit back and smile and relax those frantic hands and tell her that everything was all right and under control.

"Hey, Keely, what's happened up there? Did you burst a balloon?" She heard the disc jockey's joking voice in her headpiece, but it no longer seemed real to her.

"Joe!" she screamed as the chopper began to spin crazily, like a top off its axis.

"Sit tight, Keely," he said with amazing resignation. "We're going down, baby."

CHAPTER SIXTEEN

KEELY LOOKED OUT and saw that the ground and horizon were no longer level, but tilting at an alarming slant. The blades of the helicopter were still rotating, but there was no sound from the engine. Around and around the small craft was spinning, even as the ground rushed up toward it.

"No!" she screamed. "No, please." As the chopper pitched forward she felt the seat belt biting into her abdomen, but it wasn't enough to hold her. When it let go, her head struck the bubble windshield with a sickening thud and suddenly she was fighting nausea and pain.

"Help me!' she cried, but didn't know if anyone heard or if she had even said the words out loud. "Oh, no, please. *No!*" She tried to open her eyes, but couldn't against a blinding light. Out of it an image took form.

Mark! She saw him, beaming proudly, reassuringly. He was the smiling, guileless, exuberant boy she remembered. His eyes lighted up with happy surprise at seeing her and his smile was as jovial as ever. *Mark!* her mind screamed, *you're alive.* He wasn't in pain. He wasn't a nameless skeleton in a jungle on the other side of the world. His spirit was very much alive in this sphere into which she had been hurled.

Or had she? The light was growing dimmer. His image was becoming unfocused. She wanted to speak to him, but he waved jauntily and turned his back on her. Gradually his image receded as he rushed back from where he had come. A giant drapery was being pulled closed behind him, separating them. Darkness was fast closing in and she was losing her battle with it. She longed for the warm and light place where Mark was.

But the darkness wouldn't go away. Just before it swallowed her, Keely realized with startling clarity that her heart knew a peace it hadn't known in years. In this flash of time, suspended between two worlds, she had shared, even experienced, Mark's death. Now she could lay him to rest. Seeing him living in a brilliant and shining light, she could accept his death in this world and let him go.

Peacefully, with a surrendering sigh, she let the darkness engulf her.

"EASY NOW, JUST lie back. No, Miss Preston, lie down. Everything is all right. You're in the hospital."

Strong yet gentle hands kept her shoulders anchored to the bed, though she strained to raise them. "Adjust that bandage, Patsy. She loosened it." While hands still held her, others tampered with something just above her brow. "She needs to wake up. Miss Preston, wake up. Come on. Open your eyes and say hello to us."

She struggled to obey but her eyelids felt like lead and she couldn't lift them. But the voices coming at her out of a dense fog were insistent and she kept trying until she could see a slit of light.

"Well, hello. We didn't think you were going to be a very friendly guest. Gracie gets her feelings hurt if her patients don't speak to her."

"That's right, I do. Especially if the patient is a celebrity. How do you feel?"

The nurses' white uniforms hurt her eyes. A thermometer had been poked under her tongue. Her blood pressure was being taken.

Where…when…how? The questions bounced inside her brain, jousting with the pain already there. Then she remembered the spinning helicopter and struggled against the restraining arms again.

"Joe," she croaked and didn't even recognize her voice. "Joe."

"He's fine," she was told. "He landed that helicopter on the Superdome parking lot just like he always does."

"Landed it?" The words seemed to roll around in her mouth, trying to find an exit. "But…"

"Don't worry about that now. The details will be filled in later. You were the only casualty. Now, do you think you can sip on a 7-Up without throwing it up all over that glamorous gown we've got you in?"

She shook her head no, but they brought her the cup with the bent straw anyway and she took a few obligatory sips before she fell asleep again.

The way back to complete consciousness was long and fuzzy. Confusion blurred the times she did awaken and her sleep was so heavy that she seemed never to come completely out of it. She knew she had an IV needle in the back of her hand and every time she moved it, she felt the pull of the tape.

Her parents moved in and out of her dreams until she realized that they were actually there. Her mother wept softly. Her father looked uncomfortable and awkward, but he kissed her on the forehead when she managed to smile at him in a moment of lucidity.

Once she awakened to see a man's face bending over her. It was a comical face with frizzy blond hair ringing it like a wreath.

"Hi," he said cheerfully. "Just looking at my handiwork."

She stared up at him in confusion and he must have read the question in her eyes. "Dr. Walters. Call me David. Your friend called me in when she knew you had to have your forehead stitched. I'm a plastic surgeon. You'll have a tiny scar right at your hairline, but I'm so damn good, it will hardly be visible to the naked eye."

She smiled.

"Are you feeling all right otherwise? Need anything?"

She shook her head and closed her eyes and went back to sleep.

Then, as if by magic, the cobwebs had been swept away, and when she awoke, everything was clear. Her head ached abominably, but that was understandable. A debilitating weakness made her limbs tremble, but the nurses made her get up and walk around her room before allowing her to fall dizzily back into bed. She managed to drink a whole can of apple juice and keep it down, so the nurses took the hateful needle out of her hand. It left a blue bruise.

The rest of that day she napped intermittently and her sleep was no longer heavy and drugged. By nightfall she was able to read the accounts of the near-disaster in the newspapers the nurses had saved for her. Her room was filled with flowers she hadn't been cognizant enough to appreciate before. The nurses oohed and aahed over each bouquet and hovered nearby as Keely read the cards aloud to them.

One card wasn't signed and the nurses mourned over that fact since it went with the largest and most beautiful bouquet of yellow rosebuds. Keely didn't think the unsigned card was an accident. She plucked off one of the perfect blooms and kept it on her pillow. It caught her tears as it would dewdrops.

The next morning she was able to get up, shower, dress in her own negligee, and make up her face. A small bag with her things in it had miraculously appeared in her room overnight. When asked, her mother denied knowledge of it.

Both the doctor who had first treated her at the hospital and her own physician examined her and agreed that she could receive visitors. The manager of KDIX came in and she was touched by his concern and relief that she was still among the living. He brought her cards from the rest of the staff that were generally ribald and irreverent. They made her laugh until her head ached.

Joe Collins came in later. Tears made him look watery as he leaned down and hugged her tight. "Joe, thank you," she said. After his concern about her condition had been eased, he explained what had happened.

"Something, a tiny particle of something, blocked the fuel line and the engine conked out. Luckily I stabilized the chopper and managed to land with what is called auto rotation. The blades keep rotating for a while, you see. We were almost directly over the Superdome when it happened, so..." He shrugged modestly. "I was busy trying to keep us up and at the same time I was worried as hell about you. All I could see of your face was covered with blood."

"You saved my life, Joe."

He seemed suddenly shy and embarrassed so she switched subjects. She rested after he left and the nurses persuaded her other waiting visitors to come back later.

After dinner that evening she was propped up in bed watching television when there was a timid knock on her door.

"Come in," she said. Nicole and Charles walked in. Nicole looked meek and anxious. When Keely held out her arms to her, she lunged across the room and flung herself at her friend.

"Keely, I'm so sorry. Did you do this on purpose to pay me back for the terrible way I talked to you? Oh, God, when I heard you up there screaming, I thought I'd die."

"You heard?"

"Yes, we all did," Charles said. "Remember, you were in the middle of your conversation with the DJ. I'm afraid he didn't react with the quick skill he should have and cut your mike. Your radio audience heard the whole thing."

Keely covered her mouth and closed her eyes. "I didn't realize. How awful that must have been."

"Well, it made you a heroine," Nicole said with resilience since she knew she had been forgiven.

"Are you responsible for the plastic surgeon and my bag being here and everything?"

"Charles and I."

"Thank you." The women locked hands and stared at each other with understanding.

"About the other night, Keely—"

"It's forgotten. About many things you were exactly right."

"And many things were none of my damn business too."

"Yes, they were. You're my friend."

"That I am." They were both perilously close to tears. Charles saved them an emotional scene.

"Darling, you haven't told Keely your news," he said in a bland voice.

Keely was so shocked by Charles's calling Nicole "darling" that for a moment she stared at him before turning to Nicole and asking, "What news?"

Nicole twisted around from her seat on the edge of Keely's bed to glare at him. "You just love to gloat over it, don't you?"

"Yes," he said, rocking up on his toes and smiling broadly.

"Well, I don't think it's funny. Not one damn bit."

"Would the two of you please let me in on the mystery," Keely interrupted. "What news?"

"I'm pregnant," Nicole mumbled.

Keely looked at the top of Nicole's bowed blond head as she picked at the covers of the bed. Keely's eyes then moved beyond Nicole to Charles, who was managing to look both sheepish and smug at the same time. Her gaze came back to Nicole. Had her friend just announced that she was going into a convent, she couldn't have been more stunned.

"You're *what*?"

Nicole vaulted off the bed, jarring Keely's aching head. "You heard me. Pregnant. Knocked up. With

child. Whatever the hell you want to call it and *he*—"
she pointed an accusing finger at Charles "—did it."

Keely began chuckling softly, then the laughter built
until she was convulsed with it and tears were cours-
ing down her cheeks. It made her head throb, but the
laughter felt good and she milked it for all it was worth.
The corners of Nicole's mouth quirked until she was
smiling and then she too was laughing.

"I can't believe it," Keely said, wiping the tears from
her eyes. "When did—"

"The night we went with you and—and Dax to the
Café du Monde. Charles took me home, remember? I
used every feminine wile I have and finally lured him
into bed. He got his revenge!"

Charles winked at Keely. "You're not too upset over
it, are you, Nicole?" she asked intuitively.

Nicole bent down and whispered loudly, "Who
would have thought it to look at him? Keely, he's hell
on wheels in bed."

That started Keely's laughter all over again and she
was weak by the time it subsided. Nicole had finally
met her match and neither of them looked unhappy
about it. Charles had pulled her against his chest, his
arms folding across her midriff. "Well, are you going
to let this child be born out of wedlock?"

"Oh, Keely," Nicole began on a wail and turned her
face into Charles's shoulder.

"I'll tell her, darling, since I was the one who insisted." He kissed the tip of her nose. "We were married yesterday, Keely. Of course we would have loved
to have you there, but I didn't feel it was proper for us
to wait any longer."

Keely smiled at them and tears of a new kind came

to her eyes. "I'm so happy for both of you. I couldn't be more pleased. I've always thought the two of you belonged together."

"So did I," Charles said. "*She* took some convincing."

"You have a most convincing manner," Nicole purred and turned into his embrace.

"May I at least kiss the groom?" Keely said impatiently when their kiss lengthened with no sign of letup. Charles pulled himself out of Nicole's possessive arms and bent down to kiss Keely's cheek with his usual reserve. When he straightened, he said, "I'll be out in the hall. Don't hurry, darling." Tactfully he withdrew, giving the two women some time alone.

"Nicole," Keely said, catching her friend's hands. "You love him, don't you? And the baby? You're happy about it, aren't you?"

"Keely, I'm so happy, I feel I'm about to burst. There will never be a mother more loving or attentive. Not a day will go by that this kid doesn't know he's loved. And Charles. Charles," she said wistfully, lovingly. "I was afraid to love him, afraid of his rejection. But wonder of wonders, he loves me, Keely. He truly does. For myself, not for— Well, you know. Despite all the—the other men and my reputation, he loves me."

"I knew he did. I'm glad he finally convinced you."

"So am I." She smiled the smile that melted the hearts of thousands of television viewers every night. But the classic smile faded when she looked down at Keely's wan complexion and saw the haunted, lonely expression in her eyes. Her taut body couldn't hide the tension within. "What about you, Keely? How do you intend to solve your affair of the heart?"

"I think it's been solved for me." She looked sadly at the yellow roses, then back to Nicole, who was watching her closely. "I realized when that helicopter was going down that Mark is dead. He belongs in the past. Dax is the present, could have been the future, but...I love him, Nicole. I love him more than my life. But he will never forgive me for mistrusting him."

"How do you know? Have you asked him?"

"No, of course not."

"Then why don't you? He's right outside."

Eyes that had been dulled by weariness and despair flew to Nicole's face to see if there was any deceit there. "He's...Dax is..."

"Outside. He beat the ambulance to the hospital, Keely. He was listening to you on the radio. He's not left the hospital since you got here. I've seen raving maniacs with better dispositions than his, snarling at anyone who— Keely, what do you think— Get back in that bed!"

"No." She pushed off the covers and swung her legs to the side of the bed. "I'm going to him."

"Keely, for godsakes, let me—"

"No," she said, using her last strength to shake off Nicole's helping hands. She had to go to him on her own.

Halfway to the door she stretched out her arms in an effort to keep the room from reeling, but she wasn't about to give up. She had to see Dax, to tell him....

The door was too heavy for her, so she did allow Nicole to pull it open. Her bare feet on the cold tile floor were silent as she stepped through the door and looked down the hallway.

He was sitting in a chair, his knees wide-spread,

his hands clasped between them, his head bowed. He had assumed that position the night he had told her he was on the subcommittee. Dejection was evident in the slump of his shoulders, the mussed hair, the stubbled cheeks, the rumpled clothes. He had never looked more beautiful to her. He was speaking softly to her parents, who shared a short sofa in front of his chair.

"Dax."

His head snapped up at the sound of her voice and swiveled around to look down the sterile length of the corridor to where she stood, so frail, yet so courageous.

Shakily he rose to his feet. He stumbled on a small magazine table as he took a step toward her. Then he was rushing, his long strides eating up the distance between them. His eyes, always compelling, were even more so with the shine of tears glossing them. Fiercely he gathered her to him and wrapped his arms around her as though he'd never let go.

The power of his embrace robbed her of breath, but she gave it up gladly. Her arms folded around his waist. "Keely, Keely," he repeated into her hair.

They were unaware of the spectacle they were creating in the corridor, but Nicole wasn't. To protect them she placed a hand on each of their shoulders and backed them into the room, closing the door behind them. Dax and Keely were unconscious of ever moving.

He combed through her hair with frantic fingers. Anxiously he scanned her face. Lovingly he touched her features. "I thought you were going to die. I was listening to you on the radio, loving the sound of your voice, loving you, wanting to see you. Then I heard that engine die. I've been in too many helicopters not to know what happened the instant it did. My heart stopped beating. My screams matched yours, my darling. I thought you were going to die. Oh, my God, Keely…"

"Shh," she comforted him, stroking his hair as he nuzzled his face in the hollow of her neck. "I didn't. I didn't. I'm alive. Here with you now. Shh."

Her fingertips fanned across his lashes and picked up the moisture clinging to them. "When you learned the St. Christopher medal proved Mark was dead, why didn't you come to see me, Dax?"

"Did you really want me to?"

She laid her cheek against his chest and groaned softly, "Yes, I wanted you. I cried for you, but I was afraid. After what I said to you I didn't think you'd ever want to see me again. Will you forgive me for doubting you, Dax? I'm sorry."

Now he comforted her. "I was a fool, Keely. I shouldn't have blurted out Mark's death to you then. I was just so anxious that you know." He held her head between his hands and tilted it back to look into her eyes. "When you knew that what I told you was the truth, you didn't call me." His face looked pained. "Why, Keely?"

"Because I didn't think you'd ever forgive me for not believing you. Because you still have your career and campaign to worry about. Because you don't need any problems in your life just now. Because I saw your picture with Madeline."

A smile tugged at his lips. "Is that all?"

Her own lips tried to smile, but they were trembling too much. "Because I love you and didn't want to do anything that would hurt you."

"Keely." He reached for her again and smothered

her against him. "I didn't come to you because I didn't know what you were thinking or feeling. I thought you might be grieving over Mark. I had come on too strong and too soon once before, and I didn't want to risk doing it again."

She smoothed the collar of his wrinkled shirt with her fingertips. "No. I was relieved that Mark hadn't suffered years of imprisonment and pain. When I was in the helicopter and it was going down…"

"Yes?" he prodded when she hesitated.

"Well, I said goodbye to him, Dax. He'll always be a very fond memory, but he's been dead for a long time. I've been granted a second chance. I can't afford to waste one day of living."

He kissed her then, long and hard and earnestly. When at last they pulled part, he said huskily, "You need to be in bed."

He led her back to the high bed and eased her onto it. When she was propped onto the pillows, seemingly having suffered no ill effects for having got up, he took her hand and pressed it between his. "Keely, will you marry me?"

"Do you want me to?"

"Very much."

"I'm a recent widow."

"Twelve years? Once Mark's death is officially announced, people will understand your wanting to marry again."

"Oh, my darling," she said, smoothing her hand over his rough cheek. "I'm not thinking of what people will think of me, but of jeopardizing your campaign."

He turned his head far enough to kiss her palm. "You let me worry about that. Tomorrow, with your consent, I'm calling a press conference to announce our engagement. Van Dorf will be the first one I call."

"Van Dorf! Dax, he'll—"

"He'll be here with bells on and will probably give us a glowing write-up." He chuckled.

Her eyes narrowed suspiciously. "What aren't you telling me?"

"Lie back. You're sick, remember? I'll tell you for now that Al and I have reached an understanding." He dropped a silencing kiss on her mouth. "Enough of him. Will you marry me?"

Her brows knit in worry. "Dax, the voting public still might frown on us. Our names have been bandied around for weeks."

"Keely," he whispered, leaning over her to kiss her just beneath her jaw. "I think you'll be an asset. The public will love you. They already do. And if they don't vote for me because of the woman I married, or for any other reason, I'll serve my country as a farmer and businessman. I've never meant anything more than I mean this. I'd rather have a life with you than hold any office. I'd rather have you than anything."

"Dax." His name was a sigh before she brought his head down to kiss his lips.

"Do you think you can handle the campaign trail? I mean, with your job at the radio station and all?" His nibbling lips stopped when he heard her soft laughter.

"You're always the diplomat, the politician, aren't you?" He had the grace to grin abashedly. Tangling her fingers in his hair, she shook his head. "I think loving you will be a full-time occupation."

The ebony eyes liquefied with love. "I like the sound

of that," he said roughly. Light kisses were brushed across her brows.

"Dax?"

"Hmm?"

"Madeline."

"What about her?"

"What about her?" she repeated.

He lifted his head. "Absolutely nothing, Keely. There never was, even before I met you. There certainly never will be now. She wanted it. The press wanted it. No one consulted me. I took advantage of the publicity she attracted. That was wrong, perhaps, but I'm all done with it now. If she wants to contribute to my campaign, then she'll have to do it through proper channels."

"Stay with me tonight." Her ready acceptance of his explanation was a pledge of trust, of love. She reached up and switched off the light over her bed. When he glanced cautiously toward the door, she laughed. "Anyone who tries to come in would have to get past Nicole, and I don't think that would be possible."

Even in the shadowed darkness she saw his smile. He slipped off his shoes and lay down beside her, cradling her body along the length of his. Without another word his lips found hers, fused with them, opened. His tongue glided over her teeth, past them, into the hollow of her mouth, probing, a reminder of the times he had loved her.

One hand lay along her cheek, tenderly, possessively. The other coasted down her chest to slip inside her negligee and cherish her breast. Lightly his thumb swept her nipple.

"Dax," she murmured, rolling to face him, pressing her body to his.

"Oh, God, Keely," he groaned and pushed away from her. "This isn't going to work. I've got to go."

"No," she cried, clutching his shirtfront.

"We can't make love, Keely. You've got to rest, to sleep—"

"I will, I promise, only please don't leave me."

She found herself in a swift, sudden embrace. "Never, never," he vowed. "I love you, Keely. I'll never leave you. Never."

He pressed her head against his heart and with its strong, steady beating she felt her old anxieties fading away. This was a beginning. Yesterday's heartache was gone; today was splendored; and they could still look forward to the promise of tomorrow.

* * * * *

ABOVE
AND
BEYOND

CHAPTER ONE

"YOU'RE DOING FINE, Kyla. Take quick, light breaths. That's right. Good, good. How do you feel?"

"Tired."

"I know, but hang in there. Go with the pains now and push. That's it. A little harder."

The young woman on the delivery table ground her teeth while the labor pain held her in its fierce grip. When it subsided, she forced her body to relax. Her face, though flushed and mottled, was radiant. "Can you see him yet?"

No sooner were the words out of her mouth than another pain seized her. She pushed with all her might.

"Now I can," the doctor said. "Give me one more push…there…here we are. All right!" he exclaimed when the new life slipped into his waiting hands.

"What is it?"

"A boy. Beautiful. Heavy son of a gun, too."

"And he's got great lungs," the obstetric nurse said, beaming down on Kyla.

"A boy," she murmured, pleased. She let the blessed lethargy steal over her and sank back onto the table. "Let me see him. Is he all right?"

"He's perfect," the doctor reassured her as he held up the squirming, crying baby boy where his mother could see him.

Tears stung Kyla's eyes when she saw her son for the first time. "Aaron. That's what we're naming him. Aaron Powers Stroud." For a moment she was allowed the privilege of holding him on her chest. Emotion welled inside her.

"He's a boy his daddy can be proud of," the nurse said. She lifted the baby from Kyla's weak arms, wrapped him in a soft blanket and carried him across the room to be weighed. The doctor was attending Kyla, though it had been an easy, routine birth.

"How soon before you can notify your husband?" the doctor asked.

"My parents are standing by outside. Dad's promised to send Richard a telegram."

"He's nine pounds three ounces," the nurse called out from across the room.

The obstetrician peeled off his gloves and took Kyla's limp hand. "I'll go out now and break the news so he can get that telegram on its way. Where did you say Richard was stationed?"

"Cairo," Kyla replied absently. She was watching Aaron kick angrily as he was footprinted. He was beautiful. Richard would be so proud of him.

CONSIDERING THAT AARON had been born at dusk, she spent a reasonably peaceful night. They brought him to her twice during the night, though her milk hadn't started and he wasn't hungry yet. The pleasure of holding his warm little body against hers was immense. They communicated on a level that was unlike any other she had experienced.

She studied him, turning over his tiny hands and examining his palms when she could pry open the fingers he stubbornly kept clenched in a fist. Each toe, each fine strand of hair on his head, his ears, were investigated and found to be perfect.

"Your daddy and I love you very much," she whispered drowsily as she relinquished him to a nurse.

Hospital sounds—squeaky laundry carts, rattling breakfast trays, clanking equipment dollies—roused her early. She was in the middle of a huge yawn and a luxuriant stretch when her parents entered her private room.

"Good morning," she said happily. "I'm surprised you're here instead of at the nursery window with your noses pressed against the glass. But then they don't open the curtain—" She broke off when she noted their haggard expressions. "Is something wrong?"

Clif and Meg Powers glanced at each other. Meg gripped the handle of her purse so tightly that her knuckles turned white. Clif looked as though he'd just swallowed bad-tasting medicine.

"Mom? Dad? What's happened? Oh, my God! The baby? Aaron? There's something wrong with Aaron?" Kyla threw off the covers with flailing arms and pumping legs, unmindful of the pinching soreness between her thighs, intent only on racing down the hospital corridor to the nursery.

Meg Powers rushed to her daughter's bedside and restrained her. "No. The baby's fine. He's fine. I promise."

Kyla's eyes wildly searched those of her parents. "Then what's wrong?" She was on the verge of panic and her voice was shrill. Her parents rarely got ruffled. For them to be so obviously upset was cause for alarm.

"Sweetheart," Clif Powers said softly, laying a hand

on her arm, "there's some distressing news this morning." He silently consulted his wife once more before saying, "The American embassy in Cairo was bombed early this morning."

A violent shudder shimmied up through Kyla's stomach and chest. Her mouth went dry. Her eyes forgot how to blink. Her heart thudded to a halt before sluggishly beginning to beat again. Then, gradually gaining momentum as she assimilated what her father had said, it accelerated to a frightening pace.

"Richard?" she asked on a hoarse croak.

"We don't know."

"Tell me!"

"We don't know," her father insisted. "Everything is in chaos, just like the time this happened in Beirut. There's been no official word."

"Turn on the television."

"Kyla, I don't think you should—"

Heedless of her father's warning, she snatched the remote control from the bedside table and switched on the television set that was mounted on the wall opposite the bed.

"...extent of the destruction at this point is undetermined. The President is calling this terrorist bombing an outrage, an insult to the peacekeeping nations of the world. Prime Minister—"

She changed channels, frantically punching the buttons on the remote control with trembling fingers.

"...costly, though it will probably be hours, even days before the death toll is officially released. Marine units have been mobilized and, along with Egyptian troops, are clearing the rubble looking for survivors."

The camera work on the videotape was substandard and testified to the pandemonium surrounding the ruins of what had been the building that housed the American embassy. The shots were jerky and out of focus, random and unedited. "Taking credit for this abomination is a terrorist group calling itself—"

Kyla changed channels again. It was more of the same. When the video camera swept the area and she saw the bodies that had already been recovered neatly lined up on the ground, she threw down the remote control device and covered her face with her hands.

"Richard, Richard!"

"Darling, don't give up hope. They think there are survivors." But Meg's soothing words fell on deaf ears. She clutched her weeping daughter's body hard against hers.

"It happened at dawn Cairo time," Clif said. "We were notified just as we were getting up this morning. There's nothing we can do at this point but wait. Sooner or later, we're bound to get word of Richard."

It came three days later, delivered by a Marine officer who rang the doorbell of the Powers's house. Kyla realized the moment she saw the official car pull up to the curb that subconsciously she had been waiting for it. She waved off her father and went to answer the door alone.

"Mrs. Stroud?"

"Yes."

"I'm Captain Hawkins and it is my duty to inform you..."

"BUT, DARLING, THAT'S WONDERFUL!" Kyla had exclaimed. "Why are you so downcast? I thought you'd be jubilant."

"Well, hell, Kyla, I don't want to go off to Egypt while you're pregnant," Richard had said.

She touched his hair. "I'll admit I don't like it for that reason. But this is an honor. Not every Marine is selected for guard duty at an embassy. They chose you because you're the best. I'm very proud."

"But I don't have to do it. I could apply—"

"This is a chance of a lifetime, Richard. Do you think I could live with myself if you turned down this honor on account of me?"

"But nothing's more important than you and the baby."

"And we'll always be here." She hugged him. "This will be your last tour and it's a fabulous opportunity that will only come around once. Now you're going and that's final."

"I can't leave you alone."

"I'll live with Mom and Dad while you're away. This is their first grandbaby and they'll drive me crazy calling and checking on me. I might just as well make it easy on us all and move in with them."

He framed her face between his hands. "You're terrific, you know that?"

"Does that mean I don't have to worry about you with those mysterious Eastern women?"

He had pretended to ponder it. "Do you know how to belly dance?"

She had socked him in the tummy. "That would be a sight to see, with the belly I'm going to have soon."

"Kyla." His voice was tender as he threaded his fingers through her hair. "Are you positive you want me to do this?"

"Positive."

That conversation, which had taken place seven months earlier, played through Kyla's mind as she stared at the flag-draped casket. The soulful notes of taps were snatched from the lone trumpet by an unkind winter wind and scattered over the cemetery. The pallbearers, all Marines, stood rigidly at attention, resplendent in their dress uniforms.

Richard was being interred beside his parents, who had died within a year of each other before Kyla ever met him. "I was all alone in the world before I met you," he had told her once.

"So was I."

"You have your parents," he had reminded her, perplexed.

"But I've never belonged to anyone, really *belonged,* the way I do to you."

Because they had loved each other so much, he had then understood.

His body had been shipped home in a sealed casket that she had been advised not to open. She didn't have to ask why. All that was left of the building in Cairo was a dusty pile of twisted stone and steel. Since the bomb had exploded early in the morning, most of the diplomatic corps and clerks had yet to arrive for work. Those who, like Richard and the other military personnel, had had apartments in the attached building, had been the victims.

A friend of Clif Powers had offered to fly the family to Kansas for the burial. Kyla could only be away from Aaron for several hours at a time because of his feeding schedule.

She flinched when she was handed the American flag, which had been removed from the coffin and ceremonially folded. The casket looked naked without it. Irrationally she wondered if Richard were cold.

Oh, God! she thought, her mind silently screaming. *I have to leave him here.* How would she be able to? How could she turn and walk away and leave that fresh grave like an obscene, open wound in the ground? How could she get into that private plane and be whisked back to Texas as though she were deserting Richard in this stark, barren landscape that she suddenly hated with a passion?

The wind whistled with a keening sound.

She would and she could because she had no choice. This part of Richard was dead. But a living part of him was waiting for her at home. Aaron.

As the minister recited the closing prayer, Kyla offered one of her own. "I'll keep you alive, Richard. I swear it. You'll always be alive in my heart. I love you. I love you. You'll always be alive for Aaron and me because I'll keep you alive."

HE WAS COCOONED inside a cotton ball. Once in a while the world would intrude on his cloudlike confinement and these were unwelcome interruptions. All sounds were clamorous. The slightest movement was like an earthquake to his system. Light from any source was painful. He wanted no part of anything outside the peacefulness of oblivion.

But the intrusions became more frequent. Compelled by a force he didn't understand, finding handholds and footholds in sound and feeling, clinging precariously to every sensation that hinted he was still alive, he slowly climbed upward, out of that safe white mist to greet the terrifying unknown.

He was lying on his back. He was breathing. His heart was beating. He wasn't certain of anything else.

"Can you hear me?"

He tried to turn his head in the direction of the soft voice, but splinters of pain crisscrossed inside his skull like ricocheting bullets.

"Are you awake? Can you answer me? Are you in pain?"

It took some doing, but he managed to coax his tongue to breach his lips. He tried to wet them, but the inside of his mouth was as dry and furry as wool. His face felt odd and he didn't think he could move his head even if the pain hadn't been severe. Tentatively he tried to raise his right hand.

"No, no, just lie still. You have an IV in this arm."

He struggled valiantly and finally managed to pry his eyes open to slits. His lashes, forming a screen across his field of vision, were magnified. He could almost count them individually. Finally they lifted a trifle more. An image wavered in front of him like a hovering angel. A white uniform. A woman. A cap. A nurse?

"Hello. How do you feel?"

Stupid question, lady.

"Where…" He didn't recognize the croaking sound as his own voice.

"You're in a military hospital in West Germany."

West Germany? West Germany? He must have been drunker than he thought last night. This was a helluva dream.

"We've been worried about you. You've been in a coma for three weeks."

A coma? For three weeks? Impossible. Last night

he'd gone out with that colonel's daughter and they'd hit every night spot in Cairo. Why the hell was this dream angel telling him he'd been in a coma in where?... West Germany?

He tried to take in more of his surroundings. The room looked strange. His vision was blurred. Something—

"Don't become distressed if your vision is fuzzy. Your left eye is bandaged," the nurse said kindly. "Lie still now while I go get the doctor. He'll want to know that you're awake."

He didn't hear her leave. One instant she was there, the next she had vanished. Maybe he had imagined her. Dreams can be bizarre.

The walls seemed to sway sickeningly. The ceiling swelled and then receded. It was never still. The light from the single lamp hurt his eyes...eye.

She had said his left eye was bandaged. Why? Disregarding her caution, he raised his right hand again. It was a Herculean effort. The tape holding the IV needles in place pulled against the hairs on his arm. It seemed to take forever for his hand to reach his head and when it did, he knew the first stirrings of panic.

My whole damn head is covered with bandages! He raised his head off the pillow as far as he could, which was only an inch or two, and glanced down at his body.

The scream that echoed through the hall seconds later came straight out of the bowels of Hell and set the nurse and doctor flying down the corridor and into the room.

"I'll hold him down while you give him a shot," the doctor barked. "He'll tear up everything we've done so far if he keeps thrashing that way."

The patient felt the sting of a needle in his right thigh and cried out in indignation and frustration over his inability to speak, to move, to fight.

Then darkness closed in around him again. Soothing hands lowered him back to the pillow. By the time he reached it, velvet oblivion had claimed him again.

HE DRIFTED IN and out for days...weeks? He had no point of reference with which to measure time. He began to know when IV bottles were changed, when his blood pressure was being taken, when the tubes and catheters entering or exiting his body were monitored. Once he recognized the nurse. Once he recognized the doctor's voice. But they moved around him like ghosts, solicitous specters in a soft misty dream.

Gradually he began to stay awake for longer periods of time. He came to know the room, to know the machines that blipped and beeped out his vital signs. He was increasingly aware of his physical condition. And he knew it was serious.

He was awake when the doctor came through the door, studying a chart in a metal file. "Well, hello," the doctor said when he saw his patient staring up at him. He went through a routine checkup, then leaned against the side of the bed. "Are you aware that you're in a hospital and pretty banged up?"

"Was... I...in an accident?"

"No, Sergeant Rule. The American embassy in Cairo was bombed over a month ago. You were one of the few who survived the blast. After you were dug out of the rubble you were flown here. When you're well enough, you'll be shipped home."

"What's...wrong with me?"

A flicker of a smile touched the doctor's mouth. "It would be easier to say what's right." He rubbed his chin. "Want it straight?"

An almost imperceptible nod encouraged him to proceed in a blunt, no-nonsense manner. "The left side of your body was crushed by a falling concrete wall. Nearly every damn bone you've got on that side was broken, if not mangled. We've set what we could. The rest," he paused to draw in a deep breath, "well that will take some doing by the specialists back home. You're in for a long haul, my friend. I would say eight months at least, though twice that long would be a more accurate guess. Several operations. Months of physical therapy."

The misery reflected on the bandaged face was almost too poignant to witness, even for the doctor who had earned his stripes on the battlefields of Vietnam.

"Will I...be...?"

"Your prognosis at this point is anybody's guess. A lot of it will be up to you. Sheer gut determination. How badly do you want to walk again?"

"I want to run," the Marine said grimly.

The doctor came close to laughing. "Good. But for right now, your job is to get stronger so we can begin patching you up."

The doctor patted him lightly on the right shoulder and turned to go. "Doc?" The medical man turned at the hoarse sound. "My eye?"

The doctor looked down at his patient sympathetically. "I'm sorry, Sergeant Rule. We couldn't save it."

The doctor's stride was brisk and businesslike as he strode from the room, and belied the tight lump in his throat. The most eloquent sign of despair he'd ever seen was that single tear trickling down a gaunt, darkly bewhiskered cheek.

GEORGE RULE WAS allowed to see his son the next day. He came to the bedside and clasped Trevor's right hand. Slowly he lowered himself into a nearby chair. Trevor never remembered seeing his father cry, not even when his mother had died several years earlier. Now, the attorney from Philadelphia, who struck terror in the heart of any lying witness, wept bitterly.

"I must look worse than I thought," Trevor said with a trace of wry humor. "Shocked?"

The elder Rule pulled himself together. He'd been cautioned by the medical staff to appear optimistic. "No, I'm not shocked. I beat you here by several hours and saw you when you first arrived. It might not feel like it, but you've come a long way since then."

"Then I must have been bad because I feel like hell now."

"They would only let me see you once a day while you were in the coma. Then since you came out of it, they wouldn't let me see you at all. You're going to be fine, son, fine. I've already been talking to doctors in the States, orthopedic surgeons who—"

"Do something for me, Dad."

"Anything, anything."

The last time Trevor had seen his father they hadn't been on very good terms. If Trevor hadn't been so preoccupied with other thoughts now, he would have noted his father's drastic change of attitude toward him.

"Check the casualty list. See if Sergeant Richard Stroud made it."

"Son, you shouldn't be worrying—"

"Will you do it?" Trevor groaned, already physically taxed by his father's visit.

"Yes, of course I will," George rushed to say when he saw his son's anxiety. "Stroud, you say?"

"Yes. Richard Stroud."

"Friend of yours?"

"Yes. And I hope to God he didn't die. If he died, it's my fault."

"How could it be your fault, Trevor?"

"Because the last thing I remember is falling asleep in his bunk."

"PSST! STROUD? YOU AWAKE, buddy?"

"I am now," came the grumbled reply. "Jeez, Smooch, it's three o'clock. Are you drunk?"

"How 'bout a drink?"

Richard Stroud sat up in his bunk and shook off sleep. "Must have been a helluva weekend pass."

"'s wonderful. Ever had an orgasm?"

Stroud laughed. "You're drunk all right. Here, let me help you with your pants."

"An orgasm, an orgasm. I think I had three las' night. Or was it four?"

"Four? That's a record even for you, isn't it?"

A wobbly finger was pointed at the end of Stroud's nose. "Now shee, Schtroud. You're always thinkin' the worscht of me. I was talking about the *drink*. An Orgasm. Has vodka and liqueur and... Are my pants off yet?"

"They will be if you'll lift your feet up."

"Oops!" Trevor Rule fell over onto Stroud's bunk, dragging the other man with him. "Do you know Becky?" he asked with a goosey smile.

"I thought her name was Brenda," Stroud said, disentangling their limbs.

"Oh, yeah. Come to think of it, I think it is Brenda, I think. Great legs." He winked lewdly as Stroud helped him with his shirt. "Strong thighs. Know what I mean?"

Stroud chuckled and shook his head. "Yeah, I know what you mean. And I don't think Colonel Daniels would appreciate you talking about his daughter's strong thighs."

"I think I love her." Trevor said the words with the seriousness only a drunk can conjure. The avowal was punctuated with a moist belch.

"Sure you do. Last week you loved the brunette secretary on the third floor. And the week before that it was the blond AP reporter. Now come on, Smooch, let's get you to your own bunk."

He put his arms under Trevor's and tried to heave him up, but the other man was deadweight and only grinned up at him sappily. "I've got a better idea," Stroud said when Trevor couldn't be budged. "Why don't you just stay in my bunk tonight?"

For an answer, Trevor fell backward onto the pillow. Stroud felt his way across the dark room to Trevor's bunk. He settled down to go back to sleep.

"Nighty-night."

He raised his head to see Trevor waggling his fingers at him like a dimwit. Laughing, Stroud said, "Nighty-night."

Before either of them woke up, the terrorists struck.

TREVOR'S RECOVERY WAS harder than he anticipated—and he had anticipated that it would be a living hell.

He was in the hospital in West Germany for another month before he was transported home. The expert doctors who examined him went away grimly shaking their heads. The left side of his body was a mess.

"Fix it," Trevor said tersely. "Do what you can. I'll do the rest. But you can bank on this. I'll walk out of here."

He had had nurses read him newspaper accounts of the embassy bombing. He went through stages of disbelief, then despair, then anger. The anger was healthy. It gave him the strength he needed to fight the pain, to overcome the trauma of one operation after another, to withstand the grueling hours of physical therapy.

Once his medical discharge was official, he let his Marine haircut grow out long. He had told the nurse who came in to shave him every morning to leave his mustache. He refused to be fitted with a prosthesis for his eye.

"I think it looks...dashing," was the opinion of one nurse. There were several clustered around his bed as a doctor fitted him with a black eye patch. Half the nursing staff was in love with him. His extensive injuries hadn't detracted from his brawny build. Greatly admired and discussed at the nurses' station were his ruggedly handsome face, long limbs, wide chest and narrow hips.

"It goes with your wavy black hair."

"When you leave here, you'll have to fight the women off with a stick."

"With my cane, you mean," Trevor remarked, studying the eye patch in the hand mirror someone had passed to him.

"Don't give up yet," the doctor said encouragingly. "We've only just started."

He knew of seasonal changes only by the landscape through his hospital room window. The days bled into each other. He kept track of time by keeping a calendar on his bedside table and jotting down at least one entry on it each day.

One afternoon an orderly, who occasionally came in to play poker with him after his shift, dumped a duffel bag onto the chair near the bed.

"What's that?"

"All the stuff they could salvage from your room in Cairo," the orderly told him. "Your dad thought you might want to sift through it and see if there was anything worth saving."

There wasn't. But one thing caught his attention. "Hand me that metal box please."

It was an unremarkable green square box with a hinged top. The combination lock had only one number. Miraculously he remembered it. He turned the lock and, when it came open, raised the lid.

"What's all that?" The orderly was peering at the contents over Trevor's shoulder. "Looks like a pile of letters."

Trevor felt a constriction in his chest. It squeezed his throat as well, so much that he could barely say, "That's exactly what it is."

He hadn't remembered them till now, but suddenly he recalled that afternoon with stark clarity.

"Hey, Smooch?"

"Hiya, Stroud. What can I do for you?"

"You know that metal box you keep your poker stakes in?"

"What about it?"

"Would you mind if I put these in there for safekeeping?" Embarrassed, Stroud held up a stack of letters, bound with a rubber band.

"Hmm. Are those from that wife who keeps you as chaste as a monk?"

"Yeah," he admitted bashfully.

"I didn't think she could write."

"Huh?"

"I didn't know angels did such mundane things," Trevor teased, poking his friend in the ribs.

"Not you, too, please. The guys are ribbing me about saving her letters, but I like to read them several times."

"Mushy?" Trevor's green eyes twinkled mischievously.

"Not really. Just personal. What about the box?"

"Okay, sure, lock them away. All you have to do to open it is turn the lock to four."

"Four? Thanks, Smooch."

He caught Stroud's arm as he turned away. "Sure they're not mushy?"

Stroud grinned. "Well, a little mushy."

They had gone out for a beer and that was the last Trevor had thought of Stroud's letters from his wife. Until now.

He slammed the lid down, feeling as guilty as if he had watched them making love through their bedroom window. "Throw the rest of that junk away," he said irritably.

"You keepin' the box with the letters?" the orderly asked.

"Yeah, I'm keeping it."

He didn't know why he did. It probably had some-

thing to do with his guilt over being alive when Stroud
had died while sleeping in his bunk. He told himself a
million times through that afternoon's hand and arm
exercises that he wasn't going to violate a dead man's
privacy by reading letters from his wife.

But when night fell, when the hall was emptied of
visitors, when the last of the medication had been dis-
pensed, when the nurses had taken up their posts at
their station, Trevor lifted the box from the bedside
table and set it on his chest.

He was lonely. It was dark. He had slept alone for
more nights than he cared to count. It had come as a
tremendous relief to him to feel his body respond every
time the orderly sneaked him the monthly issues of
Playboy and *Penthouse*. That part of him wasn't impaired.

He needed a woman.

It wasn't that he couldn't have one. He knew that if
he gave any of several nurses a certain look, they would
have been more than willing to accommodate him.

But he had had about all the melodrama in his life
that he could handle. Hospital gossip being what it was,
it would be foolhardy to become romantically entangled, especially when what he wanted and needed had
little or nothing to do with romance.

Yet he yearned for a woman's touch. A woman's
voice. There was no satisfaction to be derived from
looking through the magazines on this night like so
many others. Those women, with their voluptuous bodies and abundant hair and affected smiles were as two-
dimensional as the slick pages they were printed on.

The composer of the letters was real.

The lid to the metal box opened without a sound,

but the paper rustled when he touched the letters. He yanked his hand back. Then, cursing himself for a fool, he picked up the letter on the top of the stack.

There were twenty-seven in all. He sorted them and put them in chronological order. When all the busy-work—designed to delay the commission of what he supposed was a grievous sin—was finished, he opened the first envelope, took out the plain pastel sheet, and began to read.

CHAPTER TWO

Sept. 7
My darling Richard,
It's only been weeks, but it seems like years since you left. Missing you has become a sickness. Instead of getting better each day, I grow worse. My imagination plays cruel tricks. I often think I see you, especially in a crowd. My heart begins to beat fast with excitement. Then I go through the wrenching realization that someone only reminded me of you....

Sept. 15
Dearest Richard,
I dreamed about you last night and woke up crying....

Sept. 16
My darling,
Forgive me yesterday's letter. I was blue....

Oct. 2
Dearest Richard,
I felt the baby move today! Oh, darling, I can't tell you what a thrilling experience that was. At first it was only a fluttering. I held my breath,

standing very still. Then he (I know it's a boy) moved again, much stronger. I laughed. I cried. Mom and Dad came running. They couldn't feel the movements because they are slight, but somehow I know you could. If you were here, touching me, I know you could. I love you. So much.

Oct. 25

…and your excursion to the pyramids sounds wonderful. I'm jealous. Mom and I went to NorthPark yesterday and did some shopping. If anything, the traffic in Dallas is getting worse. I was so tired by the time we got home, I could barely climb the stairs and Dad brought me supper on a tray. But we had a productive day. I won't have to buy clothes for the baby until he's six!

We all laughed over your story about the consul's wife. Does she really dress that way? And about your friend Smooch, STAY AWAY FROM HIM! He doesn't sound like a very good influence on a married man with a pregnant wife….

Thanksgiving Day

…and I want you here so badly. I went to a movie with Babs last night. I should have know better. It was sexy, steamy actually. And now I want you! I'm climbing the walls. For shame! Nice pregnant ladies aren't supposed to feel like sex kittens, are they? But it's cold and rainy and I think, given the chance, I could even lure you away from the football games on television today.

Dec. 21

My love,

I got your letter yesterday and laughed out loud.
So you want me to stay away from Babs? You've
got a deal if you'll end your friendship with
Smooch. He sounds like the kind of man I detest. Thinks he's God's gift to women, doesn't
he? Even though you say he's as handsome as the
devil, I know I wouldn't like him....

Dec. 24

My dearest,

The days are short, but they seem endless. My
spirits are down. I wish I could have slept through
Christmas. Everywhere I look people are celebrating, smiling, sharing the season with those
they love. I feel like an alien in a world made up
of couples only. Where are you? I can tell Mom
and Dad are worried about me because I've been
so depressed. They've done their best to cheer
me, but I miss you so terribly that nothing they
do works. The packages you sent are under the
tree. Dad splurged and got a Noble fir this year,
my favorite. I hope you received your presents in
time. I would trade all the presents I've ever gotten and will get on future Christmases for one of
your kisses. One of those long, slow kisses that
fulfills and tantalizes. Oh, Richard, I love you.
Merry Christmas, darling.

Jan. 11

...but I'm much better now that the holidays are
over and we've passed the halfway point of your
year away.

It grows increasingly uncomfortable to sleep.
The baby is going to be a fullback, you'll be glad
to know. Or maybe a placekicker. But in any
event, in about twenty-two years the Cowboys
will be recruiting him for sure! By the way, what
do you think of Aaron as a name? If it's a boy, of
course. Which it had better be since I've come
up empty on girls' names so far.

You would go wild for my breasts. They're
huge! Unfortunately the rest of me matches them.
I didn't realize the baby would make such a drastic change in them. Even the nipples have grown
larger. I'm preparing them to breast-feed. (That
naughty Babs says she wishes she had that good
an excuse. She's so bad!) I wish you were here
to help out on the project. (Come to think of it,
I'm pretty bad myself.)

But I can't think of anything more wonderful
than nursing our baby... Aaron....

Jan. 25

...and it was the most horrible dream I've ever
had. I woke up sweating. I won't eat any more
chili before the baby comes!

Was Smooch along on that weekend trip to
Alexandria you wrote me about? You didn't
mention him and I think that was an intentional
oversight. If you have done something indiscreet,
if you have a real lech for a belly dancer, don't
confess it to me. I feel like a water buffalo and
cried yesterday because I was so fat...at the same
time I was stuffing down a banana split that Babs
assured me would cheer me up. (Three scoops of

chocolate almond!) Sometimes I despair that I'll never see you again, Richard. Will you ever hold me? Will I ever feel you inside me again? Sometimes I think you aren't real, that you're someone wonderful that I dreamed up. I need you, darling. I need to know that you love me. As I love you... with all my heart....

"You're being released next week?"

Trevor turned away from the window. "Yeah. Finally."

"That's great, son," George Rule said earnestly. "You look as good as new."

"Not quite."

There was no bitterness in Trevor's tone. Over the past thirteen months, he had come to realize how fortunate he'd been. His strolls through the wards of the hospital had convinced him of that. He could have been confined to a wheelchair for the rest of his life, like so many he saw in physical therapy.

He could walk, with a slight limp, but he could walk. He had even gotten accustomed to the eye patch, so that he wasn't bumping into furniture any longer. It was true what was said about the body's ability to compensate for the loss of one of its members. He could barely remember what it was like to have both eyes.

"They want me to come back every week on an outpatient basis for physical therapy, but I said no," he told his father. "I think this is as good as I'll get. I can do the exercises myself."

"What do you plan to do now?" George Rule asked his son hesitantly.

Trevor's choice of career had been a bone of contention since his graduation from Harvard. His joining the Marines had been an act of rebellion against his father, who had wanted Trevor to become a lawyer like himself and had refused to listen to his son's own plans.

"What I always planned to do, Dad. Be a builder."

"I see." Rule's disappointment was apparent, but he squelched it. He had almost lost his son. Trevor's close brush with death had scared the indomitable George Rule. He didn't want to lose Trevor in another way now. He had no doubt that he would if he tried to direct Trevor's future. "Where? How do you plan to start?"

"Texas."

"Texas!" It might just as well have been another planet.

Trevor laughed. "You've heard of the building boom in the Sunbelt states. That's where the action is now. There's still land waiting to be developed. I've chosen a small town near Dallas. Chandler. It's a booming community and I intend to capitalize on its growth."

"You'll need a bankroll."

"I've got back pay from the Marines coming."

"That's hardly enough to go into business."

Trevor looked at his father steadily. "How much would a law degree from Harvard have cost you, Dad?"

George Rule nodded. "You've got it." He stuck out his hand and Trevor gripped it firmly and shook it.

"Thanks."

For the first time in Trevor's memory, he was embraced by his father and hugged tight.

Later that night, after he had packed his things, Trevor stretched out on the hospital bed for the last time. But he was too excited to sleep. He had been given a second chance at life. His first shot at it hadn't amounted to much. But this new one, which would start tomorrow, would. No more angry wasted years. Now he had a mission.

He reached for the green metal box. It was never far from his hand. The letters were worn at the creases, frayed around the edges. He knew all twenty-seven letters by heart. But he derived pleasure from looking at the swirls and curves of her feminine handwriting. He selected one, and it wasn't a random choice.

...end your friendship with Smooch. He sounds like the kind of man I detest. Thinks he's God's gift to women, doesn't he? Even though you say he's as handsome as the devil, I know I wouldn't like him....

Trevor folded the letter carefully and replaced it in its envelope. He didn't go to sleep for a long time.

SHE WAS BEAUTIFUL.

He had seen her many times in the past few weeks. But never this close. Never for this long. It was a luxury to be able to study her.

In a thousand years he would never be able to describe the color of her hair. "Blond" wasn't sufficient because of those burnished streaks threaded through it. But she wasn't a true redhead. "Strawberry blond" connoted sweetness to the point of insipidity. And there was nothing insipid about Kyla Stroud. She radiated energy and light like a sunbeam.

That indescribable hair was pulled back into a casual ponytail. The ends of it were curly, as were the strands that had escaped it to frame her face.

And what a face. Heart-shaped. With a dainty chin. Brows that arched over wide-set eyes. A smooth, high, intelligent forehead. A complexion that made his mouth water for a taste. Cheeks naturally tinted the color of ripe peaches.

She had on casual tan slacks, a striped cotton shirt with the sleeves rolled up to her elbows and a cardigan tied around her neck. Her figure was neat and trim. Perfectly proportioned.

She was…well…perfect.

He liked the way she talked to the child, as though he was understanding every word she said. And perhaps he was, because when she smiled, so did the robust toddler. They seemed impervious to the heavy foot traffic in the mall, unaffected by the Saturday afternoon crowd that was patronizing the shops and food stands.

It was at one of those concessions that she had bought the ice-cream cone. With miraculous agility she had held the ice-cream cone in one hand while she pushed the baby stroller through the crowd to a bench. She had assisted the little boy, though he hadn't needed much encouragement to climb out.

Now, they were seated on a bench and the child was destroying the ice-cream cone while his mother alternately laughed with delight and admonished him for making such a pig of himself. Her right hand governed the cone, while her left deftly wielded a napkin.

When the cone and napkin had both been mutilated to a soggy mess, she spoke sternly to the child, then left the bench to throw the refuse away in the nearest trash can.

The instant her back was turned, the toddler slid off the bench and hit the floor of the mall running. As fast as his short, sturdy legs could carry him, he headed for the sparkling fountain that gushed toward the sky-lit ceiling. Surrounding the fountain was a pool about two feet deep.

Reflexively Trevor pushed himself away from the wall where he had been indolently propped on one shoulder while he watched them. He risked taking his eyes off the child for a few seconds to see Kyla turn away from the trash can and notice that the boy was gone. Even from that distance he read in her expression the instantaneous panic only a mother whose child is missing can register.

Without thinking, Trevor began weaving his way through the crowd toward the fountain. The boy was now climbing onto the low wall surrounding it and reaching toward the bubbling water.

"Oh, God," Trevor murmured as he pushed aside a man with a pipe. He increased the length of his stride and picked up his pace. But he wasn't fast enough. He watched the child go over the wall and into the water.

Several bystanders noticed, but Trevor was the first to reach the fountain. He swung his right leg over the wall, stepped into the pool, caught the boy under the arms and scooped him out of the water.

"Aaron!" Kyla was frantically pushing her way through the crowd.

Aaron, sputtering water, looked curiously at the man holding him. With apparent approval of his rescuer, the boy smiled, revealing two neat rows of baby teeth, and said something that could have been "water."

Sloshing water, Trevor stepped out of the fountain. The bystanders fanned out to give him room.

"Is he all right?"

"What happened?"

"Where's his mother?"

"Wasn't anybody watching him?"

"Some parents just let their kids run wild."

"Excuse me, excuse me." Kyla finally elbowed her way through the gathering onlookers. "Aaron, Aaron!" She lifted her son out of Trevor's arms and clutched him to her chest, squeezing hard, regardless of his wet clothes. "Oh, my baby. Are you okay? You scared Mommy. Oh, God."

The moment Aaron sensed his mother's distress, his adventure turned into a trauma. His lower lip began to tremble, his eyes filled with tears and his face crumpled. Opening his mouth wide, he began to wail.

"He's hurt! Is he hurt?" Kyla said frantically.

"Come on, let's move over here. Please, folks, let us through. He's okay, just scared."

Kyla was vaguely aware of a large man beside her. She felt his hand between her shoulder blades, propelling her through the crowd toward an out-of-the-way bench. She was so busy examining Aaron for possible injuries that the man went unnoticed until she was seated on the bench. Finally, hugging a crying Aaron to her, she looked up at him.

It took a long time for her eyes to reach his face, so her first impression of him was that he was very tall. She wasn't quite prepared for the curving mustache, much less the black patch over his left eye, and caught her gasp just in time. "Thank you."

The large man sat down next to her. "I think he's all right. Your reaction frightened him."

She whipped her head around, showing him that her chin wasn't only dainty. It could be stubborn when she was challenged. When she saw that he wasn't being critical, she smiled with chagrin. "I guess you're right. I overreacted."

Aaron's crying was beginning to subside. She held him away from her and wiped the tears off his ruddy, round cheeks. "You scared me half to death, Aaron Stroud," she scolded. Then looking at the man again, she said, "One minute he was there, the next he wasn't."

She had brown eyes. Velvety, dark-brown eyes that he felt himself sinking into.

"He moved like greased lightning." When she tilted her head, obviously puzzled, he explained. "I had been watching him eat his ice-cream cone."

"Oh." It didn't occur to her to ask why they had attracted his attention in the first place. She was wondering what had happened to his eye. It was a shame he had lost it because the one that looked back at her was green, deeply green, beautifully green, surrounded by spiky black lashes.

It gazed back at her like a steady emerald flame. Self-conscious at having been caught staring, she looked away. It was then that she noticed his wet jeans and boots. "You went into the fountain?"

He laughed, glancing down at his legs. His jeans were wet from his knees down. He rolled his foot back on the heel of his wet boot. "I guess I did. I don't remember it. I was thinking about Aaron."

"How did you know his name?"

Trevor's heart did a somersault. "Uh, I heard you call him that when you reached for him."

She nodded. "I'm sorry you got wet."

"It'll dry."

"But those look like expensive boots."

"They're not as valuable as Aaron." He chucked the

boy under the chin. Aaron had the sleeve of his mother's cardigan in his mouth, gnawing away. Mechanically, she lifted it away from him and smoothed it back down over her chest.

"Oh, my gosh!" she exclaimed. As though to reinforce what she'd just realized—that they were both soaking wet—Aaron sneezed.

"You're wet," Trevor said.

He was staring down at her front in a way that made Kyla feel hot rather than chilled. She surged to her feet. "Thank you again. Goodbye." Holding Aaron in front of her like a shield, she rushed toward the nearest exit.

"Wait!"

"Why?"

"Aren't you forgetting something?"

"What?"

"Your purse for one thing. And Aaron's stroller. They're still over there by the ice-cream stand."

Feeling like a colossal fool, she shook her head, laughing shakily. "I'm still—"

"Upset. I can imagine. Let me get them for you."

"You've done enough."

"No problem."

He was walking away from her before she could offer another protest. Surreptitiously she glanced down at her chest to see if she was indecently exposing herself and was only slightly relieved to see that her exposure wouldn't get her arrested.

Hastily she glanced back up at the man's retreating figure. It was then that she noticed his limp. It was almost undetectable, but he definitely favored his left side. He must have been in a terrible accident to have lost his eye and partially crippled his entire left side.

But even the limp didn't hamper the lithe way he moved. For such a large man, he was graceful and had the oiled gait of an athlete. And the build. Broad shoulders and narrow hips. His hair was midnight-black, wavy and long enough to cover the tops of his ears and curl over his collar. Kyla noticed that the women he passed took a second look. None seemed put off by the eye patch. In fact, it contributed to his appeal, which was rakish and a tad disreputable.

Yet, masculine as he was, he seemed indifferent to slinging the strap of her purse over his shoulder and pushing the baby stroller through the mall back toward where she stood waiting with Aaron.

"Thank you again," she said, avoiding Aaron's swinging fist, which was aimed for her earring. She reached for her purse. Trevor slid the strap down his arm, up hers, and patted it into place on her shoulder.

She's so dainty, he thought.

He's so tall, she thought.

She leaned down and tried to seat Aaron in the stroller, but he was having none of it. His stout little body went as stiff as a board and she couldn't forcibly bend his legs. He began to protest strenuously.

"He's getting tired," she said by way of explanation, embarrassed that her child was behaving in such an undisciplined way. They were attracting attention again, and those passersby new on the scene were staring curiously at the sodden child, damp mother and the man with the wet jeans.

"Why don't you carry Aaron and let me push the stroller out to your car?"

She straightened, lifting Aaron with her. "I can't let you do that. I've inconvenienced you enough."

He smiled. His teeth were very straight and very white behind his very sexy mustache. "It's no inconvenience."

"Well..." she hedged.

The man made Kyla nervous. Why, she couldn't exactly say. He had behaved with enough courtesy to earn him a Boy Scout badge. He hadn't looked at her suggestively. More than likely he thought she had a husband out playing golf or at home working in the yard.

Still, *she* was aware that *he* was aware of her wet blouse, and even though he couldn't actually *see* anything the suggestion was there, and that made her jittery.

"Come on. Let's go before Aaron becomes more than the two of us can handle."

The boy was becoming heavier in her arms with every passing second and his fractiousness was increasing. He was squirming discontentedly, because he was no doubt as uncomfortable as she in his wet clothes. "All right," she said, pushing back a wayward strand of hair that had met with the flying fist she had tried to dodge. "I would appreciate that."

"Out this way?" Trevor asked, nodding toward the exit.

She looked uneasy. "No, actually, I'm parked on the other side of Penney's."

He could have asked why, if she was parked on the other side of Penney's, she had headed toward this exit as though the devil were after her just a few minutes ago, but in true gentlemanly fashion he said nothing and, after waiting for her to precede him, steered the empty stroller toward the department store at the other end of the mall.

"My name is Trevor, by the way. Trevor Rule." Holding his breath, he watched her face for signs of recognition and when none were forthcoming, he felt a tightness in his chest relax.

"I'm Kyla Stroud."

"Pleased to meet you." He cocked his head toward Aaron, who had stopped crying now that he was in motion again. "And Aaron, of course."

Smiles like his should be outlawed, Kyla thought. It was hazardous to the female population. His appeal crossed generational barriers. She saw a gaggle of teens openly flirt with him as they walked past. Plenty of grandmothers turned their heads. It didn't matter whether a woman was accompanied by another man or not, they all noticed Trevor Rule.

He wasn't classically handsome. There was nothing pretty about his face. It was lined. Twin grooves extended from the edges of his nostrils down to bracket his mouth and wide mustache. Kyla wondered how they could be so deeply engraved there. Pain from his debilitating accident? He couldn't be any older than his early thirties. Not much older than Richard would be.

Richard. At the thought of him that familiar pang shot through her. If he were alive, he would be walking by her side. She wouldn't need the assistance of a stranger. The first anniversary of his death had passed.

According to all the books on the subject, that was a landmark and she should be getting over the loss by now. But not a day went by that she didn't think of Richard, usually at a moment when she least expected it. Like now. And she was glad. She had vowed to keep her husband alive both for her sake and for Aaron's.

Nursing memories of Richard day by day kept him a vital part of her life.

"How old is Aaron?" Trevor asked suddenly.

"Just over fifteen months."

"He's hefty, isn't he? I don't know much about babies."

"Yes, he's hefty," Kyla said, laughing and shifting him from one arm to the other. "But his daddy was muscular."

"Was?"

Why had she left that gate open? She hadn't intended to. "He died," she said without elaboration.

"I'm sorry."

And he meant it. Or did he?

Trevor had waited for this day for months. After he left the hospital, he had marked time, waiting until the time was right. He was anxious to get his business started, but even with his father's unabashed string-pulling, there had been a million and one tedious details to see to. The hours he had spent cooped up in offices seemed endless to a man who had months of his life to catch up on. There had also been hours spent outdoors shirtless, so he would lose his sickly hospital pallor.

During it all, he had imagined his first meeting with Kyla a hundred times, asking himself where it would happen, what she would look like, what he would say.

He hadn't set out to meet her that day. But it was happening! He was living it. And having seen her, he honestly couldn't say whether he regretted sleeping in Richard Stroud's bunk that fateful night or not. Out of sheer selfishness, he was extremely glad to be alive at the moment.

"I'm afraid we still have quite a walk," Kyla said apologetically as he held the door open for her.

"I don't mind."

The parking lot was a good indicator of the crowd inside the mall. Motorists just arriving were fighting over parking spaces as they became available.

"Are you from around here, Mr. Rule?" Kyla asked conversationally as they entered the melee.

"Call me Trevor. No, I'm not. I moved here about a month ago."

"What brought you to Chandler?"

You.

"Greed."

Startled by his answer, she looked up at him. "Pardon?"

A strand of hair blew across her lips. His heart skipped a beat, just thinking about moving aside that strand of spun gold and kissing her lips. She had the most kissable mouth he'd ever seen. "I'm a builder," he said a trifle too loudly after clearing his throat. "I want to be a part of the expansion going on around here."

Maybe he should have bought a few nights with a woman before meeting Kyla. Maybe he should have cultivated some casual relationships based solely on sex. Maybe he shouldn't have subjected himself to abstention.

"Oh, I see. Well, that's my car." She pointed out a pale blue station wagon.

"Petal Pushers?" he asked, reading the stenciled logo on the side panel.

"My friend and I have a flower shop."

Fifty-two ninety-eight Ballard Parkway. He knew exactly where it was, the colors in the striped awnings over the paned windows, and what the hours of operation were. "A flower shop, hey? Sounds interesting."

He waited while she secured Aaron in his car seat and helped her put the collapsible stroller into the backseat. "I can't thank you enough, Mr. uh, Trevor. You've been awfully kind."

"Don't thank me. I enjoyed it. Everything but seeing Aaron go over that wall into the water."

Kyla shuddered. "I don't even want to think about that." She looked at him for a long moment. There seemed to be no graceful way to leave. How did she say thank you and goodbye to a stranger who had saved her child's life? "Well, goodbye," she said, feeling awkward and having absolutely nothing to do with her hands.

"Goodbye."

She slid behind the steering wheel and closed the door. He stepped back, waved and walked away. Kyla turned the key. The car made a hateful grinding sound, but the engine didn't catch. She pumped the gas pedal and tried again. Wrrra, wrrra, wrrra. Again and again. But the car didn't start. She muttered something her mother would be horrified to hear coming from her daughter's mouth. Or, more likely, her mother didn't even know that word.

"Problem?" Trevor Rule had spoken through the window on the driver's side. His hands were braced on his bent knees.

She rolled down the window. "It doesn't want to start."

"Sounds like your battery has gone dead."

Stubbornly she tried again, several times. Finally admitting defeat, she twisted the key off and flopped back against the seat. Aaron was fussing in his car seat, flailing all four limbs against the confinement. This was turning out to be a heck of a Saturday.

"Can I help?" Trevor asked after a moment.

"I'll just go back into the mall and call my dad. He'll come pick us up and send someone out to look at the car."

"I have a better idea. Why don't I drive the two of you home?"

She stared at him mutely, then looked away. A prickle of fear chased up her spine. She didn't know this man. He could be anybody. How did she know he hadn't rigged her car not to start, then befriended her in the mall and...

Stop it, Kyla. That's crazy. He couldn't have orchestrated Aaron's fall into the fountain. Still, she had better sense than to get into a car and go anywhere with a total stranger.

"No thank you, Mr. Rule, I'll manage."

The refusal came out sounding brusquer than she had intended, but she couldn't let herself feel charitable toward a possible abductor. She reversed the energy-draining process she had gone through only minutes before, unbuckling Aaron and lifting him out of the car, picking up her purse, rolling up the window and locking the car door. She struck out in the direction from which they had just come.

"I don't want to detain you, Mr. Rule," she said as he fell into step beside her.

"It will be no trouble for me to take you anywhere you want to go."

"No thanks."

"Are you sure? It would be much—"

"No thank you!"

"Is it this damn thing?" He flung his hand up toward his left eye. "I know it automatically makes me suspect, but I swear I'm not someone you need to be frightened of."

Kyla came to a sudden halt and turned to face him. *Oh, Lord.* Now he probably thought she had a prejudice against handicapped citizens. "I'm not afraid of you."

The tension in his face was gradually replaced by an engaging grin. "Well, you should be. You can't trust strangers these days." They laughed softly. Unmindful of the traffic they were blocking, he took a step closer and looked down at her earnestly. "I'm only trying to help by offering you a ride."

She felt like an idiot. Any man who would ruin a four-hundred-dollar pair of boots to fish a little boy out of a fountain wouldn't be inclined to kidnap, kill or maim. "All right," she conceded softly.

"Good."

The patience of the driver waiting to pull out of the parking space finally gave out and he honked his horn. They started walking.

"Where's your car?"

Trevor indicated the direction with a hitch of his chin. "About an acre and a half from here," he said, laughing. "Why don't you let me carry Aaron?"

With only a trace of reluctance, Kyla handed her son over to him. Aaron smacked him on the cheek with the palm of his chubby hand. He seemed to be not at all wary of the tall, dark, handsome man with the patch over his left eye, the charm of a medicine show barker and a smile that could do an iceberg serious damage.

CHAPTER THREE

HE APOLOGIZED FOR the pickup truck.

"I didn't know I'd be driving you this afternoon, or I would have left the truck at home and brought my car."

He unlocked and opened the door with his right hand while still holding Aaron in his left arm. As soon as Kyla was situated in the cab of the truck, he passed Aaron to her, setting him in her lap.

Trevor's arm brushed against her breasts. She pretended not to notice. So did he. At least he closed the door quickly. They pretended it hadn't happened, but she knew he must be thinking about that fleeting touch just as she was.

"It's warm in here," he remarked as he slid behind the steering wheel and started the motor. "The sun's been shining in."

"It feels good. We're still damp."

She could have bitten her tongue for mentioning that. He glanced down at her chest, swiftly and guiltily. She was glad that Aaron still provided her with a shield.

They fell into an awkward silence as he negotiated the traffic through the parking lot. Once he looked toward her and smiled apologetically for the delay. She smiled back and wondered if the tepid grin looked as sickly as it felt. Why couldn't she think of anything to say?

When he pulled up to the exit ramp, he turned his head. She could feel him looking at her, but she concentrated on smoothing down Aaron's soft brown hair.

Why was he staring at her like that? And maybe she should have asked that he please turn on the air conditioner. It was becoming uncomfortably warm inside the truck. Or was it her own temperature that was rising?

"I have to ask you something," he said softly.

Her heart lurched.

Are you game?

What should we do with the kid?

Are you protected?

Your place or mine?

The possibilities marched through her head. She dreaded hearing any of them. Up until now he had been so nice. She should have known it wouldn't be that easy. No man picks up a woman, gets her into his car, does her a favor and expects nothing in return.

Keeping her eyes trained on the cowlick on the crown of Aaron's head she said, "What?"

"Which way?"

A nervous laugh of relief escaped her lips on a gust of breath. "Oh, I'm sorry. To the right."

He smiled disarmingly and followed the directions she now supplied without being prompted. *He must think I'm a real ninny,* Kyla thought. He's just a nice man who is playing the Good Samaritan to a widow with a baby. Nothing more.

He might have suited the role better if he hadn't been quite so handsome, quite so...manly. His hands for instance. Large, strong, tan. When he reached for the dial on the radio she saw that his nails were bluntly trimmed. The back of his hand and knuckles were sprinkled with dark hair, sun-bleached on the tips.

He moved his right foot from accelerator to brake. Kyla noticed the supple contraction and stretching of long thigh muscles.

His lap, too, attracted her attention.

"Hot?"

"What?"

"Are you hot?"

Her face was flaming. Her insides were afire. Had he caught her staring at…that? "Yes, a little." He adjusted the thermostat and cool air began to whisper through the cab. But from that moment, she kept her eyes away from him.

Clif and Meg Powers had lived in the same house since Kyla was born. When they purchased it, it had been in a fashionable part of town. But the town's industrial expansion and its increased importance as a commuter's alternative to living in Dallas had changed their neighborhood. It was no longer fashionable.

The houses, once attractive and well maintained, now belonged to owners who didn't take much pride in them. Like frumpy matrons who had resigned themselves to middle age, the houses looked unkempt, the yards ungroomed.

The only exception on the block was the Powers's property. The deep front porch was bordered by a white wrought-iron railing, which Clif had painstakingly repainted the previous summer. The shrubbery had been pruned to make room for new growth. Flowers bloomed in well-tended beds.

As Trevor's truck turned onto the street, a sprinkler was vigorously watering one half of the yard. The grass on the other side of the center sidewalk leading up to the front porch was glistening in the late afternoon sunlight, having already been watered.

"That's it," Kyla said, pointing out the house for him.

Trevor's foot was already on the brake. He knew which house she lived in. In the past month he'd driven by it often enough to know what days their garbage was collected.

Kyla hadn't noticed his familiarity with the neighborhood because she was inwardly groaning. A familiar car was parked in the driveway. Babs. As if making explanations to her parents wasn't going to be difficult enough, she would have Babs and her vivid imagination to contend with. Maybe she could just hop out and thank Trevor without further ado. Maybe he would drive off before anyone saw him.

No such luck.

Trever had no sooner pulled the pickup to a stop at the curb than the front door opened and her father came out. He looked at the truck curiously as he bent down to turn off the water faucet and cut off the sprinkler. He looked even more curious when he recognized Kyla and Aaron sitting on the far side of the cab.

"That's my dad," Kyla said, as Clif Powers came ambling down the front walk. For reasons she couldn't explain she felt nervous and shy.

Trevor pushed open his door. "Hi," he said with a friendly air as he stepped out of the truck. "I've got some passengers who say they belong here." Clif Powers appeared dumbstruck.

Kyla already had her door open by the time Trevor came around to her side. "Better hand Aaron to me.

It's a long step down for you." Reluctantly she let him lift Aaron off her lap.

As though he'd been doing it for years, he caught Aaron under the bottom and anchored the boy against his chest. With his free hand, he helped Kyla down. He kept his hand beneath her elbow as they rounded the truck to face her puzzled father.

"Hi, Dad."

"Where's your car? Is something wrong?"

"No, nothing's wrong, but it wasn't the most uneventful trip to the mall I've ever had," she said ruefully. She wondered how she could take her son out of Trevor's arms without creating an awkward situation. She didn't want to risk touching him again. Which was ridiculous because he was perfectly harmless.

"What's going on? Clif? Kyla?"

The voice belonged to Meg Powers, who was just then pushing her way through the front screen door. Her pleasant face wore an expression of concern. Behind her was Babs. Kyla didn't even want to contemplate what Babs's speculative expression conveyed.

Meg rushed down the front steps and took the sidewalk at a trot. Her eyes were moving back and forth between Kyla and the tall, dark-haired stranger who was holding her grandson.

"Mom, Dad, this is Mr. Rule. Trevor Rule."

"Sir, ma'am," Trevor responded politely and shifted Aaron to his left arm to shake hands with Clif Powers.

"And that's my friend and business partner, Babs Logan," Kyla added.

"Hello, Ms. Logan."

Babs's eyes danced over Trevor appreciatively. "Hi. Where did she find you?"

Babs wasn't acquainted with tact. She didn't know how to exercise restraint. She blurted out precisely what the Powerses were thinking, but didn't have the gumption or lack of manners to ask.

"He sort of found us," Kyla said.

"Where's your car?" Clif repeated.

"Still at the mall."

"I think the battery has run down, sir," Trevor added politely for Clif's benefit.

"Mr. Rule offered us a ride home."

"How chivalrous," Babs said. Her eyes were still busy with their inspection of Trevor. "What did Mrs. Rule think about that?"

Kyla was going to kill her! As soon as she had an opportunity, she was going to kill her with her bare hands!

Trevor only smiled as he bent down to set Aaron on the ground. Normally Aaron would have taken off at a run. But as soon as his feet made contact with the sidewalk, he began to whine. His chubby hands clutched at Trevor's damp pant legs. Bending down again, Trevor lifted him back into his arms and patted his bottom. Contentedly Aaron snuggled against him.

"I'm sorry," Kyla murmured, embarrassed that her son had formed such an attachment so quickly. "I'll take him now so you can get on your way."

"It's all right," Trevor assured her with a soft smile.

For an instant, as their gazes locked, it was as though they were alone. They momentarily forgot that they had an avid audience of three.

"The baby's clothes are wet," Meg ventured meekly.

"Oh, yes," Kyla said, shaking herself out of the brief trance. "He fell into the fountain."

The Powerses were immediately alarmed. Babs was merely more curious. "Was this before or after the battery ran down?" she asked, amused.

"Before. Trevor reached in and pulled him out. Don't worry, Mom, Aaron was okay. Just wet."

"How did it happen?"

"I was feeding him an ice cream." Kyla gave them a condensed rundown of the sequence of events. "When I looked around, Aaron was gone, but a crowd had encircled the fountain. Mr. Rule was standing there with a dripping Aaron in his arms."

"You jumped in the fountain and fished Aaron out?" Babs asked Trevor, nodding toward the denim that was obviously still damp below the knees.

"Yeah."

"Hmm," Babs purred, looking at Kyla in a knowing way that made Kyla want to slap her.

Clif and Meg were busy thanking Trevor for his quick action and commending him for his kindness to Kyla and Aaron. None of them saw the mouthed conversation going on between the two friends.

"He's yummy."

"Shut up."

"Your blouse is wet."

Kyla immediately ducked her head and saw that indeed the damp material of her shirt was still clinging to her breasts and outlining the lacy brassiere.

Her eyes swung up in time to catch Trevor looking at her. His gaze had followed hers down. It immediately sprang back up to her face. All this happened just as Meg, who had been expounding on how quickly a toddler could get out of sight and into mischief, concluded with, "Why don't you come in and have a cup of coffee with us, Mr. Rule?"

"No!"

Kyla's cheeks turned a warm pink when she realized she had voiced aloud the word that had shot through her mind. She wet her lips. "I mean, we've kept Mr. Rule too long as it is." She reached for Aaron and virtually yanked the boy out of Trevor's arms. "Thank you again. You've been very helpful, and I appreciate the ride home." Now please leave! she finished silently.

"It was my pleasure." He pinched Aaron's chin. "Bye, Scout. Nice to meet you," he said, nodding his head toward the others. With a lean-hipped saunter, only slightly hindered by his limp, he turned and walked back to his truck. With a final wave, he drove off.

Self-consciously, Kyla faced her parents and Babs, who were staring at her expectantly. "I've got to get Aaron out of these wet clothes." She wedged past them, but they trooped after her and were surrounding her by the time she reached the wide, spacious entrance hall.

"Tell us!" Babs demanded.

She had been Kyla's best friend since grade school. Her mother had died when they were in junior high. Since then her father often worked double shifts at a manufacturing plant in Dallas. Through the secondary school years, Babs had spent as much time under the Powerses' roof as she had under her own. She considered herself part of the family and so did they.

"Tell you what?"

"About him! What gives?"

"Nothing." Kyla headed for the kitchen, ostensibly to get Aaron a drink of juice. She placed him in his high chair and opened the refrigerator. Her parents and Babs crowded around her.

"Did he really jump into the fountain to rescue Aaron?" Meg asked, moving aside only when Kyla reached around her for a glass.

"Don't make it sound so heroic, Mom. He didn't dive into shark-infested waters. It's a shallow fountain, and Aaron couldn't have been in the water for more than a few seconds."

She couldn't believe she was making light of the incident now. Only an hour ago, she was thinking that Aaron could have drowned had it not been for Trevor Rule's quick reflexes.

"What about the car?" her father asked. "How did he know about the car?"

"Well, he, uh, had walked out with me."

"All the way to your car?"

"Yes. Because Aaron was crying and I was still shaken."

"He volunteered to do that?" Babs asked.

"Yes," Kyla said tightly.

"Hmm."

"Will you stop saying, 'Hmm'? You're not making a diagnosis. And I wish all three of you would stop looking at me like I've got the lowdown on a juicy piece of gossip. He's just a man, all right? A male person who was kind enough to offer his help. Honestly," she said with exasperation, "you're acting like hungry cats who've trapped the last mouse in town."

"He didn't have to drive you home," Meg said.

"He was being nice."

"He limps. Wonder what happened to him," Clif mused.

"It's none of our business. We'll never see him again. And, Dad, you'd better call someone at the garage and have my car taken care of. Do you need any help with supper, Mom?"

They recognized her tone. It was the clipped, terse one she had started using several months ago to let them know that she was officially out of mourning for Richard. With that brusque inflection she had indicated to them that they didn't need to walk on eggshells around her anymore or speak in hushed tones as though they were still at the funeral. It clearly stated that she would brook no more coddling. They knew by that tone when to back off, and now was the time.

"No, dear, thank you," Meg said, declining her offer. "You take Aaron upstairs and change him. We're only having sandwiches and I can manage. Are you staying, Babs?"

"Not tonight, thanks. I have a date."

Kyla left the kitchen and carried Aaron upstairs. Babs followed her. "I thought you had a date," Kyla said crossly as she carried Aaron into the spare bedroom that had been converted into a nursery for him.

"I've got time."

"Anybody I know? Or is this a new one?"

"Won't work, Ky," Babs said, plopping down in the rocking chair and sitting cross legged.

"What won't work?" Kyla asked nonchalantly as she unsnapped Aaron's suspenders and took his shorts off.

"Trying to avoid the subject of your tall, dark and handsome hunk."

"He's not *my*...anything."

"Do you think he's married?"

"How should I know? Besides what difference does it make?"

"You mean you'd get involved with a married man?"

"Babs!" Kyla exclaimed, whirling around. "I'm not getting 'involved' with anybody. He offered me a ride home, for Pete's sake. What kind of day did we have at the shop?"

"Fair to middling. I don't think he's married," Babs went on doggedly. "He wasn't wearing a wedding band."

"That doesn't mean anything."

"I know. But he didn't have that married *look,* you know?"

"No. I don't know. I didn't look at him that closely."

"Well *I* did. All six feet three or so inches of him. And speaking of inches, did you notice the way he filled out the front of those jeans?"

"Stop it!" Babs had touched a nerve and Kyla kept her back to her friend because she didn't want her to see the telltale stain on her cheeks. "You're terrible."

"What did you think of the eye patch?"

"I didn't think anything of it."

Babs shivered. "I think it's wildly sexy. With that positively wicked mustache it makes him look like a highwayman or something."

"Wildly, wicked? You've been reading too many historical romances."

"And that single blue eye."

"It's green." The moment the words left her mouth, she knew she had incriminated herself. Hoping that Babs had missed the slip, she cautiously glanced over her shoulder.

Babs's smile was angelic, but there was pure devilry in her eyes. "Thought you said you didn't look at him that closely," she taunted.

"Will you go home?" Kyla pulled Aaron, now naked, into her arms. "I'm going to give Aaron a bath because he's going to bed as soon as he's had his dinner. You've got a date. And..." She drew in a deep breath. "I don't want to talk about Mr. Rule anymore. I don't even want to think about him."

"Bet he's thinking about you," Babs said, unfolding her legs and coming to her feet. She wasn't perturbed by Kyla's crankiness.

"Don't be ridiculous. Why should he give me a second thought?"

"Because he seemed damned reluctant to leave. If you hadn't acted like you'd just sat on a tack when your mother offered him a cup of coffee, I'll bet he would have accepted her invitation as an excuse to stay. *And* he noticed your wet blouse just like I did."

"He did not!" Kyla cried indignantly.

"Oh, yes, he did. Bye."

Before Kyla could offer another protest Babs was on her way downstairs. Through dinner the Powerses were just as curious about the man who had "rescued"—as Meg seemed determined to call it—Kyla and Aaron. Their questions weren't as explicit as Babs's, nor as sexually oriented, but they were just as pointed.

When she could stand their subtle quizzing no longer, Kyla stood up and said, "I wish I had just called a cab. I didn't know one man could cause such a commotion. We'll never see him again. Now good night!"

She carried Aaron upstairs and put him to bed. In her own bedroom, she tried to read, but she kept thinking about Trevor Rule. "No wonder, with everybody talking about him all evening," she grumbled, slamming her book closed.

"No matter what Babs says, he wasn't looking at my wet blouse," she averred as she pulled it off. "He wasn't!" she muttered again as she took off her brassiere.

But the thought that he *might* have been kept her awake for a long time.

"I DON'T BELIEVE IT," Babs said suddenly, making the front-porch swing rock erratically as she sat up from her lounging position.

"Don't believe what?" Kyla asked around a yawn. She was stretched out in one of the chairs on the porch. Her head was resting on the back and her eyes were closed. It was a warm, sunny Sunday afternoon and she was feeling lazy and luxuriously indolent.

"It's *him*."

Kyla opened one eye and saw whom Babs was referring to, then her other eye popped open, as well. Trevor Rule was braking a car in front of her house.

"What'd I tell you?" Babs said. "He's come back for another look."

"If you say anything to embarrass me, I'll murder you," Kyla threatened her friend. She smiled wanly at Trevor as he made his way up the sidewalk to the front porch.

"Hi."

"Hi," the women chorused.

He gave Babs a cursory glance before his gaze homed in on Kyla. She became shyly aware of her shorts and bare feet. Her sandals had been kicked aside, but to retrieve them now would have called more attention to how casually and comfortably she was dressed.

"I was worried about your car, but I see you got it back all right." He indicated the station wagon parked in the driveway.

"Yes. Dad called the garage he patronizes. He met the mechanic on the mall parking lot and they charged my battery. The car started, but I'll probably have to get a new battery."

"That would be a good idea. Did you go with him?"

"No."

"How did he locate it in the sea of cars that was out there yesterday?"

She laughed. "It was the only one with Petal Pushers painted on the side."

His rich laughter echoed softly off the porch's covering. "Well I'm glad you got it back okay."

"Me, too."

Nervously Kyla hooked a strand of hair behind her ear, wondering if it looked like it had been styled with an eggbeater.

Trevor's own nervous reaction to the cessation of conversation was to slide his hands into the back pockets of his jeans, stretching the cloth tight across his narrow hips. Kyla wished she couldn't remember what Babs had said about his build. But she did remember and it left her mind wide open for unladylike speculation.

For her own part, Babs could have throttled Kyla for acting like such a simp. She took matters into her own hands. "Won't you sit down, Trevor? Would you like something to drink?"

"Uh, no," he said, swiftly removing his hands from

his pockets. "In fact, I came by hoping I could talk Kyla and Aaron into going for an ice cream with me. I know he likes ice cream."

Kyla opened her mouth to refuse his invitation, but Babs piped up, "Now isn't that a shame? Aaron's taking his nap." Then her blue eyes opened wide with sudden inspiration. "But *you* could go, Kyla."

Flustered, Kyla stammered, "I don't—"

"Am I interrupting anything?" Trevor looked at Babs inquiringly.

"Oh, don't worry about me," Babs said, laughing. "I don't live here, but I'm not company who has to be entertained. Kyla and I are old friends. Why, her folks practically raised me. We've been working on our tans this afternoon. You see, there's this part of their roof just outside Kyla's bedroom where we can sunbathe in total privacy." She winked audaciously. "If you get my meaning."

He did. He wasn't stupid. And when it came to playing these kinds of word games, he could make even the flirtatious Babs look like an amateur. Hell, he had invented some of the games. He could have leaned down, included them both in a suggestive smile and glibly delivered a dozen witty, leading innuendos on the subject of nude sunbathing. But the smile on Kyla's face was so strained that he didn't pursue the subject.

"But it got too hot," Babs went on. "So we came in and showered and now we're just relaxing here in the shade. In fact, I was about to drop off to sleep, so there's no reason for Kyla not to go."

Trevor met her gaze and smiled. "Would you like to?"

"No, I—"

"Kyla, who's… Oh, Mr. Rule," her father said from behind the screen door. He pushed it open and came out in stocking feet, wearing only his old-fashioned undershirt over his trousers.

"Hello, sir." Trevor shook his hand politely. "I hope I didn't disturb a nap."

"No, no," Clif lied. "I wasn't finished with the Sunday paper yet. I think I'll bring it out here on the porch."

"Trevor came by to take Kyla out for an ice cream. Wasn't that nice of him?" Babs made the announcement with a broad smile, as though some monumental decision had been reached and signed into law.

"Yes, it was," Clif agreed.

"But I don't think I'd better go because Aaron—"

"He'll be fine. He and your mother are still asleep. I just checked on him. Go on. It would do you good to get away for a spell."

Kyla couldn't remember when she had last been allowed to complete a sentence. She could have gladly strangled all three of them, her father for being so accommodating, Blabbermouth Babs, and Trevor Rule for putting her in this compromising position in the first place. "All right, I'll just go in and change." She bounded out of her chair and headed for the front door.

"You don't need to change." Babs spoke with the authority of a drill sergeant. She knew what Kyla would do. She would go upstairs and wake up Aaron and use him as an excuse not to go.

Well she wasn't going to get by with that trick. She was a widow, granted. But she was a young, vibrant widow, and Babs intended to see that Kyla didn't retreat any further into her shell.

Trevor Rule was the first man brave enough to pursue Kyla despite the cold shoulder she had given him. Whether Kyla wanted her to or not, Babs was making it her business to see that he didn't get discouraged, take his losses and go away. Her inflection softened as she asked, "Does she need to change, Trevor? You're not going anyplace where she would need to dress up, are you?"

"Hardly. Kyla?"

There was such a compelling tone to the way he spoke her name that she couldn't find a polite means of turning him down. "I guess I could go," she said, nervously tugging on the hem of her shorts. "If we're not gone too long." She returned to her chair and put on her sandals. After shooting Babs a venomous look, she came to her feet again. "I guess I'm ready."

Trevor placed his hand under her elbow and they left the porch. "Don't rush back. Take your time," Clif called after them. "We'll watch the baby."

"Have fun," Babs said, waving gaily.

Mortified, Kyla slid into the front seat. She fought a compulsion to hide her face behind her hand as Trevor got in and started the car. As soon as they turned the corner at the end of the block, he surprised her by pulling the car to the curb. He put the automatic gear into "Park" and, laying his right arm on the back of the front seat, turned to face her.

"Look, I know they embarrassed you back there, but I don't want you to be. Okay?"

There was a hint of a smile at the corners of his mouth. She ducked her head and let go of a short, small laugh. "I was embarrassed."

"I know. I'm sorry."

"It was nothing you did. They acted like they wanted to hog-tie you before you ran away."

"I take it you haven't dated much since your husband's death."

"I haven't dated at all. And I don't want to."

Trevor took the news like a surprise right hook under his chin. He turned forward and contemplated the hood of the car through the windshield. On the one hand he was thrilled to know that she hadn't been seeing other men. On the other hand, she was spelling out the ground rules right off the bat and seemed in no rush to alter them. But she was in his car, right? He had gotten this far, right?

Kyla was thinking that perhaps she had been blunt to the point of rudeness and was just on the verge of offering an apology when he turned his head and said, "Not even to go for ice cream?" He took her spontaneous laugh as consent and engaged the gears of the car again. "Besides, eating ice cream is kind of like drinking."

"How's that?"

"It's no fun if you do it alone."

He drove through Chandler's streets, which should have been familiar to her, but which he seemed to know more about than she did. "I bought this tract of land."

"That's where the post office used to be before it moved into that new shopping center."

"That's what I hear. Anyway, I'm building a small office complex on this lot. Very nice. There'll be a central courtyard with plants and fountains. I hope it'll attract the professionals—doctors, lawyers—you know.

"I've bid on that piece of land but I don't think I'll

get it," he said of other property as they cruised past.
"There'll be a new supermarket over there."

"But it's a cow pasture!"

He laughed. "Give it a year. I understand there will
be a movie theater complex, too."

He seemed to have inside information on what was
going on in a town she had lived in all her life. What's
more he seemed to be one of the movers and shakers
who were making it all happen.

"Maybe Babs and I should consider moving Petal
Pushers to a new location."

"No, you're fine where you are."

She looked at him quickly. "How do you know
where we are?"

"I drove past your shop today before I picked you
up," he said easily after a slight pause. "I was curious
about any store called Petal Pushers. How long have
you been in business?"

"Almost a year. Six months after Richard died...
that was my husband." Idly she pleated the hem of her
shorts between her fingers. "Anyway, when Babs and
I were growing up, we loved the movie *My Fair Lady*
and had always said we were going to work in a flower
shop like Eliza Doolittle wanted to. So, when I found
myself at loose ends, Babs started hounding me about
it. She was unhappy with her job at the time. My parents thought it was a good idea. I needed something to
do with my life and an investment for Aaron's future.
So..." she said, drawing out the word, "we pooled our
resources and before I knew it, I was co-owner of a
flower shop."

"And has it been good for you?"

"So far, very good. The other florist in town has

dated ideas and no imagination. We're closing in on him," she said with a mischievous smile that Trevor would have given heaven and earth at that moment to taste. He had been aware of every pleat she had pressed into the cotton shorts against her smooth, lotion-creamy, flower-scented, suntanned thigh.

But to his supreme irritation he had to devote his attention to his driving. He had driven off the main highway into a lane that hadn't yet been paved. It was rough.

"Do you know about an ice-cream parlor I don't?" Kyla asked.

He smiled broadly and winked. "Maybe I'm just carrying you off into the woods." Her smile faltered and he laughed. Reaching over, he patted her knee. "Relax." *I'm touching her knee. My skin against hers. God! But don't press your luck. Remove your hand. Now, Rule, now.* "I'm building this house on spec. Some of the carpenters are working today for overtime wages and I want to make sure I'm getting my money's worth out of them. Do you mind stopping for a few minutes?"

No, she didn't mind. But "relax"? Impossible. Not when she could still feel the imprint of his hand burning into the skin of her bare knee.

CHAPTER FOUR

THE LANE WOUND through a forest of pine, oak and pecan. At the end of it stood a house currently under construction. Even at this stage of completion Kyla could see that the structure would be contemporary and impressive. The lot sloped through the woods to a shallow creek.

"This is beautiful, Trevor," she exclaimed, not even noticing how easily his name had come to her lips.

But he noticed and smiled at her as he brought the car to a stop. "Do you like it?"

"The lot is beautiful."

"Come on, let me show you around."

"I don't think I should get out." She was self-conscious of her skimpy outfit and the curious workmen, who, without exception, had suspended their labors when the car drove into the clearing.

"I'm the boss around here," Trevor said, shoving open his door. "If I say you should get out, you should get out."

The sun spread heat over her bare legs. A warm breeze caressed them. But she wasn't nearly as conscious of the elements as she was of the stares directed toward her as Trevor prodded her forward over the rough ground and around piles of building materials toward the house. They picked their way carefully. After one dark frown from Trevor, the building activity was resumed. Hammers rang out. A buzz saw shrilled. A drill whirred.

"Careful of nails," he cautioned. One of his hands was curled around her elbow. The other was riding the small of her back. When they had cleared most of the obstacles, he regretfully removed his hands. "The front door will be here. I was thinking of something with etched glass."

"How lovely."

"You'll step into an entry with a tall ceiling. Sky-lighted."

"I like skylights."

"Yeah?" One of her letters had told him so.

...and went in. It was just the kind of house I've always dreamed about. Contemporary. It was sur-rounded by trees and had a skylight.

"I saw a house like this once and loved it."

"Watch your step." Taking her hand chivalrously, Trevor led her down to the next level. "This is the liv-ing room. Very informal. A fireplace on that wall. The dining room is through there. Kitchen is that way." He pointed out the floor plan and Kyla tried to imagine what it would be like when the walls were up. Con-centrating on the house kept her mind off how small her hand felt in his.

"Can you step through here?"

"Sure," she said, grateful for the opportunity to re-move her hand from his.

But it didn't turn out that way, because he kept hold-ing her hand firmly tucked into his as they squeezed through a maze of two-by-fours. "This is the master bedroom. Of course, before too long you won't be able

to walk through the walls. You'll have to use the hallways."

"It seems a shame to enclose it."

*The rooms were so open and airy, you could get the
feeling that you lived outside.*

"Exactly what I thought. Nearly every hallway has
one wall of floor-to-ceiling windows so you won't get
that closed-in feeling."

Dappled sunlight angled in through the overhead
beams to shadow and highlight his face. The light
found each iridescent streak in his black hair. His dark
mustache spread wide over a lower lip so sensual that
it bordered on being pouty.

Kyla withdrew her hand from his and just barely
resisted the urge to wring it with her other. Casual as
his touch had seemed, she didn't think it was casual at
all. It just wasn't possible for a man to have a face and
body like Trevor Rule's and not be a lady-killer. She
could well imagine any number of female hearts dangling from his belt like trophies. The sooner he knew
she wasn't in the chase, the better.

"What goes there?" she asked, putting space between them.

"Another fireplace."

"You're kidding!"

"No, why?"

She had always pictured her dream house as having a fireplace in the master bedroom, but something
cautioned her about telling that to Trevor. "Nothing.
I think having a fireplace in here sounds wonderful."

"And romantic."

She glanced away. "I suppose so."

"Mr. Rule?" One of the carpenters had joined them,

but up until that instant had gone unnoticed. "Excuse me, but as long as you're here, could I ask you a question? It's about that breakfast nook."

"Sure. We'll be right with you." They retraced their footsteps through the framework of the house into the area of the kitchen.

"Over here in this informal dining area, you said you wanted a window. Which wall did you want the window on?" the carpenter asked.

Crossing his arms over his chest, Trevor pivoted on his boot heels to face Kyla. "Since you seem to have an instinct for these things, which wall should we put the window on?"

"I don't know anything about building."

"I'm merely asking for your opinion."

"Well," she said hesitantly, "let's see. That's south, right? And that's east?"

"Yep," the carpenter confirmed.

She contemplated the layout for a moment then said, "Why not both?" At their puzzled expressions she rushed on, "Could they meet in the corner? Maybe have one of those angled roofs that are made of glass? Then it would be like eating outdoors surrounded by trees."

The carpenter was scratching his head skeptically. "I've seen those prefab sunrooms. I reckon one might work."

Trevor, sold on the idea, clapped the carpenter on the back. "Consult with the architect tomorrow and let me know. I love the idea." He turned to Kyla. "Thanks!"

She felt her cheeks growing warm beneath his praise. "I'm sure the architect won't be too happy with me for spoiling his house plans."

"The architect has to worry about pleasing me."

They stepped out into the open again and began making their way to the parked car. "I think the house is going to be spectacular," Kyla said honestly. "I wonder who'll end up living in it."

"Never can tell. Maybe you and Aaron."

At his surprising words she stumbled over a discarded sack of concrete mix. Trevor's arm shot out, encircled her waist and secured her against his chest before she could blink.

"Careful there. Are you all right?"

She was fine except for a sudden breathlessness, a tingling sensation along her exposed skin and a curling warmth in her middle. She had forgotten how wonderful it felt to be held in a man's arms. The scents associated with masculinity—shaving soap, cologne, sweat—filled her head. She had missed those distinctive smells. He was hard and lean and strong. His breath was warm as it fanned against her cheek when he bent over her solicitously.

"I'm f-fine," she stammered and pushed herself away.

"Sure?"

"Yes. Clumsy, that's all."

The near fall had caused a strap on her sandal to become loose. She bent down to readjust it and when she did, one of the workers whistled. She sprang back up and whipped her head around. All of them were bent industriously over their tasks. And all of them looked too innocent not to be guilty.

She glanced up at Trevor, who smiled sheepishly and said with a shrug, "So they've got terrific taste. Ready?"

By all means she was ready to get away from there. She had gone on this outing to appease Babs and her father. It shouldn't have lasted longer than half an hour. How long did it take to drive to the ice-cream parlor and buy two cones?

But they had driven all over town before coming here. She had no business being on a work site with him, offering him her opinions on the house he was building. What had she been thinking of?

"You'd better take me home," she said as soon as he guided the car into the bumpy lane. "Aaron will be waking up soon."

"I promised you an ice cream."

"That doesn't matter."

"It does to me."

And that, it seemed, was that. At least if the rigid way he held his jaw was any indication. Kyla got a glimpse of another Trevor Rule then. He might be affable enough to jump into a fountain and lift a little boy out. He might be good-natured enough to push a baby stroller through a crowded mall on a Saturday afternoon. He might be kind enough to see that a stranded woman got home safely. But he also had a purely male stubborn streak. That sheer male dominance was slightly intimidating and vaguely unsettling to the woman sitting next to him in the air-conditioned car.

The car was another contradiction. She would have expected him to drive something powerful, mean, low, sleek and probably imported. Instead he was driving an all-American, conservative, middle-class family car with a full-size backseat that would accommodate Aaron's car seat.

Good Lord! What had made her think that?

"What's your favorite?"

She jumped, startled by his sudden question and her last thought. "My favorite what?"

"Ice cream. Mine's chocolate almond."

"Mine, too!"

He grinned at her. "Seriously?"

"When it comes to my chocolate almond ice cream, I'm dead serious."

On this first summery Sunday afternoon of the season, the ice-cream parlor was packed with people. Trevor seated Kyla on a high stool near the windows, then patiently stood in line. She had asked for a single dip; he brought her a double. "I'll never eat all this," she said, licking at the sinfully rich ice cream.

"Give it your best shot. Let's go outside to the gazebo. You're cold."

The air-conditioning in the ice-cream store had been turned up high and Kyla had goose bumps on her bare arms and legs. She didn't know whether to be impressed by his attentiveness or disconcerted that he was so aware of her body as to notice her chills.

As they went through the door on their way outside, a family of five came in. A little girl about six said, "Daddy, what's that thing on that man's eye?"

The mortified parents hustled the children inside and in frantic whispers admonished them not to stare.

"I'm sorry," Trevor mumbled.

Kyla was at a loss for words. She was embarrassed for him and for the parents. She certainly didn't blame the children who were naturally curious and didn't mean to be cruel.

"Does it bother you to be seen with me?" His voice was self-defensively harsh.

"No," she cried, turning to face him.

"I know the patch puts some people off."

"And attracts others." He looked at her in surprise. She explained. "Babs said it makes you look like a highwayman."

He shook his head, laughing. "A highwayman, huh?" Then his smile faded. "One who frightens children."

"Aaron wasn't frightened," she pointed out quietly.

"No, he wasn't, was he?" His tense posture began to relax. "I'm sorry if you were embarrassed by what the little girl said."

"I wasn't. It's just that I know situations like that must be awkward for you."

"I'm getting used to them." He licked at his cone, then ran his tongue along his upper lip beneath his mustache. Kyla couldn't help but wonder what that felt like. Silky or scratchy? "Sometimes I even forget what I look like to other people. Like today. I pulled on a pair of shorts, then changed my mind and put on these jeans."

"Why?"

He laughed. "If you think this damn thing is scary, you ought to see my left leg. I didn't want to repulse you."

"Don't be silly. Wear shorts around me anytime you want to."

His smile became reflective as he gazed deeply into her eyes. "I'll remember that," he said in a low, stirring voice.

Damn! Did he think she was hinting that they would be seeing each other again? To alter the course of the conversation she asked, "Were you in an accident?"

"Sort of."

Another blunder. Obviously talking about the cause of his disabilities made him uncomfortable and that topic was closed. She searched for something they could talk about and came up empty. What did they have in common but a hectic half hour at a shopping mall?

Trevor didn't seem to notice their lack of common ground as he led her into a latticed gazebo that provided shade from the new summer sun. They sat down on the bench ringing it and fell to eating their ice-cream cones.

"Better?" he asked after a long silence, nodding down toward her arm. "Your goose bumps are gone."

"Much better." If she broke out in goose bumps now it would be because his thigh was resting very near hers on the bench. Occasionally she could feel the brush of soft denim against her leg.

"You're wearing another pair of boots," she remarked. Her teeth crunched into her sugar cone.

He glanced down at his feet, which were indeed shod with another pair of lizard boots. Having grown up in Texas, Kyla knew they hadn't come cheap. "I've never owned a pair of cowboy boots until recently. Now I'm convinced I may never wear anything else."

The ice-cream parlor was situated in a row of shops and boutiques. The developer of the shopping center, who, as Trevor had told Kyla earlier, was one of the cleverest around, had created a parklike setting in the open-air mall. Willow trees bowed toward a man-made, rock-lined brook as though paying homage to the waterfowl that swam there. Halved whiskey barrels overflowed with blooming flowers. It was a pastoral place for sitting in the grass, wading in the water, walking hand in hand with someone special.

Kyla noticed that another couple had come to stand near the gazebo. Obviously the two young people were so absorbed with each other that they didn't see Trevor and herself sitting in the shadows of the interior. Speaking in soft whispers, his arms around her waist, hers locked behind his head, their middles nudging playfully, they nuzzled in the universal manner of all lovers.

"You obviously didn't grow up in this part of the country." Kyla cleared her throat uneasily, wondering if Trevor had seen the other couple. When he took a long time responding to her leading statement, she glanced up at him. He was staring at the young man and woman through the slats of the gazebo.

Feeling her eyes on him, he swiveled his head around guiltily. "Uh, no. Philadelphia. I went to school in the Northeast."

The man's hand was now strumming the woman's arm, sliding the backs of his fingers from her elbow to her shoulder. Then he loosely closed his hand around her neck.

"That's why you don't have an accent," Kyla said.

The young man kissed the woman lightly, a soft pecking kiss.

"I guess so."

The woman angled her head back and said something that made her lover laugh softly.

"Do you have a family?" Kyla's voice was light and breathy, as though it was her neck that hungry male lips were nibbling.

"Family?" Trevor repeated dully. "Oh, family. Yes, my dad. He's a lawyer."

The man's mouth nudged aside the woman's collar and disappeared between the folds of fabric. Reflexively Trevor raked his mustache with the tip of his tongue.

"That's all? Just your dad?"

The woman made a soft sound and moved one of her hands to the man's chest. Her thumb languidly stroked the vicinity of his nipple.

Squirming on the bench, Trevor coughed. "That's all. My mother died several years ago. No brothers or sisters."

The lovers kissed. In earnest this time. There was a tilting of heads. A caressing of tongues. Arms and legs moved simultaneously to bring two yearning bodies together. Thighs adjusted themselves to interlock. Groans of pleasure and murmurs of arousal were carried on the whimsical wind that danced in and out and around the gazebo.

The muscled thigh that was now pressed tightly against Kyla's on the bench, bunched and went hard. "Lick it."

At the raspy command, Kyla's eyes flew up to meet a fierce green stare. "What?"

"Lick it. Quick. Before it drips." Lips parted, eyes glazed, she stared back at him mutely. "Your ice cream."

That roused her and she immediately jumped back.

"Oh!" The melting ice cream was running over her fingers.

Trevor stood up abruptly, a pained expression on his face. "Are you finished with it?"

She glanced down at the remains of the ice-cream cone and was amazed to find that she had squeezed it to a pulp. As though it were a murder weapon she'd been caught holding, she practically threw it at him. "Yes, I'm done."

No matter how hard her mind willed it, her heart would not slow down. Her mouth was dry. Lord, what she would give for one good deep breath. Oxygen, that's what she needed to ward off this vertigo that had first hit her when he mentioned her and Aaron's living in the house he was building.

Trevor carried their trash to the receptacle near the doorway of the gazebo. Kyla stood, though her knees were wobbly, and followed him. He was stunned by how lovely she looked framed in the opening.

Sunlight struck her hair and set it aflame as it swirled around her face. Her parted lips were red and moist. She squinted against the sun, and long curly lashes crinkled around velvety brown eyes.

"Trevor? Is something wrong?"

"No," he replied huskily. "I was just thinking about you sunbathing on the roof." Color, hot and vivid, rose out of Kyla's halter and spread up over her throat and onto her cheeks. She said nothing. But his face seemed to have magnetized her eyes. She couldn't look away. "That must be a sight worth seeing."

She swallowed. "Yes. Babs has a terrific figure."

He waited an interminable amount of time before he said softly, "I wasn't thinking about Babs."

When they pulled up in front of the house, Kyla knew there was a pair of eyes at each window. She wished she could bolt from the car and race for the front door, but she knew that a gentleman like Trevor wouldn't allow that. He came around to her side and held the door for her, offering her his hand as she climbed out. She pretended not to see it. She couldn't bring herself to touch him.

On the porch, she faced him awkwardly. She hadn't been able to meet his gaze since he had mentioned what she looked like sunbathing. "Thank you, Trevor. I had a nice time."

How insipid can you get, Kyla? He probably can't wait to get away, she was thinking.

I had to go and get horny and make that comment about her sunbathing. That probably ruined everything, he was thinking.

"So did I." The new boots suddenly felt too tight for his feet and he shifted from one to the other. "Well, goodbye, Kyla."

"Goodbye."

She turned toward the front door and nearly collided with her mother, who was stumbling over her own feet in her haste to get to the porch. "Oh, my goodness," Meg said, flustered. "Mr. Rule, how nice to see you again."

Her surprise over catching them together was as phony as a three-dollar bill. Trevor knew it and Kyla knew he knew it, and she wanted to sink into a deep hole and never have to come out again.

"Hello, Mrs. Powers," he said.

"I just made some sandwiches and lemonade. We

thought we'd eat in the backyard on the picnic table. Why don't you join us?"

Tempted, Trevor glanced at Kyla. Her smile was strained. No, better not, he thought. He'd pushed just about as far as he could for one day. If he hadn't said what he had about the sunbathing.... But he had. Well, damn it, she had looked good enough to eat standing there in the sunshine, and he had had to endure watching while she made eating a damned ice-cream cone look like an erotic exercise. Oh, hell, the damage was already done.

Hating the necessity of it, he declined Meg's invitation. "That sounds great, but I've got some work waiting for me."

Meg's anxious smile collapsed. "What a shame. Well, another time."

"I'd be delighted." He smiled at them both, then loped down the front porch steps and down the sidewalk to his car. As soon as he had driven out of sight, the front door disgorged Babs and Clif.

"Well, how was it?" Babs asked. "Did he ask you out?"

"Will you see him again?"

"Did he ask permission to call?"

"Oh, for heaven's sake!" Kyla exclaimed cantankerously. "I wish all of you would grow up and leave me alone." She stormed past them and went through the front door in a huff.

But who was she mad at? Trevor? Her well-meaning parents? Babs? Or herself?

Because she was just the slightest bit sorry Trevor hadn't accepted her mother's invitation.

"No, no, Aaron," Kyla repeated for the hundredth time. "Don't touch the flowers."

They were in the back room of Petal Pushers. Meg, who sat with Aaron when Kyla worked, had needed to go to the dentist. Clif hadn't returned from an errand in time, so she had dropped Aaron off at the flower shop saying she wouldn't be long.

Kyla was keeping an eye on him while she did the month's accounting. When they had divided the labor of running the shop, Babs had volunteered to keep it open and actually deal with the customers if Kyla would do all the ordering, billing and accounting. Babs loved people but was a disaster at figures. The book-keeping tasks kept Kyla's hours flexible, which was essential since she had a child to care for.

As she ran another tape through the adding ma-chine, Kyla was vaguely aware of the tinkling sound of the bell over their front door. She didn't pay any attention to it until Babs called out, "Oh, Kyla?"

"Hmm?" she responded absently, jotting down the sum of her tally.

"You have a customer."

"A cus—"

The question died on her lips as Trevor Rule stepped through the swinging louvered door that separated the shop proper from its back room.

"Hi."

Babs was standing behind him, grinning like a Cheshire cat. "I thought you might want to deal with this customer personally."

Kyla's eyes threatened her friend with annihilation. Sunday evening had been torture. They had eaten sup-per in the backyard on the picnic table under the trees.

The old table's paint was blistered and peeling because it had been in the backyard for as long as Kyla could remember. She and Babs used to drape it with blankets and play "tent" under it.

"Aren't you going to tell us *anything?*" Babs had asked around a mouthful of Meg's famous baked beans.

"There's nothing to tell," Kyla had said. "And would the three of you stop staring at me? My nose is not going to start growing like Pinocchio's."

"You can lie by omission," Babs intoned. "I don't think it's very sporting of you to keep us in the dark."

Kyla laid her fork on her plate, stared down at it while she slowly counted to ten, then raised her head. "All right. He drove me into the woods, parked, tore off all my clothes and we made wild, passionate love in the backseat of his car. We were both like wild beasts, consumed by spontaneous lust and licentiousness."

Kyla was the only one smiling when she finished her tale. "That's not very funny," Meg said stiffly. "For months we've been telling you you're too young and pretty to seal yourself off from life. We've encouraged you to start seeing men. Mr. Rule is the first one you haven't run from. We're only excited for you."

Kyla sighed wearily. "That's my point, Mom. There's nothing to be excited about. I had a husband. His name was Richard Stroud. He'll remain my husband until I die. I'll never fall in love again, never love anyone but Richard, and am not looking for someone to love that way again."

"Love, love, love," Babs cried in exasperation. "Do you always have to bring *love* into it? Why not just go out for kicks? Have some fun. You don't have to love a guy to enjoy him."

"Maybe you don't, but I do. And you know damn good and well, Babs, that men don't take out women 'for kicks' without expecting them to jump into bed with them for a payoff. I'm sorry, Mom, Dad," she said to them when their faces paled, "but that's the way it is these days. Now, I don't want to hear another word about Trevor Rule or any other man. I'm not in the market for one. Is that clear?"

They had honored her request and changed the subject, though she could tell that Trevor Rule was far from being a dead issue. All day Monday her parents had leaped toward the telephone each time it rang. It was the same at work with Babs. Kyla was relieved that none of the callers had been the one they obviously expected.

Relieved, but a trifle disappointed, too. He could have at least *tried* to reach her and given her the satisfaction of saying she didn't want to see him again. Despite her best intentions, her thoughts often strayed back to him.

Now, seeing him filling the doorway to the back room made her insides turn to mush. A dull roaring sound, not unlike the ocean, was rushing through her head.

"Hello, Trevor."

Some smart advertising executive should hire him to model jeans, she thought. He wore them so well. His chest and upper arms filled out the cotton shirt to perfection. His hair was agreeably mussed by the wind. The patch over his eye gave him the dangerous air of a mercenary, a man who lived just beyond the pale, a man to be wary of. Extremely wary of.

Belying his macho image, Trevor crouched down

to speak to Aaron, who was standing in front of the large refrigerated cabinet that stored the flowers they used in their arrangements. "Hiya, Scout." The boy was happily slapping his hands against the cold glass. Trevor patted him on the bottom and Aaron gurgled a happy sound by way of greeting. He flashed their unexpected visitor a slobbery, toothy grin.

"I've got work to do. Excuse me," Babs said and disappeared.

For no good reason Kyla stood up behind her desk. Then, when Trevor also stood up, she sat back down. If she could have found it within herself to see the humor in their seesawing, she would have laughed.

"You look nice," he said.

She glanced down at her simple dress. It was the color of champagne, a color she knew she wore well. But it was nothing special and she wondered why he had even commented on it. Then she remembered that he'd never seen her dressed up. "Thank you." Was she supposed to tell him he looked nice, too? But he didn't look nice. He looked…sexy. She certainly wasn't going to tell him that because she had an idea he already knew.

"It smells good in here."

She forced her hands, which were gripping her ballpoint pen, to relax. "That's one of the benefits of working in a flower shop. It always smells good."

"I thought it might be you. Your perfume."

The ballpoint pen was strangled again. She tore her eyes away from Trevor's face and happened to catch sight of Aaron. "No, Aaron." She came out of her chair and rounded the desk hurriedly in an attempt to save the carnations. They were standing in a bucket of water, waiting to be used in an arrangement that had been ordered that morning. Kneeling down, she turned her meddlesome son away from the allure of the flowers and tried to distract him with his toys. "Here, play with Pooh Bear."

When she stood up again, she found herself as close to Trevor as his shadow. She stepped back quickly. "He's into everything." A nervous hand fluttered up to the gold chain around her neck, which seemed to have captured Trevor's interest. Count Dracula had never studied a neck so intently.

"Do you always keep Aaron here while you're working?"

"No." She explained about her mother's dental appointment. At that moment she couldn't have said whether she wished her mother would return and save her from being alone with Trevor. (Babs certainly was no help.) Or whether she would rather her mother never know about his visit to the shop.

But why was she herself making such a big deal of it? He was just another customer. "Can I help you with anything?"

"Oh, yeah," he said, jerking his attention back to the business at hand. "I need to order a corsage."

"I see."

Several thoughts tumbled through her head. Uppermost was whom the corsage was for. Then: If that's all he wanted, why hadn't he placed the order with Babs out front? Then: Oh, Lord, maybe he hadn't wanted to see her at all. Had Babs ushered him back here to see her when all he had intended to do was give Petal Pushers his business?

"I'll, uh, let's see, yes, here's an order pad." She

yanked up the tablet and held her pen over it. She filled in his name at the top. "What did you have in mind?"

"I'm not sure. What do you suggest?" He moved up behind her as she bent over the desk. She felt his legs brush against her skirt and madly thought about a French movie Babs had dragged her to a few months ago. She closed her eyes for a moment until the pornographic image was banished.

Drawing a ragged breath, she asked, "What's the occasion?"

"A banquet. Semiformal."

What banquet? Where? Whom was the corsage for? "A banquet. All right."

"I like orchids," he said.

"Orchids?"

"Yeah. Those big, fluffy ones. White ones."

You'll never guess what I found in a keepsake box the other day. That first orchid corsage you gave me for the Chi Omega spring dance. Remember? That's when I fell in love both with you and Bow Bells.

Kyla looked at Trevor with surprise. "Bow Bells?"

"Pardon?"

"Bow Bells. That's what you described. It's a cattleya hybrid." When he said nothing, she elaborated. "They're very pretty. They have large white ruffled petals and a deep golden throat." He was watching her lips as they formed each word. Kyla wondered how, in only a matter of seconds, "throat" had become the most provocative word in the English language.

"That's exactly what I had in mind."

"I... I have to order them from Dallas. When did you need the corsage?" Why was he looking at her as

though he were about to make her his lunch and why
was she allowing it?

"Saturday night." He took a step closer.

"No problem," she said briskly, alarmed by how
quiet it had become in the shrinking room and how
close they were standing. She could delineate each hair
in his thick mustache.

She bent back over the desk. "One flower or two?"

"Two."

"They're expensive."

"That's okay. Don't scrimp on it."

"What time do you want to pick it up?"

"Do you deliver?"

"Yes."

"Then please deliver it Saturday afternoon."

"The address?"

"Two twenty-three East Stratton."

The ballpoint pen fell from fingers suddenly gone
boneless. It rolled across the desk and dropped off the
edge. Kyla turned around and gazed up into the dark,
handsome face bending over hers. "That's my address."

"Will you go to the banquet with me?"

Speechless, she stared at him and began shaking her
head even before she found her voice. "No, no I can't."

"It wouldn't be a date," he said in a rush. "It's a banquet for bankers and other potential lenders. A group
of us developers have put together a videotape presentation on business opportunities in the community."

"What does that have to do with me?"

"You've lived here all your life. I'm still a stranger
in town. I'd like having you there to introduce me
around."

If Kyla was ever certain of one thing, it was that

Trevor Rule didn't need anyone to introduce him around. One smile like the one he was bestowing on her now and people, especially women, would flock to him. His grin was of the stuff that sold everything from toothpaste to brandy. When sex appeal had been doled out, Trevor Rule had gone through the line at least twice. He had charisma. He was the kind of man who attracted men and women alike. Everyone would want to be his friend.

"No, Trevor, I'm sorry, but I can't."

If he had posed no threat, then maybe she would have accepted. But he was too attractive. All she needed to do to start rumors flying was to be seen in the company of the newest eligible bachelor in Chandler. By Sunday morning her mother's friends would be talking wedding.

He made a small regretful sound and rubbed the back of his neck. "I never thought I'd have to resort to this to get a date with a beautiful woman, but I'm desperate."

"Resort to what?"

He looked at her cajolingly from beneath his brows. The green eye was twinkling. "You owe me a favor."

"Do either of you claim this little hoodlum?"

As one, they turned toward the door to see a vexed Babs holding Aaron in her arms. He had three drooping carnations clutched in one tight, moist fist. He had left a trail of wilted flowers from the back room into the shop. The stems had dripped water onto the floor. Aaron was waving at them with another battered blossom.

"Oh, gosh, Babs, I'm sorry." Kyla rushed forward and took Aaron out of Bab's arms.

"That's all right. He only destroyed about ten dollars worth of carnations, not to mention the vase he was stuffing his Pooh Bear into. You must have been awfully busy in here." Her blue eyes were teasing as they bounced between Trevor and Kyla.

"We were, uh… Mr. Rule was ordering a, uh, some flowers."

Babs gave them both a knowing glance before smiling benignly and leaving them alone again.

"Well?" Trevor said. "About Saturday night."

"I don't know." Kyla and Aaron were battling over possession of the carnations because she was afraid he was going to eat them and she didn't know if they were poisonous or not. When he finally lost that skirmish, he reached for her earring.

How could she wrestle with him and make a decision like this? She should coolly refuse Trevor's invitation, no matter how charmingly it had been extended. She had never written up an order for flowers she was to receive before. And that much charm coming from a man she hardly knew was disturbing.

But, she did owe him a favor, and if he considered this a business occasion…

"It wouldn't be a date?" she asked tentatively.

"No."

"Because I wouldn't want you to get the wrong idea."

"I understand."

"I mean, I'm a widow and I don't date."

"You've already told me that."

She had, hadn't she? So why was she babbling on about it? If she made too much out of it, he would think she was protesting too much. "All right, I'll go."

"Great. I'll see you Saturday about seven. And don't forget the corsage."

"You still want me to make it?"

"Sure. Goodbye, Aaron." He cuffed the boy under the chin. "See you Saturday night, Kyla."

Seconds after he had gone through the swinging door, Babs pushed it open. "'See you Saturday night, Kyla.' Is that what he said?"

"Yes. I'm going to a banquet with him."

"That's wonderful," Babs said, clapping her hands together. "What'll you wear?"

"I won't wear anything." When Babs's mouth formed a small *o*, Kyla sighed resignedly. "I mean, it doesn't matter what I wear because it's not really a date."

"Oh, sure."

"It's not. It's a business affair and he asked me to go with him to introduce him around."

"Uh-huh."

"He did!"

"Uh-huh."

"It's not a date."

"Uh-huh."

"He said so himself. It's not a date."

CHAPTER FIVE

IT CERTAINLY FELT like a date.

Kyla didn't remember being this jittery getting dressed for her first car date, her senior prom or her wedding. She didn't want to think about her wedding or Richard. But *not* thinking about them only implied that this "date" with Trevor Rule meant something, which she vowed repeatedly that it didn't.

Still, she was clumsy as she tried to apply her makeup. Nothing went right. She had to do one eyelid three times. Aaron, who seemed to have grown an extra pair of hands, was into everything. Her mother and father kept popping into her room, apprising her of the time, the current weather conditions, asking questions, offering assistance and generally making pests of themselves.

Thankfully, Babs had a "heavy date," so Kyla was spared her interference. Babs had insisted that Kyla buy a new dress for the occasion when all the while Kyla had insisted that it wasn't an "occasion."

Kyla's eventual capitulation only resulted in another argument, over which dress she should buy. Babs had gone on the shopping expedition without invitation.

"I like this yellow dress," Kyla said. Babs had mimed gagging herself by poking her index finger into her open mouth. "Very eloquent," Kyla had said sarcastically.

Placing her hands on her shapely hips, Babs asked, "Would you rather look like Mata Hari or Little Mary Sunshine?"

"I'd rather look like me."

"Try on the black one again."

"It's too...too..."

"Exactly," Babs had said, shoving the garment at Kyla impatiently. "It's terrific and it *is* you. Right?" she demanded of the intimidated sales clerk who was cowering against the dressing room wall.

"Right."

Kyla had left the store with the black dress, knowing instinctively that she was making a mistake. The yellow would have been much more suited to her. The black dress was too sophisticated. Trevor would think... God knows what he would think.

Her previous worries were compounded as she zipped up the back of the cocktail dress and caught her reflection in the mirror. The silk clung and swirled just where it was required to. Black complemented her complexion, especially since she had already enhanced it with pastel blushers and frosted eye shadows, and lip gloss the color of peach sorbet. Her hair was soft and shiny and had about it a look of artful disarray. She had left it to curl softly on her shoulders, sweeping one side back and holding it above her ear with a decorative comb. At the base of her throat lay a single strand of pearls. Pearl studs adorned her ears.

Hearing the doorbell downstairs, she reached for the orchid corsage and hastily pinned it to her dress. She pricked herself with the pins and was glad that

Aaron, who parroted everything these days, wasn't in the room to hear her soft curses.

The corsage had brought on another argument between herself and Babs as recently as that afternoon. "It's four-thirty and you haven't made that corsage Trevor ordered."

"I'm not going to," Kyla had replied.

"The hell you're not. I've already sent him a bill."

"You what?"

"He's a customer, Kyla. He ordered a corsage and I billed him for it. Now we owe him an orchid corsage."

Casting her smiling friend a stormy look, Kyla made up the corsage.

"Won't do," Babs said, surpervising over Kyla's shoulder. "He asked for two flowers."

"How do you know?"

"I overheard. And he said not to scrimp either, so put some more of that lacy stuff behind it."

"Did you eavesdrop on the entire conversation?"

"Sure. At least I think I did. Did either of you say anything you're ashamed of?"

"Of course not," Kyla said heatedly.

"Then why are you getting so bent out of shape?"

Now, as Kyla made one last inspection of herself in the mirror, she had to admit that it all went together well: the black silk dress, the pearls, the hothouse flowers.

And that was just what she felt like, a hothouse flower who had been cultured and protected and was about to be thrust into the elements for the first time.

Such qualms were juvenile. She knew they were. But knowing they were juvenile and shaking them off were two different things. She had been married. She was a mother. But she felt like an old-world, convent-bred ingenue about to meet her first man.

"This is ridiculous," she told herself in exasperation as she yanked up the small black beaded evening bag and switched out the light. "This isn't even a date." She repeated that to herself, in cadence to her trepid footsteps down the stairs.

Trevor was standing in the entrance hall holding Aaron in his arms. He was bouncing the boy up and down as he conversed with Meg and Clif.

"...should be finished in about two weeks." He swung his dark head around when he realized that something on the staircase had captured the Powerses' attention.

Only an act of will kept Kyla's feet from faltering on the next step as Trevor looked up at her. She forced herself to descend calmly. Unfortunately she had no such control over her heartbeat.

"Hello, Trevor."

"Hi."

Aaron was plucking at Trevor's mustache, but he seemed not to notice. His gaze was fixed on Kyla. She was having just as hard a time keeping her eyes off him. He was gorgeous.

His suit was charcoal-gray, so dark that it almost looked black. The crisp white shirt only intensified the color of his hair and the depth of his tan. The correct silver and black striped tie would have looked ordinary on any other man, but Kyla realized then that Trevor was by no means ordinary. He was never going to be. Perhaps his distinction lay in the ever-present eye patch, which was so familiar now, so much a part of his face, that she didn't see it as something apart.

"The orchids are beautiful."

"Yes," she said breathlessly. She touched the corsage lightly, self-consciously, where it reposed on her breast. "Thank you. Do you like them?"

"Do you?"

"Very much."

"Good."

Think of something else to say, you idiot, she ordered herself.

Aaron came to her rescue. He chose that moment to take one of those unpredictable dives that toddlers often take from one pair of arms to another. Without warning, he lunged toward her and she barely had time to get her arms up before he landed against her with a solid thud.

But Trevor, whose relaxed arms tensed around the child immediately, hadn't quite let go of Aaron yet. So his right arm became trapped between Aaron and Kyla's breasts. As she gradually got a better grip on Aaron, Trevor withdrew his arm. There ensued a few moments of awkwardness, which everyone tried to cover with loud chatter.

"Here, give me the baby," Meg said.

"You two had better be going or you'll be late," Clif said.

"Are you ready?" Trevor asked.

"Yes. I think I have everything. Good night, Aaron."

"We'll get Aaron to bed, so there's no rush about coming home early," Meg said.

"Drive carefully. You've got plenty of time," Clif called to them as they went down the walk.

Kyla was grinding her teeth. Anyone would think this was her first date. She wouldn't have been sur-

prised if Clif had posed them in the hall while Meg
went searching for the camera.

Trevor stepped around her to open the car door.
He didn't touch her and she was grateful. All too well
she was remembering the feel of his hard arm moving
across her breasts. It had left a tide of heat in its wake.

Once he was behind the wheel, he said, "I know
this isn't a date, but am I allowed to tell you how pretty
you look?"

His attempt at humor put her at ease somewhat and
she glanced over at him. "Yes, and thank you."

"You're welcome."

He reached for the dials of the radio and turned to
an easy-listening music station. His suit coat sleeve slid
up. His shirt cuff was starched and stiff and had been
skewered with a cuff link that had a smooth square of
ebony fixed in a trim gold setting.

He had impeccable taste.

"I haven't talked to you since Tuesday. How was
your week?"

"Busy," she said, silently thanking him for opening up an avenue of conversation. She seemed to have
lost all talent for making small talk. Trevor hadn't,
though, and before she knew it they had arrived at
their destination.

The Chandler Country Club was only two years old.
The landscaping was still immature, but the modern
building of native stone couldn't be faulted. Sprinklers
out on the dark golf greens were swishing as Trevor
escorted her up the footpath that connected the parking lot to the front door.

She had almost, *almost,* gotten accustomed to having his hand wrapped around her elbow. But she wasn't

prepared for him to slow his stride, lean down close to her and come near to pressing his face against her neck before standing straight again.

"This time I know that fragrance isn't flowers. It's you. And you smell wonderful."

"Thank you."

The words had been difficult to speak for the constriction in her throat. He overwhelmed her. He was so tall, so purely masculine. Around her, he had never acted like anything but a gentleman. Nonetheless she felt threatened by him. Not afraid, just threatened.

Every time he smiled down at her, as he was doing now, she remembered the discussions she and Babs used to have about kissing and how it would feel to kiss a man with a mustache.

Trevor's dark mustache was thick, but well groomed. It virtually obliterated his upper lip, while emphasizing the shape of the lower. It curved over the corners of his mouth as though caressing it. His teeth shone beneath it, startlingly white. The overall effect was disturbingly sensual.

Kyla tried convincing herself that her interest in it was purely casual, a holdover from youthful curiosity. But her powers of persuasion seemed to be taking the night off.

The cocktail party preceding the banquet had already started by the time they entered the room overlooking the golf course and swimming pool. The laughter-spiked din almost drowned out the music being provided by the combo playing a popular hit from a dais in the corner.

"Would you like something to drink?" Trevor had

to bend down and place his lips close to her ear to be heard over the racket.

She turned, stretched up and spoke directly into his ear. "Club soda and lime, please." He nodded, smiled and elbowed his way through the crowd toward the bar, leaving behind him the scent of his cologne. Kyla liked it very much. It was clean and brisk, with an air of citrus. She couldn't help but notice how well the tailored coat fit his broad shoulders and—

"Why, Kyla Stroud! I told Herbie it was you. It's so good to see you out, dear."

"Hello, Mrs. Baker, Mr. Baker."

"How are your folks?"

"They're fine, thanks."

"And your little boy?"

"Aaron's a typical toddler." She laughed softly. "Almost more than I can keep up with."

"Kyla, your drink." She turned and accepted the glass of soda from Trevor. The surprised expressions on the older couple's faces were just what she had expected and dreaded.

"Thank you, Trevor. I'd like you to meet Mr. and Mrs. Herb Baker. Mrs. Baker taught me seventh-grade English grammar and literature. Mr. Baker has an insurance company. Trevor Rule," she said, presenting Trevor to them.

"Rule, Rule," Mr. Baker repeated as he pumped Trevor's hand. "Sure, Rule Enterprises! I've seen your signs everywhere. Contractor, aren't you?"

"Yes, sir. I've just formed my own company."

"Couldn't have picked a better place to start," Baker said. "Chandler used to be a sleepy little town. Nothing but a cotton gin here for decades. We're gradually changing all that. You joined the Chamber of Commerce last week, didn't you?"

"Yes, sir, I did."

"Glad to hear it. I'm on the membership committee."

While this conversation had been going on, Mrs. Baker's eyes had been busily bouncing between the two of them. She couldn't have been more obviously greedy for information if she had had a radar detector growing out of her forehead. "Did the two of you know each other *before?*"

Before exactly what, Kyla was never to know because Trevor intervened. "Please excuse us. Someone across the room is waiting to meet Kyla. Mrs. Baker, Mr. Baker."

Trevor nodded politely; Kyla smiled vapidly and let him usher her away. "I know that makes you uncomfortable."

"What?"

"Being seen with me."

"It's not that. It's what everyone is thinking that bothers me," she admitted.

"What do you think they're thinking?"

"You know, things like, 'It's about time the little widow got out in circulation again.' Or, 'It's too soon for her to be out in circulation again.' My parents acted like they had to foist off the eldest daughter before they could marry off the other six."

Trevor laughed. "It wasn't as bad as all that."

"Wasn't it?"

"No. You're far more self-conscious about that than I am."

"I wouldn't have blamed you if you had turned and run."

"But I didn't. I'm still here."

He spoke with such intensity, that Kyla's uneasiness was far from relieved. To avoid looking at him, she gazed out over the crowded room. "Now I feel like people I've known all my life have become spies and gossips."

"You can waste a lot of time and energy worrying about what people are thinking and saying behind your back."

She sighed. "I know. But this can't be much fun for you, either. Don't you get the feeling that you're a window dressing and everyone's staring at you?"

He drew a serious face. "Don't worry about me. What people think doesn't really bother me. I don't want *you* to be uncomfortable. That's the only reason I mind it."

"We know this isn't actually a date. I just wish everyone else did."

"Short of announcing it over the microphone, what can I do to let them know this is not a date?"

For starters he could remove his hand from the small of her back. Because they had reached the other side of the room after maneuvering through the crowd—and his hand was still there, a firm, warm pressure against the arch of her back.

Then they could dispel more rumors by engaging other people in conversation. As it was, with the two of them silhouetted against the sunset beyond the plate glass windows, with Trevor's face bending close to hers in serious conversation, they must surely be giving everyone the impression that what they were saying was private and personal. It *felt* private and personal.

She moved, ostensibly to take a sip of her drink.

Actually it was to put a few safe inches between them. Trevor sipped at his own drink, a pale whiskey.

"Would it make you feel better if I told you that you look sensational?" he asked.

She traced the rim of her glass with her finger. "No, I don't think so."

"Okay. Then maybe I'd better not mention that your dress is a real knockout."

Her eyes slid up to his face and caught his teasing smile. Her own stiff, plastic, party-manners smile became genuine. "Thank you for not mentioning that."

"Maybe we should migrate toward the dining room," he said. "Some are already moving in that direction to locate their table."

On their way into the dining room they were joined by a young banker and his wife. Lynn and Ted Haskell were new to town and therefore didn't know Kyla and her past. Trevor introduced her merely as his "friend." She enjoyed their lively conversation through the filet mignon dinner.

Trevor was attentive to her every need, always making certain she had salt, pepper, butter, fresh bread, water, coffee. She found herself basking in his attention. Mealtimes with Aaron were more like battles. Attack and retreat. Sometimes when she finished, she couldn't remember having eaten because she had snatched bites between mopping up spilled milk and wiping Aaron's dodging mouth.

"Didn't you like the food?" Trevor asked as the waiter whisked away her embarrassingly empty plate.

She blushed at his teasing and laughed self-deprecatingly. "I loved it, mainly because I got to eat it in peace. Having dinner with Aaron isn't quite so relaxing. It was all I could do to keep myself from cutting your meat for you. If I start patting your napkin back into your lap, try not to notice."

He blinked, startled. Then a slow grin spread across his rugged face. Leaning closer he said, "Kyla, if you start patting my lap for any reason, I'm going to find it damn near to impossible not to notice."

She could easily have died at that moment. In fact she even prayed for a sudden death. Her cheeks were scalding. Her fingertips and toes were throbbing with an influx of blood. Never had she been so embarrassed.

"I... I meant—"

"I know what you meant." Trevor, sensing her mortification, squeezed her hand. "More coffee?"

She made no more verbal blunders and they settled back in their hard chairs for the program. After the videotape presentation, the speakers droned on endlessly, extolling the attributes of Chandler in particular and north central Texas in general.

"Bored?" Trevor whispered, leaning close.

She had unsuccessfully tried to hide a delicate yawn with her hand. "No. It's all very interesting."

"You're a terrible liar," he growled close to her ear. She laughed, ducking her head. "Do you want to leave?"

"No!" she exclaimed, knowing this evening was important to him. He was here to see and be seen.

"We can sneak out."

"No. I'm fine. Really."

"Sure?"

She nodded her head.

"Positive?"

She nodded again.

"You're lovely, Kyla."

Her head snapped up and she met his gaze, which was compelling and hot. "I just threw that in to see if you were paying attention."

Slowly he pulled away and sat back in his chair. Kyla swallowed hard and removed her gaze from his. She glanced around anxiously, wondering if anyone had noticed their whispered exchange. She caught sight of Mrs. Baker's expectant face and looked away quickly.

Her eyes landed on the banker and his wife. Lynn's hand was lying on Ted's thigh. He was idly stroking the back of her hand. Kyla smiled at such a sweet display of marital intimacy. The subconscious kind. The kind that came automatically. Those demonstrations that said so much, but that wouldn't even be remembered later.

Richard and I used to do things like that all the time.

Mentally she sprang erect. That was the first time she had thought of Richard in hours. Guilt pierced her to the core. What was wrong with her?

She concentrated on him, on his face, his smile, his funny laugh, until the final speaker concluded his speech. Trevor and she said their good-nights and were among the first to leave. They barely made it to the car before it began to rain.

Once under way Trevor asked, "Would you like to go somewhere for dessert?"

"Remember the cherry cheesecake?"

"Oh, yeah." After a pause he said, "Coffee?"

"I don't think so."

"A drink?"

"No thank you, Trevor. I should be getting home."

"Right."

He sounded disappointed. Surely she was mistaken. He must be as glad as she that this evening was almost over.

They said little, which only made the tapping of the rain on the roof of the car and the rhythmic clacking of the windshield wipers seem louder.

Apparently he wasn't accustomed to driving with both hands on the wheel because he kept his right one in constant motion while he steered the car with his left. At first he fiddled with the radio, turning the volume up, then seconds later turning it back down.

He reached for the thermostat. "Comfortable?"

"Yes, fine."

His hand was withdrawn, but was no less restless. With that fidgeting right hand he worked loose the knot of his necktie. He raked back his hair. He adjusted the volume on the radio one more time. Finally he let that hand rest.

On the seat.

Halfway between them.

From the corner of her eye, Kyla watched that hand as though it posed some grave threat.

What if it inched toward her? Would she say something?

What if it reached out and grabbed her? Would she scream?

What if it reached for her own? Would she allow her hand to be held?

What if it caressed her thigh? Would she slap it away?

Her heart was thudding and she felt her palms grow slick with moisture. Never had the house where she lived safely with her parents and baby been such a welcome sight.

The hand didn't do anything but turn off the key in the ignition after the car had rolled to a slow stop. "Sit tight," he said, when she reached for the door handle. "I have an umbrella." Turning, he stretched his arm over the seat and reached behind him for the umbrella. His coat gaped open and Kyla saw the hard muscles of his chest straining against his shirt.

He got out and popped the umbrella open. He was holding it over his head when he opened her door and reached inside to take her hand and lift her out.

How it happened, she was never quite sure. Maybe they were crowding beneath the umbrella in an effort not to get wet. But somehow, *somehow,* when she stood up on the sidewalk, she was very close to him. So close that their clothes were brushing against each other.

Instinctively, her head tilted back. His face loomed close. He was holding the umbrella with his left hand. With his right, he loosely enfolded her neck.

She felt the tickling brush of his mustache first, then his lips, warm and firm, rubbing against hers.

Oh, God, that feels good.

She pulled back quickly and lowered her head. He removed his hand from her neck. She could still feel the imprint of each finger, though he had barely touched her and his clasp could hardly be classified as such.

The rain pecked against the silk umbrella and rolled down its slick surface to drip off the edge. Beneath that meager shelter they stood still and silent…and close.

"I'm sorry," Trevor said after a long moment. "No kisses allowed on the first date?"

"This isn't a date."

"Oh, yeah. Damn. I keep forgetting that."

He turned them toward the front door. Carefully they made their way up the walkway, made treacherous by the rainfall. No outside light had been left on to aid them in reaching the safety of the porch.

Trevor swung the umbrella down and shook it hard.

"Thank you for the evening, Trevor," Kyla said, edging toward the door.

"I know we said this wasn't a date." The umbrella was dropped onto the porch. It made a lazy spin on the axis of its handle before coming to rest.

"Yes. That's what we said."

"Right. We agreed that it wasn't a date, only—"

"What?"

"I'm not pushing. I don't want you to think I'm pushing."

"I don't."

"But…" He took a step toward her. Another. "Say this *was* a date."

"Yes?"

"Would you—"

"Would I what?"

His hands came up to frame her face tenderly. Her eyes slid closed. His lips met hers again. But they stayed this time. And pressed. And angled until hers parted. The tip of his tongue dared to penetrate, to make fleeting contact with hers, to sweep her mouth once, to sink deeply. Then it withdrew. He lifted his mouth away from hers. His hands fell to his sides.

"Good night, Kyla."

"Good night."

How the words found their way out of her mouth, she couldn't fathom. After watching him retrieve his

umbrella and walk to his car, she automatically unlocked the front door and let herself in.

She drifted upstairs, telling herself every step of the
way that since it hadn't really been a date, that hadn't
really been a kiss, either.

But her alter ego was saying, "Oh, it was a kiss
all right. It was a dilly of a kiss. Babs, at her wildest,
couldn't have imagined such a kiss. If you looked up
the word *kiss* in the dictionary, a description of what
you just experienced beneath Trevor's mouth would
be the definition."

She unpinned the orchid corsage and laid it on the
dresser. She carelessly dropped her pearls amidst her
perfume decanters, when normally she would have
stored them in their velvet box. The black silk dress
was left heedlessly lying on a chair with her under-
clothes piled atop it.

She floated toward the bed, naked—for the first
time in a long time.

When she reached to turn out the lamp on the bedside table, she noticed Richard's picture.

Then she burst into tears.

CHAPTER SIX

"YOU'RE A DAMN FOOL."

He spoke softly. His breath fogged the window because the glass had been cooled by the rain. The room behind him was dark, so he was spared having to look at his reflection in the windowpane.

He sipped his drink. "A fool, a coward," he sighed, then added, "a liar."

Every time he saw her, he was lying by not telling her who he was. He knew what he was doing was wrong, but he couldn't bring himself to say, "I'm Smooch. Remember me? The guy your husband wrote to you about. The kind of man you said you detested. Egotistical. Thinks he's God's gift to women. Despoiler of reputations. Smooch." She had ridiculed him in her letters and he had deserved every reproachful word. In his place her beloved husband had died.

Clenching his teeth and closing his eyes, Trevor pressed his forehead against the window. What he was doing was manipulative and downright deceitful. There was no way he could excuse himself.

Actually there was an excuse, but who would believe it? Who would believe that he had fallen in love with a woman he'd never seen merely by reading her letters? He barely believed it himself. Certainly she would never believe it.

Sooner or later he would have to tell her who he was. But when? How? When she found out, what would her reaction be?

Impatiently he turned away from the rain-streaked window and slammed his highball glass down on the tacky table. It came with the drab, furnished apartment he hoped he was living in only temporarily.

He knew what her reaction would be when he told her. Fury. Contempt. Hate. Those weren't the emotions he wanted to see burning in her brown eyes when she looked at him.

Going into the bedroom, he stripped. The purple scars that meandered and crisscrossed down his left side were no more than he deserved, he thought with self-loathing. He deserved to be placed on the rack for not having identified himself to her when they had met.

But would he tell her the next time he saw her?

No. What good was making promises in the dark that he knew he wouldn't keep? He wasn't going to tell her. Not yet. Not until…

Lying in bed alone, he watched the rain splatter silver patterns on the windows. He thought about her. About the kiss.

"Oh, God, the kiss," he groaned.

She had such a delectable mouth. Warm and wet and silky. Beyond the restraint she had exercised, he knew there lurked a simmering passion.

You know how I've always loved rain. It's raining today, one of those relentless, steady downpours when it looks like the sun has deserted and forgotten us. I'm not enjoying it. I'm depressed. The raindrops aren't happy, sparkling drops that dance as they splash in puddles. But leaden, ominous things that would weigh me down like chain mail if they fell on me.

I've figured out the difference. Rain is something that must be shared. There's nothing cozier than seeking shelter from the rain with someone you love. But there's nothing lonelier than having to endure it alone.

As Trevor recalled that particular letter, he laid his hand on his body and moaned softly. Still tasting the kiss, he whispered to the shadows, "If you were here with me, Kyla, I'd share the rain with you. I'd share everything."

"BUT THAT'S CRAZY!"

"I don't want to discuss it, Babs."

"Because you know you're wrong. Because you know you're just being pigheaded."

"It's not pigheadedness," Kyla averred. "It's common sense."

They were washing the breakfast dishes. Kyla's friend was as transparent as the plastic wrap covering the leftover biscuits. Her early appearance for Sunday morning breakfast was unprecedented. As soon as she had cleared the back door she had begun grilling Kyla about her date with Trevor.

"I can't believe you won't go out with him again."

"Believe it."

"Why won't you?"

"That's my business."

"And you're my best friend, so I'm making it mine."

Kyla draped the dish towel over the rack and turned to face Babs. "Leave it, Babs. Don't you have enough drama in your own life to keep you occupied? Must you meddle in mine?" She left the kitchen and headed for the stairs. Babs was right behind her.

"My love life doesn't need help. Yours is at a crisis point."

Kyla halted on the step and whirled around. "We're not talking about a 'love life.' I don't have one."

"Precisely my point."

"And," Kyla stressed, "I don't want one."

"All right. Delete 'love' and insert 'sex.' Let's talk about your sex life."

Kyla resumed her trip upstairs. "That's disgusting."

Babs grabbed her arm to detain her. "Disgusting? *Disgusting?* Since when is a healthy sex life disgusting? You used to have one."

"That's right," Kyla said, yanking her arm free. "With a man I loved, my husband, who loved and respected me. That's as it should be." Tears stung her eyes and she dashed up the remaining stairs before Babs could see them fall.

The Powerses had already left for Sunday school. Kyla was to join them in time for the worship service. They had taken Aaron with them.

When Babs entered Kyla's bedroom, the latter was shrugging off her robe. She took a dress from her closet and stepped into it. Somewhat subdued, Babs sat down on the edge of the bed.

"Ideally that's the way it should be," she acknowledged sulkily. "But we're not all that lucky, Ky. We take what we can get."

"I don't. What I had was perfect. I don't want anything less."

"Well, hell, look at him! Trevor Rule is just about as perfect as you can get."

Just the sound of his name caused Kyla's hand to tremble as she tried to secure an earring in her ear. It wasn't taking much to rattle her today, not after the tearful night she had spent. Seeing Richard's picture on her bedside table had reminded her of her betrayal. She had vowed to keep him alive in her heart. Spending time with Trevor Rule, she had discovered, jeopardized her resolve to hold to that pledge.

To counter Babs's argument she said, "How do I know he's so perfect? I don't know anything about him. I only met him a week ago."

"You know how good he looks. You know that he's considerate, that he drives a nice—if rather boring—car, that he's ambitious, that he's kind to senior citizens and children, that he—"

"All right, I get the point. Besides the fact that he's good-looking, you could be describing thirty other men. I don't want to marry any of them, either."

"Who said anything about marriage?" Babs cried. "I'm talking about having fun. Going out." She glanced up at Kyla slyly, "Going to bed."

The kiss, the kiss, the kiss. Damn that intimate and evocative kiss. Why had she permitted it? Why couldn't she forget it? Why had it been so good?

"Don't be silly." Shakily she stuffed tissues into her handbag. Aaron invariably came out of the church nursery with sticky hands. "I don't even think about that anymore."

"Liar." Kyla's head swiveled around. "You might not consciously think about it, dear heart, but you think about it. Ky, you can't just cast off your own sexuality because somebody else dies. You don't dispose of it like a pair of socks that don't fit anymore. It's a part of you and you're going to have to come to terms with it."

"I already have."

"I don't think so."

"What makes you say that?"

"Because you've put on earrings that don't match."

Incredulous, Kyla checked the mirror. Babs was right. Aggravated, she began making the switch. "That doesn't prove anything."

Babs came off the bed and approached her friend. "I know you loved Richard. I'm not trying to talk you into forgetting him."

"I never will."

"I know that," Babs conceded with her kindest tone of the morning. "But he's dead, Ky. You're alive. And being alive is not a sin."

As though refuting her friend's words, Kyla said, "I'm going to be late for church."

At the front door Babs caught up with her. "Will you or not?"

"Will I what?" Kyla asked as she checked her hair one last time in the foyer mirror.

"Go out with him again?"

"No. End of discussion."

Babs pointed her finger at Kyla and glared at her with narrowed eyes. "You had a good time," she accused. "Damn it, I *know* you did."

Too good a time, Kyle thought. "I did him a favor to pay back one. Now we're even. Besides," she added as she pushed open the screen door, "he probably won't even ask me out again."

HE DID. ON Thursday of that week. She hadn't seen or heard from him until the telephone rang in Petal Pushers. Since Babs was busy with a customer, Kyla answered.

"Petal Pushers."

"Kyla? Hi."

"Hello."

"This is Trevor."

As if he needed to identify himself. She had recognized his voice immediately. At the sound of it, a delicious weakness had spilled through her.

"How are you?" she asked, wishing her voice didn't sound so breathless.

"I'm all right. You?"

"Fine. Busy. I've hardly had time to think this week. The days have flown by." She didn't want him to think she had been sitting by the telephone waiting for a call from him. Why she felt it was necessary to play these courtship games, she didn't know.

"How's Aaron?"

"Cranky. I thinks he's cutting another tooth."

A deep rich laugh filled her ear before he said, "Then he has a right to be cranky."

She twisted the telephone cord through nervous fingers. Should she thank him again for Saturday night? No, that would remind him of their date. And of the kiss.

"The reason I'm calling…"

"Yes?"

"It's short notice, I know, but the Haskells… You remember Ted and Lynn?"

"Sure."

"Well, they asked me over for dinner tomorrow

night. Steaks out on the patio. Would you like to go with me?"

"I don't think I can."

"Lynn suggested it," he rushed to say. "What I mean is, she asked if I'd like to bring someone and when I mentioned your name, she was glad. Seems you two hit it off."

"Yes, we did. I liked her very much. But Friday night is a problem. Aaron—"

"He's invited, too. Lynn said they have a wading pool. She thought all the kids—they have two, you know—could play in the pool." He laughed again and Kyla realized how much she was coming to like that rumbling bass sound. "We know how much Aaron likes water."

"I don't know, Trevor."

"Please."

Kyla gnawed the inside of her jaw in indecision. Should she accept? No. Because she didn't want to give him the wrong impression. On the other hand, how could he jump to the wrong conclusion if her baby was invited along? It didn't sound like an evening that would lend itself to romance. And wouldn't it be ungracious not to accept the Haskells' invitation? She really had liked the friendly couple. One could never cultivate enough friendships with bankers. As a business-woman, having this contact might prove to be helpful later on. She and Babs might want to expand some day and need a business loan.

Good Lord, whom was she trying to convince?

The fact was that she wanted to go if only to prove that last Saturday night, and especially the kiss, had meant nothing. Trevor was new in town and didn't know many people. He wanted her company. That was all it amounted to.

Blame all her magnified erotic memories of the kiss on Babs, who had recently been taking her to movies redolent with skin, sweat and steam. Blame it on the fact that she hadn't felt the touch of a man's mouth on hers in almost two years.

It hadn't meant *anything.* So why make a big deal of it? Why not just go out and enjoy the Haskells' hospitality?

"That sounds like fun, Trevor. Thank you for inviting me…us. Aaron and I will be glad to go. What time?"

"SEVEN O'CLOCK ON the dot."

"Actually the digital clock says six fifty-eight, but we're ready."

Kyla stepped aside and Trevor walked through the screened front door. Between the times she saw him, she forgot just how tall he was. Or did he only seem so because he was so muscular? Impressive biceps bunched beneath the short sleeves of his white polo shirt. The casual tan slacks would have elicited a comment about his buns from Babs, had she been there to see him.

"Are your folks around?"

"No. They said to tell you hello. On most Friday nights they meet with friends for catfish and dominoes. They alternate houses."

"Is that the reason you hesitated to accept my invitation tonight?"

One of them, Kyla thought. A minor reason. "Yes.

Babysitters are hard to come by. By the time they're old enough to trust, they're thinking of nothing but boys."

"Did you?"

"What? Think of boys? Of course," she said, throwing her head back and laughing softly. He liked the way her hair swirled around her shoulders. "With a friend like Babs I had no choice. All through high school we were degenerately boy crazy."

"I see you two degenerates have been working on your tans."

The white sundress showed it off. She had hesitated to wear it because it left her shoulders and most of her back bare, save for a network of straps. After her shower, she had smoothed on a lotion that gave her tanned skin a glowing patina. She had added to the luster by dusting her shoulders with a body powder that had a sheen to it. Her nose and cheekbones had been dabbed with the puff, too. With her sun-lightened hair, she looked summery and golden.

"In the afternoons," she answered, self-consciously aware of Trevor's green gaze moving over her. "There's enough sun left when I get home to get in a half hour's worth."

"It looks great." His voice sounded a bit hoarse. Just the way he had sounded before he kissed her.

She moved away quickly. "Aaron is upstairs."

"Let me help you bring him down."

"Don't bother."

"Four hands are better than two," he said as he followed her up the stairs. "Where Aaron's concerned, I'm not even sure that's enough."

When they came into the nursery, Aaron was standing up in his crib. At his first sight of Trevor, he pointed his index finger, began to bounce up and down against the rails of his baby bed and babbled something that only he could understand.

"I think he recognizes me," Trevor said, pleased. He lifted the boy out of the bed and swung him high over his head. "Hiya, Scout. Have you been a positive terror this week? Eaten any more carnations?"

It was while he was holding the baby over his head that Kyla noticed the scar on Trevor's left arm. It started at his wrist, twisted around his elbow and disappeared into the sleeve of his shirt. When Trevor turned, laughing, to address something to her, he saw where she was looking.

He sobered instantly. "I told you it was ugly."

Her eyes swung up to his face. "You must have suffered terribly."

He shrugged. "Not so much. Ready?"

He carried Aaron while she toted the diaper bag. He had looked at it dubiously when she hoisted it onto her shoulder. "I know. It looks like we're moving," she said, laughing, "but I've learned to go prepared and I'm sure Lynn will understand."

He helped her secure the house. "We'll have to transfer Aaron's car seat from your car to mine," Trevor remarked as they stepped off the porch.

"How far are we going? He can sit in my lap."

"Uh-uh. Let's do this right."

"Will you at least compromise and take my car?"

"Will you let me drive?"

She smiled up at him and dropped the keys into his free hand. "How's the house coming?" she asked him once Aaron had been secured in his car seat and they were driving through the twilit streets.

Trevor had had to push the front seat back to accommodate his long legs. He drove as he had before, with his left wrist draped idly over the steering wheel. Only this time he stretched his right arm across the back of the front seat. His fingers were close to, but not quite touching, her left shoulder.

"Great. Your idea about the dining area in the kitchen was terrific. Even the architect liked it and was miffed that he hadn't thought of it himself."

"It's such a lovely lot. It would be a shame not to enjoy those trees to the utmost."

"That's why I chose to build there."

...that a house without a tree is nothing. I'd rather live in a tree house like the Swiss Family Robinson, than in a palace that was surrounded by nothing but concrete.

Ted and Lynn Haskell had equally effervescent personalities. Kyla and Aaron, over whom they made much ado, were welcomed into the noisy chaos of a happy home. Not that their house wasn't lovely. It was. Kyla even felt a mild envy for the gracious rooms that Lynn led her through on the tour that Kyla had requested.

The couple had produced two children as handsome and congenial as themselves. The eldest, a girl of seven, bossily took Aaron under her wing and kept him entertained while the men supervised the grilling of the steaks out on the patio. Lynn was unself-conscious enough to accept Kyla's offer to help in the kitchen.

"Trevor told us that you're a widow."

Kyla's hands paused as she tore at the iceberg lettuce. Had he been talking about her? Apparently Lynn sensed her tension. "I'm no gossip, Kyla. Neither is Trevor. I asked. He told me, but he didn't elaborate. If it makes you uncomfortable, we can talk about something else."

Trevor couldn't have elaborated because he didn't know the facts about Richard's death. Curious, that he had never asked. She glanced at Lynn. "Richard died the day after Aaron was born."

"My God," Lynn said, setting down the bowl of potato salad she'd just taken from the refrigerator. "What happened?"

Kyla related the story. "It hasn't been quite two years yet."

Lynn looked out over the patio where the men were sipping at beers while they tended both the steaks and the children who were splashing in the wading pool. As she watched, Aaron bent at the waist and ducked his head into the water. Apparently he got more than he bargained for. He came up sputtering. Instantly Trevor was kneeling beside the pool, wiping the boy's face with a towel and thumping him on the back. "Trevor and Aaron seemed to have formed quite an attachment. When did you start seeing him?"

"Only a week or so ago. We're only friends. What dressing do you want on the salad?" When Kyla turned around, Lynn was looking at her with an amused expression. "What is it?"

Lynn laughed. "Only that if everything Ted says about Trevor Rule is true, you'd better be careful."

"Why? What does Ted say?"

"That Trevor is ambitious, that he knows no fear, that he's daring in business ventures and that so far they have all paid off. In other words, he usually gets what he goes after." She smiled and sent a wicked grin in Kyla's direction. "If the attention he paid you the other night at the banquet is any indication, I'd say the man's after you. Unless you want to be caught, you'd better run fast." After taking two cans of beer from the refrigerator, she passed one to Kyla. "Come on. I think they can use another."

Trevor had lifted Aaron out of the pool, then had crouched down and placed him between his knees. He was drying the child briskly with a towel, as though it were something he did every day. Kyla popped the top off the beer and handed it down to him.

"I'll take over when you want me to."

Trevor looked up at her with a heart-stopping smile. He sipped the beer and licked the foam off his mustache. "We're doing fine, but thanks for the beer."

"You're welcome." Flustered, she turned away in time to see Ted accepting his fresh beer from his wife. He said, "Thanks, hon," and swatted her bottom. His hand stayed and squeezed her playfully before falling away. Lynn bent down and planted a soft kiss on the crown of Ted's thinning hair.

Kyla felt a loneliness more encompassing than any she had experienced before.

"The house is dark," Trevor commented as he drove Kyla's car into the driveway.

"I guess Mom and Dad are still out." It was odd that they were out this late. Usually the domino parties didn't last much past eleven and it was almost midnight. She strongly suspected that their delay in coming home was calculated.

"Ted and I should have challenged you and Lynn to a rematch."

"Men will never beat women at word games."

"How's that?"

"Women are more intuitive than men."

"Well, my intuition is that Aaron's become dead-weight on your shoulder."

"This time your intuition is right."

Aaron, who had fallen asleep on the Haskells' living room sofa, hadn't taken kindly to being roused for the ride home. To prevent a tantrum to rival any recorded in history, Trevor had broken his own safety rule and let him ride in Kyla's lap rather than being strapped into his car seat.

Trevor got out of the car and came around to assist Kyla. "Is your key in your purse?" he asked.

"The side pocket."

He had found the key by the time they reached the front door. Juggling the key, her handbag and the heavy diaper bag, he barely managed to unlock the door and swing it open.

"Thank you, Trevor. I had a good time."

"I'll see you in. I wouldn't let you and Aaron go into an empty house alone this late at night."

There seemed no point in arguing, though it made her distinctly uncomfortable to have him precede her through the dark house and upstairs. He had already switched on the soft lamp on top of the bureau by the time Kyla reached Aaron's room. She lowered the sleeping toddler into the baby bed.

"Can you undress him without waking him up?"

"I think I'll let him sleep in his shirt. I'm afraid if he wakes up fully, he'll think it's time for breakfast."

Trevor chuckled as he set the diaper bag in the rocker near the bed. He watched, fascinated, as her capable fingers moved swiftly to remove Aaron's shoes and socks.

Without waking him, she peeled down his shorts and plastic pants. Automatically she reached for the adhesive tabs that held on his disposable diaper. There her hands stilled.

She became acutely aware of the man standing beside her. The room seemed to shrink, leaving barely enough room for the two of them beside the baby bed. The atmosphere became thick with tension. The air was heavy and uncomfortably warm, almost sultry. The house grew more silent.

It was silly. Ridiculous. Aaron was a baby, sexually undeveloped. But the man standing next to her *was* developed and she was embarrassed to remove Aaron's diaper with Trevor hovering so close. Looking at a naked male child would be an intimacy between them, an intimacy Kyla couldn't engage in.

Apparently he noticed that her deft fingers had suddenly become clumsy and inefficient, because he cleared his throat loudly and moved away.

Faster than she'd ever done it in her life, she changed Aaron's wet diaper. Miraculously, he didn't wake up. Trevor was standing framed in the doorway of the nursery when she turned around after covering Aaron with a light blanket and switching out the light.

"All tucked in?"

"Yes. He had a big night. I think I'll get him one of those wading pools."

She led the way downstairs. There was a tightness in her chest she couldn't account for. Her stomach was fluttering. She felt an insane impulse to talk loudly so that the encroaching silence in the dark house wouldn't smother them.

One of the stairs took Trevor's weight and groaned in protest. He laughed softly and spoke in a hushed tone. "You've got a squeaky step."

"Several, I'm afraid." She sighed as she was reminded of a problem that was never too far from her mind. "It was my parents' dream to sell this house when Dad retired. They wanted to buy one of those fancy motor homes and travel all over the country."

"Why didn't they?"

"Richard was killed." Trevor said nothing, though she sensed a hesitation in his stride before he took the next step down. "I became a liability to them all over again."

"I'm sure they don't see it that way."

"But I do." He had stopped following. She stopped leading and turned around to face him. He was poised several steps above her.

"Why don't they sell it now?"

"They don't want Aaron and me to live alone. Besides, the market for houses in this part of town isn't as good as it once was. Unless the neighborhood is rezoned, I'm afraid they wouldn't make much by selling."

"This worries you, doesn't it? You don't want them to feel responsible for you."

She smiled ruefully. "I'm just sorry they aren't able to realize their dream because of me."

They looked at each other. Silence fell like a final curtain. Even though Trevor had turned on a light in the foyer, the remainder of the house was shadowed and dark.

One side of his face was lit, the right side. She

could sense the leashed tension in his body, though they weren't touching. His wavy black hair cast errant shadows over his face. Lean and dark and intense, he looked like the brooding hero of a Gothic novel. He posed no physical threat, but was dangerous just the same. What should have been sinister was scintillating.

He made her tremble.

"I'll let you out," she said hastily, breathlessly, and turned away.

She took only one more step down the stairs before she felt his fingers in her hair, reaching, closing into a fist that caught and captured. A small whimpering sound issued from her throat, but she was helpless. The fist closed tighter around the handful of hair. It rotated once, making his hold more tenacious. Then a steady, unrelenting pull gradually drew her head back, back, until she turned on the step.

With his other arm he lifted her up even as his head descended. He stamped his mouth over hers, hard and unyielding. He didn't step down to bring them together, but hauled her up instead and drew her against him.

Her hands made futile attempts to push him away, but his chest was like a brick wall. Her heart thrummed, echoing loudly in her head. Or was that his heart? She knew nothing but the prickle of his mustache and the firm pressure of his lips against hers.

When he angrily lifted his head, she gasped, "No, Trevor, please."

"Open your mouth."

"No."

"Kiss me."

"I can't."

"Yes you can."

"No, please."

"What are you afraid of?"

"I'm not afraid."

"Then kiss me. You know you want to."

His mouth claimed hers once again. This time it brooked no resistance. It slanted and moved. His lips parted. Hers, obeying a will more powerful then her own, responded. Then his tongue was there, seeking and finding hers as it had once before. He tasted her thoroughly, until they fell apart gasping for breath.

Hotly, he pressed his open mouth against the arch of her throat.

"No, no," she said, not even recognizing that panting voice as her own.

"I can't believe I'm kissing you."

"Please don't."

"And that you're kissing me back."

"No, I'm not."

"Oh, but you are, love."

His mouth brushed the skin of her throat with light airy kisses, pausing to plant heated ones at its sensitive base. "Your skin, oh, God, your skin." His hand was caressing her bare back. His fingers slipped between the straps of her dress and pressed her closer to him. Against her stomach she could feel what she told herself was his belt buckle.

Nonetheless she clung to him. At that moment he was the only reality left in the world. Not even remembering how they had gotten there, she discovered her fingers embedded in the thick strands of his hair. Again, her mouth was behaving wantonly beneath his.

"Is it even possible that you could want me?"

"Trevor."

"Because I want you."

Alarmed, she tore her mouth free of his scalding kisses. "No, don't even think—"

He cupped her face between his hands. "Not just sex, Kyla. I want more than sex. I know this is sudden, but I've fallen in love with you."

Huntsville, Alabama

THEY HAD BOUGHT a house for their fifth wedding anniversary, and it was moving day. The house was a mess. Boxes were stacked everywhere.

"How could we have accumulated so much junk? Did you finish cleaning out the attic?"

When the accountant's wife got no answer to either question, she turned her head to see what had her husband so preoccupied. He was looking through a stack of snapshots, studying each one intently. "What's that, honey?"

"Hmm? Oh, some pictures I took in Cairo."

She shivered and moved toward him. Closing her arms around his shoulders from behind, she leaned down and looked at the pictures over his shoulder. "Every time I think about how close I came to losing you, I shudder. How many days between the time you went on leave and the terrorist bombing?"

"Three," he said grimly.

"Who's that with you?" she asked softly, looking down at the picture he now held. She knew he often thought about the men who had served on guard duty with him at the embassy, especially those who had died.

"The one on the left was Richard Stroud."

"Was?"

"He didn't make it."

"And the other one?"

Her husband smiled. "That handsome devil is Trevor Rule. A Harvard man. Distinguished Philadelphia family. He was a hell-raiser though. We called him Smooch."

She laughed. "No need to ask why. I can see where he might come by his reputation."

"He had a harem a sultan would envy."

"Did he survive?"

"He was rescued, but was severely injured. I don't know if he survived it or not."

"Will you save the picture?"

"Think I should?"

"Was Stroud married?"

"Yes. Why?"

"If the picture isn't that important to you, why don't you send it to his widow? She'd probably like to have it. You all look so happy, like you're having a good time."

"Smooch had just told one of his famous dirty jokes." He leaned back and kissed her. "Good idea. I'll send it to Stroud's widow. If I can track her down."

He tossed the picture into the box of keepsakes they would move to their new house.

CHAPTER SEVEN

SUDDEN?

Sudden? Is that what he had said? "I know this is sudden, but I've fallen in love with you." "Sudden" hardly captured the earth-shattering essence of the statement. The following morning, as Kyla thought back on the scene, she still couldn't believe he had said that.

She had thanked heaven that her parents had walked through the front door only heartbeats later. Having been struck mute and paralyzed by what Trevor had just said, she had made a valiant effort at conversation, explaining that they had just gotten in and put Aaron to bed, and no, her parents weren't interrupting anything.

Trevor, while being polite to her parents, had stared down at her with that single green eye that more than compensated for the lost one. Avoiding his stare as best she could, she had escorted him to the front door and said a perfunctory good-night before Clif and Meg could go upstairs and leave her alone with him again. Even as she closed the door on him, he had stood his ground, staring down at her. It was then that she had vowed never to see him again.

Now, in the light of day, now, with the memory of last night's kiss still burning in her brain, she repeated that promise to herself. "I can't, I won't, see him again."

But it wasn't going to be that easy. He called during breakfast.

"Kyla," he said as soon as she answered the phone, "I'm sorry it's so early, but I have to talk to you. Last night—"

"I can't talk right now, Trevor. I'm in the middle of feeding Aaron his breakfast and he's making a mess of it."

"Will the two of you have lunch with me? You and Aaron?"

"Thank you anyway, but we can't. Dad and I are going to paint my old swing set today."

"When? I'll come by and help."

"No, no, don't do that," she said hastily. "I don't know exactly when we'll be working on it and I can't let you tie up your entire day."

"I don't mind. I want—"

"I've got to go, Trevor. Goodbye."

He came by anyway late that afternoon. She feigned a headache and didn't even come downstairs to say hello. Her parents looked at her disapprovingly once Trevor had left, but they said nothing.

Babs had no such qualms about offering her opinion. Kyla had ignored her less than subtle disparaging looks and grunts. By the end of the week she had become considerably more vocal. The two friends squared off during a lull in business. "The guy has called here several times a day for the past five days."

"That's his problem."

"It's my problem, too. I've run out of excuses as to why you can't come to the telephone."

"With your imagination, Babs, I'm sure you'll invent others. *If* he calls again."

"He will. He's not nearly the coward you are."

Kyla rounded on her. "I am not a coward."

"No? Then why are you going to so much trouble to avoid him? What did he do, something despicable like try to hold your hand?"

"I can do without your sarcasm."

"Want to know what I think?"

"No."

"I think that it was more than hand-holding."

Kyla turned away so that Babs wouldn't see the color flaring in her cheeks. "As I said, you have a vivid imagination."

"Otherwise you wouldn't be running so fast and so hard. If Trevor Rule hadn't gotten to you in some way, you'd be laughing off his attempts to see you."

"They're not funny."

"That's my point. This is damned serious."

"It is not!"

Into that scene, already crackling with tension, stepped the subject of their dispute. The bell over the door of Petal Pushers jangled musically as Trevor came in. Simultaneously the two women turned their heads in that direction. He was looking at only one, the one whose face suddenly lost its high color, the one who nervously ran her tongue over her lower lip, the one who clasped her hands together at her waist in order to keep from flying apart.

"Excuse me," Babs said. She sashayed through the swinging louvered doors into the back room, mumbling something about Muhammad and mountains under her breath.

Kyla stared at the floor that spanned the distance between them. Maybe he had come to order flowers.

Maybe he had come to discuss the weather. Maybe he had come for any reason but the one she dreaded most.

His opening line instantly dispelled her hopes.

"Why are you avoiding me?"

All right, he wanted to play rough. She'd be rough. Her head snapped up proudly and she met his gaze. "Why do you think?"

"Because of what I said last Friday night?"

"Good guess."

"Did it offend you?"

"Tossing the word *love* around like that is offensive."

"I wasn't tossing the word around. I meant it."

"I find that impossible to believe."

"Why?"

She stared at him, aghast. "*Why?* Because we had seen each other exactly four times before you told me you loved me."

"You were keeping count?" Teasingly, his mustache curved above those sparkling white teeth into a lazy smile.

"Only because what you said was so outlandish." Damn his smile and damn his mustache and damn her stomach for doing cartwheels at the sight of them.

"It happens that way sometimes."

"Not to me."

"But to me. I'm in love with you, Kyla."

She turned her back on him and braced herself against the countertop with stiff arms. "Stop saying that. Please."

He moved up behind her. She felt him there even before he placed his hands on her shoulders. His warmth crept over her back the way the sun glides over the beach at dawn.

"What are you afraid of, Kyla?"

"Nothing."

"Me?"

"No."

"Are you afraid of what you're feeling?"

"I'm not feeling anything."

"You're feeling something." He moved her hair aside and trailed his fingers from one side of her nape to the other. "You kissed me back."

Her head fell forward until her chin was almost touching her chest. "It didn't mean anything."

"Didn't it?"

"Only that I hadn't been kissed in a long time."

"And it felt good?"

"Yes… No… Please. I can't talk about this with you."

"It felt good to me, Kyla. So damn good. And right."

She turned to face him, wedging herself between him and the counter. "But it wasn't right, Trevor," she said with emphasis.

"Tell me why."

"Because I love my husband."

"But he's dead!"

"In here he isn't!" she cried angrily, laying a hand over her heart. "He's alive inside me. And I intend to keep him alive."

"That's crazy. It's unnatural."

"And also no business of yours, Mr. Rule!"

She shoved him aside and moved away. When she faced him again, her breasts rose and fell in agitation. Breathing didn't come easily. "I haven't led you on. I've been fair. I told you the second day we met that I wasn't looking for a romance. I had one. A wonderful love affair that will last me the rest of my life. Nothing could top it and I would never settle for anything less."

Impatiently she dashed the tears out of her eyes with the back of her hand. "In spite of my making that clear to you, you came on to me. I'm sorry if you fancy yourself in love with me, but that's something you'll have to come to grips with. I don't want to see you again, Trevor. Now just please leave me alone."

His jaw was rigid. The muscles along it were flexing with anger. Beneath his mustache his lips had narrowed into a tight, thin line. His hands were balled into fists and tapped his thighs. Kyla couldn't tell if he wanted to strike her or kiss her, and didn't know which to fear most.

Finally, he pivoted on his boot heels and strode out the door, letting it slam closed behind him. The bell over the door made a terrible racket.

Kyla slumped against the counter, not realizing until then just how physically taxing the encounter had been. Every muscle in her body felt as though it had been wrung out like a dishcloth. There was an excruciating piercing pain between her eyes.

When she had regained a modicum of composure, she pushed herself away from the counter and turned to find Babs standing in the doorway, her arms folded over her breasts, a sour expression on her face.

"Don't say a word," Kyla warned, meaning it.

"I wouldn't think of it," Babs said airily. "You said all that need be said and quite brilliantly, I thought. Any other man would probably turn tail and flee. But not our Mr. Rule. Not by a long shot."

"Damn it!"

His foot punished the brake of his pickup truck as he whipped it off the road onto the gravel shoulder. Rocks sprayed out from beneath the wheels and clouds of dust engulfed the truck before it came to a complete stop. Trevor shoved it into Park and folded his arms over the steering wheel. He laid his forehead on his hands.

"Well, what did you expect?"

Had he really thought that he could waltz into her life and, without too much time and effort, have her fall into his arms? Into his bed?

Yes, he admitted now. That's what he had subconsciously expected. Because to George Rule's son things had always come easy.

Sports. Leadership. Studies. Popularity. Women.

To Trevor, life had been a banquet spread out on silver platters. He had even successfully thwarted his father's plans for his life. He was doing what he had always wanted to do. Except for that setback in Cairo, he had led a charmed life. Even then his good fortune had not deserted him. The bombing had left him impaired, but not totally incapacitated as it could have.

Raising his head, Trevor propped his chin on his hands and stared through the dusty windshield. The north Texas plains extended to the horizon in every direction. A barbed wire fence stretched endlessly.

Was that where his life was going? Nowhere?

Kyla's rejection was a bitter pill to swallow. Was this gnawing emptiness inside his gut only the reaction of a spoiled man to whom life had been abundantly sweet until now? Was he to be denied the only thing that was truly important? Were the gods mocking him, laughing at him because he had made one honorable gesture in his life and was to be denied the privilege of carrying it through?

But it was more than that. Honor and duty had little or nothing to do with his behavior toward Kyla now.

He loved the woman.

No longer was she just words written on sheets of inexpensive stationery, words that had filled lonely hours, and alleviated pain, and given him an anchor to hold on to when things had looked their bleakest.

She was a personality. A voice. A scent. A smile.

"And she still loves her husband," he reminded himself grimly.

Richard Stroud had been a terrific guy. Now he was a terrific ghost. And ghosts had a way of making themselves more terrific than the person they had been. One forgot the faults of those departed and remembered only their finer qualities.

But Richard Stroud wasn't his enemy and he mustn't think of him in those terms. Maybe he should give up this whole crazy idea. She loved her husband's memory. She had made her feelings known in plain, understandable English.

Give up while you're ahead, ol' boy. She doesn't want you.

Then he remembered the passion of her kiss, the taste of her mouth, the scent of her hair, the feel of her skin beneath his hands, and knew he wasn't about to give up.

"Not yet." Each precise motion indicated his resolve as he engaged the gears of his pickup and pulled it back onto the country road.

He would give her space, breathing room, time. She was entitled to it.

In the meantime, his days would be busy. He had a lot to do. And at night, in his bed, when his body ached for the appeasement hers promised, he would content himself by reading her letters. They were like her voice whispering her innermost secrets to him in the dark.

"WHAT'S ALL THAT, DAD?" Kyla asked as she entered the kitchen.

"This, oh, this is nothing," Clif Powers said quickly and began gathering up the papers scattered over the table.

"It's *something*." She hadn't missed her father's haste in removing the documents from her sight, nor the covert glance that passed between her parents. Their expressions were as guilty as Aaron's when she had caught him uprooting her favorite ivy.

Placing her hands on her hips, she said, "All right, you two, confess. What gives?"

"Sit down and have a cold drink, why don't you, dear?" Meg suggested.

"I don't want a cold drink. I want to know what it is the two of you are trying so hard to hide."

Clif sighed. "We might as well tell her, Meg."

Kyla sat down in a chair across the table from her father and folded her arms over the laminated table-cloth. "I'm listening."

"The city council was petitioned for this street to be rezoned as commercial property. We, your mother and I, contested it, but none of the other home owners did. The petition passed in a vote of the council last night."

Kyla assimilated that, for the moment thinking only of what this would mean to her parents' future. "Why did you contest it? Won't that escalate the value of your property?"

"Well, yes, dear, but we don't want to leave this house," Meg said. "Not that they're rushing us. We have a while, but..."

"You don't want to leave because of Aaron and me," Kyla said softly, realizing the reason for their secrecy. "We'll manage. I've always told you that."

"We know, but we never wanted to sell the place out from under you."

"Well it seems that the city council has taken the decision from you. I'm glad. This is what you wanted, to sell the house, buy a motor home and travel."

"But you and Aaron—"

"I'm a grown woman, Mom. Aaron is a well-adjusted child. We'll get a home of our own. It will be good for both of us."

"But we promised you when Richard died that we would never leave you alone," Clif argued.

Kyla reached out to cover his hand. "I appreciate your concern, Dad. You've been wonderful. But you and Mom have your own lives. You've earned these years together. You shouldn't spend your retirement shackled to me." She glanced down at the folded documents. "You've already had an offer to buy the property, haven't you?"

"Well, yes," Clif finally admitted. "But we've got eighteen months to vacate. We don't have to take the first offer that comes along."

"But who knows what will happen in eighteen months?" Kyla said. "Opportunities like this don't come along every day. If this is a fair offer, accept it."

"No," Meg said, shaking her head stubbornly. "We promised you that we wouldn't desert you."

"But, Mom—"

"Until you and Aaron are settled someplace, we won't even think about selling this house. And that's final, young lady." Meg stood up. The discussion was closed. "Do you want that cold drink or not?"

Several hours later Kyla lay in bed and stared at the changing patterns of shadow the moonlight cast on the ceiling of her room.

She was worried about her parents' reluctance to sell the house. The sale would ensure them financial security for the rest of their lives. She didn't want them to put it off until they were too old and feeble to enjoy their retirement.

It was for her sake that they hesitated to jump at this chance. Didn't they realize how guilty their sacrifice made her feel? They had already postponed fulfilling their dream for almost two years, as a result of Richard's death. Granted, she would miss them. She would be sad to see the old house razed to make way for office complexes and filling stations. But growing pains always hurt.

It was time she experienced some of her own. Whether her parents sold the house or not, wasn't it time she made a home for Aaron and herself? How to convince Clif and Meg of that was the problem.

With a tired sigh, she forced her eyes to close.

And it happened again.

Trevor Rule's image was projected onto her eyelids. For hours each night, until she finally fell into a frustrated, exhausted sleep, he haunted her. It was as though he were communicating with her on some spiritual plane that she had no understanding of. Her obsession with him was irritating and unnerving.

It had been a month since their showdown in Petal Pushers. She wished she could forget how angry he had looked then. She wished even harder she could forget how he had looked last week when she had accidentally crossed paths with him.

It had been during the heat of the day. She and Babs were making a delivery in downtown Chandler. It had been an order large enough to require both of them, so Clif had volunteered to watch the shop while they were gone.

"Look at that," Babs had said.

"What?" The potted mums had leaked water on Kyla's hands and she was busy shaking them dry.

"Across the street. Yum-*my!*"

Using one damp hand to shade her eyes from the glaring sun, she followed Babs's gaze to the hardware store across the street. Trevor was stepping off the curb into the street where his pickup was parked. He was carrying a bag of concrete mix on his shoulder. As they watched, he swung it down into the bed of the pickup. From that distance, one would never guess he'd been in a terrible accident and had the scars to prove it. He had executed the chore with the strength and grace of an Olympic discus thrower.

Babs smacked her lips. "May the good Lord strike me blind if he's not gorgeous."

"Don't—"

"Hello, Trevor!" Babs sang out.

Gasping in outrage and mortification, Kyla turned her back and opened the car door. She scrambled in and slammed the door behind her. "I'm going to murder you," she whispered to Babs through the open window.

"If you act like an idiot, I'm going to murder *you*," Babs retorted.

Trevor had spotted them instantly and waved. While he was waiting for a car to pass, he took off the slouchy, straw cowboy hat that was shading his head and wiped his perspiring forehead on his rolled-up sleeve. He started toward them before the oncoming car had completely passed, even going so far as to step around its rear. He jogged the remainder of the distance across the street.

"Hi."

God was cruel. No man should have that much sex appeal and be left to run around loose, making a hapless victim of any woman he met.

He combed his fingers through his thick, black hair, pushing back the sweat-waved strands before pulling the cowboy hat back on. With the eye patch, he looked rakish and daring and piratical.

His throat was darkly tanned. At its base lay a rolled and knotted white bandanna. His sleeves had been rolled up so far and so tight that they looked like ropes encircling the teak biceps. The blue work shirt had been left unbuttoned. Kyla envisioned him working shirtless until it was time to drive into town and then pulling on the shirt in haste. Because of the heat, he hadn't felt inclined to button it.

In any event, the long shirttails flapped against his thighs, and his chest was left bare, save for the carpet of dark, damp curly hair that covered it. And covered it beautifully, from the fan-shaped cloud that blanketed the curving muscles of his breasts and swirled around the flat nipples, to that slender, silky line that divided his corrugated stomach and eventually flared around his navel. His chest was magnificent, marred only by an arcing scar that curved under his left breast from beneath his arm.

His jeans had that snug fit and softly faded look that no less than a thousand washings can give them. He wasn't wearing a pair of shiny lizard boots this time, but a pair that had been abused by seas of mud. A pair of worn leather work gloves covered his hands and curled back over his wrist bones.

Most stirring of all was the wide leather carpenter's belt that was strapped across his lean hips. It rested there like a gunslinger's holster and symbolized masculinity just as flagrantly. The building tools dangled against his trim thighs, rubbing against the muscles with every supple movement they made.

He was a living, breathing fantasy, masculinity incarnate.

"What brings you out? It's hot as the dickens."

Babs laughed. "You're even beginning to sound like a Texan. Isn't he, Ky?"

Kyla, inside the sweltering car, sat as rigid and wooden as a mannequin. "Yes, he is."

He braced one forearm on the top of the car. The shirt gaped open wider. Some of the springy hairs on his chest were beaded with sweat. He ducked his head to speak to her directly. "How are you?"

"Fine. You?"

"Fine. Aaron?"

"He's fine, too."

"Good."

"You seem to be working hard, Trevor," Babs said.

Kyla could tell by her strained tone of voice that Babs was irritated with the way the conversation was being conducted. Well, let her be! She was the one who had hailed him over like a streetwalker hollering, "Hey, sailor!" Let her chat with him.

She had thought she would be relieved when he straightened up to talk to Babs. But his doing so had left her with an unrestricted view of his torso. It fascinated her.

She watched a single bead of sweat form on the low curve of his right breast. It gathered itself there until it was a full, liquid pearl. Heavily, it detached itself. Slowly it began to roll downward. Kyla's eyes followed its undulating descent over each rib. It could have gotten lost in the soft hair that dappled his stomach, but it had too much momentum now and continued to slide over the bronzed skin. At last, it angled inward toward his navel and funneled straight into that hair-whorled dimple as though it were a chalice fashioned for such a treasure.

"Won't we, Ky?"

Kyla jumped. "What?" Babs had asked her something, but she was helpless to say what.

"I told Trevor that we'd come out to see the house he's building as soon as it was finished."

"Oh, yes, I'd like that," she said vaguely. *Don't look at him anymore. Keep your eyes on the horizon or the parking meter or anything but him.*

Right now her own body was pouring perspiration, and the midsummer heat was only partially responsible. She willed Babs to get in the car and leave.

But it was Trevor who said goodbye first. "I've got

to be going. The concrete man is waiting on me. It was great seeing you."

"Bye-bye, Trevor," Babs said.

"Goodbye, Babs. Kyla."

"Bye," she answered in a thin voice.

Only when she knew he had turned his back and was almost at his truck, did she raise her eyes. Then she wished she hadn't. His shirt was plastered to his skin, stuck there by the healthy, virile sweat of a working man. The clinging cloth emphasized the breadth of his shoulders. And the jeans were as flattering to his behind as they were to his front.

Now, struggling to go to sleep more than a week later, she still saw him that way. His slight limp only accentuated the swaggering walk that never failed to make her mouth go dry.

Sighing resignedly, she turned onto her side and, surrendering to temptation, mentally followed that salty drop of perspiration down his chest again. This time her tongue followed it straight into his navel.

SHE WOKE UP CRANKY.

Her mood didn't improve when she reached across the coffeepot on the breakfast table to answer the phone.

"Hi, it's Trevor."

She glanced quickly at her parents. The one time they had ventured to ask why Trevor didn't come around anymore, she had cut them short by saying, "I told you we were just friends. He's probably found a girlfriend." Unwilling to reveal the identity of the caller now, she simply said, "Hello."

"I got it finished."

"Finished?"

"The house."

"Oh! Congratulations."

"Thanks. Will you come see it?"

Her parents were looking at her curiously. Meg mouthed, "Who is it?" Kyla pretended not to understand the exaggerated pantomime.

"I don't know if I can," she hedged.

"You said you would," he reminded her.

"I know, but I've been awfully busy."

"Before I put it on the market, I'd like your advice on decorating."

"I'm not qualified to give you that kind of advice."

"You're a woman, aren't you?"

Yes, she was a woman. Otherwise her heart wouldn't be throwing itself against her ribs as though looking for a means of escape. Otherwise her thighs wouldn't feel like melting wax and her palms wouldn't be slippery and she wouldn't be thinking about his mouth and her breasts.

"I don't know anything about decorating a house like that."

She saw Meg's eyes slice to Clif, saw Clif's brows bob up once then slowly lower.

"Will you come anyway?"

"When?"

"This afternoon."

"This is my Saturday to work." She and Babs swapped off Saturdays.

"After work. I'll pick you up when the shop closes."

Kyla twirled the telephone cord, wondering if she dare use Aaron as her excuse. Trevor would only tell her to bring him along. And her parents were digesting every word she said right along with their crunchy granola, so she couldn't use something involving them as a reason not to go.

What did she care how flimsy her excuse was? She had told him in no uncertain terms that she never wanted to see him again. He had a nerve even to call and ask.

But wouldn't it be rude to turn down this particular invitation? She had seen the house under construction. It was obviously important to Trevor to get it just right. His career could be riding on the success of this house. Perhaps he *did* want her opinion on suitable decor and that was the extent of it. He needed a sounding board, someone whose taste he trusted.

"All right. I'll see you at six o'clock."

"Great."

She was busy in the shop all day, but the hours seemed to crawl by. And she stayed hungry. Or was that sinking feeling inside her dread at the thought of seeing him? Or expectancy? She didn't want to know.

At exactly six o'clock, he entered the shop, looking devastating in a sport shirt and slacks. He smelled as though he had recently showered and shaved. His hair was still damp. It curled around his ears and fell over the eye patch with breath-stealing appeal.

"Got any flowers left to sell?"

She laughed, relieved that he was being friendly and treating this date with the lightness it deserved. "A few."

"Ready?"

"Let me get my purse and turn off the lights in back."

In less than a minute she was back. He escorted her

out and waited for her to secure the front door. His hand was beneath her elbow as he helped her into his car, but his touch was impersonal. So far, so good.

They made light, inconsequential conversation as he drove through the streets of town, then out into the countryside toward the wooded lot and the new house. He inquired about her parents and she told him they were well. He asked about Aaron and she filled him in on his latest antics. They didn't speak of the argument that had taken place over a month ago.

"Oh, my heavens!" she exclaimed, when the house came into view. "I can't believe it."

He braked the car in the curved driveway that was lined with boxwoods. "Like it?"

"What's not to like?" Without waiting for him to assist her, she opened her door and stepped out, staring appreciatively at the house. "You didn't tell me it was going to have stained-glass windows on either side of the front door."

"You didn't ask," he replied teasingly. "Come on inside."

It was like stepping into the pages of *Architectural Digest.* The style overall was casual. The house had been designed for comfort and convenience, but no amenity had been spared. The rooms were spacious, but had a feeling of warm coziness about them.

Kyla gave a glad cry when she entered the dining area of the kitchen and saw how well her idea of the sun room had worked. "And look, a boiling water tap in the sink," Trevor said proudly, demonstrating it. "And a built-in refrigerator and freezer."

"It's perfect, perfect," Kyla said, smiling.

"You really like it?"

"It's wonderful!"

"Come outside. I want to show you the backyard."

Redwood decking extended for several yards beyond the house to the lawn, which had already been
landscaped. Clusters of azalea bushes encircled the
trees, which had been shaped and pruned. Flowers of
every variety bloomed in tubs placed strategically on
the deck. A fern-bedecked gazebo housed a bubbling
spa. In the distance, the creek shone like a silver ribbon threading itself through the leafy trees.

"I can't believe it, Trevor," she said in awe. "You've
done wonders. It's beautiful. What decorating you've
already done is perfect. You won't have any trouble
selling this house."

He took both her hands in his and turned her to face
him. Kyla was surprised. Up until that moment he had
hardly touched her. He'd been jocular and funny as he
had led her through the rooms of the house, showing
it off with the enthusiasm of a ten-year-old with a new
bike. Now he was staring at her with an intensity that
set her pulse to racing.

"I've stayed away from you, as you asked me to."

"It was for the best."

He shook his head. "I stayed away, but that doesn't
mean that I liked it or that I didn't think about you."
Kyla swallowed. "Quite the contrary. I think about you
all the time."

"Trevor, please, let's not argue."

"I don't intend to."

"Then don't say any more."

"Let me finish." When he saw that she would grant
him that, he went on. "You know how I feel about you.
Don't you?"

"You… You said…"

"That I love you. And I meant it, Kyla."

"Please, don't pressure me about it. I can't."

"Can't what?"

"I can't be involved in an affair."

"I know. That's why I'm asking you to marry me."

CHAPTER EIGHT

"MAY I SIT DOWN, please?"

His mustache twitched with a smile. "That shocking, huh?" He led her to an old-fashioned porch swing similar to the one on the Powers's porch. It had been attached to the rafters over the deck.

Kyla was too stunned by his proposal to comment on the swing. She'd always had a fondness for porch swings. Any other time she would have remarked on it. Now she could barely command her limbs to move.

Trevor sat down beside her, but didn't touch her. For a few minutes the only sound between them was the faint squeak of the chain as the swing rocked gently. Crickets chirped from their hideouts. Cicadas had begun their nightly concerts from the dense branches of the trees. Words and phrases flitted through Kyla's head like fireflies, but they blinked and burned out before she could vocalize them.

"I don't know what to say."

"Say yes."

She looked at him through the gathering dusk. "Trevor, where did you get the idea that I wanted to marry you? To marry anybody?"

"I got no such idea. You've made it clear on several occasions that you aren't in the market for a husband."

"Then why did you ask me to marry you?"

"Because I love you and want to be your husband. I want to take care of you and Aaron, be a father to him."

"But that's crazy!"

"Why?"

"Because you know that I don't love you."

He stared down at his hands, turning them over and studying them as though seeing them for the first time. "Yes, I know that," he said finally. "You're still in love with Richard."

She felt compelled to touch him and shyly laid her hand on his knee. "Are you hoping that I'll change, that love will come in time?"

"Will it?"

She removed her hand. "I'll never love any man the way I did Richard."

"I still want you."

"How can you even consider wasting your life that way? Why would you want to marry a woman you know doesn't love you and never will?"

"Let me worry about the whys and wherefores. Will you marry me?"

"You're a very attractive man, Trevor."

He smiled broadly. "Thanks."

Her exasperation showed. "What I mean is, six months from now, or next week, or tomorrow, you might meet another woman, one who loves you."

"I won't be looking."

"But you should be."

"Look," he said patiently, "this fictitious woman could come up and pinch me on the ass, and it wouldn't matter. I've found the woman I want to give my name to."

"But you barely know me."

I know you inside out, he thought. *I know that you*

*love porch swings and sky lights and stained-glass
windows and houses surrounded by trees. I know that
in the tenth grade you went with a boy named David
Taylor and the bastard broke your heart. You have a
patch of freckles under your right arm that you consider your birthmark. And you're self-conscious about
your breasts because you think they're too small. But I
think they're lovely and I can't wait to see them, touch
them with my fingertips and tongue, make love to them
with my mouth.*

Trevor cleared his throat and shifted uncomfortably
on the swing. "I didn't believe in love at first sight either until I saw you in the mall that day. I thought you
were beautiful, but you were more than just a pretty
woman who caught my eye. I liked the way you talked
to Aaron. I liked the way your hands moved as you
tended to him." He grinned lopsidedly. "If he hadn't
taken a mind to jump in the fountain, I would have
devised a way to meet you." He inched closer to her.
"Marry me, Kyla. Live with me in this house."

"This house!" she exclaimed softly. "You built this
house with the intention of *our* living in it?"

Pleased that he had surprised her, he asked, "Why
do you think I paid such close attention to detail?"

Behind her, beyond the walls of glass that opened
onto the deck, Kyla could see the well-arranged rooms,
rooms that, had she designed them herself, couldn't be
more to her liking. "We have an uncanny similarity in
taste. It is a lovely house, Trevor, but that hardly con-
stitutes a good reason to marry."

"Right now, it's just a house. I want to make it a
home. For Aaron. For you. For us."

She studied him for a moment, shaking her head. "It just doesn't make any sense."

"It makes perfect sense. I want us to be a family. I want to assume responsibility for you and Aaron."

The idea came from nowhere, but struck her with the impact of a speeding freight train. He wanted a wife and child. Now why would a man with Trevor's looks and Trevor's charm, a man who could have any woman he wanted, be proposing marriage to a widow with a child? Unless he couldn't come by them any other way.

Of course! All of Trevor's disabilities weren't visible. Was her main attraction that she didn't and couldn't return his love? Did he need a wife who would make no physical demands on him? To have a child, did he have to marry a woman who already had one? In a quaint fashion, was this to be no more than a marriage of convenience?

"Trevor," she said hesitantly, "your... When you were hurt...?"

"Yes?"

"Did...?"

"Did what?"

"What I mean is... Are you...?"

"Am I...? What?"

She took a deep breath. "Are you capable of intimacy?" She felt small and the world closed in. It had a stranglehold on her throat. Garnering all her courage, she raised her eyes to look at him.

"You've kissed me, haven't you?" he asked in a deep, throbbing voice.

"Yes."

"I've held you."

"Yes."

"Close."

"Yes."

Her eyes fell away and when she didn't say anything for an interminable time, he prodded, "Well then?"

She fiddled with the fringed sash at her waist. "I thought maybe since I was a widow with a child, and if...that...had happened to you, then..."

He tilted her head up with his hand beneath her chin. "I'm not only capable of, but eager for intimacy with you." Each word sent a vibrating current through her body that continued to hum, like harp strings long after deft fingers had plucked them. "And just so there's no misunderstanding later, I'll tell you right now that this marriage would carry with it all that the relationship implies. I want to be your husband in every sense of the word. I want you in my bed, Kyla. I want to make love to you. Frequently. Do you understand?"

She nodded her head with no more willpower of her own than one hypnotized. Neither of them ever remembered how his fingers had come to be loosely caging her neck, but both became conscious of it at the same time. They sat very still. His single green eye held hers in thrall as his face moved closer. The instant she felt the brush of his mustache against her lips, her eyelids closed.

What a waste, Kyla thought as his fingers threaded up through her hair to settle against her scalp. What a shame that a kiss like this had to be wasted on a woman who didn't and couldn't love him. How regrettable that the lips that were both fiercely possessive and gently persuasive, enough to cause hers to part as though they were hungry, couldn't be kissing a woman who could return such passion.

Lightly she rested her hands on his shoulders in order to keep from tottering off the rocking swing and the rocking universe.

Trevor's other arm encircled her waist and drew her against his chest. A low masculine growl purred in his throat as his tongue penetrated her lips and tasted her mouth at will.

Kyla had a difficult time restraining her own low moans. The silky lash of his tongue made her think how lamentable it was that this kiss wasn't being bestowed on a woman who could appreciate it.

Then it occurred to her that she was giving every semblance of appreciation. Her back was arched, pressing her breasts against his chest. Her hands had wadded the fabric of his shirt in death grips. Her tongue was responding to the love play of his.

She broke away, experiencing an alarming scarcity of breath. Standing quickly, she wondered what ailment had befallen her knees. They were trembling so badly that they could hardly support her. "I've got to go."

Trevor was having a difficult time breathing too, if that rasping sound filtering through his lips was any indication. "All right," he agreed without argument. It took him a long time to stand up. One swift, forbidden glance down his body made a mockery of her earlier speculation.

Virtually at a run, she went back through the house and waited for him at the front door. Gratefully she sank into the front seat of the car when he held the door for her, not sure when her legs would collapse beneath her.

Trevor didn't attempt conversation as he drove her home. Kyla was relieved. Midsummer madness might have been responsible for his proposal. Maybe he'd only been joking. He could already be regretting that he'd asked her to marry him.

But she knew such was not the case when he cut the car's engine at the curb in front of the Powers's house, turned, and laid his arm on the back of the seat and said, "Kyla?" in a blood-stirring tone she couldn't mistake.

It was shocking to discover his taste lingering on her lips when she nervously swept them with her tongue. "I don't think it even warrants further discussion. You can't be serious about this."

"Kyla." He waited until she cautiously turned her head and looked at him. "I'm serious. Do you think I could have kissed you like that if I hadn't been serious?"

"I don't know," she said with a trace of desperation.

He chuckled softly, finding that amusing. "I've kissed many women, but I've never proposed to one. At least I've never proposed marriage. Rest assured that I'm serious." Taking her hand he raised it to his mouth and kissed the palm. "I know I've taken you by surprise. I didn't expect an answer tonight. But promise me you'll think about it. Think about what our getting married could mean to you and Aaron. To your parents. Sleep on it."

TREVOR RULE WAS a dirty fighter, Kyla thought angrily as she checked the digital read-out on her bedside clock for the umpteenth time. She had charted each hour of the long night, and he was to blame for her sleeplessness.

For one thing her body refused to relax. It was restless, alert to every sensual stimulant. Hadn't her bare legs ever felt bed linens against them before? If so, why were they sliding against the sheets as though that were a new indulgence? And why was this old cotton nightgown irritating her breasts? Why, tonight, were her nipples supersensitive to every brush of the fabric against them? Why did they need soothing? And why, every time she thought of them being soothed, did she imagine Trevor's lips against them?

Repeatedly she swore that these physical manifestations had nothing to do with his kiss. Was she about to have her period? That could be the cause for the achy pressure between her thighs. Could she have gotten into poison ivy? Was that the reason her skin felt itchy and in need of caressing?

"I'm *not* aroused."

Her body argued with her, saying otherwise.

Damn him for using such sneaky tactics. He knew the right button to push. He had subtly suggested that if she didn't marry him, she was being selfish.

All right, she'd play devil's advocate.

It *would* be good for her parents. They would feel free to make their own plans, knowing that she and Aaron would be under Trevor's protection.

And it would be good for Aaron. A growing boy needed a father. Clif Powers had filled that role in Aaron's life so far, but how long could he keep pace with his grandson? Would he be healthy and energetic enough to participate in sports with him in a few years, take him fishing and camping, and do all the myriad, physically taxing things a father does with his son?

But Aaron had a father! Kyla argued. Richard Stroud was Aaron's father. She had sworn to keep Richard alive for his son and she was determined to hold to that vow. It would take more than Trevor's smooth manner and glib tongue to sway her from that.

Besides, a woman didn't commit herself to a marriage because it would be beneficial to the people around her, no matter how attractive the man was. Granted, Trevor Rule was attractive and good husband material. She was aware of the strides he was taking in the community. He was constantly being quoted in the business pages of the newspaper. Obviously he was a man of integrity, honest in his business dealings and respected for his innovative ideas for commercial growth. Physically—

No. It would be better not to think about his physical attributes. Her burst of inspiration that he could have been emasculated as a result of his accident had been disproved only moments later.

No, leave his physical attraction out of this. Thinking about that tended to cloud her mind and color her judgment. The only way to approach this problem was pragmatically.

That was what she did until dawn, when she finally reached a decision. She would find a place for Aaron and herself to live. She would move from this house so that her parents could sell it and carry on with their plans.

Marriage to Trevor wouldn't be necessary. Financially she was holding her own. When he was old enough she would see that Aaron had a close association with other boys his age and their fathers. She didn't need a man in her life.

However, she supposed she should thank Trevor for his proposal and for goading her into making decisions that she had postponed since Richard's death. The sooner she turned him down, the better.

While her parents were dressing for church the next morning, she made the telephone call. He answered in the middle of the first ring. "Hello, Trevor. I hope I didn't wake you."

"Hardly."

"I've come to a decision. I—"

"I'll be right over."

He hung up before she could say another word. Disgruntled, she replaced the receiver. It would have been easier to turn him down over the phone and spare them both the awkwardness of meeting face-to-face.

Since she and Aaron were already dressed, she carried him and his plastic beach ball outside. If she met Trevor on the front lawn, this could be over and done with before her parents knew about it.

Trevor must have been standing by the telephone with his car keys in his hand because he got there in a matter of minutes. Kyla was surprised to see him emerge from his car wearing a dark suit. His hair gleamed darkly in the sunlight. He gave the large plastic ball a tap with his foot and Aaron toddled off to chase it.

"Good morning," he said.

"Good morning."

She was nervous. This was going to be more difficult than she had thought. While she was trying to concentrate on how ridiculous the idea of marrying him was, her mind ventured onto how good-looking he was. She was remembering the feel of his mustache against the palm of her hand, the way he had of kissing her throat and touching her neck with fingers that seemed to know just the right amount of pressure to apply.

"Trevor," she began, licking her lips quickly and clasping her hands damply together. "I—"

The dog seemed to drop out of the sky. Suddenly it was just there, dancing around Aaron and yapping loudly. The white poodle's movements were frenzied, quick and, to the fifteen-month-old, terrifying. What to the poodle were playful thrusts and parries, to the child must have seemed like vicious attacks.

Aaron screamed, but his screams only seemed to excite the dog more. It bounded around the child like a fluffy white dot, its barking as sharp and rapid as the rat-a-tat of a machine gun.

Aaron took several stumbling steps forward, seeking escape. The dog reared up on its hind legs. Aaron toppled over backward. Then, as agilely as he could, he scrambled to regain his footing and ran blindly toward safety.

Or rather not so blindly. He had a clear choice of whom to run to. But he didn't choose his mother. The child ran toward the large, strong man, who bent down to scoop him up just as Aaron's solid little body barreled into his shins.

The stout little arms wrapped around Trevor's neck. Aaron buried his tear-streaked face in the crook between Trevor's neck and shoulder. Trevor lowered his head over the child's and rubbed his back soothingly. "There now, Scout. It's all right. You're okay. I've got you and I'm not about to let anything hurt you. That puppy just wanted to play with you. Come on now, you're okay."

The animal's owner, a heavyset middle-aged

woman, came huffing down the sidewalk. She grabbed up the poodle and swatted him on the rump. "You naughty thing, you. Why did you scare that little boy like that?" Tucking the poodle under her arm, she came rushing toward them. "Is your son all right?" she asked Trevor.

"He's fine. Just frightened." Trevor continued to rub Aaron's back. The boy hadn't moved. His face was still pressed against Trevor, but he had stopped crying.

"I'm sorry. I let go of his leash and he shot off like a rocket. He wouldn't bite. He only wanted to play."

"I think Aaron was overwhelmed." Trevor's large hand covered the back of Aaron's head and held it securely against his neck.

"I'm so sorry." The woman continued on her way down the sidewalk, still admonishing the dog.

Trevor patted Aaron's back. He nuzzled his cheek with his mustache and kissed his temple. "He'll be okay. I think he just—"

His words faltered when he noticed Kyla's face. She was standing close, looking up at him with an expression that arrested his gaze and halted his speech. Tears were standing in her eyes. Her lips were tremulous and slightly parted. She was looking at him as though seeing him, really seeing him, for the first time.

For long moments, they stared at each other, not even aware that the Powerses had rushed out onto the front porch to see what the commotion was about. Meg started down the steps, but Clif caught her arm and held her back.

Trevor, still holding Aaron, reached out his left hand and folded it around Kyla's chin. He made a pass across her lower lip with his thumb. "You were interrupted. What were you about to tell me?"

In that instant, she knew what her answer would be. Aaron needed a father. A living father. Richard's memory would be kept alive, but he wasn't there as a safeguard against the day-to-day terrors of the world, like energetic puppies.

Trevor obviously cared a great deal for her son. Aaron had instinctively sought him out for protection. He was tender and loving and kind and generous. Where else would she find a man willing to take over the responsibilities of rearing another man's child, a man willing to marry her knowing she didn't love him?

"I was about to tell you that I'd be pleased to marry you. If…if you still want me to."

"If I still want you to?" he repeated gruffly. "God, yes, I still want you to."

He closed the space between them and with the arm that wasn't holding her son, embraced her. She didn't know what she had expected. A handshake to seal the bargain? A premarital document to sign? Certainly not the kiss she got. It was a Sunday morning. They were standing in broad daylight, in full view of any neighbor who might venture outside or any motorist who happened to drive by.

But Trevor exercised no decorum in kissing her. He tilted his head to one side, aligned his mouth with hers and kissed her in a greedy, manly way.

Kyla felt a blow to her middle, as though a velvet fist had socked her. It sent ripples of pleasure throughout her body. Vaguely, in the back of her mind, she was disappointed that he was still holding Aaron and therefore unable to pull her against him and complete the circuits of sensation that were popping and sizzling. Everything feminine inside her was craving to be pressed against that hard, virile frame. She wanted to be filled with him.

When he finally raised his mouth from hers, she reeled slightly. His strong arm was there to steady her. It turned her around and guided her toward the house, where she saw her parents hovering on the front porch. Aaron was happily tugging on a fistful of Trevor's black hair. Trevor was smiling broadly and every few steps he laughed out loud.

"Mrs. Powers, Mr. Powers, Kyla has done me the honor of saying yes to my marriage proposal."

Meg immediately burst into tears of gladness. Clif hurried down the steps to pump Trevor's hand. "That's wonderful. We're very happy. We're…well, we're happy. When?" he asked his daughter.

"When?" Trevor echoed.

"I, uh, I don't know." Now that she had made the decision, she felt as if she was being swept along by a tidal wave. "I haven't had time to think about it."

"How about next Saturday?" Trevor suggested. "I came dressed to go to church with you. We can check it out with the minister after the service."

"I think that's a lovely idea," Meg said enthusiastically. "Here at the house, of course."

"Yes, why wait?" Clif added.

Yes, why? Kyla was asking herself. Why did she feel like applying the brakes? Accepting Trevor's marriage proposal had seemed like the thing to do just moments ago, but now she was realizing the enormity of her decision. This was for real. She was about to become Mrs. Trevor Rule. What would everyone think?

Babs left no doubt as to how she took the news. As was her habit she came over for Sunday dinner. Trevor answered the door when she knocked. Clif was cranking the freezer of homemade ice cream Meg had insisted on making for dessert in celebration of the occasion. Kyla was feeding Aaron so he could be put down for his nap before they ate. Meg was spooning up fresh green beans. Trevor was the only one available.

Babs stared at him in wordless awe as he pushed the screen door open and stepped aside. "Come on in. Everyone is in the kitchen."

Kyla hadn't told Babs that she was going to see Trevor. Babs hadn't seen him since that afternoon in town over a week ago when Kyla had acted like such a ninny. Now, where his carpenter's belt had been strapped, a blue and white gingham apron was tied in a bow. He had insisted on helping Meg get lunch ready.

Babs padded into the kitchen behind him. No sooner was she through the door than she demanded of Kyla, "What's going on here?"

Kyla's eyes swept across the other expectant faces, but when no one seemed inclined to answer Babs, the chore fell to her. "Trevor and I are getting married."

Babs's wide china-blue eyes found Trevor. He grinned engagingly. "Surprise!"

"You're getting married!" Babs exclaimed. When he nodded, she clasped his face between her hands and smacked a hearty kiss directly on his mouth. "Since you're marrying my best friend I think I'm entitled to that."

Laughing, Trevor hugged her around the waist and laid another sound kiss on her mouth. When he released her, he said, "I think so, too."

Everyone laughed, including Aaron, who didn't understand anything but the gaiety going on around him. He pounded his spoon on the tray of his high chair.

Lunch was a joyous affair. There was a lot of teasing and talk about the wedding and matrimony in general. Kyla couldn't get accustomed to the idea that in less than a week she would be a bride. Nor could she get accustomed to the affectionate way Trevor treated her.

He sat close. He took advantage of innumerable opportunities to touch her. His arm was often resting across her shoulders. Caresses seemed to come as naturally to his fingertips as kisses came to his lips.

Kyla wasn't annoyed by these demonstrations of affection. Quite the contrary. She found that she was beginning to look forward to them. That anticipation turned to guilt. As far as she was concerned, this marriage *was* a marriage of convenience. Wasn't it?

Trevor spent the afternoon with them. He acquainted them with his background. "I grew up in Philadelphia. Went to prep school, then to Harvard."

"Your mother is dead?" Meg asked him.

"Yes, she died several years ago. I'll notify my father about the wedding, but I doubt he'll be able to make the trip on such short notice."

"He's a lawyer?" Clif asked.

"A very successful one. It was a disappointment to him that I didn't want to follow in his footsteps and make the name of the firm Alexander, Rule and Rule."

"But surely he's proud of your success in your own field," Clif said.

Trevor became reflective. "I hope so."

By that evening everyone in town seemed to know

about their forthcoming marriage. "Mrs. Baker has offered to give you a shower."

Horrified, Kyla turned away from the countertop in the kitchen where she was preparing a tray of sandwiches to take out to the men, who were sitting on the porch. "Oh, no, Mom. I don't want any of that folderol. Please thank anyone who calls to offer, but kindly refuse."

"But, Kyla, everyone's so happy for you."

She shook her head adamantly. "I don't want any parties. Nothing. Please. I had all that once and it was lovely. This...this marriage isn't like that."

Meg looked at her with undisguised disappointment. "Very well, dear."

Her parents, whose heads were in a cloud of romanticism, would never understand her motives for marrying Trevor. She wasn't certain Trevor understood them, either.

She escorted him outside after he had bidden her parents good-night. As soon as they stepped through the screen door and into the deep violet shadows of the porch, he gathered her in his arms and lowered his mouth to hers.

The kiss was intimate and evocative, a mating of their mouths. His tongue stroked hers. His hands slid from her back to the front of her waist. They glided up over her ribs and pressed her breasts. He moaned.

"God, I don't know how I'll make it till Saturday night." His hands fell away. "Do you know how much I want to touch you? But I can't touch you now. If I touch you now, I won't be able to stop until there's no cloth between us and I'm holding you, kissing you, your mouth, breasts, stomach, everywhere."

The last word was sighed into her ear. Then his open mouth slid from just beneath her jaw to the base of her neck. His mustache was a pleasure-giving, conscience-ridding, memory-banishing instrument that left her tingling and warm and moist. If he had strengthened the embrace, she would have allowed it. He didn't.

"Good night, love."

The darkness swallowed him up. Long after she watched the taillights of his car disappear, Kyla stood there on the porch, trembling at the thought of their wedding night. She tried convincing herself that the shivers plaguing her were caused by dread.

But she didn't really think they were.

EVERYONE'S MOOD THE following week was festive. Her parents were more animated than she had seen them since Richard's death. It was plain to see that they adored Trevor and trusted him to make their daughter and grandson happy. Babs's enthusiasm was uncontainable and by midweek was wearing thin.

"But I don't need anything like this," Kyla said of the sexy negligee Babs was holding up to her.

"Every bride needs something like this. Not that they last very long," she said with a naughty wink. The implication made Kyla's stomach feel queasy.

"I've got plenty of nightgowns," Kyla objected in a muffled voice.

"I've seen them. They're wretched. At least for a honeymoon."

"We're not taking a honeymoon. Not right away. We're moving directly into Trevor's house."

"*Your* house and you know what I mean about a honeymoon. You don't have to leave town to have one. Or for that matter, you don't have to leave the bedroom to have one." She laughed gaily. "I've had several myself. So which is it going to be, the peach or the blue?"

"I don't care," Kyla said petulantly, plopping down on the chaise in the boutique's dressing room. "You're the one who insisted I needed a new negligee, you pick it out."

"Boy!" Babs said in exasperation. "What's the matter with you?"

Babs wouldn't believe her if she told her, and she wasn't going to tell her. When you were insane, you rarely went around announcing it to your friends. "Nothing."

"Well, you're sure grouchy. I can't think of a better way to improve your mood than to spend a few days in the sack with Trevor Rule."

She turned to call the salesclerk and missed Kyla's stark expression. She wanted to get caught up in the spirit of the occasion but couldn't allow herself to. Getting excited about the wedding would be disloyal to Richard. No one had mentioned his name in days. It seemed that he had been blotted from everyone's mind but hers.

She clung to his memory more tenaciously than ever, but inevitably it seemed to be slipping from her grasp. She noted these lapses of memory the most when she was with Trevor, who was playing the role of bridegroom to the hilt.

Every evening they went shopping for household items. He wanted her input on everything from blenders to bolsters. He could have read her mind and not picked out furniture she liked better. Their taste in everything coincided. Often she felt like Cinderella having all her wishes granted at once. He spared no expense. As the interior of the house began to take shape, she felt like pinching herself to make sure this wasn't some bizarre dream.

That was how she felt the evening he led her into the master suite to show her the final product of their combined efforts. "They delivered the chairs and bed today," he said, switching on the lamp with the lotus-shaped silk lampshade. "I think everything came together real well."

The room was lovely, out of her dreams. Her eyes surveyed it slowly, and when they came back full circle to the man, he was staring at her intently. Her hair was limned by the lamplight and her body was cast into silhouette through her soft voile dress.

"What is it?" she asked on a soft breath.

"Let's try out the bed."

She reacted with a sudden intake of breath, a lurch of her heart, a blinking of her eyes. He reached for her and within a heartbeat, she found herself lying on the bed with him bending over her. Holding her eyes captive with his gaze, his hand drifted down the side of her neck until it came to rest on her breast and the first button of her bodice. He unbuttoned it. The second. The third.

Still she couldn't move. Not even when he slipped his hand inside her bodice. Her breathing accelerated. Involuntarily her eyes closed.

He wedged his fingers beneath her bra strap and pushed it down over her shoulder. Down, down, until the top curve of her breast swelled over the lacy cup.

"God, you're lovely." He laid his hand on her and

rubbed the gentle curve of her breast, then moved lower to graze the responsive crest.

He sighed her name an instant before his mouth claimed hers. His kiss wasn't tempestuous as she had expected. But infinitely sweet and tender and loving. As loving as the hand that continued to fan lightly over her nipple.

He pressed his mouth to her ear. "I want to be inside you, Kyla. I want to feel you coming."

He trapped her gasp behind another deep kiss. His fingertips soothed the flesh that shrank even tighter in response to his bold words.

"Please, love, don't make that sexy sound. Please don't feel this good," he groaned, as his fingers caressed her breast. "Or I won't be able to stop. And I want to be your husband the first time I take you."

Exercising tremendous control, he refrained from other caresses. He restored her clothing and drew her up to stand beside the rumpled bed. She sagged against him weakly.

Smiling into her hair, he returned his hand to cover her heart. "I'll make you happy, Kyla. I swear it."

She buried her face in his neck, not out of passion, but despair. He made her body sing. But she couldn't reciprocate his promise of happiness or love. Because keeping that one would jeopardize the one she had made long before she ever met Trevor Rule, the one she had made to Richard the day he died.

CHAPTER NINE

BABS FILLED THE house with flowers. Meg laid out a sumptuous buffet. The bakery delivered a multitiered cake. What Kyla had hoped would amount to no more than a small family gathering with their pastor, began to look very much like a wedding.

She fretted over it in her bedroom upstairs. "Everyone is making too much of this." She reached for the buttons on the back of her bodice.

"Everyone should. This is a wedding, for heaven's sake." Babs turned her around to do up the unreachable buttons.

"A *second* wedding."

"So what are you bitching about? Some of us have yet to see one."

Kyla stared at Babs in surprise. "I didn't think you ever wanted to get married."

Babs looked chagrined at having said something she wished she could recall. "Not to anybody I've met so far. But if one Richard Stroud or Trevor Rule came into my life I'd rope him and drag him to the altar."

Properly chastised, Kyla stepped into her skirt. "I'm sorry, Babs. I know how lucky I've been."

"Oh, hell, don't pay any attention to me. I'd hardly call it lucky to have a husband killed by a terrorists' bomb. I'm just jealous because not one wonderful man has loved me and you've had two groveling at your feet."

She laughed at the mental picture Babs's words painted. "I doubt Trevor would ever grovel."

Babs laughed, too. "Come to think of it, so do I." She sighed. "Jeez, Kyla, he's such a stud. But a nice stud and those two qualities rarely go hand in glove."

Kyla didn't want to think about the man who was waiting downstairs for her. Every time she thought of Trevor and the night to come, she began to quake.

"Are you sure this dress is appropriate?" she asked, changing the subject. "I feel like I should wear something simpler."

"It's perfect."

The two-piece silk design had detailed stitching at the shoulders and on the waistband of the dirndl skirt. The pale yellow color and the fabric's icy sheen made it look like lemon sherbet. The only jewelry she wore was a pair of pearl earrings.

"Don't you think you should take that off?"

Kyla followed the direction of Babs's gaze down to her left hand. "My wedding ring." She hadn't even thought of it because it was as much a part of her hand as her fingerprints. Tears welled in her eyes at the thought of removing it. It hadn't been off her hand since the day Richard had slipped it onto her finger with a solemn vow to love her until death.

Slowly, with a twist and a wrenching tug, she removed the ring. Reverently she laid it on the velvet lining of her jewelry box and closed the lid.

"Are you ready?" Babs asked.

"I suppose so," Kyla answered shakily. Parting with the wedding ring had been an emotional upheaval as violent as that of leaving Richard in his grave. All week she had been making light of this occasion. But she couldn't any longer. She was about to marry another man. In a matter of minutes he, not Richard, would be her husband. "Has Dad already taken Aaron downstairs?"

"You're a bride! Stop worrying about Aaron. Surely your parents and I can handle him." Babs reached into a large square box she had carried into the room earlier. "Trevor asked me to give this to you before you came down."

It was a bouquet of white orchids, the Bow Bells that she loved, garnished with white rosebuds and clumps of baby's breath. "My Lord," Kyla breathed, taking the lavish bouquet from Babs's outstretched hands. "There must be—"

"A dozen orchids in all. He was very specific." Her blue eyes were twinkling. "I'm telling you, Kyla, the man is a jewel, and if you make a mess of this marriage, I'll snatch him up without an apology or a smidgen of conscience."

"I'll do my best to make it work," Kyla murmured as she walked dazedly toward the door.

Downstairs, Babs preceded her into the living room. Kyla heard the hushed conversation cease. She took a deep, hopefully steadying, breath. Everyone was looking at her when she entered.

Meg had a damp lace handkerchief pressed to her cheek, but she was smiling. Clif swallowed a lump of emotion that made his Adam's apple slide up and down. Babs was grinning with the romantic mischievousness of a wood nymph. The Haskells, Ted and Lynn, were standing together, unusually solemn.

Finally Kyla looked at Trevor, who was so handsome that she went mushy on the inside. He was wearing the same dark charcoal suit he had worn to the banquet. This time his shirt was ivory. An ivory tie with black pinstripes matched the silk handkerchief folded into his left breast pocket.

Trevor moved toward her, but Aaron, who could move like a streak of lightning when one least expected him to, darted forward and reached her first. Meg and Babs took simultaneous steps forward to prevent him from tearing her stockings or wrinkling her skirt.

But Trevor reached down and picked the boy up into his arms. "Your mom looks beautiful, doesn't she, Scout?" he asked on a husky whisper when he straightened up.

Aaron babbled something that sounded like "Mama" repeated several times, then stretched forward to smear a rough, wet kiss on Kyla's cheek. He seemed content to remain in Trevor's arms, which was just as well since Kyla didn't know how she could hold her son and the bouquet of orchids at the same time.

"It seems like I'm always thanking you for flowers."

"Do you like them?"

"They're beautiful. Of course, I love them. You were too extravagant."

He shook his head. "This is my wedding day. You are my bride. Today nothing is too good for us, love."

They stared at each other for ponderous moments until Aaron began to wiggle within the grasp of Trevor's arms. Trevor shook himself out of the trance Kyla's appearance had induced and took her arm. Together they moved farther into the room where the others were grouped around the minister.

"Kyla, Trevor, this is a happy day," the minister began.

Though it was the middle of the afternoon and sunshine streamed in through Meg's polished windows, Babs had insisted on having candles. They flickered like winking eyes from every nook and cranny of the room, filling it with the heady scent of vanilla. Someone had thought to put an album of romantic instrumentals on the turntable of the stereo. Surely Babs had depleted the inventory at Petal Pushers because flowers, not limited to white but covering the spectrum of the rainbow, filled vases and baskets scattered throughout the room.

The service was by necessity informal. During the recitation of vows, Aaron sneezed, spraying Trevor's shoulders. Automatically Kyla reached for her mother's hanky, blotted the damp spots on Trevor's coat and dabbed at Aaron's nose. Trevor smiled on, fondly. Once that housekeeping chore had been attended to, the pastor continued. When he called for the bride's ring, Trevor shifted Aaron in his arm and reached inside his right coat pocket. Kyla stared down at her hand as he slid the circlet of diamonds onto her finger.

Trevor noticed the pale band of skin around the base of her finger and, realizing what had caused it, swiftly lifted his gaze to her face. Her soft look carried with it an apology. An expression she couldn't decipher flashed across his features, but was instantly gone. He pushed the dazzling ring into place on her finger and clasped her hand tightly. The awkward moment passed with only the two of them knowing it had occurred at all.

Several minutes later, the minister said, "Trevor, you may kiss your bride now."

They faced each other. Kyla's eyes came to rest on the knot of his necktie and seemed disinclined to move away. Finally they shyly climbed up his chin, along the sensual mouth beneath the thick brush of his mustache, over the chiseled perfection of his nose to meet that brilliant green gaze. She swallowed timidly.

Trevor angled his head and lowered his lips to hers. His were parted, damp and warm as they pressed her mouth with a tender, yet possessive kiss. When he withdrew, he smiled down into her face, then kissed Aaron's cheek.

"I love you both." He spoke softly to Kyla's ears alone and she felt a sudden urge to cry.

Before she could, she was spun around and embraced by her parents. Babs made a beeline for Trevor, taking advantage of the opportunity to kiss him again. Ted and Lynn joined in the exchange of kisses.

To record the day, Clif got out his camera. Kyla smiled for the lens, but she couldn't help but think about the white padded satin album upstairs in her closet that was filled with pictures of another wedding.

As Kyla filled her plate with food from the buffet, Trevor moved up beside her. "If you don't like the ring, I'll get you something else."

"I didn't expect it," she said, looking down at the unfamiliar ring. "But I like it very much." And she did. It was simple and elegant.

"The diamonds are from my mother's wedding ring. Dad sent it to me last week. The mounting was gaudy and didn't look like something you would choose, so I had the stones reset."

"You took your mother's diamonds and had a ring made for me?" she asked, flabbergasted.

"She told me before she died to give her ring to my wife."

"But Trevor, you should have saved it for—" She broke off when she realized that she was about to say, "For a woman who loves you."

"For whom?" The back of his hand made a resting place for her chin and he tilted her head back slightly. "You are my one and *only* wife, Kyla." He bent down and kissed her lightly before dropping his hand.

"I'm sorry I didn't have a ring for you." She couldn't admit to him that it had never occurred to her. Indeed she hadn't thought of wedding rings at all until Babs— God bless her—had reminded her to remove hers only minutes before the ceremony. "I wasn't sure you would want to wear one. Some men don't."

"Well, I've been giving that some thought." He popped an olive into his mouth and chewed it slowly and exaggeratedly as though pondering a tremendously important decision. "I thought I might want something different. Untraditional."

"Like what?"

"Like maybe a gold ring in my ear."

Her mouth fell open and she stared up at him. Then she realized that he was teasing her and she burst out laughing.

"What's the matter?" he asked, pretending to be offended by her laughter. "Don't you think a pierced ear would go well with my eye patch?"

"Yes, I do," she said honestly. "Pierced ears for men is the 'in' thing and I think you would wear an earring with panache."

"Well then, why the levity?"

"I was just wondering what the guys on your construction sites would have to say about it?"

"Hmm, you're right. Maybe I should reconsider."

They laughed together and when it subsided, he said, "That's a start."

"What is?"

"I finally managed to remove that guarded, tense expression from your face and replace it with a genuine, relaxed smile. You actually laughed."

"I laugh all the time."

"Not with me. I want to see you laugh often." He leaned down and added on a whisper, "Except when I take off my clothes."

The thought of that rid her mind of all laughter. "I promise not to laugh then."

She could have kissed her father for interrupting them at that point to take another picture. They were photographed. They ate; they drank numerous glasses of Meg's punch; they said goodbye to the Haskells with a promise to get together soon.

Babs left for a date. "Poor guy," she told Trevor and Kyla at the door. "He doesn't know what he's in for tonight. All this wedding sentiment has put me in a very romantic mood." With a seductive wink and a jaunty wave, she left.

"Mom, let me help you clean up this mess."

"No, no, no," Meg said, shooing Kyla out of the kitchen. "You and Trevor get on your way."

"But not all of Aaron's things are packed yet. I thought I'd change and—" She fell silent when she realized the other three were staring back at her as though she'd taken leave of her senses. Only Trevor seemed faintly amused. She had come to know that the twitch of his mustache usually heralded a grin. "What's the matter?"

"Well, we, your mother and I, just assumed that you'd leave Aaron here for tonight at least," Clif said uneasily.

Kyla opened her mouth to speak, only to find that she had nothing to say. She closed her mouth without uttering a word.

"Thank you, Clif, Meg," Trevor said to fill an awkward silence. "We appreciate the offer. If Aaron won't be any trouble we'll leave him here tonight. Tomorrow when we come for him we'll bring the pickup. Kyla still has some things to move, don't you, love?"

"Yes," she croaked. "I'll finish packing and get it all out of your way by tomorrow evening."

Since the announcement of her marriage to Trevor, the Powerses had officially sold their house. Kyla knew that the sooner she moved all her possessions out, the sooner the sale could be closed.

However, she wasn't thinking about that now. She was thinking about the night to come when she wouldn't have Aaron to act as a buffer between her and her bridegroom. She dragged out their leave-taking as long as she could without it being obvious.

"Meg knows how to throw a great party," Trevor said once they were alone and on their way home.

"She's always been a gracious hostess."

"I appreciate her efforts."

"She loved doing it."

"I like your dress."

"Thank you."

"Silk?"

"Yes."

"I like the sound it makes when you move."

"Sound?"

"That secretive rustling sound that makes me wonder what your body is doing underneath it."

Her eyes swung quickly to the horizon. "I didn't know it made a sound."

"It does. Each time you move. I find it terribly sexy." He reached across the seat for her hand and laid it high on his thigh. "And exciting."

Her heart slammed against her ribs. Breathing was difficult. She tried to concentrate on how the fabric of his tailored slacks felt against the palm of her hand, but her brain seemed determined to dwell on his excitement, the extent of which she could measure should she move her hand up a scant few inches.

The headlights swept across the front of the house as he braked the car to a stop. "Do you need the bag tonight?" He had carried a small suitcase to the car for her.

"Yes, please. It has makeup and…stuff…in it."

"Oh, I see. Stuff." His grin did nothing for her heart or her lungs, both of which seemed to have shut down operations for the night. "Well you can't do without your stuff, can you?"

On the porch, he set the suitcase down and unlocked the front door, pushing it wide. Before Kyla could prepare herself, he swept her up into his arms and against his chest. "Welcome home, Kyla."

He carried her inside. As soon as he crossed the threshold, he lowered his head and kissed her. And kissed her again. And again. Until soon it was hard to tell where one kiss stopped and another began.

Both of his hands were occupied. Kyla could have turned her head away and ended the kisses, but she lacked the will to do so. His mouth was incredibly sweet and warm. She felt an irresistible compulsion to see just how nimble his tongue could be. It thrust again and again into her mouth with a greediness tempered only by tenderness.

He relaxed the arm beneath her knees but kept her anchored to him as she slid down against his body. Finally she was standing toe to toe with him. And still the kiss went on uninterrupted.

With his arms now free, his hands explored. They slid up and down her back. She felt the pressure of his palms on her bottom, urging her closer to his hard middle. Once she was secured there, he made vees of his thumbs and index fingers and bracketed her breasts in the notches. The vees closed and opened rhythmically, gently, causing his thumbs lightly to brush the peaks of her breasts.

She caught her breath. Trevor's hands fell away immediately, but he didn't retreat. He folded his arms around her protectively and pressed her head against his chest.

"I'm about to get carried away," he whispered into her hair. "Making love standing up in the entrance hall isn't the way I planned our wedding night." Chuckling, he put space between them and looked down into her face. "Not without closing the front door first."

When he turned to do that, Kyla moved as far away from him as possible without making it look like an escape. "Are you hungry?" she asked hopefully. "I'll fix you something."

"After that spread Meg had prepared?" he asked

incredulously. "One more marinated artichoke and I'd have burst. But I do have some champagne chilling. Would you like to change first?"

First. First. He kept dropping in that one-syllable word that implied so much to Kyla. She knew what was at the culmination of all those "firsts."

"Champagne sounds good." Could he detect the tremors in the corners of her mouth when she tried to smile?

As he walked into the kitchen, he shrugged off his suit jacket and worked at the knot of his necktie. Casually he tossed both of them into one of the chairs at the kitchen dining table as he went by. He unbuttoned the top three buttons of his shirt and, after unclipping his cuff links, rolled the cuffs of his sleeves up to his elbows.

He seemed perfectly at ease. Kyla envied him that nonchalance. She would dearly love to slip out of the new shoes, which had made her toes numb, but she didn't even feel comfortable enough with their privacy to do that.

"Ah, good and cold," he said, swinging the bottle of champagne out of the industrial-size refrigerator. Kyla noticed that the shelves inside it had already been stocked with food, including Aaron's favorites. Didn't Trevor ever forget anything? "Would you get down the wineglasses, sweetheart? They're in that cabinet there," he said nodding toward one. "I put everything up, but you can rearrange it all if something's not convenient for you."

"I'm sure everything is fine," she said woodenly.

She found the champagne glasses and brought him two. She jumped when the cork popped out of the bottle. Laughing, he poured the foaming wine into the glass. Some of it washed over Kyla's hands. She began laughing, too. The icy effervescent wine tingled on her skin as the tiny bubbles burst one by one.

Having set the glasses on the countertop, she was shaking the moisture from her hands when Trevor captured one and lifted it to his mouth. "Allow me."

She watched it. She watched her finger disappear between his mustache and lower lip, but she didn't really believe that it was actually happening until she felt his tongue laving the pad of her finger.

Stunned, Kyla was powerless to do anything but watch as he finished with that finger and sucked the next one into the silky heat of his mouth. He slid his tongue between the next two fingers, gathering up all traces of the spilled wine. It curled around the beautiful wedding ring he had placed on her finger earlier.

Delicious sensations wound through her. His tongue's deft caresses never ventured beyond her fingertips, but seemed to touch her everywhere, in forbidden places. They coaxed responses from her body she had thought were buried with that flag-draped casket in Kansas.

That melting sensation in her middle. That aching in her breasts that made her want to feel Trevor's tongue there, doing what he was doing to her fingertips. That quickened respiration. That pounding of her heart.

Finally he turned her hand over and kissed the palm, whisking it with his mustache before relinquishing it. She had the impulse to tuck her hand under her arm as one does when one has been stung or has pricked a finger with a pin. Or did she want to hide that hand

in shame because it had been guilty of such erotic responses?

"Here's your champagne." Trevor handed her a
glass. "To us." He clinked their glasses together and
they each took a sip. Then he lowered his head and
kissed her softly. "Know what?" he asked while his
lips were still resting against hers.

"What?" What cologne does he wear? her mind
was asking distractedly. It was as intoxicating as the
champagne.

"You taste better than champagne." His tongue
swept her lower lip. "In fact you taste better than anything. I could make a glutton of myself on you. I could
indulge until I was sated and drunk on you. And I still
wouldn't have enough. I'd want…one…more…taste."
Between the words, he pecked soft kisses. After the
last word, his mouth stayed and he sent his tongue deep
into her mouth.

Unmindful of the sloshing, he removed the wineglass from her hand. None too steadily, he set hers and
his on the countertop without ever having released her
from his kiss.

Slowly he raised her arms to his shoulders. Involuntarily they bent at the elbows to enclose his neck. His
hands met at the small of her back. The kiss deepened.
He inched forward until she was sandwiched between
him and the counter. He rocked his hips from side to
side, massaging her softness.

"Oh, God." She sighed when he left her mouth to
plant one of those treacherous kisses on her vulnerable throat. Her head fell back. Her eyes drifted open
and she gazed at the ceiling hazily as his open mouth
touched her skin.

Why was God doing this to her? Why had he sent such a temptation into her life? The marriage itself had been a betrayal of Richard. She didn't love this man, yet she wanted him in a purely carnal way. It was wrong! How could she withstand such an inundation of sexual provocation and not submit to it?

"Would you like some privacy in the bedroom before I join you?" he asked roughly.

Witlessly, she nodded her head and he released her. Like a sleepwalker she turned and wended her way to the other side of the house and into the bedroom. Trevor, having followed her, set her suitcase just inside the door. "I'll be back shortly." The door closed softly behind him.

She carried the suitcase into the bathroom and opened it. As though programmed to do so, she automatically unpacked her cosmetics and toiletries and arranged them on the dressing table. When she chanced to catch her image in the mirror covering the wall, she froze.

Her eyes! What had happened to her eyes? They were aglow, lambent, limpid. They hadn't looked like that since the night she had discovered she was in love with Richard Stroud.

In love! Good Lord, yes. That's what she looked like, a woman in love.

The thought extinguished the light in her eyes immediately, extinguished it so quickly that she could almost convince herself that it hadn't been there at all, that it had been a trick of the lighting, a product of her imagination.

In love with Trevor Rule? Impossible. She hadn't known him long enough. She loved Richard. Solely.

Exclusively. There was no room in her heart for any other man.

Even if she allowed Trevor the use of her body that night, she wouldn't be betraying Richard. It was, after all, just a body, material and impermanent. Her body had nothing to do with the personality inside it, the heart and soul and mind of Kyla Stroud.

Kyla *Rule,* a malicious imp reminded her.

Kyla *Stroud,* she insisted.

She would sleep with Trevor because she had made a bargain and she intended to uphold her end of it. She would swap him bedroom privileges for the parenting he would extend to Aaron. He would have access to her body, but never, never to her heart. She had promised her heart and love to Richard. Trevor Rule would never be allowed to violate that covenant.

She and Babs had moved her clothes the night before. Her entire wardrobe, all seasons included, filled only a fraction of the closet space Trevor had built into the master bedroom. After a quick shower, she slipped into the negligee she had bought under duress and brushed her teeth and hair. Almost as an afterthought, she applied perfume to the backs of her ears and the base of her throat.

In the bedroom she turned down the bed. She left only one lamp burning. When the soft knock sounded on the door, she whirled around, clasping her hands together. "Come in, Trevor."

He stepped through the door. When the soft lamplight fell on him, Kyla momentarily regretted that she didn't love him. The black pajama bottoms hung low on his hips, held there by a black cord. His chest was most impressive, shadowed by that cloud of dark hair that arrowed down past his navel. She didn't even want to think of what that stripe of hair pointed to. The scar that arced beneath his left breast intrigued her as it had before. She wanted to touch it, soothe it somehow. His feet were bare. There was a network of scars on his left foot.

Only after she had cataloged his body did she raise her eyes to his face. He was staring at her, a hint of a smile hiking up one corner of his mustache.

"You're beautiful, Kyla." He moved into the room until he was standing an arm's length away.

She couldn't have guessed how appealing she was to him at that moment. This was the woman of the letters, the woman who had spoken to his heart before he even met her. Now, she stood before him, naked, save for a few scraps of peach-colored silk and satin. His most erotic fantasy was close enough to touch. She was breathing, stirring the hair on his chest with each light exhalation.

The golden glow of the lamp enhanced her spectacular coloring. It made her hair shine like copper and her skin take on the richness of old satin. He wanted to wrap himself up in her. Her eyes were velvety dark, unusually wide, incredibly bright.

The nightgown was sheer and curtained her body like a veil. A ribbon was tied beneath her breasts, making their fullness more pronounced. Her nipples were dusky temptations beneath the filmy fabric. Above the brief bodice, the small mounds of her breasts swelled creamy and full.

Her body was cast in shadow against the lamplight. As his eyes moved down it, his manhood grew thick with desire for her. Her waist was incredibly narrow, especially for someone who had carried a child. He was transfixed by the shadowy cleft between her slender thighs, the heart of all that made her a woman. He wanted to honor it, cherish it with his caresses and his mouth.

Unable to stop himself, he extended his hand and cupped it over that soft delta. Shifting the material of her gown so that only one layer was between her and his hand, he pressed. "You're so warm," he whispered fiercely. "Standing here with you like this, I feel weaker than I did after my accident when I couldn't even move." His hand drifted up over her belly to her breast. "I want you so much it's painful."

His finger moved over her nipple and, when it responded beautifully, he made a hissing sound and crushed her against him. His mouth covered hers and he kissed her with all the fervency burning inside him. He fondled her breast lovingly as his other arm closed around her waist.

Kyla tried to keep herself indifferent. She wanted to step outside herself and observe the embrace from that viewpoint. But it was difficult to remain passive when the heat of his body was seeping into hers, when she throbbed where his fingers had just stroked her. The passion he transmitted delivered with it a lassitude that threatened her resolve not to participate with her mind.

Through the sheer nightgown, she could feel the crisp texture of his chest hair, the erection of his nipples. His thighs were hard and straining against hers. His maleness nestled in the cove her body offered it. He was hard and she wanted him.

Her body and her mind waged war. She struggled

to keep her emotions intact. But in doing so, her body unwittingly went as unyielding as her heart.

Suddenly, Trevor withdrew his mouth from hers. The movement was so abrupt that her head snapped back and she fell victim to a cold green gaze.

He gripped her upper arms and shoved her away from him, holding her at the end of stiff, strong arms fully extended. "No thank you, Kyla."

She looked at him fearfully. He was furious and it showed. His dark brows were pulled down low over his eyes. His nostrils flared slightly with each breath.

"No thank you?" she repeated in a thin voice. "I don't understand."

"Let me explain it then." He spoke in a tight voice she knew he must be having a hard time keeping below a shout. "I don't want a sacrificial lamb beneath me going through the motions of making love."

The hasty lowering of her eyes was as good as a signed confession. "You're my husband. You can demand—"

He laughed harshly. "If only you knew how laughable that was. Demanding isn't quite my style, Kyla. I certainly don't intend to exercise caveman tactics on my wife!"

He released her so abruptly that she reeled against the bedside table. "You may relax," he said scathingly. "You're safe from me. I won't impose my lust on you tonight. Nor will I ever."

Her eyes snapped up. "That's right, Kyla," he said silkily, reading her surprise. "I still love you, but it's not conditional on whether you go to bed with me or not. But I warn you," he said, pointing a finger at her, "that loving you as I do, it will be impossible for you not to love me back."

In a heartbeat, he was towering over her, his left hand knotted in her hair. With his right arm he hauled her high against him and positioned them so there could be no doubt of his readiness to take her if he chose to. He pulled her head back until she was forced to look up into his glowering face.

"I promise you this," he said with soft emphasis, "no one has ever loved you as much as I do. No one has ever made love to you as well as I can. I'll bury myself so deep inside you that when I'm not actually there, you'll feel like a vital part of your body is missing." He lowered his head and branded her breast with his mouth. "Now when you exorcise those ghosts that haunt you, come to me and I'll be more than glad to demonstrate what I'm talking about."

Releasing her, he spun on his heel and stalked to the door. "Sleep well," he tossed over his shoulder, a second before the door slammed behind him.

CHAPTER TEN

"GOOD MORNING."

It wasn't the tone of voice she had expected, nor that, she secretly admitted, she probably deserved.

Surly, peevish, snide, cruel. Kyla would have expected him to be any of those, but not congenial and seemingly in a good mood.

"Good morning."

She skirted the table where he sat reading the newspaper and made a beeline for the coffee maker on the countertop. There was an empty mug waiting for her. She poured the fragrant, steaming coffee from the pot.

"I hope I didn't make it too strong for you."

She sipped. "It's fine. I like it strong."

"So do I."

She didn't realize he had come up behind her until his breath stirred her hair. She turned around quickly to face him. His arms slid around her waist and pulled her close. Ducking his head, he kissed her surprised mouth. It wasn't a passionate kiss, but a tender one that was almost as unsettling. "How was your night?" he asked solicitously.

Her night had been wretched. After Trevor had slammed out of the picture-perfect master bedroom suite he had created for his bride, Kyla had collapsed onto the wide bed and wept for what seemed like hours.

She longed for familiar surroundings, her own bedroom, Aaron, the comforting presence of her parents.
She longed to roll back the clock. She longed for Richard.

And she longed for Trevor.

That particular longing had brought on another wave
of weeping.

She had finally fallen asleep shortly before dawn,
and had awakened with a dull headache and puffy eyes.
When she left the bedroom wrapped in an old robe
that she had managed to sneak past Babs's eagle eye,
she hadn't known what to expect from her husband of
less than twenty-four hours, a husband to whom she
had denied a wedding night, if not by deed then by attitude. Sullen fury at best.

She wasn't prepared for the cherishing embrace with
which he enfolded her now. Nor for the soft kisses that
he employed to trace her hairline. Nor for the gentle,
tension-ridding massage his hands were giving her
back.

Kyla felt anxiety slowly leaking out of her. She
rested her cheek against the muscles of his chest, which
were delineated by the tight white T-shirt he was wearing over a pair of ragged cutoffs.

"Can you cook?"

"What?" she mumbled sleepily.

"I asked if you could cook."

She raised her head and took a step backward. "Of
course I can cook," she said with some asperity.

His mustache curved over a grin. "Then how about
some breakfast?"

"What would you like?"

"What can you cook?"

"Anything," she boasted with a coquettish toss of her reddish-blond hair. "If you'll get out of my way, I'll prove to you what a good cook I am."

He bowed deeply from the waist, sweeping his hand wide. "The kitchen's all yours, milady. I'll just return to my newspaper if that's all right with you."

A few minutes later she set a frosty glass of orange juice in front of him. He tipped the corner of his newspaper down. "Thanks."

She smiled at him. "You're welcome."

"It smells good."

"It's almost ready."

He folded up the scattered newspapers and pushed them aside so she could set the table. Apparently she had found everything where he had had it stored. She laid out place mats and used the casual stoneware and silverware for their place settings. He watched her hands as she expertly folded linen napkins and arranged them in rings in the centers of the plates. Before she could turn away, he reached for her hand and drew it to his mouth. He kissed the back of it.

"It doesn't take long to get spoiled. I think I'm already used to having a wife make such a fuss over me," he said softly.

The way he looked up at her from his chair sent a warm tide of pleasure spilling over her middle. She felt a blush rising out of the unglamorous neckline of her robe.

She tugged on her hand, "I, uh, don't want it to burn."

He released her hand and she scurried toward the range. Moments later, she was bearing a platter of aromatic food to the table. She set it down, then stood by, nervously awaiting his reaction.

"Eggs Benedict!" he exclaimed in delight. The dish had been arranged appetizingly on the platter and garnished with fresh orange slices and sprigs of parsley.

"Do you like them that way? I didn't know."

"I'll eat just about anything that doesn't move off the plate. And rutabagas. Don't ever try to feed me rutabagas."

She laughed. "I think that's the only thing that wasn't stocked in the pantry or refrigerator."

During this exchange she had carried the coffeepot to the table and refilled his mug. As she set it on a trivet, Trevor rose from his chair and pulled hers out for her. She looked up at him in surprise and when she did he pecked a quick kiss on the tip of her nose. "Thanks for breakfast."

"You're welcome." She sank into her chair. Her hands were trembling slightly, but she filled his plate, then her own.

"Delicious!" he pronounced after taking an unabashedly huge first bite. "Where did you learn to cook like this?"

"My mother taught me the basics. And I took a cooking course while—" She stopped abruptly. Trevor's head came up, a question in his expression.

"While?" he prodded.

"While my hus...while Richard was overseas."

She had never mentioned the cooking class in her letters. Why, he wondered.

"What did Richard think of your cooking classes?" Had he missed some letters? He was suddenly, unaccountably, furiously jealous of anything she might have written to her husband that he, Trevor, hadn't been privy to. What else had he missed?

"I didn't tell him."

Trevor's grip on his fork relaxed. "Why?"

She took a drink of juice and blotted her mouth with her napkin before answering. "I wanted to surprise him with all kinds of exotic recipes when he came home," she said, cutting into the slice of Canadian bacon. "Babs and I took the class together. It was great fun. Babs was the worst student. She ruined everything she tried, but it wasn't a total waste of her time because she ended up dating the chef."

She was chatting now because she was nervous. Trevor could tell because she wouldn't look at him directly, but glanced at a spot just off his shoulder. They weren't even at the point where she could mention Richard's name without feeling awkward about it.

"I'll bet you were at the top of the class, because this is great." Her head came up and she blessed him with a shy smile that melted his heart and made up for the hellish night he'd spent alone in the guest room. Well, almost. "I've always ridiculed the former jocks who get married and go to fat. Now I can see how it happens." He winked at her.

"Were you a jock?"

"In school."

"What sports?"

"Hmm, let's see." He sipped his coffee. "Track. Basketball. Rowing."

"Rowing?"

"I don't think you have it in Texas."

"That must be what developed your shoulders and thighs."

When her gaze dropped to his long legs, she noticed the scars. There they were, ugly pink raised seams in his flesh, running the length of his left leg, intersecting and meshing like railroad tracks.

Trevor lowered his fork to his plate and watched her. Bracing his elbows on the table, he folded his hands in front of his mouth and waited for the revulsion he prepared himself to see in her expression. It never came. When she raised her eyes to his face, there was only compassion in her brown eyes.

"I told you it wasn't pretty," he said, a definite edge to his voice.

"It's not so bad, Trevor."

"It's not so great, either."

She looked at his leg again. "It must have been awfully painful."

"It was."

"You've never told me what happened to you."

He shifted uneasily and she attributed that to self-consciousness. "It doesn't matter."

"You once said you were embarrassed to wear shorts. You shouldn't be."

A wry grin slanted his mustache upward. "You don't think all the ladies on the beach would cover their eyes and run in terror?"

"Not at all. You're too attractive."

He sobered instantly. Leaning forward, he speared her with his green gaze. "Do you think so?"

"Yes."

Several moments ticked by while Kyla was held transfixed by the gruff intensity in his voice and the hypnotizing power of his stare.

She willed herself out of the daze and stood up hastily, bumping the table with her thighs hard enough to rattle the glassware. "If you're finished, I'll clean up the dishes."

She spun around, but was brought up short when Trevor dug his fingers beneath the tie belt of her robe at the back of her waist. Giving it a swift tug, he turned her around and pulled her between his wide-spread thighs so that her middle bumped into his chest and his face was on a level with her breasts.

"Thanks for breakfast." The words, spoken in a low, rumbling voice to begin with, were almost completely muffled by the fabric folded over her breasts.

"It was the least I could do."

She lowered her eyes to the top of his head where the dark wavy hair swirled from the crown. It wasn't easy, but she resisted the urge to thread her fingers through the ebony strands to see if they felt as alive as they looked.

Her eyes battled to stay open when he rubbed his hard cheek against her breast, but they lost the contest and flickered closed. She felt the vibration of the moan that issued up out of his chest as his nose nuzzled her.

"You bathed this morning." It wasn't a question.

"Yes."

"You smell good. Like soap. And powder. And woman."

He made gentle gnawing motions with his mouth that sought and finally found the peak of her breast through the cloth. He didn't actually kiss her. He didn't actually suckle. What he did was rub his open mouth back and forth over her until he felt her flesh respond, then he touched her with his tongue.

"Breakfast was delicious," he whispered. Her skin

became damp where his breath filtered through the robe. "Is there any dessert?" He pressed his face deeper into her softly giving flesh. But he pulled back almost immediately and looked up at her. "Hmm?"

When he saw her tremulous expression, he chuckled and stood up, pushing her gently away from him. "Never mind. Let's get dressed and go get that kid of ours before your parents spoil him rotten." He checked the clock on the oven. "By the time we get there, they should be getting home from church. I'd like to take everyone to lunch. The Petroleum Club goes all out on its Sunday buffet."

"We're not members," Kyla found enough voice to say. She was still feeling aftershocks of delight at having Trevor's mouth on her breasts.

"But I am." He tweaked her nose. "I'll clean up the kitchen—you go get ready. I want to show you off." He kissed her swiftly and gave her rump a husbandly pat.

Kyla left the master bathroom twenty minutes later, after having applied her makeup and arranged her hair. That was when she came to the startling realization that she and Trevor might not be sharing a bed, but they were still sharing a bedroom.

She caught him in the act of stepping into a pair of dress slacks. A fleeting impression of light-blue briefs registered on her brain before she spun around and said, "Excuse me." She almost made it to the bathroom door before his stern voice halted her retreat.

"Kyla."

"What?"

"Turn around."

"Why?"

"Because I want to talk to you."

Slowly she came around, studiously keeping her eyes aimed at a point above his head. Casually he zipped up the trousers and, still shirtless and barefoot, crossed the room toward her. "I showered in the guest bath so I wouldn't disturb you, but my clothes have all been stored in the drawers and closets in here. It will be damned inconvenient to move them."

She wet her lips rapidly. "That's fine, fine. We'll just, uh, try to stay out of each other's way."

"I won't." He laughed, but when he saw her frown he said, "Okay, we'll split the differences. You can get in my way any time you like, and I'll try to stay out of yours. Deal?"

It was too complicated to think through, especially looking at his bare chest as she was. So she merely parroted, "Deal."

"Good." He turned his back—a smooth expanse of darkly tanned skin stretched tautly over rippling muscles—and returned to his closet, where he proceeded to take out a shirt and pull it on with the nonchalance of a person alone.

Kyla forced her feet to move to her own closet. She stood there motionless, working up her courage to take off her robe.

You're behaving like a child, she told herself angrily. The nightgown she had faced him in last night was a thousand times more revealing than the bra and half slip she had on beneath the robe. Swiftly, before she could change her mind, she whipped it off.

"I've been thinking."

At the sound of Trevor's voice, she jumped as though she'd been shot in the back now exposed to him. "About what?"

She willed her fumbling hands to hang the robe on a hanger properly and return it to the metal bar in the closet. It required tremendous concentration because she knew he was probably looking at her back and the slender ivory satin straps of her bra.

"About Aaron."

She hazarded a glance at him over her shoulder. He wasn't looking at her at all. He was tying his necktie, using the mirror he had had mounted over the bureau that was built into his closet. His shirt had been buttoned, but he hadn't tucked in the shirttail yet. The stiff collar had been flipped up against his square jaw. "What about him?" She reached for the dress she had chosen to wear.

"Maybe we should be locating a proper day-care center for him."

"Do you think he's old enough?"

"You're more expert on that than I am. I was just wondering what we'll do with him during the day if Meg and Clif get that motor home and strike out for parts unknown."

That had been a concern of Kyla's, too. "I suppose he should be around other children his age. There's an education in that."

"No doubt. How else will he learn all the dirty words?"

She laughed with him. "But I'd want to investigate the school's reputation."

"Absolutely. It will have to be sterling. We both have to be sold on the facility and faculty before we enroll him. Need any help?"

Before she could formulate an answer, his hands were pushing hers aside. They had been at her waist in back grappling with the lowest button on her dress. How could a man of his size move so silently? She stood ramrod straight as his fingers negotiated the buttons. After securing the top one, his hands smoothed down her back and settled on her hips.

"No one would ever guess you'd had a baby. Was it a difficult pregnancy?"

"Not at all."

"You're so slender," he said softly, squeezing her hips lightly before his hands fell away. "Can you give me some help here?"

Unwisely she turned to face him. Only a few inches separated them. "Help you? How?"

"Check to see if my collar is turned down properly all the way around. Sometimes I don't bend it down just right and my tie peeks out from underneath."

She gave it a hasty inspection. "It's not quite folded down all the way in back."

"Would you fix it for me, please? It's hard to reach."

"Sure." She spoke with far more carelessness than she felt. Actually she was wondering how she was going to keep her hands out of the black hair that curled beguilingly over his collar if she came that close to touching it.

No sooner were her arms raised and her hands occupied adjusting his collar over his tie than he flipped up his shirttails and unzipped his trousers. Her hands froze. Her eyes sprang up to his. His expression was bland as he casually began stuffing his shirttail into his trousers. Occasionally, too occasionally, his knuckles bumped into her middle.

"Anything wrong?" he asked.

"No, no, nothing," she gasped and quickly folded his

collar down. She patted it firmly into place just as the
rasp of his zipper reached her ears. Her arms slid from
his shoulders. He finished fastening the fly of his pants.

And then they stared at each other while time was
held in suspension.

"Thanks," he said after a long, still while.

"Thank you, too." His eyebrow quirked with humor.
"For doing up my buttons," she added hastily.

"Oh. You're welcome."

They fell into another staring spell. Kyla was the
first to move away, and she did so by turning her back
to find her shoes in the closet.

It took the familiar pandemonium that went with
corralling Aaron to restore her equilibrium. But even
that didn't erase an image in Kyla's mind of light-blue
briefs stretched over tight, rounded buttocks.

The Powerses were impressed with the number of
people who greeted their new son-in-law as they ate
lunch at the exclusive Petroleum Club. Even Aaron
seemed awed by his surroundings. His behavior during the meal was above reproach.

After lunch Trevor drove the Powerses out to the
house he had built for Kyla and Aaron. After a tour
that left them speechless, Trevor followed them back
to their house in his pickup. The remainder of the afternoon was spent packing and loading Kyla's things
that still had to be moved.

"He's a tired little rascal tonight," Trevor said of
Aaron as they tucked him in. He patted the boy on the
seat. Aaron's eyelids were already at half-mast. His
stuffed animals were lined up around the slats of the
baby bed like sentinels.

"Which is probably just as well," Kyla remarked,

pulling a light blanket over her son. "The first night in a new place might be traumatic if he weren't so ready to go to sleep."

"Don't you think he likes the room?"

She heard the anxiety in Trevor's voice and looked up to find that he was genuinely concerned about it. "What little boy wouldn't like it?"

She gazed around the bedroom, which had been decorated in a railroad motif. The Little Engine That Could was puffing up the hill painted on the wall. A steam-engine-shaped toy chest, filled to capacity, took up a good portion of another wall. A miniature track had been run around the molding six inches below the ceiling. At the flip of a switch a tiny freight train circled the room at a clicking pace, belching puffs of white smoke every so often and tooting its horn periodically. Aaron had clapped his hands in glee and only frowned in frustration when he realized he couldn't reach it.

Her gaze returned to Trevor. "What I meant was that sometimes when a child sleeps in a strange place it upsets him. Apparently Aaron isn't bothered by it." Aaron was already snoring softly. Kyla covered a huge yawn with her hand as they left the room.

"You're worn out, too." Trevor clasped her shoulders and within seconds his strong fingers were working the knots out of her shoulder muscles. His thumbs magically pressed the tension from the base of her neck. Moving closer and laying his cheek against hers he said, "Want to spend a few minutes in the hot tub? Does that sound good?"

It sounded heavenly. She couldn't think of anything better than being immersed in hot bubbly water.

"I'll meet you out there."

Or anything more dangerous than sharing such a sensual experience with Trevor.

She eased from beneath his massaging hands. "If you don't mind, Trevor, I think I'll just go to bed. This weekend has been so hectic. It's taking its toll."

"All right."

She could tell he was trying not to let his disappointment show. This man had taken her as his wife, knowing she still loved another man. Wasn't she being a rather poor sport? "Unless you really want me to," she added.

He shook his head impatiently. "No. I know you're tired. Good night."

He bracketed her neck with his hands and tilted her head back with both his thumbs beneath her chin. He planted his lips firmly over hers, parted them, waited for her to accommodate him and, when she did, slipped his tongue into her mouth like a velvet sword.

It was a torching kiss that conveyed all the passion that smoldered within him. His practiced technique ignited her desire until she could swear that tiny tongues of flame were licking at her body.

When he released her at last, she all but sagged against him, so totally had his kiss depleted her. "Good night," she said huskily and moved away toward the bedroom in what she hoped wasn't a staggering walk.

TREVOR SAT IN the dark, idly rocking the porch swing with his heels against the decking.

A terse expletive summed up his mood of the moment. He tossed the remainder of the whiskey he'd been sipping onto the ground. He didn't need alcohol. He didn't need anything to make him any warmer, nothing to increase the heat that simmered in his loins.

He needed Kyla. Naked. Beneath him. Sheathing that part of him that ached with its need for her.

Cursing again, he thumped his head against the thick chain holding up the swing until it hurt badly enough to feel good.

Would she ever love him? Would she ever want him as he wanted her? So far he'd accomplished everything he had set out to. She and Aaron were living under his roof, sharing his life, enjoying his protection.

But she wasn't in his bed yet. Would she ever return his love?

Possibly.

But never if she knew who you were.

He had had every intention of telling her he was the legendary Smooch before they got married, but he had talked himself out of it. Better to be legally bound before breaking the news.

Then he had decided to tell her the morning after their wedding night, after she had had a night of his loving and they were bound not only legally but physically. So much for good intentions.

Well hell, it wasn't his fault that they hadn't had a wedding night, now was it?

But you should have told her by now, his conscience argued.

"Yeah, I know," he answered it out loud.

But how? When? What time was ever going to be right to say, "We didn't meet by accident. I orchestrated everything because I knew before I ever saw you that I was going to marry you and provide a home for you and your son. Why? Well, because I'm responsible for your husband's death and I felt like I owed it both to him and to you. Oh, but I do love you."

He repeated that curt obscenity and pushed himself out of the swing.

Would Kyla believe that he loved her after he told her who he was? Hell, no. *He* wouldn't believe it were the tables to be turned.

Propping his shoulder against the outer wall of the house, he stood at the edge of the deck and stared sightlessly into the near space.

"What the hell am I going to do?" he asked the night.

He knew that with just a little finesse on his part, he could get her to surrender to his sexual advances. He knew enough about women to know that she wanted him, if only she would admit that to herself. But that was the key to it, she had to admit it to herself. When they came together—*Lord, don't let it be too much longer*—she would have to initiate it. He wouldn't be accused later of taking advantage of her that way, too.

You've got to tell her, he was reminded by that relentless conscience.

"But I've got to win her first."

He didn't have to tell her tonight. Or tomorrow. Or even next week. He would take it one day at a time. When she knew he loved her, he would tell her. When the time was right he'd know it.

And if there's never a right time? his conscience taunted him.

But he didn't listen anymore. He began thinking of the woman sleeping in his bed. He envisioned an hourglass with sand the color of her hair sliding through its slender passage. One grain at a time. One kiss at a time. One caress at a time. And her resistance was lessened that much more.

"Your time's running out, Kyla." The hoarse whisper wasn't a threat. It was a promise.

"SORRY, I'M LATE," Kyla said breathlessly as she sailed through the back door of Petal Pushers. Her arms were full of order blanks and ledgers and catalogs. All were slipping to the floor despite her efforts to keep them secured between her arms and her chest. She piled them on the desk and paused to draw a breath. Her hair had been whipped to a fiery madness by the wind. Aaron had slobbered on her blouse.

"What kept you?" Babs asked sweetly. "Did something come up this morning?"

Kyla pretended not to catch the double entendre. "You can't imagine what a circus it was trying to get the three of us dressed, fed and off for the day." Kyla eased herself down into the chair behind the desk and drew a deep breath.

Babs laughed. "Honeymoonitis?"

"What?" Kyla frowned as Babs hiked a hip over the corner of the desk and leaned forward with an eager expression on her face.

"I know what made you late this morning. Is he as good as he looks?"

Kyla pushed herself out of the chair on the pretext of picking up the papers she had dropped. "Who?"

"Who? For God's sake, Kyla, whom did you just marry? Trevor, of course."

"Oh, Trevor," Kyla said absently, deliberately keeping her back to her perceptive friend. "Good at what?"

"You aren't going to tell me, are you?"

Kyla faced her friend. "About my sex life? No."

"Why?"

"In the first place it's none of your business. And in the second place I can't imagine why you would want to know."

"But I do," Babs said, hopping off the desk and stalking Kyla into the shop. "Every scintillating detail."

"Do we have any orders today?"

"Is he the rowdy, reckless, tempestuous type?"

"Maybe we should change the window displays this week."

"Or the slow, leisurely, languid type?"

"I'm not listening."

"Is he a moaner?"

"Has the mail arrived?"

"Does he talk to you? I'm sure he does. What does he say?"

"Babs!" Kyla shouted to stop the barrage of questions. "We haven't had a conversation this ridiculous since we were in the eighth grade."

"And then you told me everything."

"I've grown up. Why don't you?"

"You even told me what Richard's kisses were like when you first kissed him. Can't you at least tell me that much? What are Trevor's kisses like."

"Indescribable," Kyla said truthfully. "Now can we please change the subject?"

"One more thing."

Sighing, Kyla crossed her arms over her chest and feigned boredom. "What?"

"Is he positively breathtaking naked?"

Kyla swallowed. Then, because she couldn't even imagine what Babs's reaction would be if she told her she didn't know, she simply retorted, "What do you think?"

And from that Babs had to draw her own conclusions.

CHAPTER ELEVEN

THEY LEARNED TO live together. Kyla discovered that her husband existed on very little sleep. He enjoyed staying up late, but he was a jovial, early riser. She had always dreaded getting up in the morning whether she had slept three hours or thirteen. Trevor learned to give her a wide berth in the mornings until she had had at least one cup of coffee.

He was prone to drape clothes over the nearest piece of furniture as he disrobed, and to scatter sections of the newspaper as he finished with them, and to leave empty glasses on end tables. But he was also conscientious about picking up after himself and helping her with household chores without even being asked.

The first week they were married, Kyla wore herself out trying to keep Aaron quiet and well-behaved around Trevor. He wasn't accustomed to having a young child underfoot. She was afraid Aaron's constant activity and incessant racket would disturb him.

But Trevor never showed signs of irritation, not even when Aaron was behaving at his worst. He spent a great deal of what psychologists called "quality time" with the child, doing everything from playing with him on the deck while she prepared dinner, to reading him books, to bathing him when she had both hands full.

As for being a good father, Kyla could find no fault with Trevor Rule.

As for his being a good husband, she could find little to complain about, either. He was considerate and good-natured. Each night he left her alone in the master suite while he slept in the guest bedroom. He exercised no modesty in changing clothes in front of her. Often one surprised the other in various stages of undress by opening the wrong door at the wrong time. Such scenes never failed to disconcert Kyla, but Trevor seemed to take them in stride.

He was generous with his embraces and kisses, too. Anyone would think they were a happily married couple madly in love with each other. He would frequently slip his arms around her from behind and nuzzle her neck, complimenting her on her hair or her complexion or her figure. He never asked permission for a kiss, but took them as his due. Often his good-night kisses were so tantalizing that as she closed herself up in the bedroom alone, she would curse herself for a fool.

"He's my husband. I owe him conjugal rights. And if being with him would alleviate this jittery feeling inside me, why not?"

Then she would open the drawer in the bedside table where she had placed Richard's picture. (She had had enough sensitivity toward Trevor's feelings not to display it openly.) Gazing down into the beloved face, she would promise him again that he still lived in her heart, that she would never betray his memory by falling in love with another man, and that he would always be her *true* husband.

But her body wasn't so easily convinced. As she lay alone in that wide, empty bed, it wasn't Richard's face that haunted her, but Trevor's. His smile. His hair. His rugged, sun-baked features. His kiss. All vivid.

As the days merged into weeks, that jittery agitation inside her continued to brew until, like all boiling kettles, it had to blow.

It happened after a particularly arduous day in which she had haggled with a wholesaler in Dallas who had billed her for a shipment of roses that Petal Pushers had never received. To top that, she had argued with Babs over her offer to keep Aaron for the weekend while Kyla and Trevor treated themselves to a Dallas hotel's weekend getaway package.

"I think you need the time away. You look like a tightrope walker who has just lost her knack for it," Babs had observed badgeringly. "I keep waiting for you to lose your balance and fall off."

"I'm fine."

"Something is wrong with you, and I intend to find out what it is, if I have to ask Trevor."

"Don't you dare!" Kyla shouted, spinning around to confront her friend. "Stay out of my business, Babs."

She regretted her sharp words the moment they left her mouth and apologized for them. But for the rest of the day, Babs was sulky. Trevor had offered to pick Aaron up at his day-care center, but the job of marketing fell to her. She couldn't find everything she needed because the clerk had rearranged the shelves; the lines were impossibly long and the checkers incredibly slow. Several times she was tempted to leave the groceries in her basket and walk out without them.

By the time she arrived home, she was physically and emotionally exhausted. To save herself a trip back to the car, she tried to carry all three grocery sacks at one time. She was juggling them as she stepped up onto the deck and headed for the back door.

Her turbulent mood wasn't improved by the sight that greeted her. Trevor was lounging in the hot tub, a cold beer near his hand. And Aaron—

"Aaron!" she cried angrily. "What in the hell is *this*?"

"This," Trevor said, smiling, as yet unaware of her bad temper, "is pudding painting. The teacher at the school said he loved it, so I decided to try it out at home."

Her child, who was sitting at the small table Trevor had bought for him and placed in the shade on the deck, was covered from head to toe in dark sticky goo that Kyla was monumentally relieved to learn was chocolate pudding.

Thankfully, he was wearing only his diaper. His chubby hands were scooping the pudding out of a bowl and slapping it onto the sheet of butcher paper Trevor had provided for him. He smeared it around, then raised his hand to his face and licked the pudding from between his fingers. Apparently that wasn't the first time his stomach had taken precedence over his artistic endeavors. His face was covered with pudding. He smiled at her through the chocolate mess and chattered something.

"I think he said 'bird,'" Trevor explained. "At least that's what I suggested he paint a picture of."

"He's filthy!" Kyla cried.

She could feel her anger rising as surely as the mercury in a thermometer. Knowing it was unreasonable to get so upset over practically nothing, she nonetheless couldn't control the inevitable eruption of her temper.

"He'll wash," Trevor said pleasantly. But between his arching brows a V had formed and was deepening. "The teacher said it was a very creative exercise for him."

"The teacher doesn't have to clean up the mess," she retorted vituperatively. "And neither do you. I'll be the one who has to. Or didn't you and teacher get around to discussing that in the cozy little chat you no doubt had together?"

She stalked to the sliding glass door and tried to wedge her foot through a crack so she could open it. It wouldn't budge and with her hands full of the grocery sacks, which were beginning to sag under the slipping contents inside, she was helpless.

Finally, gritting her teeth, she looked at her husband. "I hate to interrupt your bubble bath, Trevor," she said with brittle sweetness, "but I think the least you could do is get out of the hot tub and help me."

"Any other time, Kyla, but—"

"Well, never mind then!" she shouted. "I'll do it all myself."

He shot out of the hot tub then, angry and—

Naked.

His feet slapped against the redwood decking, slinging water with each long stride. Kyla stood rooted to the spot, even when he reached her and yanked the grocery sacks from her arms. He secured all three of them in one fist and slid open the glass door with such impetus that it rocked in its track. Heedless of both his nakedness and the water he was dripping everywhere he stormed into the kitchen and virtually slung the sacks of groceries onto the tiled countertop.

Then, with one hand propped on his hip and his right

knee slightly bent in an arrogant, belligerent stance, he turned to face her. She read his expression loud and clear. If she could have captioned it, it would have said, "Well, you asked for it, lady."

Furious with herself for making such a scene and furious with him for letting her, she fled into the bedroom and rattled every pane of glass in the house when she slammed the door behind her.

"AM I STILL in the doghouse?"

Dusk was thick and purple just beyond the plantation shutters on the bedroom windows. Kyla lay on her side, her knees drawn up to her chest. After a long bout of crying, she had showered and put on her nightgown. The sheet was pulled as high as her waist. Her cheek was resting on her hands, which were folded, palms together.

She raised her head slightly. Trevor was at the door, peeking around it as though he might be pelted with flying objects if he dared go any farther into the room.

"No. I'm sorry."

He came in. He was dressed in nothing but a pair of cutoffs and Kyla closed her eyes before returning her head to the pillow. All too well she remembered how his body had looked, soaking wet, the sunlight flickering through the trees and falling onto every silver rivulet that trickled down through that forest of hair on his chest. She recalled the hard, corded muscles of his stomach, the length of his limbs, the impressive sex nestled in a thatch of dark hair.

She had wept hot, bitter tears of regret—regret because she had noticed just how magnificent his nakedness was, regret that in spite of her best intentions she wanted him, and regret that she had denied him to herself for so long.

Now she felt the mattress sink with his weight as he lay down behind her and curved his body around hers. His fingers sifted through her hair, lifting stray curls off her cheek. He arranged the loose strands on the pillow just so. His ministrations were soothing.

"Hard day?" His breath was warm and soft in her ear.

"A bitch."

He chuckled. "Then I guess you weren't ready to see your son looking like something out of a minstrel show, were you?"

I wasn't ready to see you rising out of that hot tub like a male version of Venus, either. "I'm sorry I made such a fuss. It was a combination of things."

He was propped on his right elbow, leaning over her. His index finger swept back and forth over her cheek. "Now you understand why I didn't jump out of the hot tub to help you with your load right away."

"Yes."

"I wasn't expecting you home so early or I would have already been out and had Aaron bathed and ready for supper."

"It wasn't your fault, Trevor. None of it. It was mine." She sighed. "I don't feel well and—"

"What's wrong?" He was instantly alert, his body tensing behind hers.

"Nothing."

"Something. Are you sick? Tell me."

She turned her head up and back and stared at him in a way that conveyed her message.

"Oh," he said in a chagrined voice. "That."

"Yes, that." She turned to her original position.

"When?"

"I discovered it when I came in. I should have known. I was acting like such a viper."

"You're forgiven." He touched her tentatively, laying his hand in the shallow of her waist. "Do you… does it hurt?"

"Some."

"Did you take anything?"

"A couple of aspirin."

"Will that help?"

"A little."

"Not much?"

"No. It has to wear off."

"I see."

Moving slowly, he eased down the sheet. The nightgown was short and had narrow straps. It was made out of some thin, white material that reminded him of his most expensive handkerchiefs. There were flowers, white also, embroidered on the hem. Beneath it, he could see the outline of white panties. She looked vulnerable, virginal, and his loins began to ache with desire.

He touched her waist again. She didn't stir. Gradually he slid his hand down and around, giving her time to protest. When she didn't, he pressed his palm warmly over the lower part of her abdomen. "There?"

"Uh-huh."

Moving his hand in slow circles, he massaged her. "Better?"

She nodded.

"Poor baby." He kissed her temple lovingly.

She sighed and her eyes closed sleepily. "Trevor?"

"Hmm?"

"Have you ever lived with a woman?"

His hand paused, but so momentarily that the hesitation was barely discernible. "No, why?"

"Then what do you know about this?"

"Only that I'm glad I don't have to go through it every month."

Without opening her eyes, she smiled. "Typical male answer."

"But honest." He took a love bite out of her bare shoulder.

She didn't actually think about moving her legs. A message to them wasn't consciously transmitted. They just moved, unfolding away from her body, straightening and providing him greater access to her swollen, cramping tummy.

"Did you and Aaron manage dinner without me?"

"Like clockwork."

"What did you do?"

"Well," he said, sliding his legs against hers, catching the backs of her knees with his and filling her insteps with his toes, "first I hosed him down to get all the chocolate pudding off."

She laughed. "By the way, I approve of the idea of pudding painting. He was certainly having a good time. On any other day, I probably would have put on a swimsuit and joined him."

"As we both know by now, you had a right to be out of sorts."

"I shouldn't have yelled at you."

"I liked the part about Aaron's teacher and me having a 'cozy little chat.' The way you said it made me think you might be jealous." This time his mouth found her ear. His tongue delicately stroked the lobe. "That's so soft. A little fuzzy."

"Go on," she said in a breathy voice.

"I forget where I was."

"You…you…hmm… You, uh, hosed him down."

"Oh, right, yeah, and then I fixed his dinner."

"What did he eat?"

"His favorite."

"Hot dogs?"

"Uh-huh."

"Without the buns?"

"Of course." He kissed her neck and she moaned softly. "Tomorrow morning the birds in our woods will have three hot dog buns for breakfast. I hope they like mustard."

A low laugh issued from her throat and she didn't know whether it was because of his joke or because his mustache was dusting the column of her neck as if it were an object made of rare porcelain. "Did you—"

"I know what you're going to ask and yes, I did. I watched Aaron take every bite and made sure he chewed it."

"Thank you." Her mouth searched for his.

"You're welcome." His lips found hers.

The kiss acted like a spark at the end of two very short fuses. He ground his mouth against hers hungrily and her lips parted for the introduction of his tongue. Her body followed her head around until they were lying face-to-face.

Her arms locked around his shoulders. The tips of her breasts strained against the front of her nightgown until they touched the furry wall of his chest.

He pressed her down, covering a side of her body with his own.

"Kyla, you—"

"Trevor, I—"

"What?"

"Trevor?"

From the bed came sounds. Gratified groans. The silky shifting of linens. Soughing breaths. Incoherent whispers. Whimpers of pleasure. The music of mating.

His hands moved with restless greed. He touched her thighs; for a fleeting second her calf filled his palm. He ran his fingers along her fragile collarbone. He cupped her breast.

"Ahh." Her back arched and she tore her mouth free of his kiss.

"What's the matter?"

"It's tender."

"Oh. I didn't...it is?"

"Yes."

"I'm sorry."

"No, it...actually it felt good."

"It did?"

"Oh, yes." She sighed as he gently caressed her again.

"Like that?"

"Hmm."

"And the nipples?"

"Yes, yes."

"Tell me, if—"

But he never finished the sentence, because her fingers wove themselves through his hair and drew his head down for another avaricious kiss.

When it ended, he lowered his head. It moved from

side to side ardently pressing hot, random kisses into her breasts. His hands formed a brace for her ribs. He shifted her beneath him. His knee separated hers. The nightgown was pushed to her waist. She tucked his hard thigh high between hers. She moved against it. Rotating. Rubbing. Reaching.

"Damn!"

He lay atop her, his breath thrashing like a strong wind in her ear. She could feel the rapid thudding of his heart where his chest crushed hers. Between his powerful hands, he was holding her head immobile. His fevered face was buried in her hair.

"Don't move, sweetheart."

"What is it?"

"Please don't move, my love," he groaned. "Be still for just a minute."

She did as he asked. Several moments later, he slowly raised his head. His face was infinitely sweet and his expression compassionate. One corner of his mustache crawled up to form a rueful grin. "Wouldn't you know it? I get you just where I want you and it's the wrong night."

Embarrassed, her eyes fell away from his face. He kissed her cheek and moved away, coming off the bed completely. Bending at the waist, he laid his palm against her flushed cheek. "Are you all right?"

She wasn't in pain, except for the lower part of her body, which was aching abominably, and not with the miseries of menstruation. "I feel better," she said inanely.

He straightened and uncomfortably shifted his weight from one foot to the other. His fingers raked strands of ebony hair off his forehead. "You skipped supper. Are you hungry?"

"No. Did you eat?"

"I nibbled. I'm fine." They looked at each other briefly, then away, realizing at the same time how banal this conversation was after the passion that had seethed between them only moments ago. "Well, I'll leave you alone now. Good night."

He turned and headed for the door. The muscles of his back rippled beneath the smooth skin. The cutoffs gloved his buttocks.

"Trevor?"

He spun around. "What?"

"You…" *Don't stop now. You've gone this far.* She swallowed her pride and her better judgment. "You don't have to go."

Trevor looked at his wife. She was propped up on her elbows. The nightgown's embroidered hem was riding her upper thighs. Her tousled hair was tumbling over her shoulders like spun pink gold. His kisses had left her lips wet and berry-colored. The fabric of her nightgown was damp where his mouth had been. It clung to her breasts, transparently molding to the tips, which were making rosy inverted dimples against the soft white fabric.

He grimaced and rubbed his moist palms down the legs of his cutoffs. "Yeah, I do. I have to go. If I stay…"

If he touched her again there would be no stopping him from consummating his marriage and quenching his raging desire. Hell, he wasn't fastidious. But the first time they made love, he didn't want her to feel embarrassed or uncomfortable or to regret it for any reason.

"But hold the thought," he added on a husky whisper seconds before he left the room.

AARON WAS ALREADY in his high chair and Trevor was turning strips of bacon in a sizzling skillet when Kyla warily approached the kitchen the following morning.

"Good morning, baby." She leaned down to kiss Aaron. He affectionately bopped her on the nose with a soggy piece of bacon. "Thanks a lot," she muttered.

"It was either get him up or let him jump in his bed until all the springs broke," Trevor said, taking the skillet off the burner and moving toward her.

"Thank you for seeing to him."

"My pleasure."

He clasped her waist lightly and drew her forward. He gave her one of those morning kisses that smelled like after-shave and tasted like teeth recently brushed. Kyla wouldn't have minded if it had lasted longer, but after smacking another quick kiss on her mouth, he said, "Sit down. You must be starving."

She glanced worriedly at the clock. "I've got to hurry. I overslept."

"Take your time. I called Babs and told her not to expect you on time this morning. Aaron's school isn't expecting him until around ten."

He set a platter of bacon and homemade waffles in front of her and sent her salivary glands into delirium. "I am starving."

"How are you otherwise?" He bent down and slid his hand past her waist. "Tummy still hurt?"

"It's much better."

"And here?" He palmed her breast and gently rolled her nipple between his thumb and finger.

She could barely breathe and gasped out, "Fine... much fine... I mean much better."

"That's good." He kissed the top of her head and sat down across from her. While she fumbled with her napkin and tried to remember how to use a fork, he buttered a waffle for Aaron and slid the plate onto the high chair's tray. "Here, Scout. Attack."

They laughed at the child's atrocious table manners and Kyla remarked, "We've got to start doing something about that." When she realized she had included Trevor in that statement, making the "we" sound so permanent, she glanced up at him. His expression was warm and flooded her body with a golden heat.

"How did you sleep?" he asked.

She noticed that his fingers were so long and strong that they barely fitted in the crook of the coffee mug's handle. Yet they could be so gentle when they touched her body, as they had been only moments ago. Getting a bite of waffle past her thickening throat was no small task, but when she did she answered, "Fairly well."

She had dreamed of him and awakened perspiring, with her heart pounding and her breath coming in short, rapid bursts. At least she could now satisfy Babs's curiosity and tell her without any exaggeration that Trevor was breathtaking naked.

"I didn't sleep too well last night," he said.

"I'm sorry. What was wrong?" He had certainly taken her breath when he came out of that hot tub. His chest and thighs and—

"It was too hard."

Kyla's fork clattered to her plate and when she reached for it, she knocked over her orange juice.

Aaron pointed and said, "Uh-oh! Uh-oh!"

Trevor scraped back his chair and lunged for a dish towel. He blotted it against the spreading puddle of juice. "I was referring to the bed in the guest room."

"What?" Kyla's head swiveled around. His mustache was twitching with his need to laugh.

"The *bed* was too hard."

Her cheeks were bathed with hot color. Thankfully she was spared further embarrassment when the telephone rang. Trevor answered it.

"Dad!" he exclaimed.

Kyla lifted Aaron, who had polished off his waffle in record time, onto her lap. He reached for the food left on her plate and between her kisses, he ate that, as well. She glanced at Trevor, who was smiling broadly into the receiver.

"Sure, no problem. What time…? For how long…? Is that all…? Well, that's better than nothing…. Okay, we'll be there. Bye." He hung up.

"Your father?"

"He's flying down today to spend the night with us. That's all right with you, isn't it?"

"Certainly. I know you were disappointed that he couldn't come down for the wedding."

"I want him to meet you and Aaron. He can only stay one night and then he has to make a trip to L.A. for some case he's working on." He popped a piece of bacon into his mouth and chewed vigorously. "I want to drive him around town and show him some of my buildings. You know we— Say, I'm sorry. I didn't mean to get carried away."

Actually she was enjoying his enthusiasm. "Go on," she urged. "What were you about to say?"

"We didn't get along very well. Not until after my accident."

"He wanted you to be a lawyer?"

"And I had other ideas. But while I was in the hospital, we came to an understanding and now everything's great between us."

Her smile was genuine. "Are you driving to Dallas to pick him up?"

"If you don't mind. He gave me his flight number. I thought we'd all have dinner in the city."

"Aaron included?" she asked worriedly.

"Of course, Aaron included. He's part of this family." He scooped the child out of her arms and held him high over his head. Aaron squealed in delight. "Dad loves to eat Italian." He named a famous Dallas restaurant. "Should I call and make reservations?"

She hated to dampen his excitement, but apparently he didn't realize what a risk it was to take a fifteen-month-old child to a sedate restaurant for a leisurely meal. "I don't know if that's a good idea, Trevor. I'm not sure they welcome children there."

"Hey, if they don't want our kid in their restaurant, we'll take our business elsewhere."

FROM THE MAÎTRE d' to the lowliest dishwasher, everyone in the family-owned establishment was charmed by the three men, George Rule, Trevor and Aaron. Kyla's anxiety was all for naught because Trevor had spoken with the maître d'personally when making the reservation and the staff was prepared for Aaron before the party arrived.

Her initial meeting with Trevor's father, amidst the confusion at the airport, had gone more smoothly than

Kyla had had any right to expect. At first Aaron was shy with the tall, white-haired man with the authoritative voice. But no more so than George was with the child.

Deliberately Trevor seated them in the backseat of the car together and by the time they reached the restaurant, located in Dallas's prestigious Turtle Creek area, the two were fast friends. In fact it was George who carried Aaron inside and showed him off to everyone as his grandson.

"Trevor tells me I'll miss meeting your parents," George said on the drive back to Chandler.

"We got a postcard from them yesterday from Yellowstone," Kyla said. "They're having the time of their lives."

She explained to George that the Powerses had sold their house within days of her marriage to Trevor. What furnishings Kyla didn't want, they had sold at auction. Trevor had helped Clif pick out the motor home that best suited their needs. Meg had furnished it with the giddy excitement of a little girl with a new dollhouse. Two weeks later they had left.

"She gets homesick for them," Trevor said teasingly, reaching across the front seat to tug on a lock of Kyla's hair. "They spoiled her rotten."

"So do you."

His head swung around. She had been as surprised as he to hear herself make that statement, but she realized after vocalizing it that it was the truth. Trevor glanced out the windshield to make sure he wasn't endangering them, then looked at Kyla again.

"I'm glad. That's what I want to do."

They continued staring at one another until George

coughed loudly and said, "I don't know about you, Aaron, but I'm beginning to feel like a fifth wheel."

There was enough daylight left when they reached Chandler for Trevor to walk George through some of the building projects he was working on. Kyla remained in the car, watching their silhouettes move against the darkening sky. Trevor had hefted Aaron to his shoulders where the boy rode, his legs straddling Trevor's neck. They made a poignant picture.

"But that should be Richard," Kyla whispered, fighting the tears that blurred her eyes.

She wept because she couldn't convince herself of it. If the man should be Richard, why did it look so right for her son's fat fists to be trustingly clenching handfuls of Trevor's black hair? Why did it touch her heart so achingly to see Trevor swing Aaron down carefully and unabashedly give him a hearty hug? And why did she want to feel those same strong arms holding her?

George was justifiably impressed with the house and heaped unqualified praise on his son. Kyla carried Aaron off to bed and after a brief visit with George, excused herself to give Trevor and his father some time alone.

"I've got a bruise on my shin the size of a fifty-cent piece," George said. "Any particular reason why you kicked me under the table when I mentioned your stint in the Marines?"

Trevor had been glad Kyla was involved wiping spaghetti sauce off Aaron's mouth and had missed his father's inopportune comment at dinner. "I'd rather Kyla not know about that. She doesn't know how I got hurt."

"Any of it?"

"No."

"Hmm."

Trevor knew his father well enough to know that even a "Hmm" was never casually spoken. "You certainly fell in love and married quickly, didn't you?"

"Is that so odd?"

"For you it is." His son looked at him sharply and George smiled. "Your reputation with women reached even your ol' dad's ears, Trevor. This sudden romance is out of character."

They were sitting out on the deck in the comfortable chaise lounges. George was puffing on a cigar, which his doctor had advised him to give up. Trevor was glad the darkness covered his uneasiness. He didn't like the direction the conversation had taken. "I love her, Dad."

"I don't doubt that now that I've seen you with her. It's just strange that 'Smooch,' as your buddies used to call you, fell so hard and so fast."

"I've been in love with her for a long time," Trevor said, almost beneath his breath.

George rolled the cigar between his fingers, studying its glowing tip. "She wouldn't have anything to do with those letters you pored over and wouldn't let out of your sight while you were in the hospital, would she?"

Trevor should have known better. Nothing, not the most trivial scrap of evidence, slipped past the shrewd George Rule. To him nothing was insignificant. Trevor got out of his chair and walked to the edge of the deck. He propped his shoulder against the wall and stared out at the darkness as he had done weeks before while ruminating on how to tell Kyla who he was. "Dad, I'm going to tell you a story you're going to find hard to believe."

When he concluded his tale, several ponderous

moments of silence followed. Finally George said, "I promised never to interfere in your life again, Trevor, but you're playing with fire."

"I know," Trevor admitted, turning around to face his father.

"How do you think this young woman is going to react when she learns the truth?"

Trevor hung his head and slid his hands into his trouser pockets. "I hate to think about it."

"Well, you'd better think about it," the older man warned, "because she *will* find out." He pulled himself to his feet and ground out his cigar in the ashtray Trevor had provided for him. Laying a hand on Trevor's shoulder, he said, "But who knows? It might work out. If you love her enough."

"I do."

"Does she love you?"

Trevor hesitated, his eyes slicing toward the darkened master bedroom windows. "I think she might be coming to. Or maybe she's just getting used to having me around. Hell, I don't know."

George smiled. Then his fond gaze rested on the eye patch and he was reminded once again of how valuable his son was to him and how close he had come to losing him. Moisture gathered in his eyes and he pulled Trevor forward for a fiercely emotional, if short-lived, embrace. "After what you went through, son, you deserve to be happy."

"No, Dad," Trevor said roughly over his father's shoulder, "after what she's been through, she deserves to be happy."

Soon afterward they said their good-nights and

George ambled toward the guest room where Trevor had placed his suitcase.

Trevor approached the door to the master suite with the dawdling, shuffling footsteps of a boy who had been sent to the principal's office. His stomach was doing handsprings. His heart was thudding.

Just what the hell was wrong with him? Was he excited at the thought of her welcoming him into bed? Or frightened at the thought of her rejection?

Frightened? Of a woman weighing no more than one hundred and ten pounds? Don't be ridiculous.

Then why are you standing out here like a moron, staring at this door with your stomach in knots and your heart pounding and your palms sweating and your groin...

Oh, God, no, don't think about your groin.

Were his knees really shaking? Why, for God's sake?

He was a grown man, not a schoolboy. This was his house. He had built it. He had financed it. He had a right to sleep in any damn room he pleased.

She was his wife, wasn't she? And yeah, he *had* been spoiling her for the past few weeks. He'd walked around on eggshells, doing and saying everything he could to please her and nothing that might upset her.

Hadn't she been pleased when he installed her old repainted swing set in the backyard for Aaron? Hadn't she been pleased when he built that sandbox? And hadn't she laughed when he engaged her in a tickling match as soon as they had filled it with soft, cool sand? And hadn't she returned the kiss that wrestling match had resulted in?

Hell, yes she had! His nickname hadn't been Smooch for nothing, you know.

But he hadn't carried that or any other kiss further than he thought she wanted it to go. He had been acting like a lackey to win her approval. He'd slunk around with his tail between his legs until it was getting damned uncomfortable. Well, it was high time he started letting her know that he was the man in the family and that as such, by God, he had some rights!

The door burst open under his hand and he closed it with a resounding slam. Kyla bolted upright in bed and clutched the sheet to her breasts. "Trevor? What's happened? What's wrong?"

"Nothing's wrong. All right, I'll tell you what's wrong," he snarled as he stalked into the room, armed to the teeth with righteous indignation. "My dad is sleeping in the guest room. So for tonight, Mrs. Rule, we share this bed."

CHAPTER TWELVE

"ALL RIGHT."

Her softly spoken concession effectively disarmed him. His inflated wrath went as flat as a fallen soufflé. He rolled his shoulders to collect himself. "Well, good," he said tersely. "I'm glad you see it like that."

For some reason, her obliging conciliation only served to make him madder. He didn't need her to patronize him. No, sir!

He tore off his clothes with jerky, angry pulls and pokes and punches. One by one the garments were slung away from him. They were left wherever they happened to fall. When he was down to his briefs, he yanked back the covers and thrust his feet between the sheets. After brutalizing the pillow with his fist, he ground his head down into it.

"Good night."

"Good night, Trevor."

He turned his back to her, rocking the entire bed while he adjusted himself into a comfortable position with all the querulousness of a fairy-tale giant.

There! Guess I showed her.

If that were the case, why was it *his* body that was stiff and burning with lust? Why was it *his* heart that ached with love denied release?

KYLA AWAKENED TO find him watching her. He lay on his side facing her, his tousled dark head pillowed on a bent elbow. Silent and still, the only part of him that moved was that single green eye that wandered over her face and hair as though cataloging every detail.

She didn't realize she had lifted her hand until she saw it move into her range of vision. Lightly she touched the black eye patch. "You never take it off."

"I don't want you to see it."

"Why?"

"It's so ugly."

"It wouldn't matter to me."

"Curious?"

"No. Sad. I was just thinking how pretty your eye is and what a shame it is that the other one was lost."

"I'm grateful that one was spared."

"That goes without saying."

"If for no other reason than for this moment. I wouldn't trade looking at your face right now for anything in the world." His voice was rough with emotion.

Kyla's throat ached with the need to cry. Her hand moved from his eye patch down to his mustache. Her fingers coasted over it lightly. Then she touched his upper lip.

Trevor's breath hit the back of his throat. Heat filled his sex.

She had never touched his face. Now she engaged in an orgy of touching. The bones in his lean, dark face were pronounced. His brow bone jutted over his eyesockets. The wing-shaped brows were sleek and thick. A bristly beard stubble covered the lower half of his face. His mustache, which her fingers couldn't leave alone, was amazingly soft. With her fingernail, she languidly traced the shape of his lower lip.

"Be careful, Kyla."

She withdrew her finger a fraction. "Why?"

"Because for almost seven hours I have been lying here wanting you. Do you understand?" She nodded. "I don't think it's too smart of you to touch me now. Unless…"

He left the condition unspoken, but they both knew what it was.

Outside, bright sunlight was already filtering through the leafy branches of the trees and casting wavering patterns against the closed shutters. Birds were chirping happily. Squirrels chased each other through the upper branches. Butterflies flitted from flower to flower. Redbirds and bluejays looked like brightly feathered arrows as they darted among the trees.

The activity in the bedroom was considerably less obvious, but no less energetic. Emotions seethed between them like huge swells in the Atlantic. Longing was so thick it was palpable, desire so potent it could be breathed. If auras could be seen, the air around them would have shimmered with a red glow of mounting passion.

Her body didn't demonstrate its longing as blatantly as his, but she suffered from the same affliction. At that moment, Kyla thought of nothing more than satisfying her need to be cosseted, caressed, covered, completed.

She touched his lower lip again.

In one fluid motion, he brought them together, positioned her beneath him and captured her mouth in a hot, hungry kiss. Hard and bold, his manhood sought the heart of her femininity. Found it. Favored it with urgent caresses.

"God, I want you." He frantically groped for the hem of her nightgown. Her hands plucked at the elastic waistband of his briefs. One hand slipped inside and touched the taut curve of his buttock.

Groaning, his mouth found her nipple and closed around it while he enjoyed the silky smoothness of her panties and the contours they confined. She sighed his name and raised her knees. His fingers slipped into the waistband of her panties.

The bedroom door flew open and with the impetus of a miniature cyclone, Aaron came bounding into the room. He was chattering as raucously as were the bluejay and squirrel outside.

The breath leaked out of Trevor's body in a slow steady hiss, relieving the tension in his chest. He pressed his forehead against Kyla's and wished he could relieve the pressure in his loins as easily. A laugh began deep inside him and left his lips on an expulsion of air against Kyla's mouth. "Remind me to throttle him later."

Kyla, too, was feeling the agony of forcibly subduing passion. Sighing, she pressed her face into the warmth of Trevor's neck. "If I don't get to him first."

Trevor rolled off her, but kept her locked in the security of his arms. Together they turned their attention to Aaron.

"He must have talked his indulgent grandfather into releasing him from his crib," Trevor observed.

Attuned to the adoration of his audience, Aaron took center stage and performed some of his cutest tricks. Their laughter only encouraged him. Wearing a sappy grin, he started turning in slow circles. Heedless of their warnings that he was going to get dizzy, he circled faster until, drunk, he reached out to break his fall.

What his hand grasped was the decorative pull of the bedside table drawer. Gravity tugged at Aaron and he was too dizzy to counteract it. His bottom landed solidly on the carpeted floor and the drawer came out of its mooring to drop into his lap.

He wasn't hurt, but the two adults reflexively sat up when they saw that the inevitable was about to happen. Aaron stared at them in stunned surprise, then glanced down at the drawer lying in his lap.

The framed eight-by-ten picture of the Marine in full dress uniform was the only thing in the drawer. Aaron slapped the nonglare glass with his hands and said, "Da. Dadadada." He smiled up at his spectators, fully expecting an ovation for his brilliant performance.

The arms still holding Kyla in a loose, affectionate embrace went as hard as steel. Gradually they released her. She felt their warmth being taken from her by slow degrees. Then, with one violent motion, Trevor came off the bed on the far side and swept up the trousers he had left lying on the floor the night before. He shoved his legs into them and zipped them with a vicious tug as he strode toward the door.

"Trevor, please!"

He spun around, bare-chested, barefoot and furious. His jaw was bunched with rage and there was a cold glint in his eye as it took a bead on the woman now sitting up in the bed, her hair a mess, her face pale, her lips tremulous, her eyes pleading.

"I won't be a stand-in," he growled. "As long as

there's another man living inside your skin, madam, there's no room for this." He crudely cupped himself. His chin bobbed once for emphasis before he stormed out.

"IT'S LYNN HASKELL," Kyla reported, holding her hand over the mouthpiece of the telephone receiver. "She's invited us to a picnic at the lake on Labor Day. Do you want to go?"

It had been a week since George Rule's visit. The most miserable week of Kyla's life. The tension in the house crackled like old paper and was just as flammable. The suspense of not knowing what would touch off the inevitable conflagration was nerve-racking in the extreme.

Trevor never lost his temper, never raised his voice. Kyla would have welcomed it if he had. He was rather like a brooding, dark thunderstorm that refused to break. It lurked overhead, ominous and threatening.

He treated her no less politely than he ever had, but there had been a noticeable suspension of his demonstrations of affection. He rarely touched her, and then only out of necessity. With Aaron he behaved in the same loving way. With her, he was remote and mechanical.

Which was the way I wanted it in the first place, she rushed to remind herself every time she had a yearning for his brilliant smile…or a meaningful glance… or a touch…or a kiss.

Now, in response to her inquiry, he shrugged noncommittally. "I'll leave that up to you, Kyla. Whatever you want to do."

She shot him a withering look. He ignored it and

bent back over the wooden puzzle with the oversize pieces that he was patiently working with Aaron for about the tenth time that evening.

She couldn't keep Lynn on the phone indefinitely. She had to tell her something. But what? The Haskells were Trevor's friends. Whether he said so or not, she was certain he wanted to go. Lynn was too astute to see through a lame excuse. Getting outside and spending a day at the lake would probably be good for all of them. Hopefully it would relieve some of the tension.

"Lynn, we'd be delighted to join you." From the corner of her eye, she saw Trevor glance up at her, but he immediately returned his attention to Aaron. "What can I bring…? No, no, I insist."

INVARIABLY, THE FIRST Monday in September in Texas was cloudless and blisteringly hot. This Labor Day proved to be no different from its predecessors.

"Kyla, they're here," Trevor called from the front porch where he had hauled their gear and stood waiting with Aaron. The Haskells had suggested that they all travel to the lake in their van since it would hold both families and the picnic paraphernalia, as well.

"Coming." She went through the house checking to see that doors were locked and that she hadn't forgotten anything vital. When she reached the front porch, Trevor and Ted were loading the back of the van and Lynn was giving Aaron a "pony ride" on her knees.

"Hi. Climb aboard while there's still room for you," Lynn said, her holiday spirit showing.

During the drive to the lake Ted teased Kyla about her packing. "If I'd known you were going to bring along that much stuff, I'd have rented a trailer."

She wondered if the other couple noticed that she and Trevor could banter and joke with them, but that they had little to say to each other.

He had dressed in faded cutoffs, jogging shoes in sore need of retirement and a gray sweatshirt with the sleeves cut out. He had also enlarged the neck so that the crisp, dark pelt on his chest filled the jagged, uneven V.

Kyla had pulled her hair back into a ponytail. She had worn a pair of old shorts over her bikini trunks and had tied the tails of a matching shirt at her waist. It gapped open to reveal the bikini bra underneath. She was glad she hadn't tried to look nice. By the time they reached the lake, she had been mauled by Aaron, who had caught the infectious holiday mood from the rambunctious Haskell children.

They reached the lake, found a spot they all agreed was perfect and began the chore of unloading the van. When they were finished, Trevor celebrated by taking a can of beer from the cooler and gulping it down in three swallows.

He drank another to squelch the flames of desire that licked his belly when Kyla stripped down to her bikini after Lynn suggested that they work on their tans.

They trekked to the water's edge with the children. Aaron splashed about happily and wasn't satisfied until his mother had been showered with the cool lake water. When her nipples pouted against the cold, Trevor grumbled a feeble excuse and went back to their picnic spot for another beer.

He carried it down to the lake and offered Kyla a drink. When she accepted it, she accidentally touched his hand. And when her head tilted back, he wanted nothing more than to open his mouth over her exposed throat.

While he and Ted stayed in the shallow water with the children, Lynn and Kyla swam out to the dock that was buoyed in deeper water. Trevor watched every graceful arc her arms made through the water. His gaze was trained on her when she pulled herself up the ladder. Standing up to wave to Aaron, her slender body was silhouetted against the summer sky. Water sheeted on her thighs and coursed down her flat tummy.

"I'll be right back," Trevor muttered.

"Where are you going this time?" Ted asked him, shading his eyes against the sun and looking up at Trevor.

"I, uh, I think Aaron wants a cookie."

He picked up Aaron, who was perfectly content piling lake mud onto his knees, and carried him up to the van. Aaron got a cookie and Trevor drank another beer.

After a lunch that would have fed a caravan of gypsies, the children napped in the shade. When they woke up, everyone walked to the baseball diamond. The annual citywide "Skins and Shirts" game was a tradition among local businessmen. Anybody who wanted to play was to bring his equipment and meet at the diamond where they were divided into teams.

Trevor had just one eye and he walked with a limp, but months of physical therapy and a daily exercise program that he kept to religiously had put him in far better physical shape than the pencil pushers who had thirty or more pounds of sedentary living to lose.

Kyla gnawed on the knuckle of her index finger when he stepped to the plate in the ninth inning. The Skins, the team both he and Ted were playing for, were behind by three. The bases were loaded. There were already two outs. It all depended on Trevor. He rose to the occasion, knocking in a grand slam home run.

Kyla, like everyone else rooting for the Skins, went wild. Trevor received the hearty congratulations of his teammates. Then he and Ted came jogging toward their families.

"You were great!" Lynn said enthusiastically to Trevor.

"Hey, what about me?" Ted asked, affecting hurt pride.

"You were great, too." Lynn wound her arms around her husband's neck and kissed him soundly.

"I was holding my breath," Kyla said, laughing excitedly. As she smiled up at Trevor, her face was bathed with sunlight and her eyes were squinting against the glare. Behind a thick screen of curling lashes, he could see that they were shining. Her hands were pressed against her chest as though she were trying to contain her jubilance.

"It was a lucky shot," he said modestly.

They took hesitant steps toward each other. Paused. Then Kyla flung herself against him and, coming up on tiptoe, pressed her mouth against his for a kiss befitting the hero of the day.

Trevor, reacting instinctively, wrapped his arms around her waist. The taste of her delicious mouth for the first time in over a week sent a shaft of pleasure spearing through him. It exploded like a fireball in the bottom of his belly. Lost in her taste, drowning in it, his tongue thrust deep. Heedless of the daylight, the crowd, everything, his hands slid to her derriere and lifted her against his swelling manhood.

Something, possibly Ted tapping him on the seat with his baseball glove, but something, reminded him of where they were. He raised his head and, looking down at Kyla, laughed shakily.

Kyla gazed up at him, a bewildered expression on her face. Her eyes were smoky. Her breasts were rising and falling rapidly with each breath. Her lips were red and wet and slightly roughened by his mustache. Lifting three fingers to them, she touched them tentatively, as though they'd been scorched.

"Ready to get back?" Ted was standing with Lynn, their arms linked loosely around each other's waists. Each had a child by the hand and Aaron was terrorizing a doodlebug at their feet. "How 'bout a beer, Trevor?"

"Yeah, sure, a beer."

He drank that one in two swallows, went swimming to rinse off the sweat and grime of the game, then chased his swim with another beer.

They nibbled on leftovers for supper and gradually a healthy tiredness settled in. Trevor was mellow and feeling no pain by the time the van was loaded and they started the drive home. Traffic was congested. He was happy to relinquish the responsibility of coping with it to Ted.

In fact, he relinquished every responsibility except that of finding a resting place for his head against Kyla's shoulder. He leaned against her heavily and let his arm slide down her side until his elbow nestled in the valley between her thigh and lap. His hand curled around the inside of her thigh. He stroked the smooth skin with a lazy thumb and found that it felt good to move his arm slightly so that the hairs dusting it dragged against her smooth flesh.

Once he thought he turned his head and kissed her neck, but he wasn't certain if he actually carried out the intention or just thought about it so hard that he imagined he did.

When they reached home, he concentrated on not appearing tipsy—as he had a sneaking suspicion he was—in front of their hosts. He soberly thanked the Haskells for a great time and bade them good-night.

He realized just how rubbery his arms and legs were as he tried to carry their picnic gear up to the porch. After taking a few staggering steps and dropping the picnic basket twice, he mumbled, "Think I'll wait till tomorrow to put all this stuff up," and dropped it all onto the ground.

"That's fine," Kyla said, pressing her lips together to keep from laughing. "But could you please unlock the front door?" Aaron, who was asleep in her arms, was becoming heavy.

"Sure, sure."

Stupidly, he just stood there looking at her while the seconds ticked by.

"You have the key, Trevor."

"Oh! Of course I do." He went on an uncoordinated search through his pockets until he produced the key. Holding it up inches in front of her nose he said, "Ta-da! See, I told you I had it."

She suppressed another laugh, but he seemed not to notice as he wrestled with the lock.

"Someone has changed the lock!" His exclamation was spoken just as Edison must have said of the first light bulb, "It works!"

"Turn the key so the teeth are up."

He did as Kyla instructed. When the lock clicked

open and the door swung wide, he gazed down at her and said, "You're wonderful. Did you know that? Wonderful."

She rolled her eyes with a long-suffering expression and pushed her way past him, going straight to Aaron's room and putting him to bed with dispatch. Minutes later when she came back through the living room, Trevor was sprawled on the sofa, one arm and leg dangling. She checked to make certain he had relocked the front door, then moved toward the couch and bent over him.

He was asleep. She brushed back a strand of wavy black hair that had fallen over his forehead. He awoke. "Kyla?"

"Hmm?"

"You're sweet."

"Thank you."

"So sweet and beautiful."

"Oh, yes, I know."

He missed the wry inflection in her tone. He had no idea he was being humored. All he knew for certain was that the pale moonlight, spilling through the glass doors, looked beautiful on the face of the woman he loved.

He hooked her behind the neck and pulled her head down for a kiss. Kyla, not prepared for this sudden move, much less the passion behind the kiss, lost her balance and fell atop him. Trevor struggled to right the situation but only succeeded in rolling them both to the floor.

For several moments, he didn't comprehend that the soft pillow his head was lying heavily on was Kyla's breasts. Not until he lifted his head and gazed down at her. Then he lowered his face and nudged aside the shirt she had retied at her waist before the trip home. He touched her with his lips.

"You smell like sunshine." His nose rooted in the valley between her breasts. "I love the smell of sunshine."

He shifted so that his thighs came to be settled between hers in a snug fit. If it registered with him that her arms were lying listlessly at her sides and that her hands were turned up in an attitude of surrender, he didn't comment. He merely rearranged them so that they rested above her head, then with his index finger traced the inside of her arm from palm to armpit as though drawing a path for her veins to follow.

"If sunshine had a taste, it would taste like you, too." His mouth moved over her breasts, lips opening and closing as though taking bites. He got caught up in what he was doing and made a savage attempt to untie her shirttails. When they finally came undone, he cast them aside and attacked the front fastener of her bikini.

When she lay bare beneath him, he whispered huskily, "God above, you're beautiful."

He touched her reverently, his fingertips brushing back and forth across the soft flesh. He took his time. He made no apology. Because he was convinced she was just another dream. One of many about Kyla. But God, this one seemed real!

He cupped a breast in each hand and reshaped them with kneading motions of his fingers. Lightly he pinched her nipple between his thumb and finger, then lowered his mouth and entrapped it.

The sounds he made were those of a starving man who had just found sustenance. He suckled both breasts. He rubbed his mustachioed lip over the nipples now made glossy by his kisses. He made a sharp point of his tongue and played with them, tempting them to shrink, to become harder. And they complied.

Vaguely he became aware of the writhing movements beneath him, speaking to his body in a language it understood even if he wasn't translating too clearly.

He levered himself up and unfastened her shorts. Unerringly his hand wedged itself past them and into the damp bikini trunks. He cupped the delta that fitted his palm to perfection. He rubbed it, pressing, luxuriating in the soft fleece that covered it. His fingers curved down into the sweet mystery below.

His groan started in the bottom of his soul and rumbled through his entire body. "You're wet for me."

Passionately he kissed the throat from which a sobbing sound emanated and introduced his fingers into the fount of that seductive wet heat.

His breath rushed in and out of his body. Or was it Kyla's? He wasn't sure. He solved the riddle by clamping his mouth over hers and kissing her until neither of them could breathe at all. His tongue reached for her throat.

Her shorts came off easily. The trunks required considerably more patience and skill, both of which had deserted him by the time he whipped them from her ankles. Frustrated and clumsy, he freed himself from his clothing.

God, her skin was cool.

And he was so damn hot.

Her body accepted him. He sank into her silky wet femininity and shuddered with the pleasure. He was enveloped by warm, creamy womanhood, and it was the best it had ever been.

His mouth settled against her ear. "I've waited for this for so long. I've wanted… But it's much better… You're…my love…."

With his hands beneath her hips, he lifted her higher against him and moved with swift, sure thrusts. Her body began to quicken around his. The breasts beneath his mouth trembled and the nipple against his tongue pearled into a hard round button.

And just as he felt the sweet rush of her release pouring over him, he came in a torrent.

Huntsville, Alabama

"I'LL NEVER MOVE AGAIN. We're living here for the rest of our lives."

"Fine with me," the man said tiredly. "Helluva way to spend Labor Day. Laboring!"

"But we got everything put away. Finally. Everything except that box with all your Marine junk in it."

"It might be junk to you, but some of it means a lot to me."

She patted his hand. "I know. I was only kidding. Come to think of it, did you ever send that picture to that guy's widow? Stroud, wasn't it?"

"Yes, and no, I never did. I'll do that tomorrow." His brow wrinkled. "But I don't know how to find her."

"Why don't you send it to the Marine Corps? I'm sure they could forward it to her."

"Good idea." He stood up and offered his hand to help her up. "Let's go to bed. I'm exhausted. But don't let me forget to fish that picture out and send it off tomorrow," he added as he switched out the light.

CHAPTER THIRTEEN

IT TOOK HER a moment to remember why she was sleeping on the floor. Without pillow or blanket or anything to alleviate the discomfort, she had slept a dreamless sleep for the first time in weeks.

Moving nothing but her eyes, she looked through the glass doors and saw that it was still very early. Hesitantly she stretched her cramped legs and tried to sit up. His fingers were snared in her hair.

It took some gentle tugging, but at last she was free. She picked up her discarded shorts and tiptoed toward the hall. On the way to Aaron's room, she refastened her bikini bra, the cups of which had passed the night bunched up under her arms.

Aaron was still asleep and showed no signs of waking up anytime soon. He had had a strenuous day yesterday and it was taking its toll. Kyla was thankful. Right now, she had to think and needed no distractions.

She pulled on her shorts and crept back through the house. Trevor hadn't stirred from his place on the floor in front of the living-room sofa. He wasn't snoring, but his breathing was deep and steady. Kyla slipped outside without awakening him.

She took a towel from the stack they kept in the closet near the hot tub and walked through the woods toward the creek. The morning was still. The new sun hadn't yet penetrated the dense branches of the trees. The undergrowth was cool and damp against her bare feet.

The creek flowed lackadaisically. Heavy rain turned its current into a series of rushing swirls. Otherwise it was calm and provided a great breeding ground for crawdads. Aaron had clapped his hands in delight over one when Trevor—

Trevor.

His name echoed through her mind, eradicating all other thought. Sighing, Kyla spread her towel on the deep grass near the creek bank and sat down. Raising her knees to her chest, she propped her chin on them.

It had happened.

She closed her eyes as tremors of pleasure shimmied through her at the memory. Pressing her forehead against her knees she tried not to recall the splendor of his lovemaking, but her efforts were to no avail. Her brain might not want to remember, but her body was relishing every sweet recollection.

Why hadn't she resisted? She could have. He'd had too much to drink. When he collapsed on top of her, she could have shoved him away from her and he probably wouldn't have known the difference. Why hadn't she?

Because I wanted to make love with him.

There. She had admitted it.

She raised her head and stared at the creek as though expecting it to debate with her. It continued on its unconcerned trickling course toward lower ground.

Kyla had wanted him to make love to her since the kiss following the baseball game. That kiss had been a turning point. Even now, she could remember exactly how he'd looked as he came jogging toward her, limping more than usual after the exertion of the game.

His grin had been a wide, white swath beneath his mustache. Pointed clumps of black hair, wet with perspiration, had striped his forehead. The waistband of his cutoffs had been damp with sweat, stretched and slightly curled away from his navel. His legs, even the scarred left one, rippled and bunched with sinewy muscles as he came toward her.

Never had she seen a man so rawly masculine. Trevor epitomized the male animal and everything inside her that was woman gravitated toward it as surely as the creek flowed toward the lake.

The kiss he had pressed onto her mouth had been salty, gritty. The sweat that had plastered down his chest hair also plastered her to his chest. When she felt his hands, powerful and manly, anchoring her against his aroused manhood, she had known then that she wanted him, and that she would have him, by her own design, if not by his.

Later, when he had started kissing her breasts, she wished with all her might that nothing would interrupt this time.

Call it wicked.

Call it unfaithfulness to Richard.

Call it what you like, but she had wanted to feel Trevor Rule inside her.

"Kyla?"

She jumped and whipped her head around. Trevor was standing behind her wearing only his cutoffs, the shadow of a beard and a wary expression.

"Hi."

"Are you all right?"

She returned her gaze to the creek, finding it difficult to look at him after last night. Her chest hurt with the effort to breathe. "Yes, I'm fine. I woke up early and the morning was so pretty…. Is Aaron awake?"

"He wasn't when I left."

"I guess yesterday wore him out."

"I guess so."

He crouched down beside and slightly behind her. Idly he plucked bunches of grass, examined them, then scattered the blades back onto the ground. "What time are you going to work this morning?"

"I'm not. Babs and I traded off, last Saturday for today. That's why I was in no hurry to get Aaron up."

He acknowledged the information with a brief nod and stood up again. He was restless. Neither was talking about what was uppermost in their minds.

From the corner of her eye Kyla saw him wander toward a tree. He stopped. He turned and looked back at her. When he finally got to the tree, he raised his arms and propped them on one of the lowest branches slightly above him. He draped his wrists over the rough bark and hung his head to stare at the ground.

She laid her head back on her knees and prayed for something to break the silence.

"Did last night really happen, Kyla?"

Just as she had always thought, God had a sense of humor. Be careful what you pray for.

She glanced in Trevor's direction. He was now pinching pieces of bark off the oak and flicking them into the water. "Don't you remember?"

"I remember either an incredibly erotic dream—" he took a deep breath "—or the best thing that's ever happened to me." Her head came around quickly, swinging her hair like a red-gold cloak around her shoulders. He saw the tears standing in her eyes. A spasm of monumental regret twisted his features. "God, I'm sorry."

"It's all right."

"The hell it is."

"No, really."

"I was drunk."

"You were relaxed."

"Did I hurt you?"

"No."

"Force you?"

"No."

"Was I abusive?"

"No."

"Because I could never forgive—"

"Trevor, I wanted to!"

The hundred and one apologies he had cataloged in his mind, died on his lips. "You did?"

"Yes." She drew a shuddering breath and started plucking at the same grass he had deserted. "I've been doing some thinking."

"About what?"

"That you might…might want other children, other than Aaron, I mean. Some, at least one, of your own. It would have been unfair of me to…to withhold—"

Her lips were stopped by a long, tanned finger being laid against them. No longer could she avoid that piercing green eye. It beamed straight into her soul. "I would like to have at least one child of my own. And I appreciate your willingness to accommodate me. But is that the only reason you wanted to make love to me?"

"No," she whispered, shaking her head. "I just didn't know what else to say."

"Why did you want to make love with me, drunken and stupid as I know I must have been?"

She turned her cheek into the palm that had provided a resting place for it. Her eyes closed and two of the tears that had collected in her eyes rolled down her cheek. But when she opened her eyes, she was smiling. "You weren't drunken and stupid."

"Could've fooled me."

Laughing, she reached up and touched his hair affectionately. "You were as you've been since I first met you."

"Which is?"

"Kind, generous, fun to be around."

"Please, no more. I don't want to get a swelled head. But are you describing me or Santa Claus?" He assumed the wheedling expression of a little boy asking for one more piece of candy. "Don't I have any attributes of a more romantic nature?"

Her laughter was as sparkling as the creek water in the sunlight. "Need your ego stroked?"

"For starters," he drawled.

She shot him a shy look, but continued playing the game. "All right. What do you want to hear? That you're dashing and as handsome as the devil? That my best friend thinks you're a hunk and a stud, but a nice stud and that's rare?"

"Your best friend? How she'd get in here? I want to know what you think."

"All of the above," Kyla confessed in a raspy voice.

"Is there more?" His nose got lost in the loose curls above her ear.

"Should I go so far as to say that the mere sight of your body sets my blood on fire?"

"Sounds good to me."

Her head fell back when his lips found her throat. "You're incredibly good looking and sexy and—" She clamped her lower lip with her teeth.

"And?" he prodded, bringing her head up to meet his gaze.

"And," she added slowly, "I'm very glad I'm married to you."

He called upon a deity, whether in prayer or vain, Kyla was never sure. He applied the lightest pressure to her shoulder and she lay down on the towel. He followed her down, partially covering her body with his.

"I love you, Kyla Rule."

Her arms folded across his back. Their bare legs entwined. What their bodies had done only hours before, their mouths now reenacted.

"You're taking the day off?" he asked gruffly several moments later.

"Uh-huh."

"Then so am I. But let's get Aaron up, feed him and take him to the day-care center anyway."

"Why?"

Her husband grinned down into her face with a roguish gleam that made her heart flutter and her thighs liquefy. "Because I want to spend all day in bed tumbling my wife."

"...YES, YES..."

"Like that?"

"Yes!"

"I'm afraid when I press so deep, I'm hurting you."

"No... It...ah... Trevor...yes..."

"Sweetheart... Kyla... I can't... How much longer do you think?..."

"Not yet. I want it to last forever."

"So do I, but…"

"Now, now, now…"

"YOU'RE SO BEAUTIFUL."

"You make me feel beautiful. And naughty."

"Naughty?"

"I've never been set in front of a mirror to be admired. It's decadent, isn't it?"

"Purely. But this way I can see all of you at once. Lift your arms."

"How? Like this?"

"Perfect. Did you breast-feed Aaron?"

"For a while. Why?"

"Just wondering. Your breasts are so pretty. Did I say something wrong?"

"No, it's just—"

"What?"

"Some of the things you say embarrass me."

"Don't be embarrassed. I love you. Does it bother you for me to touch you like this?"

"Bother me? Hardly, I…ah…"

"Oh, God, look at you. I barely touch you and…"

"You know just how to touch me…how to…"

"You taste like milk."

"Use your mustache—"

"Sweet, sweet milk."

"And your tongue—"

"You taste like Kyla."

"SO DON'T SAY it's ugly."

"Every man should have a left side with a racetrack carved into it."

"Do the scars ever hurt?"

"No."

"Never?"

"Well, sometimes."

"Why does this one curve all the way from your spine to your sternum?"

"Right now I'm glad it's there."

"Glad?"

"Yes. Because your lips feel so good against my chest."

"I'd kiss it even without the scar."

"Would you, love?"

"Yes. I've wanted to kiss your chest for a long time."

"That's not my chest any longer. That's my navel."

"Close enough."

"Speaking of close...hmm, hon..."

"You got me off the subject. Why did they cut you like that?"

"I was bleeding internally from several organs."

"Oh, Lord."

"It's all right. Just keep doing what you're doing and I don't even remember it."

"Like this?"

"Oh, baby, that feels good. Kyla... Kyla... Oh, sweetheart, oh... That's the first time you've touched me."

"The first time I saw you—"

"Yes?"

"When you got out of the hot tub—"

"Yes?"

"You were breathtaking."

"No, this is breathtaking.... The way you're touching me now...that's breathtaking."

"…BUT I TOLD Babs there was no way I would sneak onto the bus with the football team."

"You were a good girl."

"I was a coward, always afraid of getting into trouble. So I rode home with the band where we belonged."

"And Babs?"

"How did you find that little patch of freckles?"

"Just lucky, I guess."

"That's my birthmark."

"Yes. Now tell me about Babs."

"Well, when we got back to the school, she came off the bus with this guy she had previously called an 'ugly moose.' She was wearing a… I don't know…a *look*, and I knew what had happened. That's also when I knew that she and I were different. I couldn't just have sex for the sake of sex."

"Damn! Sure about that?"

"Trevor, stop it now. I thought we were going to talk."

"Then stop lying there looking so delectable. All right, I'm sorry. Let's talk."

"I forgot what we were talking about."

"Were you a virgin when you got married?"

"The first or second time?"

"Very funny. Answer the question."

"That's not what we were talking about."

"You're right. Sorry I asked. It isn't any of my business."

"Yes, I was a virgin."

"You almost sound ashamed of it."

"I'm afraid you'll be turned off by my lack of experience."

"Would I be doing this if I were turned off?"

"I don't know which I like best. What you're doing or the expression on your face while you're doing it."

"Look at the way it curls around my fingers. It's such a pretty color. And soft. And so is this."

"Trevor…what?…"

"Relax."

"But what… No!"

"I want to."

"No, I…"

"Please, Kyla, let me love you."

"But…oh, my God… Trevor?…"

"Yes, love, yes. You're infinitely sweet."

"NO MORE, PLEASE. I can't stand it. My sides are hurting."

"One more. This one's about a man who goes into a pet store to buy a parrot."

"Trevor, I mean it now, no more of your dirty jokes."

"You're laughing."

"That's my point. I shouldn't be. I'm a lady."

"How can you pretend to be a lady while you're straddling my lap and I'm making lunch out of your nipples?"

"Trevor!"

"Ouch, hon. Be still or you'll cripple me more than I already am. On the other hand, go ahead and squirm. They look damn cute when they jiggle."

"You're outrageous."

"Wait till you hear the joke."

"There's no stopping you?"

"No. Now be a good wife and listen. This guy goes into the pet store and… Kyla, I thought I told you to be still. This guy goes into the pet store and the owner

says, 'I've got this terrific parrot.' 'Can he talk?' the
man asks. Kyla, you're asking for big trouble. Now stop
that. 'Sure he can talk,' the pet store owner says, 'but
there's one problem.' Kyla, I'm warning you. 'What's
the problem?' the guy asks. 'The parrot can talk, but he
hasn't got any feet.' Kyla… So the guy says, 'Then how
does he stay on his perch?' And the pet store owner
says… Oh, to hell with it."

"That's the joke?"

"No, but I just thought of a better punch line."

"THAT WAS THE hardest part to accept. There was nothing the Marines could send me. No mementos. Nothing. It was as though he had never existed. That broke
my heart. There wasn't even enough of him to fill the
casket."

"Don't, don't, sweetheart."

"He deserved a better death. And dealing with the
military was frustrating. They couldn't or wouldn't
tell us anything for security reasons. The details were
so sketchy."

"For instance?"

"Richard wasn't even in his own bunk that morning. Why? Why didn't a single thing belonging to him
survive the blast? I wanted something tangible, something of his that I could hold in my hand. A razor. A
wristwatch. Anything."

"Shh, shh. If it's going to upset you, don't talk about
it anymore."

"It's not as painful as it sounds. In fact it feels good
to talk about it. And you're a dear to listen."

"I love you, Kyla. We've needed to talk about Richard. I wanted both of us to have the freedom of speaking his name out loud."

"I loved him, Trevor."

"I know."

"And do you know that I love you? I didn't think I could ever love another man, but I love you. I just realized it. I love you! Trevor, are you crying?"

"I love you so much, Kyla."

"You won't ever leave me, will you?"

"Not a chance."

"Swear it."

"Never."

"I CAN'T BELIEVE it's raining."

"Just an afternoon thundershower. It'll be over soon. Then we'll dress and go get Aaron."

"But not yet. Let's enjoy the rain."

"Rain is no fun unless it can be shared."

"How do you do that?"

"What?"

"Read my mind."

"Do I?"

"From the very beginning, you seemed to know what I was thinking. How?"

"Because I love you."

"Yes, but—"

"Turn around, Kyla."

"I don't understand how you—"

"Are we going to make love one more time before we go get Aaron or not?"

"Hmm, Trevor, not fair. You know when you touch me there I melt."

"Where? Here?"

"Yes, yes."

"And when I kiss you there?"

"I die a little."

"Then kiss me at the same time and we'll die a little together."

Huntsville, Alabama

A LETTER WAS MAILED.

HUMMING, KYLA CHECKED the pot roast. Even Meg Powers would have been proud of it. Kyla replaced the lid on the roaster and turned off the heat in the oven. It would keep warm until Trevor and Aaron returned. Trevor had taken the child with him to run an errand, leaving Kyla at home to prepare dinner, a task she now took pleasure in.

In fact she was finding pleasure in just about everything she did these days. For the past three weeks, since Labor Day and the night following, she had lived in a bubble of happiness.

"A few days off has certainly done wonders for you!" Babs had exclaimed the day Kyla went back to work after the holiday. "You're shining like a new penny. And I'd be willing to bet that Trevor is the one who polished you to that glow."

Kyla's laugh at the ribaldry had been lusty. "You're right, I'm in love."

"Well it's catching, because Trevor has already called twice to see if you'd arrived yet, and he said to give you a kiss for him when you did, which I refused to do. What's happened to the two of you?"

"Nothing," Kyla lied airily, as she reached for the

telephone to return Trevor's call. It had been all of half an hour since she had seen him.

"I'll bet you've been renting X-rated movies for the home VCR."

"Nope."

"You ordered that kit of marital aids I showed you in *Playgirl?* What did Trevor think of the edible panties?"

"Will you hush!" Kyla had said, laughing. "I did no such thing." Then into the telephone she said, "Hi, darling. You called?"

"You're taking ginseng tablets?" Babs had persisted. "Feeding him oysters on the half shell every night?"

"No! I'm sorry, Trevor. Babs just wanted to know if I was feeding you oysters on the half shell every night.... What?... No, I can't tell her that.... No... Oh, all right. Babs, Trevor said to tell you that if he were eating oysters on the half shell every night, we'd have to buy a new mattress. Now be quiet, please. I told you I'm in love and I want to talk to my husband."

And I am in love, Kyla thought happily, as she now went through the living room, picking up the toys Aaron had left in his wake. Noticing the unopened mail lying on the hall table, she took it into the kitchen on her return trip and sat at the bar on a high stool to sort through it while waiting for her men to come home.

One envelope in particular caught her eye. It was from the Marine Corps. Slashing it open, she found another envelope inside with *Please forward* stamped on it. The name printed in the upper left-hand corner sparked her memory, but she didn't recall why until she noticed the return address. Huntsville, Alabama. Hadn't one of Richard's friends been from Huntsville, Alabama? Curious, she slit open that second envelope and took out the single sheet of plain white stationery. A photograph dropped to the bar.

The letter was brief. It introduced the sender, who expressed sympathy over Richard's death. It explained that the sender had recently found the photograph and thought that Kyla might like to have it. It ended with a heartfelt wish for her future happiness.

Laying aside the letter, she picked up the snapshot. Smiling at her from the center of a trio of Marines was Richard Stroud. He looked just as she last remembered him. He had a military haircut, high over his ears and short on top. He was in his full dress uniform, but there was a jocular smile on his face, as though someone had said something exceptionally funny just before the shutter was snapped. The lens had captured Richard's sweet, spontaneous smile.

He was standing between two other Marines. Their arms were companionably resting on each other's shoulders. The sender of the picture had considerately captioned it for Kyla. He had identified himself as the man on Richard's right. He had an open, down-home face, a toothy grin and big ears. One wouldn't hesitate to buy a used car from a man with a face that honest.

Kyla's eyes slid to the other side of the picture. "Smooch" had been neatly printed under the man on Richard's left. One would be wise to exercise caution before buying a used car from him.

Could anyone that good-looking be trustworthy? He had the grin of a hungry alligator, a brilliant white smile that slashed across his darkly tanned face. Mischievous green eyes viewed the world through spiky black lashes. He looked ready to wink, and Kyla got the distinct impression that he had made the funny remark that the other two men were laughing at. Smooch's smile was smug, unapologetically arrogant, indubitably conceited.

And familiar.

It was her husband's smile.

There could be no mistake. Even with the skinhead haircut of a Marine, without the eye patch, without the curving mustache, there was no mistaking that smile.

Kyla dropped the photograph as though it had burned her fingers. She stared down at it where it lay on the bar, but couldn't bring herself to touch it again.

There had to be a logical explanation. Richard and Trevor arm in arm? Trevor a Marine? How had a picture of Trevor come to be captioned "Smooch," a nickname she remembered well from Richard's letters to her from Egypt?

Smooch was the womanizer. The shameless playboy. The friend of Richard's she knew she couldn't stomach should they ever meet.

And she was married to him.

The implications associated with that rushed at her like a swarm of killer bees. She covered her head. She bit her lower lip to catch the sob that rose out of her chest. She forced down the scalding bile that suddenly filled the back of her throat.

There had to be some explanation. Of course there was. Trevor would come in and see the picture and say something like, "Gee, that's spooky. Can you believe that guy looks so much like me?" Or, "They say everyone in the world has a twin. Guess this Smooch is mine." Or, "It's amazing what they can do with trick photography these days."

It had to be a mistake.

But there was no mistake and she knew it.

She heard his pickup pull into the driveway. Her insides were roiling, her blood was churning, her head was thundering, but on the outside, she looked as immovable as a wood carving.

"Before you get mad," Trevor began the moment he stepped through the door, "Aaron and I took a vote and decided unanimously that it wasn't too close to dinner for him to have a cookie. So we broke open the package on the way home. That's why his shirt—What's the matter?" He had chanced to glance up and noticed her condemning expression. Cookie-smeared hands didn't warrant the intensity of it. "Kyla?"

He moved toward her and when he reached the bar, he saw the picture. He muttered an obscenity and spun around. Reciting a dictionary of curses, he went to stand in front of the windows. Shoulders hunched, he slid his hands, palms out, into the back pockets of his jeans.

"Come here, Aaron." With much more composure than she felt, Kyla picked up her son. She felt like screaming until she couldn't draw another breath, like bashing her head against the wall, like bashing Trevor's against it.

Lifting Aaron to the sink, she washed his face and hands, then set him on the kitchen floor and surrounded him with brightly colored plastic measuring cups, which were among his favorite playthings.

Finally she returned to the bar, picked up the snapshot and studied it for a moment before she said, "You take a good picture."

Trevor came around slowly, pivoting on the heels of

his Western boots, which Kyla knew now were as false and phony and affected as everything else about him.

"So now you know."

"Yes, I know," she snapped. "It's true what they say, isn't it? Clichés always have an element of truth to them. The wife is always the last to know."

"I would have told you."

"When, Trevor? When? When we're old and gray? When I was too feeble to hate you with every fiber of my being as I do now?"

"Me or what I've done?"

"Both! I can't stand the sight of you. *Smooch!*"

She uttered the name as though it were the most loathsome epithet. He winced. "I knew how you felt about Smooch. That's why I never came right out and introduced myself to you."

She laughed, a bit hysterically. "Smooch. I'm married to Smooch, a man known for his sexual conquests. A man who would tumble anything in skirts because all cats are gray in the dark."

"Kyla—"

"Didn't you tell Richard that once?"

"Yes, but that was before—"

"I don't want to hear it," she shouted, slicing the air with her hands. "I don't want any explanations from you except one. Why did you do this? What purpose did it serve? What sick, sick game have you been playing?"

"It isn't a game." His reasonable tone contrasted jarringly with her shrill one. "It was never a game. Not from the beginning."

She reined in her temper and drew in several restorative breaths. "And just when was that? I assume our meeting wasn't accidental."

"No."

"Then when did this start?"

"When I woke up in a hospital in West Germany and discovered I was alive. Missing an eye, injured almost beyond repair, but alive."

"What did that have to do with me?"

He took a step toward her. "You wanted to know why Richard wasn't sleeping in his bunk." She nodded, though no question had actually been asked. "I came in drunk the night before the attack on the embassy. Richard helped me get undressed. I barely remember it, but I do remember falling into his bunk. He was sleeping in mine when that bomb went off."

One hand flew to her mouth, the other gripped her stomach. Tears sprang to her eyes.

"My sentiments exactly," Trevor said grimly. "When I realized that Richard had been killed in my place I didn't care if I lived or died." He looked away, reliving all the pain, literally feeling it rack his body again, reducing him, making him less than a man. "But I lived. With the help of an orderly who befriended me I found out about you and Aaron. When I was well enough to leave the hospital, I came looking for you."

Kyla folded her arms across her stomach. She paced the length of the bar, rocking slightly forward and back from the waist, as though excruciating pains were tearing her insides to shreds.

When she rounded on him, she cried, "In my opinion you have carried your military duty too far. You went above and beyond the call. I don't want a husband who married me out of a sense of obligation, thank you very much!"

Her voice was so loud and vitriolic that Aaron stopped tapping the cups against the floor and looked up at her. His bottom lip began to quiver. "Ma-ma."

Wrested from a pit of humiliation by the tremulous sound of her child's voice, Kyla knelt down beside him and smoothed her hand over his head. "It's all right, darling. Play with your cups. See? Oopsy-daisy. They fell over. Stack them back up for Mommy."

Temporarily mollified, Aaron went back to his play. Kyla faced Trevor again. His face was almost as stony as hers. His lips barely moved. "It isn't like that."

"Then tell me what it's like," she sneered. "Tell me what motivated you to move here and seduce me into—"

"*Marriage,* Kyla," he said with angry emphasis. "What's so dishonorable about that?"

"Because it was all a setup. I can't believe I was gullible enough to fall for it, to fall for you. Your manners, your concern for Aaron, your instant attraction to me, your...your everything. Your damn conservative car! You stepped straight out of the Widow's Guide for A Dream Second Husband, didn't you? Why did you go to so much trouble? What made you do it?"

"I love you."

She stretched her arms out in front of her as though warding him off. "Don't...don't you dare play word games with me." She virtually spat out the words because she didn't want to alarm Aaron with her loud voice again.

"I'm not, Kyla. I was and am in love with you."

"That's impossible."

He shook his head adamantly. "There's one essential part of this story that you don't know yet."

"Then pray tell me what it is."

"Your letters."

She fell silent, dumbfounded by what he'd just said. "My letters?"

"Your letters to Richard."

She sank onto the stool as she stared up at the man who had reverted from a loving husband into a stranger again. It had happened so quickly. Seeing the picture of him had ripped the rug out from under her. Now she felt as though the floor had just dropped away. When would she hit bottom?

"You read them?" she asked with an inflection that clearly indicated she thought that was the most heinous crime he had committed so far.

"They were sent to me by mistake when I was in the hospital." He told her about the metal box and of his granting Richard the favor of using it. "When they sent me my belongings, that box was among them. I opened it and, yes, Kyla, I read your love letters to your husband."

He reached across the bar and covered her hands with his own. "I don't expect you to understand, but I swear to you, I credit those letters with keeping me alive. Every precious word did me more good than any medicine, any surgery, any therapy. They made me want to live again, so that I could meet the woman who wrote them. I memorized each one of them. I could recite them word for word to you now. They're engraved on my mind more deeply than the Pledge of Allegiance or the Lord's Prayer. They—"

"Oh, please. Save it for your next victim." She

snatched her hands from beneath his. "I don't want to hear it. Do you think I'd ever believe another word you said after the way you've tricked me?"

"I didn't think of it as tricking you, Kyla."

"No? The orchids, the house." Coming off the stool she began to pace again. "Everything. It all falls into place now. The way you seemed to read my mind. And all the time you *knew*. You knew because you had read my letters."

"And responded to what they said."

"No wonder you could manipulate me so effortlessly."

"I was giving you what was in my power to give."

"Courting me and being so nice to my parents and—" Suddenly, her body yanked to attention. Her brown eyes narrowed as she glared at him. "My parents. *You* managed to get their property rezoned at such a propitious time, didn't you?"

He closed the space between them in three long steps and laid his hands on her shoulders. "Now, Kyla, before—"

She flung off his hands. "Didn't you?"

"All right, yes!" he shouted back.

"And the sale of their house? The sale that we all marveled over because it commanded such a premium price. The sale that went through in record time without a hitch just in time for our wedding. You arranged all that, too, didn't you?"

His face was closed and hard and as guilty as sin.

"I see," she said on a soft laugh. "Well it's no wonder you felt like you could marry me and take Aaron to raise. You had bought and paid for us, hadn't you?" Her hands were running up and down her arms vigorously, as though washing away a feeling of uncleanliness.

"Stop that. Damn it, I've told you that I love you."

"I can't tell you what a comfort that is coming from a man known to his cronies as Smooch."

"Those days are over."

"No doubt they are. But you went out with a bang, didn't you? You made certain that your final conquest was a woman who was most unlikely to refuse you, a poor lonely widow lady with a child to raise. Come on, Trevor, confess. Didn't you think, in that manipulative, conniving, devious mind of yours, that I might accept you when other women would scorn you now that you aren't quite so handsome? Widows are more desperate for a man, aren't they? Wouldn't poor little Kyla Stroud be so anxious for a man to take care of her that she would overlook an eye patch and a limping, scarred body?"

She wouldn't let herself feel ashamed for the flicker of emotion that crossed his face.

"That's not true."

"Isn't it? When you were once again sure of your sex appeal, how did you plan to dispose of Aaron and me? Or did you plan to? Was I to be so grateful for what you did to me in our bed, that I'd overlook what you did in others'?"

His head dropped forward. "What do you want from me, Kyla?"

"I want you to leave me alone." She picked Aaron off the floor, protectively hugged him to her chest and stormed to the back door. "You've done so much for me, Trevor. You've lied and manipulated my future. You married me out of pity and because you were afraid that I was the only woman who would have you now. But there's one more thing you can do for me, Mr. Rule. You can get the hell out of my life."

CHAPTER FOURTEEN

"YOU'RE JUST PLAIN STUPID, you know that?"

Babs had sat enthralled while Kyla poured out the entire ugly story. She had arrived on Babs's doorstep an hour earlier. To say she was upset was putting it mildly. Aaron had been fed a grilled cheese sandwich, bathed, dressed in one of Babs's T-shirts and diapered from a supply that Babs kept for his visits. He was sold on the idea that it would be great fun to sleep in Aunt Babs's bed, and that was where he was.

In the living room of the small apartment, Babs sat on the floor, legs crossed, while Kyla occupied a corner of the short sofa. Two glasses of white wine stood on the coffee table.

Kyla had fully expected Babs to share her outrage over Trevor's treachery, taking up arms if necessary to railroad him out of town. "Stupid?" she repeated, thinking she'd heard Babs wrong.

"Stupid. Dumb. A real... Oh, never mind," Babs said irritably, getting to her feet. "I'm going to bed."

"Wait a minute," Kyla exclaimed. "Haven't you listened to a single word I've said?"

"Every self-pitying syllable."

"And that's all you can say about it?"

"That's all I'm going to say about it. If you expect

me to sit here with you and hash over what a louse Trevor Rule is, then you're in for a disappointment."

"But he is! Didn't I just tell you—"

"Yeah, yeah, you told me all about it. About how he woke up in a military hospital on foreign soil, half-blind, half-paralyzed, not knowing if he was going to live or die, and if he did live, if he'd be able to crawl, much less walk, much less make love or anything else a normal man has the privilege of doing. He woke up to find out that his friends had been blown to kingdom come by a bunch of fanatics, but miraculously his life had been spared. But to an insensitive cad like our Trevor, I doubt that bothered him much."

Scorn dripped from her voice like the water from the wineglass she had just rinsed out in the kitchen sink.

Stung by Babs's sarcasm, Kyla said, "All right, I'll concede that physically he had a difficult time."

"Now don't go exaggerating things, Kyla."

"It was *hellish,* okay? But what about the letters? Reading them, memorizing them like some pervert."

"The creep! How could he do something like that? Even Van Johnson never did anything that sentimental in his movies. Imagine Trevor doing something that horrible. Imagine him having the nerve to rearrange his future just so he could be near the woman who composed those letters. Imagine him, a man who could have had any woman he wanted with a crook of his finger and a come-hither look, going to all that trouble to meet you, his soul mate. And he didn't even have the decency to lure you into his bed first. No, he had to go and marry you!"

"Only out of pity," Kyla tightly reminded her unsympathetic friend. "Only to pay me back for Richard's death because he felt responsible."

"Right, so he'd be considered a martyr. Any other man would have come to see you, paid you his respects, humbly apologized for being alive when your husband was dead, offered you his help, probably his money, and when you refused he would have gone away with his conscience salved. But not Trevor. Oh, no. No doubt he wanted the world to think he was a do-gooder. So he hung around and got to know you, married you, took your son under his wing and built you a house a Rockefeller wouldn't be ashamed to claim." She made a tsking sound and shook her head. "What a creepy, sneaky heel. What a rat."

"You don't think it was sneaky the way he manipulated the rezoning of my parents' property?" Kyla exploded angrily. "You don't think it was underhanded the way he helped push the sale of their house through?"

"What a dastardly deed," Babs cried, shielding her eyes with her arms and feigning horror. "He handled all the dirty work so they wouldn't be bothered with it. He exacted a top price for their property, closed the sale and got them on their way to doing what they'd been wanting to do for years. The man has no heart. And the way he treats Aaron is positively sickening. Doesn't he know that most fathers don't treat their natural children that well? If he wanted to be a real father to the boy he should throw in a few harsh words, a little neglect, a lot of impatience."

"Enough, Babs. Soon I'll have to roll up my pant leg." Kyla rubbed her throbbing temples. "I might have known you'd take up for him."

"Take up for a louse like that? No way. If I were doing that, I'd probably tell you straight out what a selfish bitch you are."

"Selfish?"

"You wouldn't know something good if it came up to you on the street and bit you in the butt. If I were taking Trevor's side, I'd point out that some people prefer martyrdom to happiness."

"Stop it!"

"It's safer. There's no risk involved. When you don't love, you don't risk losing."

"You've got stars in your eyes for him. That's what this sermonizing is about. You've had a crush on him from the beginning."

"Granted. I've always had a weak spot for hunks with a sentimental streak."

"Well, the two of you would get along great. You both think with your genitals."

Babs sucked in her breath and held it for a long time. Gradually she let it go, but her body remained rigid. "Before I smack you, which is something I've miraculously restrained myself from doing so far tonight, I'm going to bed. Aaron, whose mature company I much prefer over yours, can sleep with me. You, my friend, can fend for yourself."

"Come back here. You can't just walk away from a fight."

"Watch me."

"I'm sorry for what I said. That was dreadful and I didn't mean it. Babs, please, tell me what to do."

Babs spun around and confronted her. "All right, you asked for it, here it is. You're not fighting with me, Kyla, you're fighting with yourself. And it's not me you're angry with. You're not even angry with Trevor. You're mad at yourself."

"What do you mean?"

"You were the Honor Society student. You figure it out. Now, good night."

Babs went down the hall and closed the bedroom door behind her. Tears smarted in Kyla's eyes as she returned to the living room. She prowled it aimlessly, nursing her indignation with self-pity.

So much for friendship. She felt betrayed. Murky waters could be closing over her head for the third time while she waved frantically at the shore where Babs stood mocking her, and she wouldn't feel more forsaken.

She had counted on Babs's unqualified allegiance. She had expected Babs to rally to her side and chant like a cheerleader, "That's a girl, that's telling him. Way to go. Right on." Instead Babs's sympathy had lain solely with Trevor.

Kyla flopped down on the couch and took a hefty draft of wine. "No wonder," she mumbled. Babs was female. She had fallen under *Smooch*'s spell. She, like hundreds before her, had been dazzled. That was it. Babs had become a traitor over a pair of muscular biceps and a dark curving mustache. What was loyalty to a friend when weighed against the way Smooch filled out his jeans?

Scoffing, Kyla took another sip of wine.

And what had she meant by the crack about Kyla being mad at herself?

Nothing. Absolutely nothing. Babs loved to drop little half-finished, underdeveloped tidbits of thought like that into conversations, like spoonfuls of cookie dough onto a baking sheet. And that's what they were, half-baked.

But if that were so, why did she keep dwelling on it?

Why was she giving any thought to the possibility that she *was* angry with herself? What did she have to be mad at herself for?

For falling in love with Trevor.

She slammed the glass of wine onto the coffee table and stamped to the window. Pulling viciously on the cord of the blinds, she raised them to peer out. She saw nothing but her own image reflected in the glass. Face-to-face with herself, she was forced to argue.

Admittedly she was smitten by him. She wasn't immune to a nice pair of biceps, either. And what about his generosity? And his constant kindness? And his lovemaking?

To stifle a sob, she crammed her fist against her lips. She didn't want any reminders of the way she had gloried in his tender loving. Guilt had a brassy taste. Somewhere along the way, living with and loving Trevor had become more important than keeping Richard alive in her heart. She had let the signal fire go out and that was an unpardonable offense.

Babs was right. She was angry with herself for loving him despite it all.

She couldn't hold it against him that he'd been in Richard's bunk the morning the embassy was bombed. That had been a quirk of fate. He hadn't used her letters to exploit her, but to grant her her heart's desire. He was an exemplary parent to Aaron. He was ambitious and successful, but not one of those men enslaved to his work for the sake of making a buck.

True, he had lied by not telling her that he had

known Richard. Yet if he had introduced himself as Smooch, she would have run just as hard and fast as she could, and forever been without him. If he had married her out of a sense of duty, then he was an actor of Olivier's caliber.

Love like that which Trevor had given her couldn't be faked, nor could it be summoned on command. It had to come from the heart.

If a love was that strong, what could be wrong with it?

She fled Babs's apartment. Once in the car, a thousand possibilities flickered through her mind like the insects caught in the headlights' beam. What if he had already left? What if she had lost her love for the second time? The first time, she had had no control over the loss. But this time she would have thrown it away.

As Babs had said, she was just plain stupid.

She released her pent-up breath on a wave of relief when she saw both his car and his pickup still parked in the driveway of the house. Entering through the front door, she saw that there was a feeble light on in the bedroom and rushed toward it.

Trevor was sitting on the edge of the bed, his head bent over a sheet of paper, which had been folded so many times that the creases were worn thin. She recognized it as one of her letters. Others were untidily stacked at his side. The light she had seen came from the fireplace where an unseasonable fire was burning. He was reading by firelight.

He glanced up when he heard her come in. His inquiring gaze held hers until she reached him, then she looked down at the frayed letter. Taking it from his hand, she read it. When she came to the line that said,

"He sounds like the kind of man I detest," her eyes clouded with tears.

Moving quickly, she snatched up the scattered letters one by one, envelopes included, until she had them all. Crossing the room, she moved aside the brass fire screen and threw them onto the dying fire.

"Kyla, no!"

The paper caught, crackled and curled, making a pastel pyre atop the logs. The flames were short-lived. Within moments the letters burned themselves out, shooting sparks up the chimney.

Kyla's face was streaked with tears when she turned to face him. "You don't need another man's leftovers, Trevor. If you want to know what I think, what I feel, ask me. Let me open my heart to you. Richard..." She paused and drew a deep, rattling breath. Her nails bit into her palms. It was the most painful thing she had ever had to say, but she finally voiced the truth that she had ignored for so long. "Richard is dead. I loved him. We created another human being through that love. I'll always be grateful that Aaron is a living testimony to it. But Richard is gone. I love you."

"Kyla." His voice broke on her name.

She threw herself into his arms. They wrapped around her, drawing her small frame against his. He buried his face in her neck. "I love you, Trevor. To know it, all you have to do is look at me. Read it in my eyes."

"No, DON'T LEAVE ME," she protested. With amazing strength, she clasped his thighs between hers.

"Aren't I getting heavy?"

"I like it."

"You're weird." He raised his head from the pillow to smile down at her.

"*I'm* weird? You're the one who fell in love with a woman through her letters to another man." She angled her head back to see him better. "What if I'd been a troll?"

"If you'd been a troll, if you'd been anything except exactly what you are, I would have introduced myself, offered my condolences, offered my financial assistance and bade you farewell."

"That's what Babs said."

"She did?"

"When she was still speaking to me, that is."

"Have I missed something?"

"I'll tell you all about it in the morning. Right now I'm busy." She allowed her tongue the unbridled pleasure of investigating his ear.

"I presume our son is safe," Trevor murmured around the tip of her breast, which responded beautifully.

"He's sleeping with Babs."

"You consider that safe?"

They laughed and when they did, Trevor grimaced. "Does that hurt?" she asked.

His lips tilted into that hungry alligator grin. "Laugh some more."

Instead they kissed. When she felt his body filling with renewed desire for her, she clasped his head with both hands and raised it above hers. "Forgive me. I said some terrible things to you. About your scars."

"I knew you didn't mean them."

"And about your eye patch." She touched his cheek

lovingly. "I think I know why you chose that over a prosthesis."

"Why?"

"You wear it out of defiance of the disability it represents. It would have been easy for you to wear a glass eye, to cover your scars. But you never take the easy way, do you, Trevor?"

"Not anymore. I used to. Before this happened to me, I didn't take anything seriously. I thought life was a series of parties held in honor of me. I found out the hard way it just ain't so." He pondered his next thought as he let strands of her hair slide through his fingers. "Or maybe I used the patch as a shield. Beneath it is the ugliest scar of all. Maybe I was afraid that if you saw that, you'd see the ugliest part of me, which was my deception."

"No more secrets between us, Trevor."

"None. Never. All my defenses are down."

His fingers got lost in her hair and his voice turned soft and raspy. "You were justifiably furious, Kyla. I *did* trick you into marrying me. But after I saw you, and you were even more beautiful than the things you had written, I simply had to have you, by fair means or foul. It was never my intention to replace Richard in your heart, but to create a place there for myself."

"I guess your biggest transgression was impatience."

"How's that?"

"If you had introduced yourself as Smooch—"

"You would have hated me on sight."

"Initially, maybe. But not after I got to know you. What I'm trying to say is that I feel like this was inevitable."

"You mean that no matter how it came about, we

would be married, lying here, doing this?" He moved inside her.

"Yes," she gasped softly. "Remember when you said that as long as there was someone else living inside me there was no room for you?"

Chagrined, he smiled lopsidedly. "Very crudely put, if my memory serves me."

"Crudely, but accurately." She touched his mouth with hers and left it there against his mustache. "You fill me completely, Trevor. Body, mind, and soul."

Then very gently, and with no interference from him, she threaded her fingers up through his hair and removed the eye patch.

* * * * *